The Werewolf of Paris

GUY ENDORE

The Werewolf of Paris

A NOVEL

PEGASUS CRIME
NEW YORK LONDON

The Werewolf of Paris

Pegasus Crime is an Imprint of
Pegasus Books LLC
80 Broad Street, 5th Floor
New York, NY 10004

First Pegasus Crime cloth edition 2012

ISBN: 978-1-60598-353-0

10 9 8 7 8 6 5 4 3 2 1

Printed in the United States of America
Distributed by W. W. Norton & Company, Inc.

These creatures live onlely without meats;
The Camelion by the Air,
The Want or Mole, by the Earth,
The Sea-Herring by the Water,
The Salamander by the Fire,
Unto which may be added the Dormouse,
   which lives partly by sleep,
And the Werewolf, whose food is night,
                    winter and death.

(AN OLD SAYING)

TO
HENRIETTA PORTUGAL

The Werewolf of Paris

-Introduction-

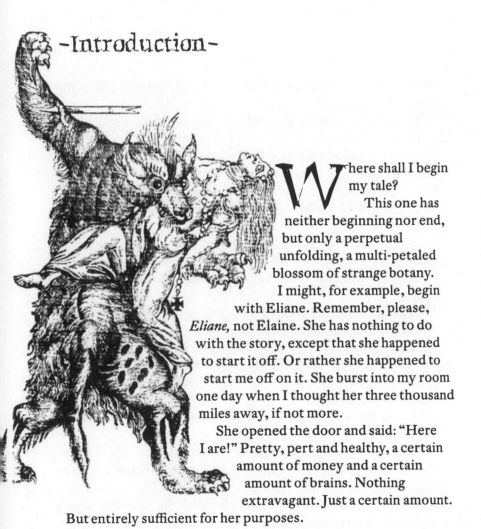

Where shall I begin my tale? This one has neither beginning nor end, but only a perpetual unfolding, a multi-petaled blossom of strange botany.

I might, for example, begin with Eliane. Remember, please, *Eliane,* not Elaine. She has nothing to do with the story, except that she happened to start it off. Or rather she happened to start me off on it. She burst into my room one day when I thought her three thousand miles away, if not more.

She opened the door and said: "Here I are!" Pretty, pert and healthy, a certain amount of money and a certain amount of brains. Nothing extravagant. Just a certain amount. But entirely sufficient for her purposes.

I did my best to express "Welcome to Paris," but I'm afraid I didn't do a very good job of it. We weren't really such great friends back home. But in the torrid atmosphere of Paris, a nodding acquaintance ripens quickly to intimacy. At any rate among Americans who have just come over. As for myself, I considered myself an old resident and Paris a quiet city in which to do a hard piece of work.

"I want to go to Zelli's and see the Folies Bergère and oh! just everything. I'll have to work fast because you see I've got only a week."

"Yes, of course," I said, only half interested, "and don't forget le Louvre."

"And I want to go to the Dôme and the Select and eat in the Dingo and at Foyot's."

"There are fine things in the Musée du Luxembourg," I added. But she went right on:

"And I've got to see the Moulin Rouge and the Rat Mort."

"And the Cluny," I reminded her.

"Oh," she said, "all the places I've read so much about. Montmartre and Montparnasse. And you'll go with me."

"I'll go what?"

"You'll go with me. Oh! I know you haven't any money. Of course, I mean to pay for both of us."

"I have no money," I said severely, "and I have no time. I'm busy."

"Busy with what?" she asked innocently.

"Why, my dear child, do you see all these books?"

"Yes, of course," she replied, "but they're written already, aren't they? What are you doing, writing them again?"

"You may put it that way," I said, somewhat offended by her refusal to be impressed.

She picked up a volume: "*De Rerum Natura.* Of things in nature," she translated.

"Of the nature of things," I corrected harshly.

"What's the difference?" she asked. "Say you'll come. Don't be mean. There's no one else in Paris whom I know. If you won't take me around I'll have to go rubbernecking with the rest of the tour's gang. And I'm just sick of them."

"And my work?" I reminded her.

"It'll keep," she said. "Besides, why don't you write fiction? Then you'd make money. I read the swellest book on the boat coming over. *Flaming Youth*. Have you read it?"

"No," I said with decision.

"You should. It's about the new generation that's growing up with freedom. I wish I could get mom and pop to see it. They just won't understand. But you're young, you ought to be with us. Be modern. Not a stick-in-the-mud."

"It's you who is the stick-in-the-mud," I said. "Look, I'll show you. Here," I said, opening up a volume, "is a quotation from an ancient Egyptian papyrus. *The young people no longer obey the old. The laws that ruled their fathers are trampled underfoot. They seek only their own pleasure and have no respect for religion. They dress indecently and their talk is full of impudence.* Do you find yourself depicted there? There always was a younger generation and there always will be. And the younger element will always think it smart to thumb its nose at its elders."

But my superior wisdom was of little avail against her persistence. We went to Zelli's. The champagne was, as usual, excellent and expensive and all that, but I don't care for it anyhow. I like beer. I remember reading in a German restaurant: *Ein echter Deutscher mag kein Franzen nicht, doch seine Weine trinkt er gern.* A real German can't stand a frog, but he drinks French wine with pleasure. Many French feel the same way. They don't like Germans but they like their beer well enough. In fact, the beers in Paris are never spoken of, but they are really fine. I ordered beer at Zelli's. The waiter must have thought me crazy.

Eliane drank champagne. I forget how much. She danced with me. Then with a dark-skinned fellow, a Cuban probably. Then she decided we would go elsewhere—just when I had decided that we ought to be going home. The taxis would be charging double fare soon. Eliane had no such compunctions. She was beginning to find Paris a huge lark. So it is, for people who don't have to count pennies and work hard for a Ph.D.

We went elsewhere and then elsewhere again and then some-where else. I forget just where all we went. There are any number of places to go in Paris. You would think there are no such places in the United States. They are full of Americans. The waiters speak English, the band is American, the customers are from back home. What's the use of being abroad? Now *MS F.2839*, on which I was writing my thesis, was not to be found in America. So I had to be in Paris. But dives? There are dives all over the world. And all over the world they are the same. That is because sin is the same all over the world. And sin is always the same. You might rack your brain from now till doomsday and you won't manage to think up a new sin.

By three o'clock I was saying to Eliane that, well, now, this was enough. But she had learnt from someone that there is an all-night restaurant at Les Halles where one could have onion soup and she wanted that. So off we went and landed there. By that time I was myself a little hazy and there were two or three other people in the party. I can't remember how they joined us or if they joined us at all. But one of them was a nice young man and he and I were soon deep in a discussion of mimicry. It was long since I had read anything on the subject, but in my drunkenness it was as fresh as if I had studied it only the day before.

"There's the pinthea," I said, "that imitates bird excrement, looks just like the dropping of a bird. There's a harmless insect that imitates a wasp. And a beetle that looks like a dangerous ant."

"Can't you people ever stop that?" Eliane said. "God, what are you men made of?" Whereupon she rose and began to dance around by herself. We continued our talk. He had some very interesting points to make. I forget what they were. Then I noticed that Eliane was singing at the top of her voice.

"I'm hot," she said, and quickly loosening her dress she slipped out of it and began to pirouette in her silken panties and brassière. The proprietor came running out and began to upbraid her and all of us as *sales américains*. But Eliane was not to be stopped so easily. She cast herself into the arms of a strange man and said: "Take me; I'm yours. I want to belong to you. To you only."

He put his arms around her and led her over to his table, where she was at once at home on his lap, her arms slung tightly around his neck and their mouths as if glued together.

22

I went over to him and expostulated. Eliane promptly abandoned him and said to me, "Don't be jealous, I'll be yours. Yes, I'll be yours. Take me with you quick."

Right there I made my mistake. For what I said was: "Now come along, Eliane, get your clothes on and let me take you home." I should have pretended to fall in with her plans. Instead I summoned her to be decent. That was precisely what she did not want to be.

"If you won't have me, then anyone can have me. Who wants me?" she shouted, "Who wants me? I want a man! I'm a virgin and free and white and good-looking, too. I'll show you," and she began to tug at her brassiere.

I tried to hold her arms, but she pushed me away. "Eliane!" I said.

The stranger on whose lap she had sat came up to her and said: "You know, darling, you are mine. You shall come with me. We belong to each other. All night long I shall worship your sweet body," and other rubbish of the sort, which, it is true, I have said to women myself, but it does sound like rubbish when you hear someone else saying it. Things like that are not meant to be overheard. That's boudoir talk and should be born and die there.

She took him seriously and melted onto his shoulder. Literally melted. Became limp all over and clove to his body. He pulled her away and talked her into putting on her dress. Then he took her downstairs and called for a taxi.

I have a faint notion that I kept following her all about and trying to make her see reason and reminding her of her mother and father. And I have the same notion that my friend of the mimicry discussion kept following me and talking to me all the time about insect mimicry.

I tried to get into the taxi with Eliane and her friend, but he pushed me out gently, she less gently. Well, such is the world.

And my friend was saying: "Unless you taste insects, you can have no clear conception of how far this mimicry goes: there's a butterfly of the Euphoadra family that tastes just like one of the Aletis, without looking like it."

"Haven't you got things a little mixed?" I said. We had walked up to the Tower of Saint Jacques and were proceeding toward the Seine.

Just then a young girl stopped us and invited us to partake of her. My friend asked at once: "How much?"

She mentioned a sum. "That's too much," he said. She came down. Still he shook his head.

"Come," she said finally, with a weary expression on her sallow face. "I don't want any money. I just want you."

Whereupon he took his watch out and said: "It's too late. Sorry, some other day, if you don't mind." And taking me by the arm he started to move off. She caught and held me.

"For nothing," she repeated with despair in her deep-sunk eyes. "For nothing," she breathed. "For nothing. I don't want any money. See, I'm rich." She opened her purse and pulled out a roll of bills. Rolls of bills mean nothing much in France, but indeed she might have been rich. She was well dressed, I noticed. Nothing extravagant, but certainly not poorly. Her whole body trembled as if in fever. And the tremors coursed through her hand and communicated themselves to me.

My friend tore me away. As we hastened on, I looked back and saw her standing where we had left her, her hands covering her face.

"Why did you do that?" I asked. The action of my new acquaintance had disgusted me. He had meant only to tease her.

"I wanted to see how far down she would come. I've had them come down to two francs, but never to nothing. But her case can't count because she wasn't after money. She's a pathological case."

"I think that sort of sport is pretty cruel," I said. I thought to myself: I'll be glad to get rid of you.

"It's a disease," he went on to say. "They are as if possessed by a beast. Did you know that there is a new school of psychology that is returning to the old belief in possession?"

He waited for an answer so I said briefly: "No." It would have done no good to say yes, he would have continued to impart his information to me anyhow.

"You've heard of Hyslop, of course?" he said. "Well, I should

24

think he would have thought the two examples we saw tonight evidences of possession by the spirits of beasts."

"Are you sure you're right?" I asked. I was slightly skeptical of the security of his knowledge. It threatened like the Tower of Pisa.

"That was the ancient psychology, too. The Romans, for example, thought of insatiable sexual appetite as due to possession by a wolf."

"I thought the billygoat was the symbol of sexual insatiability."

"You are wrong," he answered. "The word *wolf* is to be recognized in the Latin vulva, and in the word *lupanar,* a brothel, *lupus* being Latin for wolf. You know the Roman festival of the Lupereales. It would correspond to our carnival and was characterized by a complete abandonment of morals."

"Wasn't Lupercus another name for the god Pan?" I asked.

"So it was, but the name means the protector against the wolves. It had something to do with the nursing of Romulus and Remus by a she-wolf, but its sexual significance is shown by the fact that at the sacrifice of goats during this festival, the women who wished to be fruitful allowed themselves to be beaten with bloody strips cut out of the goat's hide."

"I find those theories usually built on too shallow a foundation," I objected. "It sounds like Frazer and there's nothing I care for less. Besides, there are theories for which I don't care no matter how good they are."

"You mistake me," he returned, and went on to fill my ears with a lot of arguments which I have forgotten. I wasn't particularly interested, and a one-sided discussion always annoys me. Moreover, I was thinking of Eliane. When would I see her again? What would she say to me then? As a matter of fact I didn't see her until some years later and then she was married, I think to the man who drew her out of the restaurant. But I could not ask either of them. Delicacy forbade. It would have been a romantic conclusion to that night's adventure, but I'm not sure I dare set it down as true.

But something did come of this night. As it was beginning to dawn, my friend, whom I hoped never to meet again, found his fountain of words drying up and said that he was going to his rooms in Rue de l'École de Médecine. Was I going that way? I was, or ought to have been, for I lived nearby, but I said no, I was going the other way, and so we separated at last.

I walked along the quai, then toward a little park at the river's edge, and there I sat down on a bench. My mind was vacant, ringing yet with all the myriad sounds that had been poured into it, as one's legs sometimes will tingle when one halts after a long walk.

Two men came along, each with a sack slung across his shoulder, and they began to lay out on the ground the spoils of a morning's tour of inspection of the city's rubbish. They broke electric bulbs, separated the brass base from the glass, and took out the tungsten filament. They had bottles and bits of string, and pieces of rag and buttons, and one of them had a roll of paper bound with a ribbon. He untied the ribbon and spread out the roll. There were several sheets laced together and evidently covered with writing. That was as much as I could see from where I was sitting.

I wondered what might be written on those bound sheets. Some schoolboy's composition, no doubt: the proud effort of a youthful author with high aspirations. Or some commercial report, perhaps even of recent date, for the use of the typewriter is still unknown to many French businessmen. Then again it might be a really valuable production of a famous writer, a manuscript which would fetch a high price.

Bitten with curiosity I arose and walked over to the men. They looked up at me from their squattering position and answered my greeting. I made some general comments on the difficulties of earning a living. It will be recalled that at this time the franc was plunging like a wild horse, and a little reference to this secured me the men's goodwill. There is no beggar so poor but that he likes to think his status involved in international finance, too.

Then I bent and picked up the manuscript, saying apologetically: "What is this machin-là?"

One of the men hastily assured me that sometimes such things brought in a deal of money. The other, seeing which way the wind was blowing, chimed in with a rapid story of one Jean Something-or-other who had retired upon a single find of that nature. The first

26

knew of even a more surprising case. In short, it seemed there was little doubt but that the men had struck it rich that morning and were quite prepared to retire on their prospective earnings.

One look, however, had made me keen to own the manuscript. That look had happened upon the words: *The lupercal temples became the later brothels or lupanars. Still today in Italian, lupa signifies both wolf and wanton.*

I offered one franc. The men shrugged their shoulders. They went on separating their bits of metal and rag and exchanged a few rapid remarks, in argot, which I could not catch.

Then I did a brave thing, though my heart pounded in fear. I threw the manuscript down at their feet and saying: "Bonjour, messieurs," I walked off. I had taken ten steps, and with difficulty had restrained my desire to look back, when I heard one of them cry out:

"On vous le vend pour cinq, monsieur."

I turned back, took the manuscript and said as calmly as I could: "Va, pour cinq," and handed them a little bill of five francs.

Thus through Eliane, in a way, I came into possession of the Galliez report: thirty-four sheets of closely written French, an unsolicited defense of Sergeant Bertrand at the latter's court-martial in 1871.

I had thought at first of publishing the defense as it stood and providing this curiosity with the necessary notes to help the reader to an understanding of the case. But on second thought, I determined to recast the whole material into a more vivid form, incorporating all the results of my own investigations. For I confess that the report by Aymar Galliez was of such compelling interest that I set aside my Ph.D. thesis for the moment and concentrated on it.

From its very first words, the manuscript exerts a curious fascination. Its wisdom is as strange as that of the pyramidologists of our day, those strangely learned men who prove at great length that the pyramids of Egypt were built to be a permanent storehouse of a scientific knowledge greater than that which we possess at present.

Galliez begins:

"The vast strides of our generation in the conquest of the material world must not mislead us into thinking that when we have plumbed the physical world to its depths we shall thereby have explained all there is to explain. The scientists of a former day strove mightily to fathom the depth of the spiritual world, and their successes and conquests are all but forgotten.

"Who can estimate what thanks we owe to those courageous priests of old who went into the forbidding Druidic forests and with bell and book, and swinging censer, exorcised the sylvan spirits, banished the familiars, expelled the elementals, cast out the monsters and devils of old Gaul? Who can estimate the debt we owe to them for helping to slay all the strange and unnatural beasts that formerly cowered in every dark cranny and recess, under ferns and moss-covered rocks, waiting to leap out at the unwary passerby who did not cross himself in time? Not all of these monsters were equally evil, but all constituted unwelcome interferences in the destiny of man.

"If today the lonely traveler can walk fearlessly through the midnight shadows of the silent forests of France, is it because of the vigilance of our police? Is it because science has taught us to be unbelievers in ghosts and monsters? Or is not some thanks due the Church, which after a millennium of warfare succeeded at long last in clearing the atmosphere of its charge of hidden terror and thus allowed for the completer unfolding of the human ego? We who have profited thereby should not allow pride to blind us to our debt. Future clearer thinkers will support my contention."*

Before I enter into the further contents of the script, let me tell something of its author. Who was this Aymar Galliez who could champion such a curious theory as is expressed in the above excerpt? The Bibliothèque Nationale failed to enlighten me. By chance I happened to consult a *Tout Paris* of the year 1918. There was an Aymar Galliez, sous-lieutenant, etc., etc. That was all I needed. They must be relatives.

---

* Some strange hand has scribbled in the margin of the MS: "Quel cauchemar!" (What a nightmare!)

28

In short, I wrote. I was invited to present myself and seized the opportunity to do so. It isn't very often that the French are so obliging to an American.

I found Aymar Galliez, now a lieutenant, a pleasant dapper little fellow, with a black mustache, dimples, dark eyes framed in sweeping dark eyelashes, a ready smile perpetually revealing fine teeth, the color and texture of blanched almonds. His geniality delayed our getting to the point. Finally, I asked (rather abruptly terminating a sprightly discussion on Carpentier vs. Dempsey):

"Aymar Galliez is an infrequent name, is it not?"

He laughed: "I don't think there has ever been more than one at a time."

"I mean that I was sure that you must be related to the Aymar Galliez of the last century."

"I suppose we have the same person in mind. He was my great-uncle. I don't believe there were any other Aymar Galliez'. I would be interested in knowing how you came across his name."

That was precisely what I didn't wish to tell. "Oh..." I said hesitatingly.

"You have run across some of his work?"

"His work?"

"Yes, his writings."

"No," I faltered, thinking rapidly: so his work is known, after all. But the lieutenant's next words reassured me:

"In the Bibliothèque Nationale they have many of his pamphlets but all listed under Anonymous. My mother is rather anxious to have that corrected, and has been on the lookout for signed copies presented to friends. How then did you come across his name?"

"Why...you see, I am editing some correspondence and found his name mentioned."

"I see."

"And since I am annotating the material I find it necessary to say at least a word or two about the man."

"Yes, of course. Well, he was born in eighteen twenty-four and died in eighteen ninety. He was badly wounded in the street fighting in 'forty-eight and my mother rather thinks he was slightly cracked ever thereafter. He did quite a lot of political pamphlet-eering and then suddenly decided to study for the priesthood. He didn't make a very exemplary priest. He went in for spiritualistic séances and table-tipping and after clerical authorities had long frowned on his penchant, he retired from the Church. He had his parish in Orcières and he lived nearby until his death and lies buried there. That's all I can think of at the moment. My mother remembers a lot more."

"That's quite enough," I said. "I'm grateful to you." I put away the slip of paper on which I had made my notes.

"May I ask in what connection you found his name mentioned? My mother will be sure to ask me that."

"Well, he appeared as witness at the defense of a man. Did you ever hear of Sergeant Bertrand?"

"Connais pas."

"Well, this man was tried by court-martial and your great-uncle evidently was interested in helping him out."

"What was this Sergeant Bertrand being tried for?"

"He was being tried for…" and there my tongue failed me. For nothing in the world would I have dared say it. I could not have pushed that word over my tongue had I tried with all my might. There are some things that cannot be done. Who has the courage to attempt a handstand on the corner of Fifth Avenue and Forty-second Street? Certain atmospheres are violently hostile to certain ideas, no matter how charming otherwise. So I finished lamely:

"…for some infraction."

"For some infraction?"

"For rape," I said decisively. Rape sounded best in the pleasant atmosphere of the dapper lieutenant. Yes, rape sounded best. At any rate better…

30

Chapter One

It is only inasmuch as Aymar Galliez begins his script with the tale of Pitaval and Pitamont that I shall do the same, allowing myself, however, the privilege of elaborating his often too bald treatment. The incident herein noted would seem at first glance to have nothing to do with the case. Neither does digging a well below a house seem to have anything to do with the typhoid that carries away one victim after another. The sources of moral diseases, too, often lie far back in the past.

Pitaval and Pitamont,* then, are two castles in France, which lie on opposite sides of a little streamlet, called *le Pit*. I am aware, of course, that the Joanne Gazetteer contains no mention of a Pit of any kind. The fact is that the two castles, of which hardly a vestige remains, now look at each other across a dry valley. When lumbering removed the topsoil of these hills, the river dried up. But its course can still be traced by a trail of rocks winding upwards. Local archoeologists, if there are any in that mountainous and infertile region twenty-five miles west and south of Grenoble, will resolve the disappearance of these place names.

---

* In Celtic *pit* means point or peak. Pitaval and Pitamont might be rendered as Peak Downstream and Peak Upstream, or Peak in the vale and Peak on the mount.

If the traveler today can see little if anything in this region, one visitor certainly saw plenty. I refer to Viollet-le-Duc, who went into ecstasy at this spot and drew complete plans and an imaginary reconstruction. This, if I am not mistaken, the reader may find under the discussion of "barbette." There is a reference too under the subject of "latrine." It will be recalled that Viollet-le-Duc was always keen on any vestiges of medieval sanitary engineering. Possibly there was more to see in his day.

As far back as history can recall, the castles of Pitaval and Pitamont, though the families were offshoots of one original house, were at constant war with each other. In the early days the two houses had divided between them an extensive and fertile territory. The hillsides yielded a superior wine. The forests fattened pigs, produced charcoal and chestnuts. The peasantry was hardy and cheerful and paid its taxes to lord and priest generously and usually peacefully.

But the constant warfare between the two houses eventually proved too much for the local peasantry, though surely there is nothing in history to equal the permanent patience of the sorely tried poor. They abandoned their farms and moved on. There was still free land in Europe at that time, so why stay where life was insecure?

As the estates began to yield less and less, the Pitavals and the Pitamonts, pressed for money to carry on their feud, began to make trips down the hill to the city of Grenoble, where there was a Datini factor, or even to Avignon, where the great banking firm of the Datinis had its head office. Bit by bit, they mortgaged what they had. The interest piled up. Once in a while the Pitavals would rob the Pitamonts and pay up some of what they owed to Datini. Again it was the turn of the Pitamonts to stage a clever coup and find themselves momentarily in cash.

One night, a begging friar, benighted in these mountains, found hospitality in the Pitaval castle. The women, miserably treated among their brutal menfolk, were glad for the appearance of a strange and kindly face. The venerable monk entertained the ladies with tales of the land of Italy, whence he had just come.

32

"It is all sunshine and warmth down there," he said, and played meditatively with his long beard.

The ladies shivered with yearning. Outside the wind howled. The draft came in under the door and disturbed the rushes on the floor. A dog—or was it a wolf?—howled beyond in the forest. They crossed themselves. The monk added a few words of Latin.

One young giant of a Pitaval slapped the table with his chunky hand and laughed hoarsely: "I hear that the men there, and elsewhere too, for the fashion has spread, write poetry, which they sing to the ladies while they twang on a lute. Is that so? Do men do that?"

The monk added: "It is a pretty and gentle custom. Our Lord too loved peace."

The ladies looked wistfully at the friar. He seemed to have some of that southern sun and some of that gentle poetry of love clinging to him. But the men, red from much wine, had already turned away from the monk and were discussing their next boar hunt.

The fire in the chimney had died down. The smoking candles had burned low. The men and women retired. The monk was permitted to stretch himself out on the floor, with a few sheepskins to protect himself from the cold.

The silence in the castle was extreme. The darkness complete. The monk threw off his sheepskins and rose slowly. From the folds of his cowl he drew a long, sharp dagger. He, a Pitamont, disguised by a beard grown in secret, was free in the Pitaval castle at night. His breath came and went softly through his parted teeth. He had marked where the men and women had gone to retire and now directed his steps slowly toward the chambers of the sleeping Pitavals.

He reached the first room. Faint light, from clouds lit by the moon behind them, shone through the narrow window. He dropped to his hands and knees and crept up to the bed. The curtains were parted. Holding his dagger with both hands he drew it aloft and brought it down full force on the man who lay sleeping there. A slush was the only sound, like that which a foul apple gives when you step on it.

33

"What is it, Robert?" the lady beside him whispered sleepily. Already the Pitamont had freed his dagger and brought it down again.

Silence.

Pitamont stole softly out of that room of death and on to the next. Not a Pitaval was to be left alive in that castle by the morning. This was to be the end of them.

But as he groped his way along the wall, his foot caught in a crevice and he went down on his face. His dagger was torn from his hands and went clattering down a short flight of steps.

"Holà! Hugues. Holà! Jouffroy. Light!"

"'Tis only I," said the monk. The young giant Pitaval, naked, had come up and collared him.

"And what are you doing up here?"

"I was only looking for a place to relieve myself," the friar explained.

"The ashes of the hearth are not good enough for you?" By this time everybody in the castle was awake, everybody but the two who slept forever.

In the morning, the new master of the castle of Pitaval was the young giant, heir to his father's estate. Pitamont, the false monk, was locked in a little cell, where he pondered on the curious mischance that had ruined his plans, so near success. "I am not afraid to die," he said to himself, with a sneer on his lips.

In the great central hall, the young giant sat with his pretty wife and thought. "Now what shall we do with your sunny Italian?" he laughed. She turned away and wept.

He summoned the stone mason from the nearest village. The two sat together for several hours and then the mason called for his assistants and went to work.

In an interior court of the castle stood an old well that was not often used, a larger and better one having been dug at a more convenient point. The old well was now enlarged down to near water level, a fairly permanent level, and there heavy iron bars were laid across the water-hole. A cesspool was constructed close to the well, with two pipes, one opening at the water-level shelf

34

in the well, the other, for ventilation, leading up to the surface of the earth. Fifteen or twenty feet above the shelf, a dome was constructed. Before it was completely done, the false monk, half asphyxiated with smoke, was lowered onto the shelf. Then the dome was finished, all but for a small central orifice, which remained for ventilation. The whole affair had been lined with smooth hard stone cut to fit without a crevice. Above the earth was a small superstructure, likewise of stone, and barred by a heavy iron door. Within, a flight of steps led down to the ventilating chamber directly above the dome. Three times a week a servant, accompanied by the master, went into the chamber and threw a heavy chunk of meat and suet into the aperture. It fell with a thud onto the iron bars over the water-hole. For months there was no answering sound.

When Jehan Pitamont awoke from the effects of the smoke, he found himself in a dark cold chamber. He was naked, and shivered. His first thought was that he was dead, and that this was the afterlife which the priests promised. But he had soon undeceived himself. As he groped around, he discovered that his new abode was a small circular cell. Standing in the middle, on an iron grating, with outstretched arms, his hands easily touched both sides. There was only one break in the circular continuity of the wall that lined the cell, and that was a slight recess. In the floor of this niche in the wall was a circular hole about half a span in width. Jehan guessed at once what this was for. The only furniture of the room, if furniture it could be called, was a small iron dipper attached by a short iron chain to the grating. With this, one could reach down and secure a drink of water.

Cold sweat stood out on Jehan's body when he had fully realized the nature of the dwelling place to which he had been transferred. He was in an oubliette, a forgetress, so to speak. He had heard of them, but had never seen one. Now he himself was in one. But he did not despair. He even had moments when he laughed to think how he had deceived these stupid Pitavals. And how he had killed the old Pitaval himself and his wife in their sodden sleep.

He would soon be out of this place. His brothers and his father would never leave him here. Any moment now he expected to hear the ring of an axe against the walls of his prison. His side had slaughtered all the Pitavals and were coming to free him!

But nothing happened. There was not a sound. And still he waited expectantly. They would come. First, of course, they had to prepare themselves. They would come in force, storm the castle walls and kill the damned Pitavals, man and mouse, every single one of them. Then they would search for him. And they would find him, no matter how well he had been hidden. But surely by this time, he said to himself, a horrible doubt arising in his mind, they would have already been here, had they come at all. Perhaps they had been repulsed at the storming, and had withdrawn to gather more men. Surely they were not going to leave him to rot here.

No. But he must give them time. How long had he been here? Who can tell time in the darkness? He had remained two days in the room where they had kept him locked up at first. Then they had made him dizzy with smoke and had brought him here. Now, how long was it since they had put him in here? It seemed like days, but it could be only hours, for they had not yet given him any food, and he had not slept once. No doubt they would throw food to him once a day, and he would feel sleepy once a day, so that he could count time that way. He determined to keep track of his imprisonment.

Time passed. He dozed and woke, dozed off again and woke once more. He was famished. Would they never feed him? Had they put him here to starve? Good, then, he would starve. Better so. He was not afraid to die.

Time passed. He was weak from lack of food. He heard sounds above him. A jingle of keys. Someone was in the chamber above him. He heard faint whispered voices. He was about to shout out: "Poton!" thinking it must be his brother. Then he bethought himself. He would wait and see. How his jailers would laugh at him if he made that mistake. He waited. It was not Poton. It was young Pitaval.

"Here's food for you, my solitary monk! Do you want a prayer stool? Or a lute to twang on?"

Jehan made no answer. "Ach! if I could lay my hands on your fat

36

neck," he thought. The sharp fragrance of roasted fowl came to his nostrils. Something fell from above and landed on the grating over the water-hole. The footsteps passed on. A door banged shut.

His hands went to seize the roast. No. He would not touch a bite of it. He would starve himself to death. He was thirsty too. His throat ached. He would have a drink of water, that could not harm, and would serve to help him resist the pangs of hunger. He found the dipper in the dark and slipped it through the grating. The water was cool and sweet.

That meat was tempting. That roasted crust of fat fowl, how often he had bitten through it. Why, only the other night as a monk at table with the Pitavals…but he had forborne helping himself too liberally. As a monk, it behooved him to be frugal. He regretted that he had not eaten more of it. What could it have harmed had he eaten a larger portion? The table had been loaded down with food when they had risen to go to bed. There was fowl and venison. And a dish of chopped greens and cold prawns in a sauce of vinegar. Good, that! His mouth watered. In the two days that he had been locked in the other cell, they had fed him nothing but bread, dry bread.

Why was he thinking so much of food? Food was a matter of the past for him. He meant to die. He was through with food. But this was agony with that roasted fowl filling the cell with its odor.

He would kill himself and end this torture. If only he could lift up that grating and drown himself in the water. But the grating was fastened too securely. If he could hitch himself up the wall and cast himself down. But while he could reach the opposite walls, they were tantalizingly beyond the reach of a good muscular purchase. Had they measured him to make sure of adding that extra torture to this prison?

He beat his head against the wall. He made it bloody by hammering against the grating. He fainted. But when he came to, the first thing that struck him was the odor of roasted meat. Damn that meat. He would get rid of it. He would throw it down into the cesspool. Yes, that was it. Down the cesspool, and away with all thoughts of food. Out of reach, out of mind.

The fowl was a large one. A goose, no doubt. It would not go into the opening. He tore it into pieces, dismembered it and put the separate pieces down. He heard them fall far below. The great bulk of the fowl, however, stuck in the pipe. He had to push it down. He pushed it down as far as he could and there it remained stuck fast.

There, that was that. Good God! What had he done? He had cast away his only food. He was about to cry out in despair. No, he must not make any sound. That would be shameful. They were waiting somewhere for him to cry out, that they might laugh at him and taunt him. No, never a sound must come from his lips. He stilled the cries in his throat, pushed his hands into his mouth to deaden any sound that might strive to issue from his agonized body.

He found himself licking his hands, greedily licking his fingers, smacking his lips, searching with his tongue between his fingers to find yet another bit of grease remaining from the fowl he had thrown away. Perhaps he could still reach that big piece that he had had so much difficulty pushing down into the drain. He put his arm down. He could just feel the fowl below the fingernail of his longest finger. In vain he attempted to hook his fingernail under some projection and thus draw it up. The meat was too far down.

A stick! But he had no stick. The dipper! But it was fastened by a short chain to the grating. Perhaps with his leg. That would reach down farther. But alas his clumsy toes contrived only to push down the roast still farther. He wept, he gnashed his teeth. He would have liked to howl out loud. But no sound would he allow to come from his mouth. He rolled around in agony on the cold floor, too short to permit him to lie at full length, another torture that had been only too well calculated.

He tried in vain to kill himself by breathing water up his nose. He could not do it. The will in him to breathe air was too great. If he could have wound the dipper-chain around his neck; but no, nothing would succeed.

It was days, weeks, months, years before there were sounds again above him. But no voice cried out tauntingly to him this time. He heard as if in a daze, for he was weak from lack of food, a heavy body

38

fall into his cell. Then the footsteps mounted upwards and a door was closed. Not a ray of light came into the cell during this procedure.

As soon as the door had closed, he threw himself like a wild man on that which had fallen into his chamber. It was a large piece of raw meat fat with suet. He buried his teeth in it, and lay sick and belching afterward.

He had striven hard to keep track of time. He dozed so often and was so famished waiting for food that he figured he was being fed once a week, instead of three times a week as he actually was. He had counted a year when scarcely four months had passed. He had counted four years when one was hardly over. And then he began to lose track. He ceased to hope each day that there would be a great clashing above of iron on iron and that Poton's rough voice would cry out: "Jehan, dear brother, are you there?" That would never happen. Insensibly, by stages too gradual to portray, he reached a state where he thought of nothing.

In his underground cell there was never a change of temperature. Outside the winter storms might howl, or summer thundershowers beat upon a parched earth. Within it was forever cool, forever moist, forever dark.

Nothing mattered to him now but food. He had grown to be hungry at the same hour three times a week, and then if the meat was late in being cast in, he would bark and bay like a dog.

Years passed. Now and then a Pitamont fell afoul the Pitavals. Now and then it was the turn of the Pitamonts to execute a bloody revenge. "For brother Jehan," they would say, thinking him dead this many a year.

And thus time passed and was gathered into seasons and years, and years were grouped into decades. Fully fifty years had passed since that night that Jehan Pitamont had come as a monk to beg admittance to the castle of the Pitavals, and still out in the courtyard, three times a week, the old master of the castle, his great bulk bent with age, went with his keys and his steward, and opened the door of the superstructure leading to the ventilating chamber above the oubliette.

"Let us wait a moment or two," Pitaval would say to his steward and smile.

"It is precisely noon, by the shadow," said the steward.

"If we delay but a minute or two, he will begin to howl," said Pitaval, and nodded his head in pleasant anticipation.

One day, at his office in Avignon, old Datini, the banker, took a sheaf of papers from his files and said that it was time to settle this Pitaval and Pitamont business. "I have not seen a groat of the money due me in two years, from either of those two snarling kennels. It is time we brought this matter to a conclusion."

The journey to the mountains was long, but Datini did not mind. He beguiled himself with a copy of Petrarch's sonnets to Laura. Moreover, he promised himself the pleasure of stopping off at Vaucluse on his way back and visiting the fountain there, immortalized in one of Petrarch's verses.

Thus one day the Pitavals were privileged to entertain a visitor who turned them out of their house. Indeed there was not much to be turned out. It was years since a horse had neighed in the stables; of the family there was left only the shriveled giant of former years. Of servants there was only the steward, too old and weak himself to seek fortune elsewhere. They received Datini and his bailiffs with courtesy.

"It is lucky you have come," said old Pitaval. "We slaughtered our last pig yesterday. If you have brought food along, we are prepared to welcome you."

Datini had brought food with him. They ate and discussed business.

"I have relatives in Orange," said Pitaval. "I think I shall go there."

A lugubrious howling, seeming to come out of the bowels of the earth, filled the hall.

"Do not be frightened, Master Datini," said Pitaval with a smile. "It is only a wolf that we keep in a pit in the courtyard. Here," he said, turning to his servant, "take him this piece of meat." Then he added: "Have we any ratbane? Then smear some on the meat and we shall be rid of a useless pet."

40

"A wolf," said Datini sententiously, "prefers death to captivity, anyhow."

"Aye," Pitaval agreed. "A wolf. But this one has little spirit and thinks only of his meat. Well, I am ready to leave, your factors may take charge at once." He rose heavily. The howling had ceased abruptly.

"There is no such hurry required of you," Datini returned. "I have still business to do with the Pitamonts across the way."

"So? Are my friends over there to share my fate? Then I shall have pleasant companionship on my departure."

"Shame on you to speak thus of two old ladies," said Datini. "I think I shall let them stay there the rest of their days. They are both over seventy."

A few hours later, as Pitaval and his steward were ready to leave, their packs on their backs like the lowest of peasants, an old woman came hurrying up to them.

"Sir, she cried, throwing herself on her knees and clasping her arms about the legs of old Pitaval, "you will not be so cruel as to leave this land and not tell me where my poor Jehan lies buried?"

"How could I be so cruel?" Pitaval protested, secretly giving his steward a nudge in the ribs. "Here," he said, "is the key to the vault in which he lies buried. No king ever had a more fitting tomb. Nor monk either," he added. "In the rear courtyard you will find a door to which this fits."

Come to think of it, it is strange that there should still exist and function in Genoa an asylum for poor children founded by this Datini, and that snot-nosed bambinos of that town should there enjoy the money that Datini made on the Pitavals and the Pitamonts. For it was the severe Genoan businessmen whom Datini put in charge on the former estates of the warring families who decided that lumbering would pay best and make quickest returns. The results were that Datini was repaid and that the region was permanently impoverished by erosion of the topsoil.

Records of any Pitavals in the following centuries are scarce. In fact, I find only one, Gayot de Pitaval, in the eighteenth century, who wandered up from Lyon to Paris and led a wretched existence as a law clerk, writing some miserable gossipy works on the side. It was not, in fact, until he had the brilliant inspiration to gather into a volume the gory tales of crime and detection that he picked up around the courts of law that his fortune changed and he became known all over Europe.

Think of it: he had the only volume of detective stories on the Continent. He had imitators enough in a short while, but managed to publish some twelve volumes to follow up his success. The German translation of his compilation carried an introduction by Schiller. Although practically unknown* today, the army of detective-story writers that have enriched themselves since his discovery should tax themselves to erect him a statue in gold.

As to the Pitamonts, we shall keep them company through the rest of this book and recognize them despite their disguises.

---

* As recently as 1903, there appeared in Germany a series called *Pitaval der Gegenwart*. (*The Present-day Pitaval*). Lately the book stalls have carried a volume called *Der Prager Pitaval* (*Criminal Stories of Prague*).

Chapter Two

Whoever has looked into Favre's excellent history of the morality police of Europe has not failed, I am certain, to notice and store in his mind that particularly striking case which Favre with grim (some will think it cheap) sense of humor entitled: "Suffer little children to come unto me..."

The case that Lieutenant Galliez considers briefly on page three of his defense is evidently the same, although no names are mentioned except that of Pitamont. Favre's description is very complete and precise as to names and dates. I follow his account in the main.

In the early 1850s, in Paris, there dwelt a widow by the name of Mme Didier. Her husband and she had come from the provinces and he had established himself in the jewelry business. He was successful in a fair way and left his wife well situated when he died. They had just moved to one of the fine new apartment houses on the Boulevard Beaumarchais not far from the Boulevard des Filles-du-Calvaire.

There is a particular reason for mentioning that, for in this adjoining street there lived and officiated a priest by the name of Pitamont who was Mme Didier's favorite father confessor.

Mme Didier dwelt pretty much alone, except for the frequent visits of a nephew, a young man who had been badly wounded in the street fighting in February, '48, and since had devoted himself to pamphleteering in support of Napoleon. The latter's rapid veering toward conservatism and imperialism had been a little bit too much for Mme Didier's nephew, who still retained his hatred of the Church and the aristocracy. For the moment he was undecided whether to follow his leader or continue along his own course.

At this time, Mme Didier took into her house a young girl of about thirteen or fourteen, an orphan from her own home village. Josephine had been recommended to her by the mayor of the village as a good and dutiful girl who would be useful to her in the household.

The nephew was sitting by the window and looking out on the street. It was a warm day, unseasonably so for the middle of March. The sky had suddenly become overcast. "I say, is it going to rain?" he exclaimed.

"Do you think so?" Mme Didier asked.

Just then there came the rumble of thunder and in the distance the play of lightning was visible. "Do you hear that?" the nephew replied.

"Bon Dieu," Mme Didier ejaculated. "And I have not a drop of holy water in the house."

"Holy water?" her nephew laughed. "Good heavens, you don't still practice that nonsense, do you?"

"You save your sarcasm for your pamphlets, my friend," his aunt returned calmly. "I've always sprinkled holy water about when a thunderstorm threatened. Do you wish us all to be struck by lightning?"

She laid aside her knitting needles. "My mother did the same. And she lived to be eighty. But whom can I send?" she wondered suddenly. "Françoise is out." Françoise was the cook and the only other person of the household.

44

"Send Josephine," the nephew suggested. "Unless you want to wait until I hobble there and back."

"But Josephine has been here only three days," she objected. "She doesn't know her way about yet."

"Good Lord, you don't have to know all Paris in order to go around the corner."

So Josephine, the little girl from the provinces, was called and given explicit directions how to get to the little chapel around the corner and find Father Pitamont.

"And hurry, please," said Mme Didier, as another burst of thunder resounded through the room. Josephine ran out, and directly into the thick of a violent thunder shower. Breathless she raced around the corner, repeating to herself over and over again the directions Mme Didier had given her. And thus she reached the chapel and almost flung herself headlong into the dark interior.

She was wet to the skin. Her garments clung to her, revealing her slender feminine form. Her breasts had but begun to grow. They caused her light dress to swell up. The nipples were hard with chill and chafing. Of late they pained her. Françoise had said to her sagely: "You have growing pains, everyone has them."

Lit by the golden light of the flickering candles, she made an enticing picture, thought Father Pitamont. He stood for a second and watched her, particularly her heaving, tumultuous breast. Before he could catch himself, he was overtaken by a wave of desire that shut off the voice of his conscience.

"What is it, my little girl?" he said, and came out from the pillar behind which he had been standing.

Frightened and now completely at a loss, an incomprehensible flood of words tumbled from her lips.

"Why, you are all chilled," he said kindly. "Come and warm yourself up with a glass of wine." He ushered her gently back into the sacristy, poured out two generous portions of consecrated wine, and made her drink one while he himself emptied the other.

Dazed and dizzied, she permitted him to fondle her and press her close to his cassock. She was warm there and comforted. But her fright rose again when she felt him touch her in precisely the way

45

Françoise, but the day before, had been warning her not to allow anyone to touch her. Now she wished to release herself, but her limbs were as if paralyzed. She struggled a little, but his strength was greater. And he kept pouring strange consoling words into her ear. She permitted him to lead her to the couch and do with her as he pleased.

She left without saying a word of her mission. Indeed she had quite forgotten the original purpose of her coming. In her ears resounded only the father's oft and insistently repeated caution that she must never utter a word of what had happened. He had made her swear by the cross.

The thunder shower had just ceased when Josephine returned. She came walking in, looking around out of wide-opened eyes, one finger pulling down her lower lip, as if she could no longer recognize her surroundings.

"Why, what is the matter with you, Josephine?" Mme Didier asked. She had been only a trifle worried at Josephine's absence, and that largely because she reproached herself for not seeing to it that the girl took her cloak along. When Josephine had not returned at once, Mme Didier had surmised that, caught in the thunderstorm, the girl had taken refuge and would return when the rain had abated. Which was precisely what happened. But why should she return as if she had seen the devil in person?

But Josephine would not answer and only shook her head.

"Come, Josephine, do not play the stubborn. Tell me what is the matter with you." Still the girl only shook her head.

"She has caught a cold. That's it!" Mme Didier exclaimed. "Why, your clothes are dry. No, they are a little damp. Tell me, were you caught in the rain? Or did you get to the chapel in time to miss the worst of it? Good heavens, why won't the child answer?"

Still Josephine made no reply. Then Mme Didier lost her patience and declared roughly, shaking her: "Then go to bed at once. And don't let me see you again until you find your tongue."

"Come now, my dear aunt," her nephew spoke up from his chair by the window. "Give the little girl a chance. Before you were all

46

for thinking her incapable of going around the corner. Perhaps she really did lose her way. Let me talk to her."

But his efforts were no more successful than those of his aunt. Finally Mme Didier said, as if the idea were an inspiration from on high:

"I know, she shall come with me to Father Pitamont. Surely she will not refuse to talk to him."

And truly her words were inspired, for all of a sudden Josephine let out a torrent of words, but so intermingled with sobs that one could make neither head nor tail of them. At the same time she threw herself down on the floor as if possessed.

Mme Didier was herself so taken aback that she could not summon her wits. But her nephew, fed on anti-clerical literature, cried out at once: "What did he do to you?"

"He did what Françoise said I shouldn't!" Josephine cried out, redoubling her sobs.

The nephew laughed sardonically. "So that's your Father Pitamont. A pretty bird."

"But I don't understand what Father Pitamont has to do with this," Mme Didier expostulated, completely at sea.

The nephew was suddenly resolved. Now was the time to break with Napoleon, who was at the moment off on a visit to the Pope, and throw this juicy bit of scandal into the public pot. He was so taken by his resolution that he forgot the matter at hand, and rose from his chair by the aid of his stick, determined to seek out the editor of *La Solidarité*.

Mme Didier, however, would not let him go until she had learned what all this business meant. And when she had heard, again she would not let him depart until she had sworn him not to say a word of it to anyone. Her reason was that the child was hysterical and that it would never do to believe her until the matter had been more fully investigated. His reason was simpler: all or at least most of his money came from his aunt, and further, he hoped to inherit from her some day. He could not afford to be a political pamphleteer without his aunt's support.

Mme Didier, however, herself went to the chapel and, seeing no one about, boldly knocked at the door to the sacristy. Receiving no answer, she entered. Father Pitamont was asleep on a couch. Asleep, he no longer looked the holy man she had usually taken him to be. He seemed old and coarse. His heavy features, particularly his bushy eyebrows, joined together by a heavy growth of hair above his nose, lent him a strange, almost beastly expression. In that moment, Mme Didier almost believed, but restrained herself for fear of doing him an injustice.

Feeling the weight of her glance upon him, he opened his eyes. "Why, madame, it is you," he exclaimed and rose at once.

Cutting short his greeting, she plunged quickly into her story. He nodded his head as if the matter were grave and interesting, but of no special concern to him.

"A young girl of about fourteen, you say?" he asked, as if he were trying to recall whether he had perhaps not seen such a girl somewhere.

At that moment, Mme Didier spied her bénitier, the vessel which she had given Josephine to hold the precious holy water. It was lying on the floor near the couch. At once he saw it too. How could he have forgotten to remove that! Throwing aside the rôle he had assumed, he cast himself at her feet. But she rose hastily and ran out, overcome with horror.

She disregarded the advice of her nephew, and made no complaint to the police, but went instead to the bishop and laid her case before him. With the result that Father Pitamont was called to account. The bishop, however, contented himself with transferring the culprit to another parish. There he had soon made a bad reputation for himself. The truth was that he could no longer hold himself in check. His temptations led him ever further astray into the world of sin. At night he slipped out of his cassock and, dressed in civilian clothes, frequented the most disreputable haunts of the city.

One night Mme Didier, leaving the theater late with her nephew, caught sight of him entering a voiture de place, gallantly helping in a young lady first. The broad expression of pleasure on his face, the

48

extreme of fashion in which the young lady was clad—lacy décolleté without shoulder-straps, leaving her shoulders and bosom bare down to just above the line of her nipples, long tight skirt flaring at the ankles—all this left little doubt as to the nature of the commerce that obtained between these two. Mme Didier shuddered. Her nephew had the kindness to make no comment. Subsequently she learned that Pitamont had been reported to his superiors again and again and was finally requested either to make a lengthy retreat among the forever silent Trappists, or lay down his frock. Pitamont expressed his decision by disappearing suddenly along with some valuable articles belonging to the church to which he was last attached.*

"We are well rid of him," thought Mme Didier. In truth she was far from being rid of Father Pitamont, although she never saw him again.

Her nephew, Aymar Galliez, had of late given up his own rooms and moved over to his aunt's apartment. This was partly to save money, and partly to be near his aunt, for his badly healed wounds left him a prey to fits of melancholy in which he could not bear solitude.

He was sitting at his favorite place near the window one day, and making an occasional note on a pad of paper. He had the itch to distinguish himself in the field of literature but was not quite sure of the form of the great work which he proposed to write. So many fine things were appearing lately, in all lines. Only recently the younger Dumas had electrified Paris with his *Dame aux Camélias* and a revolution in writing was taking place. Those in the know were all talking excitedly about the new way of writing. The password was *realism.*

He was being annoyed by the constant entry and exit of Josephine. "What the deuce can that girl be wanting in here every minute?" he asked himself irritably. For like all melancholic natures, much as he hated solitude, he was irritated by the presence of

---

* The report of this theft to the police uncovered the whole tale and thus came to the knowledge of Favre, who included it among the various cases in the chapter: "Suffer little children to come unto me…"

others. But after a while he became interested in the girl herself, wondering if here were not the subject for an incisive little sketch: a young girl seduced by a priest and thereupon rejected by her legitimate suitor. Or perhaps one might have the girl fall in love with the priest and he abandon his religion in order to marry her. But that was all old stuff, he had read countless things of the sort. The trouble with literature was that every subject had been done. There was nothing new for the pen to tackle.

As his thoughts ran on so, he almost forgot the girl. Gradually, however, he began to notice her strange demeanor. There could be no doubt of it, she was trying to attract his attention. Though ostensibly engaged in straightening the room and tidying up, she turned toward him every few moments, looked at him with big eyes, then suddenly looked away as if abashed. Meanwhile her body contorted itself in a positively indecent fashion. Her torso was in constant sinuous motion like the body of a snake. Her breast rose and fell as she sighed audibly.

When she saw that he was looking at her, she ceased. But a moment later she came up to him and, picking up a piece of paper from the floor, she asked: "Is this yours?" And when he thanked her she continued: "Shall I open the window a little more?" And again: "Are the curtains blowing in your way?" All of which he found most annoying. In leaning across his little table to reach the curtains and tie them back, she brought her young body up against his face. He breathed the warmth of her flesh. Despite himself he felt a powerful compulsion. Thoroughly disturbed, he found some excuse or other to dismiss the girl, and remained for a long time incapable of concentrating on his literary endeavors.

Chapter Three

One day as he was hobbling out, the door to the kitchen opened and Aymar heard himself called softly by Françoise: "M Aymar! *Psst!*"

He turned around. She beckoned him mysteriously to come into the kitchen and when he had followed her call, she first closed the door, and then whispered to him: "Do you know what terrible things are happening here?"

"Why, no," he said innocently.

"I mean about Josephine."

"Why, what's the trouble with her?" He had wanted to say: "Why, what's the trouble with her again?" but had restrained himself, not being quite sure that Françoise had been informed of the Pitamont affair, Mme Didier having been so anxious to keep the matter quiet.

"Her conduct is...how shall I say, monsieur...c'est une dévergondée!"

"What do you mean?"

"I mean that the butcher's boy, the concierge's young son, the greengrocer himself, everybody, simply everybody has had her. And if they have not had her, then it was only because they were decent enough to refuse. Yes, monsieur, I never thought that would happen to this house. A young country girl. Why, when she came here she acted as if she didn't know A from B. Monsieur, the whole neighborhood is talking about it!"

"Are you sure of this?" said Aymar, though he himself was convinced at once. "How do you know that this is not simply malicious gossip?"

She then told him how she had seen things with her own eyes. How she had caught the girl and the concierge's son up in the garret in a manner that left no doubt. Thereafter she had forbidden the girl to leave the house, but she had run away. Of course, people would say there was another girl ruined by the wicked city, but she knew better. That girl must have brought those habits with her from the country.

Aymar let her talk on, wondering himself. Could it be that that first display of bewilderment and grief and shame had been mere acting on Josephine's part? No. Impossible. The girl had been pure before. It was Father Pitamont who had unleashed this beast in her body. The mayor of Mme Didier's own home village would never have recommended a girl with a bad character.

"What I want you to tell me, monsieur, is how I shall break the news to Madame. I'm afraid to go to her with all this trouble. She has had sorrow enough, poor Madame."

"Leave that to me," Aymar consoled her. "I'll take care of everything."

"Yes, but do it at once. For who knows what may happen? Last night I woke up and found her gone from our bed. I waited, thinking she had gone out for only a moment. But when she didn't come back, I got out of bed and looked for her. I must tell you, monsieur, that she was not in the house at all. She had unlocked the door and gone out. It must be Jeannot the concierge's son who unlocked the door downstairs for her. I fell asleep again and when I woke up she was back in bed and denied that she had ever been out. What shall we do with such a creature?"

52

"Leave it to me," Aymar said again, and wondered what he could do.

But that evening Josephine waited on them at the dinner table as usual. And as usual she brought herself annoyingly into contact with Aymar. Nevertheless, her girlish face expressed nothing but purity and innocence. How could those tender, immature lineaments have expressed anything else? When she had retired to the kitchen and was busy with her own meal and with the washing of the dishes, Aymar opened up on his aunt.

"Do you see any change in Josephine since that terrible event?"

"Fortunately, no. She seems to have gotten over it and I hope will soon have completely forgotten it."

"Do you really think she was an innocent thing when she came here?"

"Why, yes, of course. What makes you ask?"

"Just so."

She pursued a pleasant thought of her own: Josephine had been the cause of the seduction and Father Pitamont had fallen to her wiles. But at the very moment she thought thus, she realized that it couldn't be so. Pitamont's subsequent actions did not endorse this view. "Why do you ask?" she repeated.

"Her behavior has not been irreproachable of late." He understated the matter, entering the thin edge of the wedge before he pounded home.

"What has she done?" Mme Didier asked.

He told her in a few words, reducing the case to its minimum and omitting all embellishments likely to cause Mme Didier to worry too much. Mme Didier remained in thought for a while and then decided sagely that Josephine should be put in a room somewhere where she would be safe and watched over and where she would remain until the mayor of her village acted upon her case. "Pull the bell for Françoise and we'll see if she knows of some good house where we can keep the girl."

Françoise appeared and listened to her mistress' decision. Meanwhile she fidgeted about and cast certain glances at M Galliez,

53

as if to say, There is something else I must tell you about. Until Aymar could not help exclaiming:

"Come right out with it, Françoise!"

Françoise sucked in her breath as if to gather courage; then jerking back her head with self-righteousness (she certainly wasn't to blame for anything), she delivered herself of this: "Josephine is pregnant."

There was a moment of deep silence, then particulars were demanded. Since when? Françoise couldn't say, but from what Josephine had told her it might be two, three months.

"Why, she has been here only three months!" Mme Didier exclaimed.

"Oui, madame," said the obedient Françoise.

"It's that damned Fa..." A look from his aunt made Aymar cut his sentence short.

"Bring her in, Françoise, I'll talk to her alone," said Mme Didier.

A moment later Josephine came in. Simply clad, demure, the bloom of rustic innocence still on her cheeks. Only when she happened to look up did her dark, blazing eyes belie her modesty and humility.

"My poor child," said Mme Didier, and put her hands on Josephine's shoulders. "Do you know that you are going to have a baby?"

"Oui, madame."

"And you are so young."

"Oui, madame."

"You poor thing."

"Is it because I go with the boys, like Françoise says, madame?"

"Oh, child, why do you do that?"

"I like it so, madame. Must I really stop? I've tried very hard not to do it, but I can't stop myself. At home I saw all the animals do it and no one ever stopped them."

"But, Josephine, my child, we are not animals. You never saw human beings do such things, did you?"

"No, madame. There was only mamma and myself at home..."

54

"Yes, to be sure," said Mme Didier and bit her lip.

"Don't men and women do it ever?"

"Hush."

"But Father Pitamont was the first to do it to me."

"Hush! Hush! Was he really the first?"

"Yes, madame."

"You unfortunate wretch. What shall we do with you now?"

"Françoise says you will send me away because I am bad. Don't send me away."

"I shall find a nice home for you." She was thinking of the Duchess of Angoulême's home for wayward girls. But a second's thought brought her to the decision not to attempt to put the girl in a home. She wanted as little explaining as possible in the case. The best thing to do was to take the matter upon herself completely, give Josephine as good a room to stay in as could be found and let things take their natural course. All wounds heal over in time, and those that are not healed are covered by the grave.

Josephine seemed to have quite resigned herself to her fate. It was only for the first few days that she suffered from lack of her nightly escapades. Here in the room they had found for her there was no running away at night or indeed at any time, but to compensate for that there was nothing to do, and in all the years of her life Josephine had been busy from early morn to night, not only at the little poverty-stricken farm where she had lived with her widowed mother, but also at Mme Didier's where under the stern direction of Françoise there was a constant succession of tasks to keep her actively at work all day long.

This sudden leisure was the first ray of sunlight in her short and bleak existence. She lolled around, doing nothing, and was quite happy at it. She sat by, the window and pretended she was M Galliez. Sat silently thus for hours.

Mealtimes she enjoyed the fullest. Not that she was a glutton, but being waited upon was to her such a novel experience that she could never have enough of it. And being called Madame by the girl who brought in her tray, a young girl much like what she herself had been but a few days before! Josephine did her best to act like Mme Didier.

Being thus, by turns, Mme Didier and then M Galliez, Josephine had really quite a nice time of it. And when every second day or so Françoise came to see her, she could not prevent herself from putting on little airs before Françoise, who was still Françoise, whereas she, Josephine, was now Madame, and feeling herself thoroughly in her rôle, it annoyed her considerably that once in front of the servant-girl, Françoise should speak quite openly of "our mistress." Josephine felt she had been humbled.

Occasionally (but rarely, being a woman of great weight) Mère Kardec ascended to the top floor of her Maison d'Accouchement to visit her most curious patient, a young girl who was not to give birth for some five months. Mère Kardec was a stern-visaged person, square hewn as if a stone carver had left her unfinished. She asked no questions. Her fortune had been acquired by her absolute lack of curiosity. The women who came to her house could be sure of being well taken care of. Mère Kardec sent a constant stream of children out to her relations in Brittany, and the mothers who left her place need never concern themselves about the matter again, beyond paying the required sums. A countess with a name known all over Europe might come to Mère Kardec's and register as whatever she pleased and have twins if nature so ordained, and Mère Kardec would make it right with the authorities, and never a word of it would go beyond her doors. A thousand romances on the brink of scandal or tragedy had come for salvation here behind the inconspicuous exterior of her house. Even the *Almanach de Gotha* must have its cesspool or sewerage system.

When Mère Kardec entered Josephine's room, she unloosened her dour visage and emitted a greeting to which she expected no answer. If one came, as in the present case, when polite words came tripping from Josephine's tongue, Mère Kardec paid no attention. She passed her hand over the furniture to see if the servants were cleaning properly, she jabbed at the bed to see if the feather mattress had been well shaken up, and looked under the bed for those fluffy accumulations of feathers, hair and dust that tend to gather there. Having satisfied herself as to this, she asked curtly about the satisfactoriness of the food, and without waiting

56

for more than a sentence of the answer, she excused herself and walked out.

To make up for these cold visits, there was the weekly call by Mme Didier herself, accompanied by M Galliez. Aymar sat down at once by the window. Sometimes he was much shaken by the arduous walk up the many flights of stairs, and this not only because the climb was difficult, but because the hall was often full of the horrible moans of women in labor. He sat by the open window and wiped his brow with his kerchief. Josephine could not take her eyes off his pale, thin face, his long delicate fingers, his silken handkerchief moistened with perspiration.

Once he came alone. Then she was so shy that he could not get a single clear response from her. Finally he arose to go. But she threw herself toward the door as if to bar his way, and taking his hand in hers she begged: "Don't go! Don't go yet!"

She slung her arms around his body and cuddled up close. He put his hands on her shoulders and said gently: "Why, Josephine, pull yourself together."

She did not answer but continued to cling to him. Then still holding her by the shoulders he sought to push her away. Only her head went back and her eyes looked up into his. Without knowing why, he bent and kissed her chastely on the lips.

Kiss me again, her eyes begged. He obeyed. Then her tongue darted out of her mouth and pushed itself between his lips. Her hot moist tongue stirred him to the depths of his bowels. Weak with sudden lust, he subsided on the bed with her.

Downstairs before her office stood Mère Kardec like the threat of doom, arms akimbo, glaring straight ahead. Aymar shrank within himself as he came in sight of her. He thought she was about to say something to him, but not a sound came from her firm lips. She had no intention of saying anything, as a matter of fact, but he, conscious of his guilt, slunk away like a whipped cur.

On his way home he came to the decision that there was only one way out for him and that was never to go to see Josephine again. Having so determined, his conscience was soothed and his ego revived from the chilling shower Mère Kardec had administered.

At home, across the table, Mme Didier said: "You look exhausted, my poor Aymar. You shall not go there again."

He controlled his great fright. "On the contrary," he assured her, "I feel exceedingly well. And if the long walk there and back has exhausted me I shall sleep all the better."

And after a moment, he added. "It is you who are looking peaked, my aunt. Why don't you run away to the country for a while? You should not have given up your plans for a vacation this year." She objected that with conditions as they were and what with Josephine and the fact that in any case she would not return to her village where she had usually spent her summers, all this made a vacation in the country impossible. He argued with her persuasively, and so well, as a trained pamphleteer like himself could do, that she capitulated.

Two days later he had the pleasure of seeing his aunt and Françoise off to the South. A moment after the train had pulled out he was in a fiacre and on his way to Josephine.

This time there were no preliminaries. They clutched at each other like two struggling in dark water and about to be engulfed.

He could not suppress a feeling of joy when he learned that Mme Didier was feeling very poorly and had been advised by the doctor to extend her stay in the Midi as long as possible. What kind of a monster am I? he asked himself and gazed at himself in horror. He shut himself up in his room, determined to write, to work on that great opus of his, to which he had not put a hand for weeks. He looked out of his window, down on the hot August boulevard. Men and women, horses and cabs, drenched in the sun, hastened by in both directions. What was the meaning of all this? His mind was empty of any thoughts. The whole world had no meaning. Nothing but hot dust, eye-searing colors, people who did not know what they were about.

He changed his mind about not going, and at once the world took on order and meaning. When he was out on the street, hastening like everyone else, then he found that the streets were not so hot as he had feared. A cool breeze was blowing. It was a balmy day with a climate such as one imagines is eternal in Paradise.

"Why do you never say a word about Josephine in your letters?" his aunt reproached him. "Don't you ever go to see her? You know I wanted you to watch out for her."

He saw that he had made a big mistake. She must not be suspicious. And there was Mère Kardec who could have told her that he had been there every day and sometimes twice.

"I remembered your injunction concerning Josephine," he wrote, slyly. "I have been to see her often. When I go to see my friend Le Pelletier as I do now and then, or when I go to see the group at the Café Palissot, then since I am passing by there anyhow, I usually drop in to see how she is faring. Indeed she has been quite well up until now."

The facts were true enough. The implication was a clever lie. He detested himself for stooping to such procedure. No longer could he have shouted "That damn Father Pitamont, that devil in priest's garb!" He felt himself to be as low, as rascally, nay, even lower than Pitamont. At the club it was noticed that he no longer inveighed so fiercely against priest and capitalist. He had come to the consoling thought that "we are all sinners together." That was the only excuse he could find for himself.

As for Josephine, now that she had him, she would not let him go. She could not bear his absence, and when he had to go she would make him swear to return at such and such a definite time, insisting that she would throw herself out of the window if he were but a minute late.

The child she carried troubled her much by its liveliness and prevented her from sleeping at night. But when Aymar was around she forgot completely about it. The small pleasure which she had had at first on finding herself treated as Madame and with no work to do had palled on her. There was for her only one satisfaction in life and that was being with Aymar.

Late in October, Mme Didier returned. Aymar promptly settled into a melancholia from which nothing could arouse him. Apathetically he listened to Mme Didier's tales of her experiences in the South. Twice he ventured to make a visit to Josephine, but his nerves were so jumpy from fear of exposing the whole sordid connection that he stopped completely thereafter. The last time, indeed, he saw Françoise mounting the stairs as he was coming down. Fortunately, she had not seen him yet and he had time to step into a dark recess, which she passed unsuspectingly. Shattered by this experience, he took to bed for a whole day.

Josephine, realizing that now everything was over, and unable to deceive herself long with the pleasant thought that after the birth of the child she would be able to return to the old conditions, demeaned herself like one gone insane and threatened so often to commit suicide that at last Mère Kardec transferred her to a room where the window was barred and took the additional precaution of leaving a nurse in the room both day and night.

And now the babe within her never stopped squirming and kicking and gave Josephine not a second's peace.

Chapter Four

One day late in December, to be precise on the twenty-third, Mme Didier and Aymar sat at the dinner table and ate with little appetite and conversed desultorily. Aymar ate out of some vague sense of duty, while Mme Didier had, ever since her girlhood, been accustomed to eat whatever was set before her and finish it down to the last particle, a trait that the French are fond of instilling in their children, perhaps to give the lie to the notion that the French are a race of gourmets.

Suddenly Mme Didier spoke up: "You know, I am beginning to be worried."

"What about?"

"Of course you will think me superstitious."

"No fear," said Aymar ironically. "You? Superstitious? Never!"

"Now don't make fun, Aymar. I have seen a good deal more of the world than you have."

"What, for example?"

"Do you believe in Christmas?"

"Of course I do," said Aymar. "Everybody believes that Christmas comes on the twenty-fifth of this month, and they are one and all right."

"If you will stop your silly jesting, I'll go on."

"Do go on, I've always wanted to know about Christmas."

"Do you believe that the animal world is conscious of the coming of Christmas?"

In spite of himself, Aymar smiled: "Are you going to tell me that the cattle kneel in their stalls on Christmas night?"

"That is precisely what I am going to tell you. And more, that I have seen it with my own eyes."

"Of course you have seen it. Anyone going into a stable any night of the year can see some or, if he is lucky, all of the cattle kneeling."

"I knew you were going to say that. But it isn't true. And what is more I went one night, as the birth of our Saviour was approaching, and heard the bees sing in their hives."

"Bees always sing in their hives."

"Come, Aymar, in the dead of winter bees certainly don't sing in their hives."

"And you say you heard them?"

"If you can't get me one way, you will have me another. Is that it, Aymar?"

Disconcerted because she had worsted him, he remained silent for a moment and then brought the conversation back to the beginning. "And so that is why you are worried?"

"No, of course not. What worries me is that Josephine is about to be delivered, and as like as not it may be at the very hour of Our Lord's birth."

"Why should that distress you? I should think, on the contrary, that you would see reason to rejoice."

"It is because I am superstitious, if you like me to put it that way. But let me tell you this. I knew a man who came to no good end, and it had always been said of him that he was doomed from the beginning, for he had been born on Christmas Eve."

"And naturally everybody did his little bit to make it come true," said Aymar bitterly.

"Do you number me among those?" Mme Didier reproached him, and went on rapidly: "And in our village and in other villages

62

where the people are God-fearing, the wives stay away from their husbands during most of the month of March and a week or so of the month of April, in order that they may not have children born on that day."

"Now, will you tell me what sense you can see in that practice?"

"I spoke only of superstition, my dear Aymar, but if you wish me to speak of sense, which is more rightly your province, I suppose, then I have this to say: When people believe in a thing, they like to show their respect for it. I have noticed that the first thing the revolutionaries do, after they have torn down a lot of old statues, is erect a lot of new ones, and after they have ruled out a lot of old holidays, institute a lot of new ones. I don't suppose that would strike you as being superstitious?"

"That is neither here nor there," said Aymar.

"Very well," Mme Didier continued, "but you will grant that people like to show their respect for what they believe in, and those who believe in the beautiful and gentle life of Christ like to honor him. Now, tell me, can they practice any finer act of homage than the renunciation of carnal conception during that period when the Virgin Mary conceived immaculately? Tell me, must not even such as you admire therein a refinement of taste and a delicacy of worship which has no parallel in your modern boisterous attachment to one political leader after another?"

"It is not lacking in beauty," Aymar admitted. "But what does it mean?"

"It means as much as all your cockades and colors and speeches," Mme Didier retorted. "What do you mean? How many times in my life has blood been shed here in France in order that people should be happier, in order that there should be no more poor? I cannot see that anyone is any better off for all this fighting."

"You have told me that you see no meaning in politics, but you still haven't told me what sense there is to worrying about a child being born on Christmas eve."

"Aymar, my dear nephew, is it not already enough of evil that Josephine should bear the child of a priest? Is that not already enough of an insult to heaven that a priest should be guilty of such misconduct, without adding to this sad birth the characteristic of being a mockery of the birth of Christ?"

In spite of himself Aymar was moved. "That's a Mother Goose story," he said irritably.

"In my opinion," Mme Didier continued, "Josephine was an innocent little girl, but when the devil tempted Father Pitamont, he did not spare her. The devil is in her now and I see it every time I go there. She is dangerous."

"Nonsense," said Aymar, but he was startled nevertheless. Somewhat unnerved and more than a little vexed, he wished to stop the conversation and therefore rose with the excuse that he had to get back to his writing.

He retired to his room and lit his Quinquet lamp. But he had no desire to work on the story he had chosen to tell, namely, that of a young man who strives to lead the world on to happiness for all and who succeeds only in losing his life.

Annoyed, he pushed away the sheets of paper. "The world is too big to be cramped up in a book," he said. Then he wondered: Why had he no ability to stick to what he had decided to do? After all, the idea wasn't a bad one and people didn't expect you to put the world into a volume. This was now the tenth or twelfth idea he had thrown into the discard. Every time a new book appeared and drew to itself the plaudits of the critics, then he found it to be on a subject he had once thought of doing himself, an idea that he had rejected for one paltry reason or another.

He leaned over on his desk and rested his head on his outstretched arms. So Josephine was going to have a baby in a day or so? What did she look like, now, with her body swollen to term? He could not picture her. In fact he could not call her face to mind. What is it I have loved? he asked himself distractedly, if her image has already faded? What he had loved was a softness and a clinging warmth, a gentleness and a vivacity. And now she would have a baby and moan like those others he had heard as he climbed the steps of Mère Kardec's Maison d'Accouchement. He found himself thinking of that baby, thinking of it with fondness and wishing that it were his own. Wishing that he and the baby and Josephine were one family.

64

Late the following night, Françoise returned from Mère Kardec's.

"Well?" Mme Didier asked.

"Not a sign yet," she reported to her mistress.

"Very well, Françoise, come, hurry up or we shall not find places for the midnight mass. And you, Aymar, you are not coming?"

"I think not, my aunt," he mumbled, his mind occupied with a bold scheme. While they were secure in the packed church, he would slip over to Mère Kardec's and be back before they returned.

No sooner were they well off than he had hastened out toward the Maison d'Accouchement. Well known to all the servants, he had no trouble in being admitted despite the lateness of the hour and went upstairs as fast as his bad legs could carry him.

A woman bustling out of Josephine's room with a large pail of red-tinted water caused him to stop in dismay. The first thought that struck him was that Josephine had died in agony. When the woman came back with her pail filled with fresh water, he appealed to her for a word of news, but she only smiled at him and entered, closing the door rapidly, before he could get a distinct view of what was inside. He had caught, however, a glimpse of Mére Kardec and a man, the doctor evidently, for though Mére Kardec was an accomplished midwife, she always called in a doctor.

Aymar waited without for what seemed to him hours. In vain his mind strove to interpret the sounds he heard, sharp phrases, the swishing of water, and feet moving back and forth. Suddenly there was a piercing scream, a long drawn-out blood-curdling yell that wound and wound, growing shriller and shriller, stopping suddenly with a deep dark gurgle as though all that vast sound were being sucked back and down into a waste-pipe. The silence that followed was so intense that the shivering Aymar could hear the responses of the people in the church across the street. Even the tinkling of the bell announcing the miracle of the transubstantiation of the wafer and wine into flesh and blood could be heard distinctly. And precisely then another sound came from the room, the strangest, queerest squeaking and mewling. Thereafter came that same medley of rapid commands, the splashing of water, the clatter of pottery, all dull and low as if heard through a dream.

Suddenly the door was pulled back and a tall man stepped out. Aymar pressed himself against the wall as if he would have liked to sink into it. But the tall man had seen him. "So you're the fortunate father?"

"Yes," Aymar stuttered.

"Well, let me be the first to congratulate you on the birth of a son."

"Is she dead?" Aymar breathed.

"Who? The mother?" he chuckled with professional satisfaction. "Never had an easier case. Slipped out like a kitten. Work would be a round of pleasure for me if they were all as easy."

"But that scream..."

"Bound to be a little pain, of course. Better not to see her now. She's sleeping. Come back in the morning." And with an amicable pat on the shoulder, he dismissed Aymar from his mind and hurried down the stairs.

And Aymar, recalling all of a sudden how little time he had if he wished to get back before Mme Didier and Françoise returned from midnight mass, scuttled down after him.

He had barely sat down in his favorite chair before the window when there was a noise at the door and Françoise and Mme Didier entered.

"It was marvelous," said Mme Didier.

Aymar's natural question stuck in his throat. All he brought forth was a gurgle. Mme Didier began to look at him suspiciously. He pulled himself together and asked: "What was?"

"The mass, of course," she answered. "The sermon was so moving, so touching. One could have fancied oneself actually present at the birth...Why, what is the matter with you, Aymar? Why, your face is the color of cheese!"

"I'm a little tired," he said as calmly as he could. "I think I'll go to bed."

"You're evading me," said Mme Didier severely. "Tell me now,

66

where does it hurt you? What you need is a good tisane or some rhubarb."

"No, no," he protested, "I'll be all well in the morning." She shook her head. "You don't take care of yourself," she declared. "I'll have to watch you more carefully." He shuddered. "Perhaps," she pursued, "you might have a vacation yourself. You know you haven't been out of Paris for over a year, and this city, with more gas lamps every day, is becoming really poisonous. No wonder everybody, especially women, are always fainting. When I was a girl, a woman was considered as strong as a man. Here I am forgetting all about you, thinking of my girlhood. Positively, I'm getting to radoter like an old woman. Wait, I'll go fetch you some rhubarb."

He submitted dully to the rhubarb pill for want of courage to argue against her.

Early the next morning he was already itching to be off, but neither Françoise nor Mme Didier seemed to have any thought of going to Mère Kardec's. Their calmness irritated him. How could they go about their work so stodgily? Truly women had no hearts. Josephine's scream still rang in his ears as indeed it had done all night. All night he had rehearsed the sounds of his nocturnal experience. He heard the clanking of vessels filled with water. He heard the doctor's pleasantly rough voice cutting into Mère Kardec's bass. He saw the woman rushing out with that horrible pail of pink water in which he thought he could recall the sight of swirling streaks of deep red. He shivered. He was allowing his imagination to get the better of him.

Finally, he heard Mme Didier call out: "Françoise! Françoise! How could we have forgotten?" He breathed with relief. He meant to propose to go with them just as soon as they broached the subject of going to see Josephine. But he heard his aunt continue: "There's all that linen in the chest. That's where those missing sheets must be."

With deep disgust he heard the two women scurrying away toward the chest which they opened with exclamations of surprise. They laughed and chatted about their amusing oversight, saying ever and again until Aymar thought he would die of rage: "How could we have forgotten...I never thought...I don't know what's coming over me..."

At noon the reason for the women's lack of interest was revealed. "Well, that's a stone off my heart," said Mme Didier to Françoise as she served the potage.

"Oui, madame," said Françoise.

"What's a stone off your heart?" Aymar asked.

"The fact that we haven't heard from Mère Kardec."

"Did you expect to hear from her?" Aymar managed to say, suddenly divining the whole situation.

"Why, yes, she told Françoise yesterday that she would send a messenger this morning if anything happened during the night. Well, my worst fears are over. It won't be a Christmas baby."

Aymar sputtered. "The soup's awfully hot," he said testily. "I thought I had asked you often enough to cool off my soup, Françoise."

"Oui, monsieur," she said, visibly annoyed, and could not help adding as she ran out, her whole body quivering with anger: "The last time was *three* years ago."

"How can you be so rude?" said Mme Didier, and she too was angry.

"Oof," he ejaculated, too exasperated to think of anything better. And he knew himself in the wrong, which was the worst of it. "Now everybody is going off to sulk in a corner," he complained.

"Well, you have yourself to blame, and the sooner you make it right with her the better."

And so there was nothing for him to do but go back to the kitchen and wheedle Françoise back into good humor. This involved a flood of tears, and many reminiscences on her part as to how she had been with the family for thirty years and had held Monsieur in her arms when he was just a baby and had used to wash his soiled linen often, because Mme Galliez was a weak woman and could not always afford a servant to help her, and other such details, ad nauseam.

Aymar forced himself to say: "I know, you and my aunt have

68

been more than mothers to me." He forced himself to say that, not because it was not true, not because he did not appreciate what these two women had done for him, but because there are types of gratitude which will always be annoying to a man.

When they came to the point of walking over to Mère Kardec's, Aymar declared that he would go along. He had wild visions of himself tearing in ahead of the women on one excuse or another, and warning Mère Kardec not to say a word of his visit on the previous night, for it was plain that the only reason she had not sent the messenger was because she figured that he would bring the news to the ladies.

But no opportunity of "tearing in ahead" of the women afforded itself, and as for a plausible excuse, his mind, no matter how he tortured it, would not yield a single idea of value. So he walked along through the mildly wintry day and tried his best to appear nonchalant while he journeyed to his doom. For his visit last night was bound to come out and with it all his secret relationship, that relationship he was burning to resume, and which yet he could not acknowledge to himself without revulsion.

Mère Kardec greeted the ladies in her usual stern manner, unbending only sufficiently to say: "You will see Madame nursing her baby for the first time."

In unison, Françoise and Mme Didier exclaimed: "What?! Her baby?! When did she have her baby? Why did you not send a messenger as you promised?"

Aymar looked on calmly, as if the matter did not interest him, though he would have welcomed the proverbial yawning of the earth beneath his feet, to swallow him whole.

Mère Kardec uttered no more than a "But I thought Monsieur..." Even before she had finished the word *Monsieur* she had checked herself and instead of explaining herself, she excused herself. Years of experience had taught her that one apology is worth a dozen explanations.

The ladies, however, did not wait for much apology but hastened upstairs, followed by the perspiring but happy Aymar. He had been saved on the brink of the precipice. Nevertheless, he was to go home that afternoon a much disappointed man. Two rude experiences awaited him.

He did not mind that Josephine should not give him a second glance. He accounted readily for that as being due to the presence of Mme Didier and Françoise. But he had not been prepared for that baby. Brought up with the belief that new-born babies were such as one sees borne by Madonnas in Italian paintings, or such as are depicted in the canvases of Greuze, he was shocked by the scrawny, spidery, fuzzy and wizened little monster that Josephine was gently hugging to her breast. As for the ladies, they went into ecstasies.

When the three had said good-bye and had gone down one flight of stairs, Aymar suddenly bethought himself of a handkerchief he claimed to have forgotten—though it still reposed in his pocket. And before Françoise could say that she would fetch it for him, he had dashed up the stairs and reëntered the room. The little baby had been placed back in its basket and Josephine was certainly free to give him one rapid passionate embrace, which was what he expected. Or at the very least, seeing that she might still claim to be an invalid, a look of tenderness and promise.

All he received was a quiet question as to the reason for his return. And her eyes, which formerly had blazed with ardor, were now quiet pools of maternal affection, entirely meaningless to him. He could not leave her thus. He stopped and said: "Well…"

"Quoi, monsieur?" she said. She had not meant the monsieur. It had returned to her naturally, along with her changed attitude. But to him it was suddenly revelatory of the fact that she was no longer his mistress, but his servant. Thoughtfully he closed the door and followed his aunt down the stairs.

At home Aymar had the courage to twit his aunt about the terrible fate of children born on Christmas eve. Actually, he was himself half willing to believe that there was something magical in all he had been through. No doubt about it, he had been bewitched. How else could he have let himself in for such a relationship, right on the doorsteps of his aunt, so to speak, no, actually in her house? And Josephine, she had been under a spell also. And now that spell was broken. He, too, felt that he was no longer enchanted. He could stay home now, and work on his book again. He could take renewed interest in the opposition party to which he belonged. Filled with his private thoughts, he only half listened to his aunt who was saying:

"I wish I could dismiss my fears. But I confess that I am still worried."

"The child does look a frightful mess," Aymar laughed.

"New-born babies are hardly ever very beautiful. What is strange about this one is that it should be able to lift its head on the very first day of its life. I never saw or heard of such a thing. But Françoise says she has seen that before."

"That's pretty small reason for believing the little fellow is born to be hanged."

"I haven't really any reason at all to think anything, if you want me to put it that way. But I have intuitions. And, frankly, I am uneasy."

"Well, we'll see," said Aymar, and dismissed the matter.

"Maybe we shall and maybe we shan't. Perhaps we shall never see him again."

"Why?"

"Well, he is to be sent to Brittany to Mère Kardec's sister-in-law, and we shall take Josephine back here if she will continue to be good, or else she may go back to her village. That will settle this affair."

Aymar found the whole matter of supreme indifference. A fact which surprised him. What? Could he have changed so fast?

Mme Didier was busy for the next few days. She bought a good layette for the baby and saw that a proper birth certificate was made out, one which involved neither the Church nor herself. Previous to the making of the birth certificate she paid a visit to the church where Pitamont had been priest. She spoke to the sacristan as if her sole mission in coming there was to arrange for the christening of the child. As a matter of fact she had another reason. She had never known or else had forgotten what Pitamont's first name was. Still his child ought properly to bear his name.

71

Casually she said: "I hear that Father Ernest Pitamont is now officiating in Nîmes." Her part in his dismissal was unknown.

"You mean Father Bertrand Pitamont?" the sacristan said.

"Of course," she answered.

A few days later the child was dutifully christened. Aymar had to stand godfather and give it the names Bertrand Aymar. Its last name was Caillet, which stood for the mythical husband of Josephine, who was off on a long sea voyage.

Back from church, Mme Didier began at once: "Now, Josephine, I shall let you have your choice. You may go back to your village or you may stay here."

"I suppose," said Josephine, "that if I went home, people would laugh at me for having a baby, wouldn't they?"

"They needn't know that you have had a baby, because we shall send the child to be taken care of in Brittany."

"Then I would rather stay here," she said, "because I want to be with my baby."

"But you can't keep your baby here, either," Mme Didier explained. "We can't have it here in the house."

"Then I shall go back home with the baby."

"But, child, think of what you will be exposed to! And how will you earn a living? What will you say to people when they ask you how you happened to have a baby?"

"Why, madame, I shall tell them the truth," she said naïvely.

This gave Mme Didier pause. The truth was what she didn't want told. What would they think of her at home when they learnt that her servant had had an illegitimate son as a result of being sent out on an errand to a church? And what would they think of the fact that she had done so little to secure Father Pitamont to his responsibility? Whatever happened, she didn't want this matter thrashed out among the gossips of her home village. She sat back and cogitated for a moment. If she sent the girl packing, God only knew how this business would come flying back to her doorstep again. Wherever she was, this much was certain, Josephine would link her, Mme Didier, with her condition. This was terrible, but then again, the link was there after all, and not to be denied. Only it

72

was ridiculous, this being responsible for someone else's misdeed. Again, if she put Josephine in an institution of whatever nature, there would be no evading of official papers to be made out, and of such papers Mme Didier had had her hands full these last few days, and she wanted no more of that. She took a sudden decision which, seeing that it was forced upon her, was not far-fetched.

"Well, for the moment you may stay here," she resigned herself. After all, the gossips of the whole arrondissement knew of the case, in even greater detail than she herself. Moreover, it was only Christian charity that she should continue to take care of an accident in which she could not consider herself quite without guilt. Yes, it was only Christian charity. She clung to that phrase. She repeated it to herself when she happened to meet someone of the neighborhood, before whom she would have quailed otherwise, and with the mental repetition of that saving phrase she found the strength to hold up her head and speak out without fear.

In truth she was more than resigned to her duty as a Christian. She could not very well live in the same house with a baby and fail to fall under that strange influence which all babies soon exert upon those who see them frequently. This influence, which naturally seizes first upon the mother, climbs out and attaches itself to all those within its range. Like ivy it has tentacles that hold fast whatever they come into contact with.

Little Bertrand was truly a model baby. He never cried. At night he slept curled up in a most delightful manner. When awake, between his long naps during the day, he responded cheerfully to those who bent over his cradle and talked to him. His whole face would break into a puckered smile. His soft brown eyes would glisten with amusement. He would open his mouth and a low gurgle of sheer joy would come out of his throat.

His health was equal to his spirits. He filled his belly full at his mother's breasts, and when he was weaned he ate whatever was given him and thrived upon it. He grew at a fine rate, and teethed without any trouble. No one surely could have wished for a better child. But we are proceeding too fast.

When Aymar, who took least interest of all the occupants of the

73

house in the baby's progress, would see his aunt gurgling back at the baby in that silly manner that is incomprehensible to those who do not share it, then he would tease her for her previous fears.

One day she said to him abruptly: "I'll talk to you later."

That evening when the house had become quiet, when Françoise and Josephine had retired to the room they shared with the baby, behind the kitchen, then she spoke to her nephew and relieved herself of her accumulated observations.

"I am far from having thrown overboard all my misgivings," she began. "Indeed, I am more than ever certain that Bertrand is an unusual child."

"You mean in the fact that he never cries? He might be dumb," suggested Aymar. "Children are often born dumb, I am told."

"Yes," she admitted, "he may be dumb. We shan't know until a few months from now, as to that, when the time comes for him to begin to talk. Personally, I think he will turn out normal in that respect."

"Then what are you still afraid of?"

"Have you ever noticed his eyes?"

"Yes, of course; they are very fine eyes, I should say."

"Well, I don't mean his eyes so much as his eyebrows."

"What about them?"

"They are very full and join together across the nose."

"And what do you deduce from that?"

"In our part of the country that was a sign of a low nature."

"Another superstition," Aymar said. "It might be simply inheritance."

"Now that you remind me of it," said Mme Didier, "Father Pitamont did have the same eyebrows."

"Just as I said. Like father, like son."

"That's precisely it. I'm afraid he might turn out to be just such an uncontrollable character."

"Well, that's still far from now." Aymar laughed at the picture that came suddenly to his mind of little Bertrand attempting rape. "And what else do you see?"

"A much more fearful matter, this. So rare that I myself have

74

never seen it yet, though I have heard old people speak of it as a sign that is the most sure and most terrible of all signs that mark the soul that belongs to the devil."

Her voice had sunk so low that Aymar had to lean forward to hear her, especially inasmuch as a cold March storm was rattling at the double windows. Despite himself he was moved, and either her words or a cold draft finding a crack in the window and blowing down his back made his spine shiver.

"Well?" he urged.

"I remember that when I was a little girl my grandmother used to tell me stories of the forests and the monsters that live there. The headless horseman who strikes those who see him with insanity; the tree where the Swedish hirelings hung five men. Their souls are now in that tree and that is why it will never die, until Judgment Day. The white deer who comes one night every year to look for a mate, who must be a pure young girl."

"Children shouldn't be told such stories," was Aymar's comment.

"Sometimes, so my grandmother used to say, men come to the village fair who have never been seen before and never will be seen again. They are men from the sea and are looking for prey to drag down into their underwater dwellings. They can be recognized by the fact that the hems of their clothes are always slightly moist and their hands are often webbed. Their teeth are sharp and pointed. Sometimes they are wolves from the mountains. Then they can be recognized by the hair that grows on the palms of their hands."

In the silence that followed her reminiscences, she added: "Bertrand has hair on the palms of his hands."

The cold spring with its constant rains and chill had proven too much for Mme Didier, whose health had been undermined by the vexations of the last few years. The death of her husband, the terrible days of '48 when she discovered Aymar wounded in a hospital, and this last event, the treachery of Father Pitamont and the misfortune of Josephine, which she had had to add to her burdens.

75

One day she had been out tending to various purchases. The morning had been so beautiful. There was a touch of spring in the air and the sky was delightfully blue, with that fresh clear blue that comes only after a long, hard winter, when all nature seems to have been purged of its vileness. But in a brief hour while she was in a shop looking over materials, the weather took a sudden turn for the worse. The sky became overcast, a cold wind arose and soon sheets of rain were sweeping diagonally across the streets. The flawless morning had turned into a dismal afternoon.

Upon coming out of the store, Mme Didier first noticed how bad the weather really was. She ordered a cab, but none could be found empty. She waited inside, hoping every moment that the rain would abate, but it seemed only to grow fiercer. The stuffy air of the shop, traversed by cold drafts at every opening of the door, soon affected her. She felt hot and cold by turns. Her throat had a soft painful lump in it. She wanted to get home quickly and have Françoise prepare her a hot tisane while she went to bed. That always fixed her up.

She determined at last to brave the weather to the boulevard beyond where she would either get a cab or take refuge in a café and there drink something hot. Pulling the collar of her astrakhan coat firmly around her neck, she walked out, head bowed against the driving rain. Two steps beyond the door and she had slipped and fallen into a puddle of water. In a trice she was soaked through and through. Kind people helped her up, and found a fiacre for her, so that she was soon home.

For days she lingered between life and death. At last her peasant strength, not totally rubbed off by her long existence in the city, came to her rescue and she grew better. During all of her illness she had yearned wistfully for a sight of the baby. But she had feared that she might infect it in some way and had therefore refused to permit it to be brought into the room. Françoise and Aymar, forbidden now to go near the baby, had to bring her long reports of its doings, reports which they secured from Josephine. The house was divided into two camps which communicated from a distance.

76

There came a day when she could feel that her illness was definitely behind her. It was a pleasant and true spring day, not such a treacherous one as had brought on her illness. The windows were flung open and the curtains moved in a gentle breeze.

"Today," she told Françoise and Aymar, "I shall have Bertrand brought in here."

"It will do you good to see him," said Françoise with tears in her eyes. "And shall I, too, be allowed to see him, now that you are so well?"

"Of course, of course, my good Françoise. Beast that I am, I had forgotten completely that I deprived you of him. Come, kiss me quick and say that you forgive me. Now go run quick and fetch him."

At that moment they became aware of a strange noise. A choking, howling, sobbing sound, indescribable in words. Mme Didier and Françoise looked at each other in surprise. Then Françoise dashed out. Aymar asked:

"What the deuce is that?" The noise grew louder, deeper, more resonant and less choked.

Josephine came running back with Françoise. "Madame," she cried out, "it's Bertrand! He must be dreadfully ill. Oh, do send for a doctor quick!"

"The doctor will be here soon," Françoise replied. "That must be he at the door now." She ran to admit Dr Robyot, who had come to pay his daily visit to Mme Didier.

"I don't approve of dogs in the houses of my patients," were his first words, commenting on the sad howls that filled the apartment.

"Oui, monsieur," said Françoise, trembling in every limb, and ushered him in to Madame's bedchamber.

"Ah, well, the patient is looking exceptionally well today," he said cheerfully, taking Madame's pulse in his hand. "You should get up a little now and exercise a bit. But not too much."

"I am not the patient today," said Mme Didier seriously, "but Madame Caillet's baby, who seems to be suffering terribly. Don't you hear him?"

The doctor, quite surprised to discover that these dismal sounds came from a baby and not a dog, left at once for the rear chambers with Josephine and returned a short while later. "I can find nothing wrong with the little lad. On the contrary, he seems fit in every way. A little fright or hysteria, perhaps. Did anyone scare him?"

"No," Josephine asserted. "I know because I am the only one who has been seeing him since Madame here has been ill."

"Well, I'll write out a prescription for a soothing dose that will quiet him. And when he wakes up, I suspect he will have quite forgotten about his fright."

"But that noise is absolutely terrifying, monsieur le docteur," said Mme Didier.

"He'll stop just as soon as he gets some of this," the doctor replied. "Meanwhile, you had better have the doors shut so that you will not be disturbed. Remember, you must be very careful. You have been seriously ill, don't forget that."

All doors were thereupon shut tight and only a faint sound managed still to penetrate into Mme Didier's chamber. Soon even that stopped, for Josephine had returned with the necessary concoction and the baby had fallen into a deep and silent slumber.

Mme Didier arose and sat near the window in an easy chair opposite Aymar. She put her thin hand with its pale, silky skin traversed by blue veins on his knee and said: "You've been a good son to me, Aymar. It's good to be sitting across from you."

He wanted to say: "Nonsense," gruffly, as befitted the occasion, but the words were caught in a lump in his throat. After a while he managed to say: "Now take good care of yourself and don't be off buying silly materials in bad weather anymore."

In the evening he sat by her bedside and she recalled to him the pranks he used to play when he came out during summers to their country home. A faint noise, growing louder, began to disturb him. Evidently the baby had awakened and began to cry again. Good that all the intervening doors were shut. His aunt was apparently unconscious of the renewed howling of the child. Wishing to make sure that her mind should not stray from her mood of reminiscing, he put leading questions to her:

78

"I have a dim recollection of something about a hedgehog; what was that?"

"Oh, that was very funny," she began briskly, and took his hand in hers. "You had always wanted a hedgehog and we would not let you keep one. Then one summer when we came back, we found the house overrun with cockroaches. That was when we had that lazy caretaker and his drunken wife. Do you remember them?"

"Not very well," he said. "Was I four years old then?"

"Within a month or two of five, I think. Oh, yes, I recall now distinctly when you had your fifth birthday. It was that very summer. But let me tell you about the hedgehog. You had been bothering your mother for a pet hedgehog. God only knows where you conceived the notion. Anyhow when we came out to our house and found the place just crawling away with bugs, you claimed that hedgehogs would eat them all up. Of course we didn't believe you, but you were so insistent. But if we hadn't sent it out into the garden again, I think the cockroaches would have eaten *it* up, for certainly it never touched a single one of them. Yes, I remember, too, that..."

His mind was so busy listening to the weird howling of the baby that for a moment he was unaware that his aunt had suddenly ceased talking. Then he wondered quickly: Had she finally heard it too? It was a ghastly sound, more like the baying of a moonstruck dog on a lonely farm than the crying of a human baby. No, she hadn't heard, she was asleep. He had scarcely thought this when a great fear came over him. A fear so mad that he rose in horror from his chair. His hand, which his aunt had been holding, slipped readily out of her grasp. He stood thus for a second not knowing what to do, then he ran out.

In the hall near the kitchen he came upon Josephine. "I was just going to give him another dose when he stopped all of himself. He's all right now. I don't know what to make of it, monsieur. I only hope he didn't wake Madame from her sleep."

"No," he said dully. "Madame is dead."

Chapter Five

In his unofficial defense of Sergeant Bertrand, Aymar Galliez devotes very little space to a matter which, had his intentions been otherwise, he would have undoubtedly expanded to greater length.

It appears that during the worst days of her illness, his aunt had called in her *notaire* and drawn up her will. Therein she left all her property to her nephew Aymar, with two provisos, firstly, that he was to continue to take care of Françoise and Josephine and the little Bertrand. The other proviso was that he study for the Church and prepare himself to take orders.

The scene of the reading of the will is easy to reconstruct. Mme Didier's notary was Le Pelletier, a man as yet unknown but soon destined to make himself widely hated and loved. He was indeed acquainted with Aymar, whom he had encountered in various radical groups.* Le Pelletier was outwardly a man of little prepossession, short, swarthy, he was as if crumpled up, soiled and thrown into the gutter by some vindictive force. He was an

---

* Political clubs, severely suppressed at this point, nevertheless continued as casual café meetings.

argument for that often repeated but unproven statement that revolutionaries are furnished by those whom fate has mistreated, the failures in life and love. Le Pelletier devoted little of his time to his profession and most of it to the Bibliothèque Nationale where he was gathering material for his two-volume history and eulogy of the Reign of Terror, a work which when published, at a time when the French Revolution was highly unpopular, aroused wide comment and procured for him the glory of a prison sentence.

After he had finished reading the will to Aymar, he leaned forward and leered: "So you will be a priest, hm?"

Aymar was shocked. "How could my aunt have been so cruel?" were his first words. "She knew my tastes."

Maître Le Pelletier rubbed his permanently furrowed forehead and suggested slyly: "There might be ways of getting around it."

"How?" said Aymar keenly.

"Time limit, for example," Le Pelletier opined.

"Time limit?"

"Yes. What good is a will that sets no time limit? You may, for example, draw out your studies for the priesthood until doomsday. And if you should come to die and wish to make a will of your own, who can stop you? You were simply unable to fulfill the demands of your aunt in your natural lifetime, and you may dispose of your fortune as you choose."

"This is annoying," Aymar complained. "I hate such deceit. Especially a deceit which I shall have to practice for years. It's a consolation to know that I shan't live very long."

"Come, pull yourself together," Le Pelletier urged. "After all, what does it amount to? You'll soon forget all about it. The only thing you cannot do is marry. But even for that there might be a way, and that might be the best course at that. You simply declare that you cannot follow the provisions of your aunt's will and thereupon you inherit as next of kin with no will to saddle you."

Aymar was thinking what his friends who knew his former violent pronouncements against clericalism would say when they discovered that he had joined the clergy. He wouldn't be there then, but he would carry the shame to his dying day.

"You don't have me to thank that the will isn't worse than it is," said M Le Pelletier. "True to my profession I warned your aunt that it was useless to make out a will that specified no forfeiture for violation of its provisions. She refused to consider the possibility that you might not care to follow her last wishes. 'He will do what I want him to do,' she asserted. The whole thing was most irregular and charming. You are really free to do as you please."

Le Pelletier's words stung Aymar as if they had been meant as reproaches. With the funeral still vivid in his mind, he found his eyes wet with tears at the thought that his good aunt had been unwilling to provide for any punishment. But how could he, who was turning more and more to the uncompromising radicalism of Blanqui, force himself into a seminary? It was unthinkable!

No, not so unthinkable at that. He recollected that but recently as he was reading an article by Blanqui in which the latter attacked the mysticism promulgated by the clergy, claiming that they did so only in order to maintain the lower classes the better in subjection to their masters, he had been annoyed. "You don't know everything," he had exclaimed and flung the paper away.

You don't know everything? Why, that phrase was the beginning and the end of mysticism.

"What do you think of religion?" he asked Le Pelletier.

"Moi? Je m'en fous pas mal," was Le Pelletier's coarse appreciation of that branch of the humanities.

"I mean," said Aymar, "what for example do you think of…an afterlife?"

Le Pelletier smiled wryly. "That old question? I didn't think people ever brought that up nowadays."

"Then you think it's settled?"

"Look here," said Le Pelletier. "Here's my watch." He drew forth his timepiece. "If I wind it, it marks time. It exists. It is alive. If the spring breaks, it stops. It no longer marks the hour. It is dead. Time doesn't exist for it. Same with you when your mainspring is gone."

"And nothing, after that?" said Aymar.

"Nothing, and lucky for us that that's so," Le Pelletier declared.

82

"Imagine being able to mark the passage of time while you lie in your coffin for thousands of years. Wouldn't be funny that, would it?"

"I hadn't thought of it that way," Aymar said softly. His mind was filled with the image of his aunt as she lay in her coffin. Pale, faintly smiling, virginal. Was she marking time? Counting second after second?

"You have allowed your grief to get the better of you," the notary said sympathetically.

Aymar sighed: "Do you believe," he asked, "that a dog can sense when death is approaching one of the inmates of the house, and that he will then bay lugubriously?"

Le Pelletier looked up suspiciously. "Me, I'm a believer in science. I have nothing to do with superstitions. I'm a positivist with Comte."

"But," Aymar objected, "might not science discover that dogs are capable of sensing the near demise of some person who is close to them?"

"What are you driving at, anyhow?"

Aymar hesitated. Here he was talking as his aunt used to talk, while the rôle of the skeptic which had formerly been his was played by Le Pelletier. "Frankly," he said at last, "something of the sort happened here at my aunt's death and has left me shuddering still."

"Nerves, just nerves," said Le Pelletier with confidence. "Everyone has moments when he can no longer see clearly. Grief blinds one. You will get over it."

And as a matter of fact, Aymar did get over it. Summer came and Josephine, Françoise and the baby went out to Mme Didier's property. Aymar was to follow just as soon as he could dispose of the apartment in the city. He did not think it necessary to keep it up. The women could stay on the farm where Guillemin the métayer made living cheap with his lush garden and his basse-cour overflowing with hens and pigs, rabbits and sheep. As for himself, Aymar might provide himself with an inexpensive pied-à-terre somewhere in the town, but he would spend most of his time in the country too.

He could not make up his mind whether to obey his aunt or to forget her wishes. Either way he envisaged a path of pain. In truth, life no longer held any possibility of pleasure. He could not bring himself to labor for the oppressed or to fight the administration of the Little Napoleon who was dusting off the throne of France. At times a prey to the fear of death, at other moments longing for the peace of the grave, which in the moral world is the universal solvent as water is in the physical world—thus he tossed about on his bed of painful indecision.

Would he, could he really study for the Church? What would his life then be like? He had the courage, one day, during a sudden shower, to step into a nearby church. When his eyes had become accustomed to the darkness, he examined with a certain curiosity the altars with their crosses and statues, the candles flickering in dozens of dark red glasses.

A priest came walking down the aisle. With sudden resolve, Aymar approached him. "Mon père," he said in a low voice, "may I speak to you for a while?"

"Do you wish to confess?" the priest asked briskly, ready to retire into a nearby booth.

"No, no. Just a few questions I'd like to ask."

"Certainly."

Aymar was for a moment at a loss how to begin. Then he asked: "Do you enjoy your work? Pardon me, I know it is a bold question, and you need not answer it, if you are not so inclined."

The priest laughed with a deep rugged voice. Altogether he was a healthy, robust fellow, most likable and certainly not in the least wan, pale or monastical. A joie de vivre emanated from his sturdy body, visibly sturdy despite his soutane. His eyes, his mouth showed lines eager to gather into smiles.

They talked. The priest explained his work. He had a rather cold, factual way of looking at things. He explained how he liked to perform mass, and went into details about various differences. He spoke of his literary ambitions. He wanted to write about the Bolandists and their vast labors interrupted by the Revolution.

84

Did Monsieur know about the astronomical work of the Jesuits in China, their remarkable architectural constructions? In this day when the Church was being attacked so savagely, it was good to remember what science and art owed to the Church. And greater glories were to come. He meant to be there to share them.

His eagerness was infectious. Aymar, too, wanted to be there.

"It will be the Church that will some day lead man out of this economic muddle," he asserted. "You will see. Rome, disappointed everywhere by unfaithful dynasties, will put its strength behind socialism. Then you will see a new era dawn for man."

In succeeding interviews, Aymar became more and more friendly with the priest and more and more willing to become a part of this vast organization whose history was greater than that of any country. One day, he said: "I want to become a priest. What shall I do first?"

The priest shook his head: "Not you."

Aymar said: "It is true. Hitherto I have been hostile, but you have explained much to me."

Still the priest shook his head.

"You think," said Aymar, "that my resolution will not last? Perhaps you are right. And still I mean to prepare myself for ordination. In fact, I must."

"You don't understand," the priest said softly. "You limp. You cannot celebrate mass while physically defective."

Aymar recalled having heard that long before, but still he was stricken. Suddenly he wanted badly to become a priest, now that the possibility had been snatched from him. He explained to the priest how, at first annoyed by his aunt's last wish, he had gradually grown more anxious to fulfill it.

"Wait a moment," the priest said. He left and returned with a magazine. He found the advertisement he was looking for. "Pierre-Paul Sgambati, advocate, 165, rue Saint Honoré, au premier. Correspondence bureau for all the Dicastery offices at Rome."*

"Go see this man," he said. "Look, see this list of things he does. Procures authorization to bless rosaries, crosses, medals with the indulgences of St Bridget. Secures permission for a bald priest to wear a wig when saying mass, for a priest to invest his personal fortune for profit, etcetera, etcetera. And here: Dispensation for missing left eye for ordination. It will cost you heavy, business with Rome always does, but you may secure what you want."

"Why, that's ridiculous," cried Aymar. "Shameful!"

"Well," said the priest and shrugged his shoulders. "Some priests here have objected, too. But Rome is big and complicated. It costs you money here too, no matter what you may want in the courts of justice. Think of the lawyer who has studied to know all the numerous offices at Rome and the secretaries and the paper and ink and whatnot. I guess St Peter didn't dream of this. But then life is ever becoming more complicated. The simple splits, doubles itself, quadruples itself, becomes a maze."

Aymar could not take the news so matter-of-factly. He thought the question over for many days, but unable to face the humiliation of obtaining a dispensation for his crippled legs, he ceased to go to see his friend the priest, and at last determined to drop the matter, for the time being at least.

He had had many bitter pills to swallow in his life. And more than ever recently. What was this world, anyhow, that delighted in mocking man for his ignorance? Was there mystery to it or was it all plain? Why was he a cripple now, and so many of his comrades at the barricades still alive and healthy, untouched by a single bullet? Why did his aunt wish him to be a priest, while the Church rejected him? Why, if he despised the Church, was he shocked to discover a streak of business in it? And finally, there was something a little more than coincidental in this priest telling him how to get around the law of the Church, a few days after the notary had told him how to get around the law of the State. Living and dead, sacred and profane, all were amenable to money and guile.

---

* I must apologize to the reader for a possible anachronism. Who the advocate was to whom Aymar was referred, I cannot say. Pierre-Paul Sgambati did not open his office at the above mentioned address until some five years later. See *l'Observateur Catholique*, Paris, 1857. This is the nearest my research came to finding the advocate's name.

Despite his increasing melancholia, he managed to dispose of his apartment lease to good advantage and packed off the furniture to the country. One day he stood in the empty apartment and said good-bye to all that he had experienced within these walls. He was annoyed to discover that he was not so deeply impressed as he expected or even as he would have liked to be. The walls meant nothing to him. The window where he used to sit, deprived of its curtains and of its window-cushions, and without the chair, which had been his by virtue of adoption, seemed like any other window. A silly comparison came to his mind and caused him disgust: *the impersonality of a skeleton.* His aunt, too, would lose the habiliments of her flesh and would be like that window, meaningless to him. What happened to bodies when they died? Doctors must know, he cogitated, with all those gruesome autopsies they have to perform. The afterlife? Was that the afterlife?

As he ruminated on in this dismal fashion, his eye caught with a start a brass object. Half hidden behind one wing of the door, it had apparently escaped the eyes of the packers only at the last moment, for the ticket on it showed that it had not been entirely overlooked. This brass object, Aymar recognized it with strange emotion, was the vessel in which his aunt had kept her holy water. It was a small brass bowl, hammered into the shape of a seashell and provided with a cover depicting some indefinable Biblical scene. Attached to a ring at the side was a short length of chain and suspended from the chain a so-called goupillon, a fox-tail made of brass and shaped like a small scepter. The head drilled with many holes was intended to gather water and release it in a spray when the instrument was flicked with the hand.

And all the things that had almost taken on the mistiness of unreality, of things remembered from a dream, came back with all their colors and outlines sharp and fresh. His aunt sending Josephine around the corner to fetch some holy water and the storm and—what was the name of that priest?—Pitamont, yes, and Mère Kardec's and the woman coming out of that room with her pail full of bloodied water, and that terrible night when the baby had howled and his aunt had died.

87

The apartment that a moment ago had seemed to contain no meaning was now replete with memories. They seemed to peel off the silk-covered walls, they swirled around him. In the gathering twilight the shadows took on life, stepped out threateningly from their corners, reached at him from behind so that he turned around suddenly with a distinct feeling that someone was behind him. He grappled with a hostile atmosphere that surrounded him with menaces. There came the echo of distant baying, growing louder, reverberating through the empty halls, filling his ears.

Stricken with horror, he dashed out as fast as he could. Down two flights of stairs to the hall and out of the hall into the street where his fiacre was waiting for him with his bags packed for travel. His chest was filled with a wild cry for help which he did not dare utter. One more step and he would be in the safety of his cab. Instead, he found himself rolling over and over on the curb and grappling with an adversary.

It was Maître Le Pelletier, the stunted, sallow notary, who rose with his mouth full of dust and curses. Then he recognized his assailant: "You, Galliez?" and extended a brown, bony hand to help him up. "What the deuce has come over you? Are you gone quite mad?"

"I have only a few minutes to catch a train," said Galliez breathless, brushing dust from his clothes. "Come with me?"

"No, thanks. Sorry but I've business elsewhere. You'd better hurry and not miss your train."

"Well, then, a thousand pardons, friend," and Aymar mounted into the flacre. At the station he had a good hour to wait and wonder, before his train pulled out.

Truly he was going mad.

Chapter Six

Says Galliez:

"There are mornings on which one wakes with the shreds of a dream cobwebbing the cogs of our daytime minds. One was asleep and in a different world. One was sunk in a different medium. Slowly one comes back to daylight and its world of daylight logic, but the taste of the dream lingers on, suddenly to make one conscious of a strangeness in our usual world, a strangeness that is so fleeting that no one has ever succeeded in analyzing it. But who is there who has not experienced it?

"In swamps one may sometimes witness a strange phenomenon: the dark, silent water, that seems too thick and oily to be disturbed by the breeze, appears in sudden agitation. The surface rises as if a body were in labor below, and out of the commotion comes an old waterlogged trunk that for years had lain at the bottom of the tarn, and now that it has risen to the surface, will slowly sink again to the bottom.—On the ocean once a few sailors were privileged to witness a similar event.

"A spar was seen protruding from the water. Before the eyes of the astonished mariners on a passing bark, the spar rose higher, revealed itself to be the top of a mast. A cross-spar, hanging awry, now made its appearance with shreds of rigging clinging to it. Another followed with a bit of sail hanging in wet tatters. A lesser mast had risen and now the deck itself came up, first the high bow of an old-fashioned design ornamented with an angel, with the water cataracting from it as it cleft the surface of the sea. And the whole ship rose and floated for a while on the waves, water pouring from every crevice. The ship itself was readily identified as an old Spanish galleon, such as has not been seen on the seven seas for near a century. And slowly the ship that had risen, plunging and rearing from the waters like the webfooted steeds of Old Neptune, settled into the waves again, and a moment later it was gone. And was as if it never had been.

"Many of the sailors on the bark doubted their very eyes, and one, stricken with a nameless fear, groveled on the teakwood deck. The wise ones debated the phenomenon with scientific plausibilities, while the more religious contented themselves with the sign of the cross and a prayer or two muttered under the breath along with a well-chosen oath. But the general verdict reached was that grain or other material, caught in a water-tight hold, had given rise to gas which had accumulated under great pressure and then breaking its confines with sudden force had propelled the ship to the surface, where it had floated until the gas had escaped and water had once more filled the hold of the ship and drawn it under.

"There are such ships, there are such logs in the swamps of our minds, and they rise to the surface of our thoughts for a moment, only to sink again. There are such ships sunk in the wastes of our lives. The years have washed over them. They are forgotten. And yet they rise, ghosts of a past that is ended. They float before us for a while to our own great astonishment, then they settle down again and are as if they never existed."

Thus writes Aymar Galliez in his minority defense of Sergeant Bertrand. And he continues:

"In the realm of nature, too, there are phenomena that have long ceased to be, and of which, yet, one example may survive. In the interior of Africa, some great monster of the past may still roam the

90

forests. A mammoth may be wandering now over the frozen wastes of our Arctic regions: last lonesome representative of his great race. A dinosaur in South America, a glyptodon in some unexplored area of the earth. That that enormous bowl of water that covers nearly all our globe may conceal animals undreamed of, who would have the temerity to deny at least the possibility?

"In this terrible age of disbelief and gullibility, people will swallow any tale of monsters of the past, but unless we find the bones of a centaur, no one will credit that myth. What have the scientists done but replace dragons, mermen and sphinxes with a new line of beasts? The people found the transposition easy. Where once they thought of dragons, they will have mammoths and other extinct beasts to occupy the same mental pews: these never change."

What shall one say to such language? One may be as skeptic as Thomas who had to see the stigmata, but there is so much in the Galliez script that can be verified by consulting old newspapers, etc., that one is tempted to believe at least the outward facts, reserving decision on the actual existence of a supernatural creature. While the following chapter relies almost exclusively on Galliez' affirmations, there are other episodes which can be reconstructed in entirety from documents and records.

If you go to the little village of Mont d'Arcy on the Yonne, you may perhaps still hear tales of great wolf hunts. The old inhabitants will outdo each other in the hair-raising details with which they decorate their reports. Some of these details will conflict. That is inevitable. And must not be taken to mean that the whole story is an invention of country gullibles who found the winters too long, and started the wolf-hunt merely to amuse their leisure hours and give their imaginations fall play. There is a good central core of the tale which must be accepted.

Bramond, the garde champêtre, was the first to come upon traces of the wolf. He had found two recently dropped lambs dead, lying by the side of the forest trail. The animals' throats were severed and the blood had evidently been lapped up, for the ground showed few stains. Or else the killing had been done elsewhere and the bodies dragged to this remote and lonely spot overhung with bushes.

One of the bodies had been dismembered, the other was otherwise untouched. The dry ground around showed a few indistinguishable traces of having been trampled.

The last wolf sighted in this region had been slain over twenty years ago, so that the appearance of a wolf in this quarter of the département was considered unusual to say the least. Bramond, stuffing his pipe, frowning and grunting with the effort of ratiocination, came to the plausible conclusion that the perpetrator of these misdeeds was a shepherd dog who had taken a taste for mutton. And at once he concluded that the felon was none other than César, the big shepherd dog owned by Vaubois, for Vaubois not only underfed his help, he actually starved himself.

Serves him right, he thought. But a slight grain of sand remained in that ointment: it might be a wolf, after all. Now if only he were as clever as those Indian trackers of whom his son read to him every night, then he would not be in doubt for a moment. He would pick up a hair and identify it at once. He would find a trace of claws and say that this or that animal was responsible. He would, in fact, reconstruct the whole scene. He would know from the state of the dead animals how long they had been thus, at what precise hour they had met their death and whether here or elsewhere. And he would conclude: "Now, friends, I invite you to a proof of the correctness of my observations and deductions. If I am right, the animal will appear on the third night from today, two hours after moonrise, at this very spot."

Old Bramond enjoyed his triumph the while he could, and then prepared to enjoy the distribution of a real piece of news, in a land always hungry for a good story. And the first person he came across was Vaubois' shepherd, Crotez.

They exchanged greetings and sat down on a rock to smoke together for a while. Then Bramond said: "Missing any lambs?"

"No," said Crotez, "why do you ask?"

"Just wondered. Where's your dog?"

"Must be around somewhere." He whistled. "Here, César!"

92

César came trotting out of a dip in the meadow and raced gleefully up to the shepherd. César was an ill-kempt specimen of that rather mongrel breed known as the chien de berger. They stand fairly high, have ears pointed forward, a bushy tail and a good coat of curly brown hair.

César's red tongue lolled out of his jaws and gathered coolness. He nuzzled his head under his master's arm, for that was his favorite position, with his human friend's arm slung over his neck.

Bramond scratched his head.

"What's this you said about lost lambs?" the shepherd inquired.

"There are two dead lambs up on the hill there. I was wondering whose they were." Even as he said it, Bramond realized that he should have kept quiet. Events were to prove that he had indeed made an error.

"Two dead lambs?"

"Half eaten."

"Half eaten?"

"Wolf."

"Wolf?"

"Fact."

"Jésus!" exclaimed Vaubois' shepherd, at last finding a word of his own.

From Vaubois' shepherd, Bramond proceeded down the gentle slope until he came to the Didier-Galliez place.

M Galliez, himself, was at the end of the alley of locust trees which concealed his house from the road, and was busied with his rose bushes.

After a few comments on the weather, Bramond shook his head: "Bad news, monsieur."

"What's the trouble, Bramond?" Aymar asked, scarcely looking up from his work.

"Wolves in this section. Found two dead lambs up there, half eaten. Couldn't be anything but wolves, though there hasn't been a wolf around here for years."

"You must be mistaken," said Aymar. "Wolves are extinct in

93

this portion of the country. They say foxes will take new-born lambs."

"Have you missed any lambs?"

"You'll have to ask young Guillemin," said Aymar, "he takes care of the sheep. Go right in," he invited Bramond.

Bramond walked down the alley and went around to the back of the house. Josephine and Françoise were spreading linen out to bleach on the grass. Young Bertrand, now about nine years old, was wrestling with his big St Bernard dog. None of the Guillemins were around.

Bramond made his inquiries but could secure no information. Neither of the women had heard of any lost lambs.

"M Galliez thinks it might be a fox. He says they sometimes will steal newly dropped lambs."

"A fox it might very well be," said Françoise. "We've missed a lot of chickens and ducks this last month. Young Guillemin has set traps but can't get the thief."

"I must get my boy to fix you up a trap. He makes good ones—" Bramond turned to Bertrand: "And you. How about some hunting again?" He chuckled. "Did he tell you how our last hunting trip turned out? He shot a squirrel and nearly fainted. You've got to learn to shoulder a gun if you want to be a man."

Françoise laughed. But Josephine said: "He's too delicate. And he won't eat."

"He looks robust enough to me. What's the matter with him?"

"He's always been in good health," said Josephine, "and I never had any trouble with him until this summer. I don't know what to make of it."

"A touch of the heat," suggested Bramond. "He's a bit upset. But they grow out of it."

Bertrand, meanwhile, the object of this conversation, appeared oblivious to everything but the dog whom he was teasing. Bramond excused himself and hastened on with his news. So far he had not met with the appreciation he had expected.

The next person whom he met was the mayor of the village, an important wine grower and dealer of the section.

94

"Monsieur le maire, I have a piece of bad news. I think that…"

"Yes," said the mayor, "you're precisely the man I'm looking for. Vaubois' shepherd just reported to me that he had found two lambs half eaten and to judge by the remains, evidently attacked by a large pack of wolves. Monsieur Bramond, you don't seem to be on the job."

"Wolves…" Bramond stuttered.

"Yes, wolves. Where are you loafing these days that a pack of wolves can come into our village and steal lambs right from under our noses?"

"Why—"

"And when our citizens cry for help, no one can find Bramond."

"But—"

"Vaubois has been looking for you everywhere!"

"But, monsieur le maire, it is I who—"

"Not another word. We shall overlook it this time. Now get on the job and have those wolves dead within twenty-four hours and delivered at the mairie."

"Oui, monsieur, only I was about to say that—"

"No, not a minute more than twenty-four hours." And with that the mayor betook his majestic personage away, leaving Bramond thunderstruck and furious in the roadway.

"I knew I shouldn't have said anything to that dolt of a shepherd. The thief—how could he play a scurvy trick like that?"

And even as he was standing there cursing the shepherd, up comes Le Vallon, shouting: "Bramond, mon vieux, where have you been? Have you heard the news? Everybody is looking for you. There are packs of wolves terrorizing the neighborhood. It's worth as much as your life to take the forest road."

"Shut up!" thundered Bramond.

Well, that at least is Bramond's version of how the wolf was discovered. Vaubois' shepherd, Crotez, of course, had another tale to tell, and since the whole village, with the exception of the people on the Galliez estate, had heard the exciting story from the shepherd, no one could be found to believe Bramond, no matter how often he explained.

95

"Why, Crotez brought the bodies here, to the mairie, I saw..."

"That only shows that he didn't have any sense. The proper thing to do was not to disturb them but wait for the wolves to return."

"But I told him myself—" he said to another.

"Ha, ha. My dear Bramond, we believe you, of course. What village in France can boast of a garde champêtre to equal ours?"

"I can point out to you the exact place where I found them."

"So can everybody in the neighborhood by this time."

Bramond paused and considered how an Indian tracker would deal with such a situation. No doubt he would have Vaubois' shepherd unmasked in a moment. But as for himself he could see nothing to do to recover his prestige but to get those wolves. So he shouldered his gun and was off.

In the succeeding days nothing further was seen of the wolf or pack of w\olves, though if the devil shows his tail when he is spoken of then the wolves ought certainly to have shown theirs, for nothing but wolves figured in the village conversations for the next week.

Then one day another lamb was found, its throat ripped open in just the same way, and its belly disemboweled. And the ducks and chickens continued to disappear from various homesteads, but particularly from the Galliez farmyard.

Various people, at various times, claimed to have seen the wolf. They were believed by some, but by most discredited. Toward autumn an incident occurred that brought the wolf mystery nearer home.

Little Pernette, coming home toward twilight from her uncle, who was sick, saw, as she came to the hedge of Vaubois' buck-wheat field, a huge dog, near as big as a calf. It came leaping at her. She screamed and ran. The heavy body of the animal cast itself at her and threw her down. Then she lost consciousness. When she awoke, it was quite dark, the full moon, dull red, stood above the horizon. Whimpering and trembling, she raced home and told her tale.

But she was so hysterical that she answered yes and no to questions that were alike or contradictory, and no one could make

96

head or tail out of her account. Nevertheless, a portion of the village was stirred to action and the night was soon spangled with torches of farmers armed with pitchforks, all out after the wolf. Others, convinced that Pernette had been attacked by some harvest laborer, questioned the migratory farm help. Still others remained at home in fear, being certain that this was no ordinary wolf but the work of the devil.

Bramond, beside himself with ambition to kill the wolf and rehabilitate his prestige as a hunter, which hitherto had never been questioned, did not cease to tramp his district, both day and night. His cheeks caved in for lack of sleep. When his boy wanted to read to him of the mighty Indian hunters of America, he cut the little fellow short, gruffly. Directly after supper he had taken down his gun from the wall and was out. But never a sight of the wolf, though he followed every clue brought home by nervous villagers prone to mistake every shadow for a crouching wolf.

One night, it was just before dawn, he was traversing a melancholy flat, a fen blacked with pools of stagnant water. The ground was covered with heath and fern, but near the water grew dense masses of flag and bulrushes amongst which the dying night wind sighed drearily. He was deep in reverie, wooing a pipe-dream, in which he exhibited at the next fair a whole series of wolfskins. Suddenly he stood as if transfixed. Not fifty feet away was the wolf, there could be no doubt of it. It was humped up over its kill and the crunching of bones between his jaws could be heard through the stilly night.

Despite the hammering of his heart, Bramond sighted carefully, coolly calculated on the distance and fired. The wolf scampered through a pool of water and was off, its belly hugging the ground as it took long strides. Bramond nevertheless had time to reload and fired a second shot. Then he hastened after it, certain that he had at least wounded the beast, in fact expecting soon to come upon the body. For that he had missed completely at so short a distance never occurred to him.

And yet that was what had happened, for Bramond did not see the wolf again, and as day dawned and he returned to the site where he had shot at the beast, he could find no trace of blood, except that of the poor partridge which the wolf had been devouring. He took the mutilated bird home and puzzled over the bit of fluff, the crushed feathers clotted with blood.

And as he thought and sighed, an idea struck him and he pounded the table with his fist.

"Wife," he cried, "a piece of wax!"

"What are you up to now?" she asked.

"Quick now!" he shouted.

"Rome wasn't built in a day," was her retort.

"Come now," he said, "and stop talking. Ever since the day you persuaded me to marry you, your tongue hasn't stopped wagging."

She brought him a piece of wax and stood watching him carve a small portion into the shape of a bullet, modeling it carefully after one he had taken from his own stock of cartridges. And her tongue wagged on:

"I met that Josephine, I beg your pardon, Mme Caillet, this morning. What a high and mighty lady she has turned out to be. Who would think that she was the same Josephine who was glad to kiss your feet for a piece of bread. What are you making anyhow? And she told me that Bertrand was giving her a lot of trouble. He had no appetite and she wondered whether she ought to send him away to school. Of course he would have to go away eventually since he was to study medicine, but meanwhile perhaps he could continue to go to the village school. Well, I told her a thing or two. The village school was good enough for her and she never even succeeded in winning a single prize book, she was that dumb. The nerve of her. Will you kindly inform me what you are making that for? Are you just trying to mystify me? Well, they can't pull the wool over my eyes. What do you suppose? Do you mean to say she married this Caillet man, whoever he was, the day she got to Paris? How else did she bring home a baby six months old? And since when are married servants retained along with their children? And why should her boy be going to study medicine? Where is all the money coming from?"

"From M Galliez, of course," said Bramond. "And stop leaning over my shoulder, I can't work."

98

"God only knows what you're doing anyhow. Well, of course M Galliez is handing over the money. Did you think I didn't know that? And if you think I don't know why, you are mistaken too. I'll bet anything that Josephine hasn't got both legs in one stocking."

"Stop your twaddle. You women always have things figured out."

"You men are as stupid as geese. You fall for anything. And why do you think M Galliez came back from the seminary at Langres? Wasn't he going to be a priest? But the call of family ties was a little too much, I suppose. His little Josephine needed him."

"Stop supposing so many things, and go fetch me your little silver crucifix. You women ought to be ashamed of yourselves, tearing a man's character to pieces like that."

"What are you going to do with my crucifix? I don't want it spoiled. That was blessed for me by the archbishop himself, when I went to Avallon."

"All the better. We can't have too much blessing on it."

"Before I give it to you I want to know what you're up to."

"You'll find out sooner or later, and have plenty of time to talk about it."

"Now mind if you lose it, you'll never hear the end of it." Reluctantly she fetched him the desired article. Now he embedded his waxen bullet in a cake of wet clay.

"Some hairs from your head!" he ordered. Too surprised to resist, she permitted him to draw a few from her head. He laid a number of these in various directions across the bullet and on top of all laid another cake of wet clay, pressing the two firmly together. Then he drew out the hair.

"For the air to escape," he explained briefly.

"What air?" she asked. For the first time her tongue was beginning to fail her.

He disregarded her question, being busy digging a small conduit through the clay down to the bullet in the center. This done he set the whole to roast on the stove. When the mold was dry and hard and the wax had all run out, leaving a perfect hollow model in its place, he melted up the Silver crucifix, to the loud shouting and weeping of his spouse. And thus was the silver bullet cast. It required only a little filing, sandpapering and polishing to make it perfect.

"Try and escape this," Bramond smirked. "A silver bullet, blessed by the archbishop, melted down from a holy crucifix. Beelzebub himself would fall before this."

And he took up his eternal watching and waiting. A deer might nibble at his back, he would not have wasted the single precious bullet that he had in the rod of his gun. A braconnier might run off with fifty pheasants. Gleaners might surreptitiously wield the scythe and Bramond would do nothing.

Winter came and still the wolf had not come within range of his eyes. Not that he had left the neighborhood, for reports of missing birds and lambs were still numerous as ever. But the animal seemed to be avoiding Bramond.

But one wintry night, when the ground was covered with snow and the sky was overcast, he did come upon it. The animal, intent upon its kill, had not noticed the guard; moreover, the wind was blowing away from it.

Bramond muttered a short prayer and advanced as cautiously as he could. When within twenty paces, so close that he could see every detail of the animal, its heavy coat of gray-brown, its sharp ears pointing forward, its large eyes glowing in the dark like dull marsh-fire, then he dropped to his knee and took aim. The animal, suddenly conscious of impending danger, looked up and sniffed the wind. It gathered itself to run off, but already Bramond had fired. The beast collapsed, but even as Bramond was exulting: "Got yon that time!" it was up and off, fleeing through the low scrub of the forested hillside which had recently been thinned out.

Bramond was hot after it. The tracks were easy to follow in the snow and a heavy trail of blood made it even easier. But the wolf was traveling fast, despite his injury which must be mortal, so Bramond thought. But the splotches of blood diminished to drops, sunk in the snow at rarer and rarer intervals. Then the blood spoor ceased entirely, but the animal's paws still made their legible mark. The low bushes were in its favor, but the hillside sloped down to a road and across the road was an open field, so that the animal could not get very far out of sight any more. "Limping on the left leg, too," the guard noted with satisfaction.

When the garde champêtre came down to the road, however, and looked across the fields, there was nothing to see. The road had been traveled on lately and the following of any trail on it was impossible, but it did not seem to Bramond that any wild beast would take to a traveled road. He confidently expected that it would have crossed, but on the opposite side of the road there was no sign of any animal tracks. Had it doubled on itself and reëntered the bushes? Or had it followed the road?

At a loss, Bramond stood in the middle of the roadway and gazed around. Nothing but the silent night surrounded him. He could hear nothing but his own heavy breathing. Startled by the silence and a little unconvinced of the reality of the brief episode, he hesitated. Which way? Home? Impossible! Why, he had almost had his hand on the beast. But where should he go? He stood irresolute until the cold warned him to move. Slow shivers began to crawl up his back as he walked off toward his house. He kept looking over his shoulder. It seemed to him as he walked that soft padded feet were being placed directly into his own footsteps as soon as his feet rose from the ground.

Then a genuine fear seized him and he began to run, and still he heard the soft patter of paws on the hard snow. And an old story came to his mind of the wush-hound and the pad-foit, those terrible animals that live in abandoned graves in cemeteries. And though he was ordinarily a man of strong nerves, all his muscles weakened. He tottered on limply. His gun was too heavy in his hands. Recklessly he cast it away. No sooner had he done so than he saw the wolf in front of him. It was running by the side of the road. And every once in a while it would dip back into the darkness beside the road only to reappear a moment later.

He cursed himself for the fool and coward that he was, gathered his last reserve of strength and ran back for his gun which was lying on the road where he had thrown it. He picked it up and raced back. Where was that wolf now? Gone! No, there it was. Up went his gun and bang! The beast crumpled up in its tracks. Rolled over and stirred no more. With a hoarse cry, Bramond ran up to it and, raising his gun which he held by the rod, he brought down the butt end on the wolf's head. Bones crushed through like paper, and blood, brains and teeth flew in every direction.

He wiped the cold sweat from his brow. "Thank God!" he muttered. He kicked the body. Where did I hit the first time? Then only he noticed that around the neck of the animal, hidden deep in fur, was a collar. He recognized the beast.

They found him the next morning lying beside the body of César.

Bramond lay severely ill for two weeks. Then he began to recover. When visitors were permitted, it was the mayor himself who deigned to enter his humble cottage and congratulate the guard. "We owe you a deep apology," he said, "and many thanks. You have done well, and I shall see to it that they hear of this at the prefecture."

Weak and happy, Bramond could only nod. There were tears in his eyes.

The mayor rose to go. But first he came up to the head of the bed and patted Bramond on the shoulder: "Who knows," he said with a big smile, "there might be a medal in it for you."

Even his wife was happy with him. "But I want that silver bullet, she said, "it belongs to me. And now it will be doubly dear to me."

"It's strange they didn't find it in the body," he said. "But when I am well I shall go look for it. It can't be hard to find. So it was Vaubois' dog all along," he mused. "You know that was my very first thought. No sign of any wolf since I killed César?"

"None," she confirmed. "Not even a chick missing."

Chapter Seven

That then was the great wolf-hunt of Mont d'Arcy, which lasted a little over six months and made every citizen a detective and a hero, at any rate after the culprit had been discovered.

Josephine, for one, was very glad when one morning it was reported to her that the wolf had been slain by Bramond and it was nothing but Vaubois' dog César.

"This wolf-hunt," she said, "was getting just a little bit too much. Bertrand has been complaining that he dreams about it every night."

She hastened to Bertrand's room, and cried: "Up, lazybones! The wolf has been killed and you've no more nightmares to fear."

Bertrand turned a flushed face toward his mother: "I don't want to get up, mamma. I don't feel well. And my leg hurts so badly that I can't move it."

"What's this? What's this now? You've always got some excuse to lie in bed. I declare, I don't know what's become of the good Bertrand I used to have. He used to be so well-behaved. Ate everything that was set before him with never a question and went to sleep nicely and woke up feeling fine. Come now, child, let me see your leg that hurts and then we'll get out and take a brisk walk to the village. It's a fine cold day."

She pulled the covers away from him while he moaned: "It's that one," and motioned to his left limb. "Oh my!" she shouted. The leg did indeed look bad and there was clotted blood around the calf, and what seemed like an ugly wound.

She ran out calling for M Aymar. He was down below in his study, but answered her call at once. As soon as he had seen the state of the leg, he ordered her to run and fetch the doctor. "Get Guillemin to race the bay for all she is worth," he shouted after her as she fled down the stairs.

Françoise, mumbling: "Oh, mon Dieu, quel malheur, quel malheur!" busied herself fetching warm water and linen to wash the wound. Aymar undertook the latter task himself.

The wound was a deep hole, as if, that was Aymar's first thought, the lad had fallen on a pitchfork: "Have you been jumping from the hayloft in the barn?" he queried.

"Aïe!" said Bertrand, "that hurts. No, I wasn't jumping in the barn."

There was a smaller wound on the other side of the calf, near the shin bone, and this only confirmed Aymar's first impression. For when he washed that area, he noticed that there was something hard just flush to the skin. "My heavens," he said to himself, "there's a piece of the pitchfork imbedded in the flesh." Ho pushed down on the skin with his thumbs to squeeze the object out. "Sure enough," he said as a shiny point appeared out of the opening of the skin, "it's the point of a tine." Despite Bertrand's howls he squeezed harder, until he found that his nails could get a purchase on the metal and drag it out.

At the moment, fortunately, Françoise happened to be out. She had gone to fetch more water and linen rags. This was indeed fortunate, for Aymar would not have known what to say had she been there, when he took out what he thought was the point from the tine of a pitchfork and discovered that it was a bullet, Bramond's silver bullet of which the whole village had been informed.

To Bertrand, who was still moaning out loud and had not been watching him, he said nothing. He put the bullet in a pocket of his waistcoat and waited for the doctor. The latter, when he came, found the wound clean and the prognosis for a rapid recovery good. "The pitchfork," he said, "fortunately only penetrated the heavy muscle of the calf, and didn't touch the bones. He'll be quits with a week in bed, provided no further trouble sets in, which I think unlikely."

When the doctor had gone, Aymar sent Josephine and Françoise out of the room and questioned Bertrand severely.

"You must tell me everything, Bertrand. Don't conceal a thing. Where were you last night?"

"Why, here in bed."

"Then how did you get hurt?"

"I don't know, Uncle Aymar."

"Come, come, Bertrand. You don't get wounds like this lying in bed."

"But if I tell you, uncle..."

"Bertrand," said Aymar, "look me in the eyes. Look." And so saying he caught hold of the lad's hand, to reassure him. "I shan't punish you, I only want to know the truth."

He had felt that hand before, and it had meant little to him. But now he was thrilled to the bottom of his spine. There was a distinct growth of fine hair on the palm. He recalled suddenly, it was ten years ago, how his aunt, Mme Didier, had spoken to him, with awe in her voice, of the hair on the baby's palm. For a moment he could still hear in his ears that terrible baying the night Mme Didier had died.

It was many years ago and in the meantime so much had happened. He had gone to Langres to study for the priesthood. At the last moment, he had had doubts as to the strength of his vocation and had not taken orders. Meanwhile Bertrand had grown up and with never a sign of the horrible fate that was to strike him, according to Mme Didier.

Now, across ten years, was that fate about to overtake the lad?

"Look in my eyes and tell me that you were in bed all night."

"Uncle," said Bertrand, "why should I have gotten out of bed? I slept here all night. I know because I woke up once during the night and I had had a very bad dream and I was covered with sweat. And I felt very ill and I wanted to call Mamma, but then I fell asleep again."

"What did you dream of?"

"I don't recall very well, but it was like every other night. I have had dreams almost every night now."

"I know, your mother has told me. Look, Bertrand, Tell me. You do not like to have nightmares, do you? Of course not. Now maybe I can help you, but you will have to be very honest with me. Since when have you been having these dreams?"

"I can tell you that, because I know very well what started it. I went hunting with Old Bramond last summer and he showed me how to shoot. And then he pointed out a squirrel to me and said: 'See if you can get him.' And I pulled the trigger and the squirrel squeaked and dropped. And Bramond said: 'Well, if you haven't got beginner's luck. How did you do that? But I was so sick at heart at the thought of having killed the little thing that I picked it up and wept. And then I kissed it and begged it to forgive me. I hadn't wanted to kill it. It was so pretty and fluffy and warm that it broke my heart. And as I kissed it again, and again, I tasted something warm flowing from it. And it burned my tongue like pepper, only it wasn't bitter but sweet, only not sweet like sugar. I can't tell you how it tasted, but I liked it so much that I kissed it once more and some more, only it was not because I wanted to kiss it but because I wanted to taste its blood and I didn't want Bramond to know what I was doing. And I am telling you everything just as it happened, because I know that I did wrong."

"Well?"

"Yes. Well, and ever since then I dream at night that I am drinking blood and it scares me to death. And sometimes I think I am a wolf like in the picture book, and I am killing a partridge or a lamb as it shows there. And sometimes I dream that I am the wolf Bramond is looking for. I can see him shooting at me to kill me, and I can't speak to him and tell him that I am not a wolf. Oh, it is awful when you want to talk and can't!"

106

"It is your imagination that is overwrought," said Aymar gently and patted that hairy palm. "Where do you find these lambs and partridges? Do you think of that in your dreams?"

"Yes, it seems to me that I am like a dog or a wolf and I leap out of the window and I run on my four legs and I can run very fast, very fast. And then I jump over hedges and I find a bird or a lamb...It all seems so real, just as if I actually did it."

"Yes, dreams are often very realistic. But they aren't true for all that. But if there were bars to that window, do you think you could still dream that you were jumping out of it? Now look, supposing we put bars on the window and locked your door at night, and see what happens. Maybe then you won't be bothered by bad dreams. Shall we try it?"

"Yes, uncle. Please do that. I am so afraid to go to bed. Yes, I think that if I knew that the window and door were locked, I wouldn't be able to dream of escaping from my room."

That very day then, after giving Josephine and Françoise a satisfactory explanation, without, however, revealing to them the full nature of the suffering of the child, he proceeded to put bars across the window and to oil the lock of the door.

The next morning he went eagerly to inquire of Bertrand how he had slept and was pleased to discover that the lad had not been troubled by any dreams. Thereafter it was his nightly custom to lock up Bertrand before he himself went to bed. Josephine alone was not quite satisfied with the remedy. "If there should be a fire," she suggested, "and Bertrand locked in his room and unable to escape? We would have to run and find you to get the key."

"We'll hang the key right here on this nail by his door, and if there should be a fire then someone, anyone, who is nearest can let him out."

And Josephine was somewhat contented. "Of course," she admitted, "his appetite has returned since he is no longer bothered with nightmares, still it's inviting disaster." Thereafter she rose frequently at night, wondering if by chance someone had not neglected a candle or a lamp, or if the wood-fire in the stove or fireplace had been properly extinguished.

Aymar too rose at night in order to listen at the door of Bertrand's room. There were queer sounds to be heard there at times. When the house was very quiet—that complete quietness that a house has only when the hour is late and every inmate is asleep, that complete quiet during which one can hear the beams in the walls lazily stretching themselves as if tired from long days of work, that dense quiet in which the furniture comes to life and begins to crack, speaking, in its way, of the years it has sat patiently in its corner—in such complete quietness then he could hear Bertrand breathing. Drawing one slow breath after another, as a child does in its peaceful sleep. But then the breathing would become hurried. Faster, faster, until it was no longer a breathing but a panting. Sometimes, then, but more rarely, there would follow the sharp and unmistakable noise of claws striking against the wood of the floor. Then there would be a sniffling and a snorting at the crack under the door and the claws would strike across once or twice. Silence would follow, broken perhaps by a low whine or another snort. And gradually the panting would cease. Bertrand's slow regular breathing was audible again.

"There can be no doubt of it now," Aymar muttered, and sighing heavily, quitted his eavesdropping. But this assurance never lasted. At once he would begin to have doubts again. "If only I could actually see him," he thought, but it was hard enough to hear him. Infinite precautions must be taken to get within three feet of the door. "He smells me," thought Aymar.

Occasionally he would try running up to the door and entering hastily. Sometimes even as his hand caught the knob, there would be the sound of a commotion inside, and when the door swung open there was Bertrand rolling in bed and moaning as if in the throes of a nightmare.

He complained to his mother, and Josephine in turn to Aymar: "You must stop waking him up that way, so suddenly," Josephine insisted. "He tells me you give him bad dreams. Why do you do it?" He excused himself awkwardly: "I just want to make sure of things before I retire."

Downstairs in his study, Aymar had gathered together what

material he could find on werewolves. Strange malady, that of lycanthropy. All over the world, wherever man has dwelt, people have believed in it. From Ceylon to Iceland and from Iceland to Ceylon, all the old races have tales to tell of it. From the berserkir (bearskins) of Scandinavia, the hyena-men of Africa, the were-bison of North American Indians, the cat-women of Constantinople (who eat rice with a hairpin, knowing that they will fill their bellies at the banquet of ghouls in the cemetery) to the tiger-men of India, the dread superstition is known and credited as truth.

Aymar read of the terrible outbreaks of werewolfism in France during the year 1598, when the disease seemed to become epidemic and whole families were stricken. In the house of a tailor at Châlons, barrels of human bones were found. His trial before the Parliament was so gruesome that the documents and records were ordered burnt at the stake with the criminal. That same year, however, another man tried on the same charge had his sentence of death commuted to imprisonment in the hospital Saint-Germain-des-Prés, ou on a accoustume de mettre les fols.* That very year, too, the whole Gandillon family was convicted and executed.

By the hundreds are the cases counted in France, England and Germany, to mention only three countries. An old pamphlet bears the title:

A moste true discourse, declaringe the damnable lyfe and death of one Stube Peeter, a high Jermayne (German), borne a Sorcerer, who in the likeness of a wolf, committed many murders, 25 years together; and for the same was executed in the cyttye of Bedbur near Coleyn (Cologne) the 31 of Marche, 1590. Published at London by Edward Venge.

In all these dreadful cases the criminals, aware of their misdeeds, were willing to confess how they changed into wolves and ran through the forest and fields, seeking prey of all kind.

When late at night Aymar would turn away from his reading, his head buzzing, he would find himself saying: "Impossible.

---

* "Where fools are ordinarily housed."

Ridiculous." Then he would take out of a secret little drawer in his desk the silver bullet and contemplate it. Then he would review in his mind all the strange events that he had witnessed since the thunderstorm that sent poor Josephine into the arms of Father Pitamont. And still unconvinced, he would go upstairs and listen at Bertrand's door. If he heard nothing but Bertrand's regular breathing, he would retire to his bed in a skeptical frame of mind. If, however, he heard a strange low whining and the striking of claws on the floor, he would cross himself rapidly and hurry downstairs again, unable to find sleep that night.

Could it be that these gory tales of medieval days were not mere delusions? Were there phenomena in the realm of nature, phenomena that perished like animals that became extinct? Could it be that a curious concatenation of causes, a rare and strange plexus of events, to be encountered only once in centuries, might produce a monstrous exception to the ordinary course of nature?

In the Galliez script, Aymar writes: "There are elemental spirits all about us, the souls of beasts that have died, or of more horrible beasts that have never lived. When the body of a man weakens, the soul of that man begins to detach itself from the tentacles of flesh and prepares itself to fly off the instant the body dies. And around a dying man a circle of beastly souls peer and wait. They would like to have that beautiful body for a house, that body of man which is the highest creation ever to have come from God's sculpturing hands. Man, the body with the erect spine, before which the horizontal spines of the animal world must grovel.

"It is to guard against the invasion of roaming souls that bodies stiffen in rigor mortis at once after death. Then the souls that enter man's husk find only a stiff shell left. Nevertheless it happens occasionally that the soul of a beast gains entrance into a man's body while he yet lives. Then the two souls war with each other. The soul of this man may depart completely and leave only that of the beast behind. And that explains how there are men in this world who are only monsters in disguise, playing for a moment at being men, the kings of creation. Just as a servant plays with his master's clothes.

"Of werewolves," Galliez continues, "there are two kinds. There are first those that have two bodies and only one soul. These two bodies exist independently, the one in the forest, the other in the home. And they share one soul. The man then only dreams of his wolf-life. Lying abed, he thinks himself abroad, roaming great pine-woods in a distant country, slinking by on soft padded paws, or yelling in a pack at the flying hoofs of three horses dragging a sleigh in a gallop across a snowy plain.—And in the same manner, the wolf, satiated with his kill and drowsing in his den, dreams a strange dream. He is a man, clad in garments, and is walking about, busy in the affairs of the city.

"And there are, in the second place, werewolves that have but one body, in which the soul of man and of beast are at war. Then whatever weakens the human soul, either sin or darkness, solitude or cold, brings the wolf to the fore. And whatever weakens the beastly soul, either virtue or daylight, warmth or the companionship of man, raises up the human soul. For it is known that the wolf shrinks from that which invites the man.

"These great truths are now forgotten, because in former days these monsters were so ruthlessly hunted down and expunged that we now enjoy a comparative immunity and freedom from such dangers. But it behooves us to watch sharply lest the race of mankind go into eclipse before the rise of a race of beasts, and the civilization of man go down before the anarchy of wolves or of lions or of some yet unformed monster. It behooves us to recall the procedure of the Middle Ages, when the inhuman rivals of man were almost completely extinguished by the cruel but necessary use of fire."

For a number of weeks after the finding of the bullet, Aymar actually considered the advisability of destroying Bertrand with fire. How? Take him into the woods and there burn him at one of the old charcoal huts, now abandoned? That was risky. Set fire to the house then? Why not? Burn the building and have Bertrand perish as if by accident in the flames.

III

One night as he was turning over the matter for the thousandth time, he came to a determination. He gathered together his most important papers, the replies to his letters of inquiry concerning Pitamont and his forebears, his slowly acquired collection on lycanthropy, the silver bullet, the goupillon and various other matters relating to Bertrand, and making several bundles of them, brought them out of the house into the distant carriage shed. These he wanted to keep.

Then he went upstairs, carrying a can of petroleum, as if he wished to fill his lamp. He paused in the dark hall before Bertrand's door, keeping a few feet away, lest he frighten the brute. And sure enough, he heard again that sharp striking of claws on the wooden flooring, the rapid sniffling and then the violent snort at the thin crack beneath the door.

"He smells me," Aymar said to himself, "and has prepared himself." For a moment his heart was wrung with sympathy for the poor lad who must suffer for a sin that was not his. Then he girded himself and was ready to dash the petroleum against the door and light a match, when he heard footsteps approaching.

"Who's there?" he cried nervously.

"It's me," Josephine answered and came up closer.

"What are you doing here?" he demanded harshly.

"Oh, I was just so worried, I couldn't sleep."

"Worried about what?"

"Fire," she said.

"How many times have I told you that with the key hanging there near the door there can be nothing to fear!" he cried angrily.

"I know," she said meekly, "only I couldn't fall asleep tonight, without making sure."

"You women…" he threw at her, and tramped downstairs to his study, where he flung himself on his couch in a fit of trembling. Cold sweat bathed his body. His intestines were tortured with cramps. After long hours of insomnia, he fell asleep.

In the morning Guillemin sought him out: "I found some packages of books and papers and things in the remise. What do you want done with them?"

112

Not knowing what to say, he uttered the words that were most ready on his tongue, words that seemed as if they had lain curled up in ambush on the tip of his tongue, waiting to fly out into the air: "*Those are to be burnt, Guillemin.*"

"Those metal pieces won't burn, monsieur."

"Yes? Well, batter them in and bury them with the ashes of the rest."

"Oui, monsieur."

Once he had given the order, he had plenty of time left to wonder why. Fatalistically he declared: "Perhaps it's best so." People lost in doubt, tortured by fears, unable to see a way out, or unable to choose one out of ten possible ways that suddenly occur to them, such people either go crazy or turn fatalists. There's no better rest for overwrought nerves than a little vacation in fatalism.

"The evidence is destroyed instead of the monster," he said to himself after a while. "I'll regret it." But he had ceased to worry. He turned over on his couch and fell asleep again at once.

And strange to say, Bertrand began to improve. He ceased to complain of bad dreams. No sound except his own regular breathing issued from his room at night. But Aymar did not relax his vigilance: "The wolf in him is quiet, for the moment."

Josephine said: "Bertrand is improving fast. I wish you wouldn't lock him up any more."

"When I think he's better, I'll do what is necessary," Aymar answered curtly.

But on her insistence he relented. And nothing happened.

"Perhaps he really is over it." He wondered.

"It was all those stories about the wolf that frightened him," said Josephine. "Why don't you begin to teach him again? You haven't given him a lesson in months. He won't be able to take the examinations."

Thereupon Aymar had Bertrand appear in the study again, as formerly, two hours every day.

But Bertrand was dull. He learnt slowly. He had used to be so quick to grasp. "He's been away from his studies too long," Aymar decided. "Or else he's reached the end. You can't teach an old dog new tricks," it occurred to him.

Months passed and still all was quiet. One day Françoise knocked at his study.

"What's the trouble, Françoise, you look worried?"

"Yes, monsieur." She paused. "I think, monsieur," she said suddenly and rapidly, "you ought to lock Bertrand's door again."

Aymar gaped. What did Françoise know?

"Has he had bad dreams again?"

"You and I, monsieur, needn't speak of bad dreams. I'm not Josephine, whose mother-love blinds her. I can put two and two together as well as you." She brushed the gray hair from her forehead.

"What do you know?" he demanded.

"I've heard that people can keep tiger cubs and make pets of them. But when they reach a certain age you have to put them in a cage."

"What do you know?" he repeated wearily.

"I know," she insisted. "Haven't I watched him grow since childhood? He was cute and playful. So are puppies. So, perhaps, are tiger cubs."

"But why have you come to me with this now?"

"Because Guillemin says to me this morning, 'That fox is back again.' Guillemin's son found a duck's head, chewed off."

Aymar wiped his forehead wearily: "Where will this end?"

At lunch he had an idea. He went into the kitchen where Bertrand was eating. He went up to the boy and pulled down the lower lid of the eye. "Anæmic," he diagnosed.

"He has no appetite again," Josephine complained.

"We'll give him a little raw meat, every day," Aymar prescribed. "That makes blood."

Afterwards he laughed. A good trick. We'll feed the wolf in him and keep him quiet. And he actually succeeded. Bertrand ate the raw flesh avidly. He improved in appearance. His hair grew glossy. His skin sleek. His eyes bright. He grew in weight and stature. And Josephine, noting the excellent results, tempted her darling boy

114

with larger, bloodier portions of meat, with bigger chunks of suet clinging to it.

In his lessons, too, he grew better, and it was delightful to see how he played in the courtyard. He would tire out the dog with running. When he played hares and hounds with the village boys he was always the last to be caught, if caught at all. And when he was It in I-spy, no one could remain hidden from him.

As a whole, the village suspected nothing of Bertrand's peculiar condition. Bramond's wife did indeed smell something a little mysterious in that house, but she ascribed it to an affair between Josephine and Aymar. She allowed her tongue to play with the notion that Bertrand was secretly Aymar's child, but much of her maliciousness in this was due to the fact, as her husband now and then took occasion to point out, that she was jealous of Josephine's son, who was destined to study medicine, a career she wished to provide for her own son Jacques, but which seemed an unlikely possibility in view of the number of the children in the Bramond family—five—and the narrow resources of the family income, limited to Bramond's salary as garde champêtre.

But she came back to it so insistently that she got what she wanted. Not, it is true, all at once, but step by step. First she was allowed to send Jacques to the local school. That was as much as Bramond would give in to. Then she was allowed to let him try to enter a lycée. And when he passed the entrance examination, well, he might have a year of it, but no more. And so on, until years had passed and Jacques was ready to take his baccalaureat, and after the summer he would be off to Paris to study medicine.

Bertrand was to take the examination for the baccalaureat at the same time. He had studied at home with Aymar, whom he called his uncle, and he did not expect to do as well as his friend, for though he was bright, he was frequently ill. Especially in winter, in February. Then he would get dull at his lessons and be troubled at night with horrible dreams. He was ashamed of this, his only weakness, and to his curious friends he would say no more than that he suffered of migraines.

He, himself, was curious about those strange dreams in which he would yearn to race on all fours through a forest, up hill and down dale. His uncle quieted him: "It's nothing. Occasionally boys will have that. You'll get over it."

Then he asked Bertrand: "What do your boy friends say?"

"They don't say anything. I don't tell them much."

"Hm. I see. Well, perhaps it's best you said nothing."

The spring baccalaureat examinations were held at Auxerre. Jacques and Bertrand went off together to take them. It was a matter of three days.

Aymar had at first proposed to go along with Bertrand, whom, despite all these years of comparative quiet, he hated to trust out of his sight. But Françoise had said: "If he's to go to Paris alone later, let him go alone now. It will be a test." That seemed wise, and was so arranged. After all, he had been pretty good these last six years, thanks no doubt to Aymar's trick of feeding him copious amounts of raw meat.

Arrived at Auxerre, Jacques and Bertrand put up at a little inn which was crowded with boys all there for the same purpose. The first two days there was quiet in the inn. Nothing could be heard but the turning of pages and the drone of many boys reciting to themselves, preparing for the daily hours of severe examinations. But on the third day, with only one more easy test in the offing, the tension relaxed. Voices rose to shrieks, there were shouts of laughter, two boys started to pummel each other in the courtyard.

And when the third test was happily in the limbo of the past, pandemonium broke loose. The boys raged through the town where the citizens, wise from long experience, had closed their shops. The cafés handed out only their worst china and were prepared to charge for broken ware as if it came from Sèvres.

In the evening, slightly drunk, one young man with whom Jacques and Bertrand had become friendly proposed that they go to a house he knew of.

Jacques was willing, for in the freer life of the poorer section of his village he had not remained totally pure. But Bertrand was shocked. No, he couldn't go.

Jacques taunted him: "Afraid?"

116

The other fellow said: "Garçon, a glass of warm milk for my baby."

Bertrand said seriously: "No, it isn't that. I'm not feeling well. I didn't sleep well last night."

"Who did? None of us could sleep."

"And then I think my migraine is coming on again." As a matter of fact he did feel that strange congestion and tension that he associated with a delirious night.

Jacques slapped him on the back. "Here's your cure! This is what you've been needing all along. *Une petite femme...*"

The other chap began to recite some naughty verses, which being obscure in meaning were all the more piquant:

> *Marc une béquille avait*
> *Faite en fourche, et de manière*
> *Qu' à la fois elle trouvait*
> *L'oeillet et la boutonnière.*
>
> *D'une indulgence plénière*
> *Il crut devoir se munir,*
> *Et courut, pour l'obtenir,*
> *Conter le cas au Saint-Père.*
>
> *Qui s'écria: Vierge Mère,*
> *Que ne suis-je ainsi bâti!*
> *Va, mon fils, baise, prospère,*
> *Gaudeant bene nati.*

"Well, good-bye, Bertrand," said Jacques, "don't forget your muffler or you'll catch cold—Gaudeant bene nati!"

The taunt was a little too much. He rose and said stiffly: "I'm coming with you." Thereupon the two caught hold of him by either arm and went walking down the street singing together. Bertrand allowed himself to be infected by their reckless gaiety. He lifted up his voice and sang louder than his friends.

The house to which they proceeded was on a quiet by-street. A small but portly woman opened the door and greeting the boys rather coolly, showed them the way into a tiny parlor. Small gilt chairs were arranged around the wall. A diminutive gilt piano occupied a corner. A few pictures decorated the wall and in the flickering gas-jets revealed fat, naked women, lolling on divans or near fountains and attended by black slaves. A single picture in a corner showed Mary Magdalene washing Christ's feet. An eternal light burnt before this picture in a deep ruby glass.

Three girls came into the room. They were neither pretty nor joyous. They were dressed simply, in dark severe materials. One girl, by far the ugliest, wore heavy spectacles. Since Jacques and his friend Raoul had at once approached the other two, Bertrand greeted the myopic girl, and began to dance a polka, along with the others, for Madame had sat down at the gilt piano and was playing.

When the dance was over, the mood was a little merrier. The girls were fanning their perspired faces with their handkerchiefs. Madame had left to fetch some champagne. Raoul had just finished one uproariously funny song and was beginning another.

The champagne added to his previous drinks, the dancing and singing had inflamed Bertrand a little.

Now Madame suggested delicately that it was getting late. She opened the door and showed the way upstairs.

Bertrand was alone with his girl. He was all at once prey to a terrible feeling of fatigue. He could scarcely stand up. His nerves could not bear the excitement. He wished the embarrassing preliminaries were over; in fact, he wished the whole business were over.

The girl laughed across to him. She was accustomed to shy young men. Her method of attack was to tease them. Now she said: "Monsieur must be very modest, if he intends to make love with his clothes on."

Thereupon he began to unbutton his jacket.

"Look," she said suddenly, "you must first write something nice in my book of autographs." She brought over a heavy volume.

He opened the book and was surprised to see the name of Victor Hugo, signed with an immense flourish beneath a dirty verse.

On another page was Horace Vernet beneath a miserable, filthy picture.

The next page showed a sonnet signed "Tout à vous, Adolphe Thiers."

There were Dumas, Garibaldi, and even a large crown and seal hastily sketched, beneath which was the name: Napoleon III.

Bertrand was at first taken in, in fact he was overwhelmed, and before he realized his mistake he had signed his name, Bertrand Caillet, Mont d'Arcy.

Then he understood. All this was mere fantasy. A cruel trick imagined by the first person to enter his name and perpetuated by those who followed.

"Can you read?" he asked.

She blushed, and shook her head.

He understood vaguely. She wore glasses for the same reason she kept a book of autographs: to conceal her misfortune, her lowly station.

"Aren't you going to write something more?"

He pleased her and added above his name the lines:

> *O mon amante!*
> *O mon desir!*
> *Sachons cueillir*
> *L'heure charmante!*

As Bertrand was still shy, the girl, Thérèse, suggested a little game. She would take off two pieces of her clothing to every one of his. There was a little argument as to whether he should count his cap. No, she said, for if he counted his outdoor clothes, so could she. They must start from scratch, as it were. Bertrand soon fell in with her mood and took off the jacket which he had already unbuttoned. She took off a jabot and a lace bolero. Apparently her costume, unadorned as it seemed, consisted of innumerable parts, several petticoats, corset-cover and corset, garters and whatnot else, to all of which she gave a name as she took it off with a giggle of triumph. But in the end she had only a stocking and a shift, and when Bertrand took off his last undergarment, he exclaimed: "It's a tie!"

"No, it isn't," she retorted, and took off one stocking and her eyeglasses and remained in her slip. "I won," Thérèse said, pointing to her last garment.

"But your spectacles—that isn't fair," he objected.

"Yes, it is," she asserted, "I've won, and for punishment you must take off this last piece yourself, only you are not allowed to use your hands."

She joined Bertrand, who, still a little modest, had, in his nudity, retreated to the protection of the bed.

"What shall I do?" he said, laughing nervously. "How can I take it off without using my hands?"

"You have teeth and toes left, haven't you?"

He began a little timidly to seize the thin material in his teeth.

"It'll rip," he said.

"Then you'll buy me another," she warned. "But it's very cheap," she encouraged with a laugh.

He set to work again.

"Aïe! Oh, you're biting me! Jésu-Marie..."

He had caught a piece of her skin between his teeth, along with the material. He heard her scream, he felt a drop of blood oozing through the linen. He had his arms laced about her body. He wanted to release her, but a strange rage had overcome him. Holding her down with one arm, he stopped her screams with the heel of his other hand. She, feeling his hand there strangling her cries, bit down for her part too, and fought out wildly with her fists.

Early the following morning Jacques and Raoul came to an agreement: "Let's leave Bertrand here, and run off together. It will give him a good scare."

When Madame presented her bill they paid only what they had to. Champagne, use of ballroom (!), all the other items with which the bill was decorated, they left for Bertrand.

"He'll pay," they reassured the procuress. "He's rich."

"Really?" she asked. She had herself noticed that he was much better dressed than the other two.

"Very rich," they answered.

120

She thought to herself: "In that case, I'll see if there isn't something else I can add to the bill." And filled with her plan, she bade her customers good-bye and-retired to write out a new and fancier bill. Local business wasn't any too good; the visiting traffic must therefore be made to bear all it could stand.

Jacques and Raoul returned to their inn, packed their books and waited for Bertrand. But Bertrand did not show himself.

"Let's go back and see what happened to him," Jacques suggested. But their return to normal life had brought on a feeling of shame for their escapade. Neither of them cared to return to that house in broad daylight.

Meanwhile the landlord wanted his inn cleared. "I'll have to charge for another day if the gentlemen are going to stay any longer."

Raoul, whistling a merry tune, decided to wash his hands of the whole matter and departed for his home, feeling that something was amiss and he'd better be out of it as soon as possible, for if it came to the ears of his parents he was done for.

As for Jacques, he too had become uneasy. To the bravado of the previous night had succeeded qualms of conscience.

"Well," the landlord interrupted Jacques's thoughts, "you'd better take out your friend's belongings too, unless he's holding the room."

"No, I'll take them," Jacques decided, "and I'll leave a note for my friend if he should come." Thinking thus to have solved the matter, Jacques made a bundle of his roommate's books, wrote out a brief note telling Bertrand that he had all the books and had gone on home, and thereupon set out.

Back in the village, he waited nervously for news of Bertrand. When he heard that Bertrand was sick at home, his trepidation increased. "Now the whole thing is bound to come out," he thought. But nothing happened. He ventured to ask his mother:

"What's the matter with Bertrand?"

"Oh, she said harshly, "who can ever say what's going on in that house! I hear that old Galliez beat the poor lad to within an inch of his life. Shame on the old roué! For that's all he is!"

He made no answer: he knew his mother's attitude to the Galliez establishment, and content to know his own skin still safe, he impatiently awaited his approaching departure to a distant farm where he was to work during the summer. He would be back about the middle of August and leave again at once for Paris, to attend the medical school there. Though the war started that summer, that did not alter his mother's plans. She could not imagine anything sufficiently important to delay her sole ambition.

Chapter Eight

On that morning when Jacques and Raoul had gone off leaving Bertrand saddled with the major part of the bill, the landlady had retired to evolve a new bill which was to be a masterpiece. This accomplished, she waited for her guest to arise. It was already late, but since a girl with a guest frequently slept late, she thought nothing further of the matter and went about her duties.

But at ten o'clock she became impatient and went to knock at Thérèse's door. There was no answer.

"Those rich people..." she thought to herself in disgust, her sense of propriety outraged. She went downstairs again to add on another day's lodging to her bill. That brought the figure to over a hundred francs. Would he have that much? Well, she would show herself amenable to bargaining for the limit in his pockets. "Including that fine watch he has," she determined.

At eleven she went to knock again. There was no answer. She put her ear to the door. A faint groan was audible. She turned the knob and entered.

Thérèse, but what a Thérèse, lay alone in bed and was moaning softly. Great brown bloodstains covered the sheets. Of her customer there was not a sign.

Madame's screams brought the other girls to Thérèse's room.

"Run for a doctor," Madame commanded.

"Get the police, too," said one of the girls.

"No!" cried the mistress. "Don't anyone dare." She did not stand in any too well with the authorities, and the last thing she wanted was to be further implicated. If the police were necessary that could wait until the last moment.

When Thérèse had had her wounds washed and bound and could talk, her mistress asked:

"And how could you let him do such things to you?"

"Well, I guess I must have fainted."

"And for all this, you didn't get a centime?"

"How did I know he was going to do this?"

"Men that want that kind of thing pay heavily in Paris," said Madame, to whom Paris was the arbiter elegantiarum in all matters pertaining to the tariff, etc., in establishments of her kind.

"He didn't seem that sort," Thérèse complained weakly.

"Now if only I had his name!" Madame cried.

"But I have it in my book of autographs," said Thérèse.

"Bah," her mistress exclaimed impatiently and with scorn: "your book of autographs!..."

"Yes," Thérèse answered her. Thereupon Madame took a look, just for the remote possibility of the thing, and there sure enough stood "Bertrand Caillet, Mont d'Arcy." That sounded real enough. And Mont d'Arcy could be reached in a two hours' drive.

That very day she took a hired carriage and had no difficulty in discovering that the Caillets lived in the fine Galliez house, behind the alley of locust trees. The latter were then in bloom and gorgeous with thousands of drooping yellow blossoms. The ground was carpeted with petals. The air full of a slow yellow rain.

The portly purveyor of love *en détail* was not intimidated by the exterior elegance, which she knew only too often concealed expensive vices. On the contrary, she felt assured of a good financial return from her visit, and marched up boldly to ring the bell.

Aymar Galliez had her admitted to his study.

"I've come to tell you about your son Bertrand," the proprietress of the maison tolérée began.

"Well," said Aymar.

She told him her story, embellishing it with art, but making no attempt to conceal her profession, which, in fact, at times she liked to flaunt before the rich bourgeoisie.

"And what do you want me to do?" said Aymar, boiling inside, but outwardly maintaining a certain indifference.

"Parbleu, monsieur. I wish to be reimbursed for damages and expenses. Who would have thought that such a nice refined boy..."

"It seems to me that this is a matter for the police," Aymar interrupted her, wondering if this would not be the very opportunity he wanted to get rid of Bertrand at last.

Madame suppressed her fright. While she certainly had the right and, in truth, the duty of going to the police, the fact that Bertrand was a minor and that she would thus involve herself in a criminal pursuit made it necessary to avoid that way out, which moreover could not possibly yield her a cent of profit.

While she pretended to consider the matter, actually she was busy thinking up a good excuse.

"Very well, monsieur," she said suddenly. "I shall go to the police. I thought, at first, that you would appreciate the opportunity of settling this matter without publicity, but I see that I have wasted my time and my charitable intentions."

Aymar fought with himself. Why did he feel that a werewolf was a disgrace? What stupid sense of shame was it that prevented him from facing the world boldly with this monster? A monster, moreover, not produced by him but by a stranger, and saddled onto him through a chance set of circumstances.

Whereby was he helping matters by concealing this beast-man? And yet he could not bring himself to expose Bertrand. His efforts on the boy's behalf had been crowned with so much success that he had almost shelved the whole matter, but it was plain once more that the lad was a permanent source of danger, and not, no, certainly not to be trusted to go to study medicine in Paris.

With a sigh, he gave in. "How much do you want?" he asked.

"Five thousand francs," she said, pinching her lips.

"Give me your address," he said quietly, "and I shall send you one thousand francs before tonight, and I shall expect to hear nothing further of the matter."

His quiet decision intimidated her. Even a thousand was something. She rose and departed. On the journey home she conceived a brilliant idea. The first thing she did when she reached her house was to upbraid everybody, and particularly Thérèse. "I could kill you!" she screamed at the poor, suffering girl.

"Oh, madame," Thérèse wept through her bandages.

"And we can't even get the doctor bills paid for you. In fact, I was threatened with prosecution for having admitted a minor."

Eventually she relented. "Well, I guess I'll have to pay the doctor myself," she said. "You poor fools never think of saving your money, and if I didn't pay for your treatment, you'd probably have to let yourself die."

Thérèse thanked her mistress profusely. "You'll see, madame, she promised, "I'll work hard for you."

"Go 'way," said Madame jocularly, "you'll probably work so hard and so well that someone will take you home in marriage and you won't even leave us your book of autographs to remember you by."

"Oh, madame, how can you say that?" said Thérèse reproachfully, while she let her mind go with the joyous possibility of this very thing happening some time.

This kind mistress' conscience still had a pang left and that would not be satisfied until she had bought Thérèse a dress for ten francs and even paid for the laundering of the bloody sheets out of her own pocketbook. The thousand francs, however, went to swell her neat little investment in rentes, on which she hoped some day to retire. The road to financial independence is awfully slow and difficult.

Meanwhile Aymar walked up and down his study and pondered.

126

How long had this sort of thing been going on with Bertrand? That could not have been his first visit? The sexual side of the crime was, in his eyes, not inconsiderable. Not that he had totally forgotten his own several profligacies of that nature, but having, since his studies at the Langres Seminary, succeeded in downing his own fleshly appetite, he could no longer appreciate the fact that in others these desires might be insurmountable. The more he thought over the lad's actions, the more incensed he grew. Finally he opened the door of his study and shouted out, which was much against his custom: "Josephine!"

She came running out from the kitchen and up the long hall to his room.

"Oui, monsieur?"

"Is Bertrand back?"

"Non, monsieur, not yet."

"Let me know at once when he arrives."

There was a question in her eyes but he ignored it and closed his door. He recalled a long letter that someone had sent him regarding the Pitamonts and Pitavals, and how a Pitamont was shut up in a well and fed on meat and suet and after long years could not speak any more but only howled like a wolf; "and in fact," the letter concluded (Aymar recalled this well), "it was said that there never was a good Pitamont but that one who was shut up there. And even at that he killed two people before they locked him up. Of course, it was Pitavals he killed so nobody missed them much, nor him either, except his sweetheart who waited thirty years or more to see him. But the Pitamonts were noted for leaving a trail of misery spreading out fanwise in their wake."

And Aymar pondered: "Will it come to that with Bertrand?"

If this kept on, there would be nothing else to do but lock him up. As he thought over the matter, he wondered how good a cell Bertrand's room would make. It would have to be livable, surely, at least as livable as the dungeon in which Pitamont was shut up, if not better.

Supposing that Bertrand grew as ferocious in his own home as he had occasionally shown himself outside, going beyond killing lambs and taking to lacerating people, like this poor prostitute, for example. Then it would have to be either the police or a cell at home.

Following the bent of his thoughts, he walked upstairs and flung open Bertrand's door. The young man was there, sleeping in his bed!

The sight startled Aymar, as if on a walk he had suddenly come face to face with a tiger. He controlled himself and went up to the bed. The boy's face was heavily flushed. He was breathing deeply. His head was thrown back as if he were depleted of all strength. His hair was awry. He looked as if he were sleeping off a drunkenness.

Under the influence of Aymar's gaze, Bertrand opened his eyes. They looked out in surprise at first; then they looked away.

"When did you get back?" Aymar asked.

"Why, I—I didn't know I was back. Oh, I can't remember."

"What's the matter with you?"

Bertrand did not answer for a moment, then he said: "I had another one of my terrible dreams; I don't know how I got here. Let me think, my head is so dull and my body is as if I had been running all night. I wonder—"

"What do you wonder?"

"I wonder, I wonder if it was only a dream this time? I was in the city taking examinations. How did I get home? Did I really run home, as I dreamed? And what happened before, was that a dream, too?"

"Not this time!" Aymar suddenly thundered at the boy, who jumped back in terror. "Not this time!" Bertrand's eyes were popping out of his head. A great fear had overtaken him. He retreated to the far corner of the bed and cowered in the angle of the wall, and there remained shivering like a lapdog in the cold.

"Wait for me," Aymar shouted at him. A sudden idea had come to him. He ran out, taking care to lock the door, and was off as fast as his poor legs would allow him, to the barn where he grabbed the heavy horsewhip used to tame colts to the Plow. He ran back upstairs and shouting to the women: "Away!" he locked himself into Bertrand's room.

"I'll tame the wolf in him," Aymar thought madly, and lashed away at the lad, who had remained in the same position. As the whip wound around his body, Bertrand let out a yell that was as if wrung from the depths of his being.

The whip rose and fell. "I'll tame you!" Aymar thought, clenched his teeth and called upon all his strength. "I'll tame you!" The sweat stood out in beads on his brow.

Bertrand howled until he grew hoarse and his voice thinned into falsetto. Then he whined, in little broken gasps. Finally he was silent. And Aymar ceased.

Dizzy, scarcely knowing why or what he had done, he left the room. Outside the door, Josephine was lying on the floor and Françoise was bending over her with a bottle of smelling salts. Guillemin's wife was downstairs and shouting up: "What is it? What is it? For God's sake!"

"Ce n'est rien. Allez! Vaquez à votre besogne!" Aymar dismissed her gruffly, and brushing past, shut himself up in his study.

For days the house was silent, full of unuttered anger. Only once Josephine, raising her fists, shouted at Aymar: "You've killed him!"

"Shut up!" said Aymar.

"What did he ever do to you?" she asked with a dark menacing note in her voice.

"That's none of your business."

"And you who are almost his father."

Aymar snorted with scorn.

"Yes, and if he dies, I'll kill you too!" she cried.

But the walls of righteousness around Aymar's anger were nevertheless gradually crumbling away and leaving him more and more exposed to the stirrings of repentance and sympathy.

One day he went up to Bertrand's room. The young man looked up at his uncle with his soft brown eyes. There was no hate in those eyes, no desire for revenge, only a plea and a little glint of terror: "Don't..."

"He looks like a whipped dog," Aymar thought. "Maybe I've cured him."

"Let me see your back," he commanded.

The boy's skin was striped with parallel lines of yellow, of red, of purple and green. Aymar was frightened. "How do you feel?"

"I'm better now," Bertrand said gently.

"And you'll take care not to repeat your—shall we call it—escapade?"

"I'll take care, uncle," he promised.

"See that you do." Aymar turned to go, but Bertrand called him back:

"Uncle, did I really do what I only dreamt? I mean…"

"What did you dream?"

The boy hesitated. He felt timid and shy.

"…I mean, bite and scratch…her."

"Yes, I guess you did.—And I had to pay for it. But forget it now and don't talk about it any more."

Bertrand pondered for a while. "I often have just such dreams of biting and scratching and people shooting at me." He paused.

"Well?" Aymar asked.

"But that's just dreaming."

"Of course," said Aymar. "But you see to it that you keep out of bad company."

"I promise you that.—And," he hesitated and went on: "You told Mother you wouldn't send me to Paris."

"I don't think you can be trusted alone, for a little while," Aymar said and resolutely left the room.

In the days that followed, he deliberately hardened his heart. Bertrand's back had healed, but still Aymar would not permit him to leave his room. When Josephine complained and pleaded, he cut her short. "In good time," he would say, and if she insisted, he left her standing. He would take no further chances, he determined.

But one day, old skinflint Vaubois died, and having been for so many years neighbors, it was necessary that the Galliez people attend. Bertrand was, therefore, released for the purpose, upon his solemn promise that he would conduct himself properly. As a matter of fact the young man was as well behaved as he had always been in his outward life. He was affable and at his ease with Mme Bramond.

"You've been ill?" she asked.

"Yes," he answered.

"Jacques left some of your books at our home," she said. "I'll send one of my boys over with them." He thanked her and wondered: "How much does Jacques know? How much did he tell his mother?"

"When are you going to Paris?" she inquired.

"Uncle hasn't said yet," he answered.

"You know, Jacques is coming back on the twelfth of next month, that is, August," she said. "You must come to the farewell supper. He'll be leaving, on foot, for Paris, early the next morning. Why don't you two boys tramp it together?"

"I'll ask Uncle," he replied evasively.

She went off thinking: "Just because they have a little money, they think they've got to be cold and hoity-toity. Well, his mother must earn her money and I'll bet Galliez doesn't make it any too easy for her."

While he thought: "Thank God, she didn't ask too many embarrassing questions."

The ceremony of the burial was beginning to affect Bertrand. He felt tense and uncomfortable. For some reason, which he couldn't determine, the long, slow action of the priest and others annoyed him so badly that he wanted to shout out, "Come on, get it over with!" He was almost glad to think that he would soon be back and locked up in his room. Strange thought, he reflected. But then, he was not like others. They could be open and free. He had secrets, the weight of which oppressed him when he was out among people he feared might know something of his trouble. Yes, he was safer in his room.

But in the evening, as he sat before his meal in the kitchen, for the first time in over a month, he felt differently about returning to his room. On the contrary, he wanted to be off in the fields and feel the good summer winds bearing evening coolness.

Aymar came in. "Time you were upstairs," he said.

Bertrand did not answer, but only looked down sullenly at his plate.

"Why aren't you eating?"

"I'm not hungry."

"How about the raw meat, here, for your anemia?"

"I don't care for it."

"You used to like it well enough. But of late I notice you won't touch it."

"I don't care for it," he repeated sullenly.

"Then get to your room!" he ordered sharply.

Bertrand did not answer. Josephine, hearing the altercation, had come to the doorway.

Aymar thought quickly: "He's not hungry. Eh? It's coming on again then. Of course now that he's gotten the taste for human blood..."

"I'll teach you!" he cried out loud. "Where's that whip?" He ran out toward the barn.

Josephine slipped up to Bertrand and put her arms around him: "My dear boy," she whispered, "do what he says. He'll kill you. Run upstairs quickly. I'll unlock your door later, when he's asleep."

When Aymar returned, Josephine managed to quiet him, pointing out that the lad had gone upstairs. "Whatever he's done," she said, "it can't be that bad. And don't think I don't know what he did. He's told me. But boys always do that. You did yourself. As if I couldn't remember."

"You don't know anything," he flung at her.

"I know that I'm going to the mayor if this doesn't stop."

He was frightened, but concealed it. "Whatever I'm doing is for his own good. And I'll stop when I think he's learnt his lesson. If you want to pack up and go, both of you, I'm willing." And he left her to go upstairs and lock Bertrand's door.

The next day Françoise came into his study.

"You know Vaubois' grave was found opened up this morning, and his body mutilated. The whole village is talking about it. They've arrested Crotez, the shepherd. They say he did it to get Vaubois' gold teeth, which they found in his room, too, but he claims that Vaubois, miser that he was, when about to die and unable to eat, gave the teeth to Crotez, in lieu of wages he owed Crotez, because he knew he couldn't use the teeth any more, anyhow."

"Hm," said Galliez, "I can believe it of that man."

Françoise appeared to be wanting to say something more, but she only stood there and brushed back her gray hair defiantly. "Well, Françoise?" he urged.

"I thought Monsieur would want to know that Bertrand was not in his room last night."

"Nonsense! How could he have gotten out?"

She shrugged her shoulders. "Maybe he's made himself a passkey. At any rate, I saw him slinking down the allée early this morning, when it was barely dawn. I'm sure I wasn't mistaken."

"Well, I'm tired of all this," he said and returned to his books on political economy. He was immersed just then in a study of Karl Marx, a German whose pamphlets were making much stir at the time.

But in the midst of his reading, a correlation which took place unconsciously in the back of his mind, even while he was hard at work on the difficult German sentences, popped into his thoughts. Bertrand–Crotez–Vaubois–why not? Yes, why not Bertrand? Was that what Françoise had meant? No, impossible! And yet even if she hadn't implied as much, the possibility remained. He needs human flesh, now that he's had the taste of it! And as for the door, it could only have been Josephine, with her silly excuse of fire, who had opened it.

His curiosity was so great that anger had no place in him. He went up to Bertrand's room. Though it was past nine, the young man was still asleep. His face was ruddy, his mouth relaxed, his breathing heavy. He looked just the way he had done the morning when the portly proprietress of the lupanar had come to claim an indemnity.

"He's sleeping off his orgy," Aymar thought with horror and disgust.

From that moment his mind was definitely made up. He sought out Josephine. "You've opened the door for your son. I've wished to spare your feelings heretofore, but understand that your son is a dangerous character. And that hereafter I shall carry the key to his room on my person, fire or no fire. And if that doesn't suit you, you may go to the police."

"I certainly shall," Josephine began shrilly.

"The upshot will be that your son will be behind the bars of a state institution and not behind the bars at home. Have your choice!" With that he dismissed her.

She ran to Françoise, but the latter would give her little information.

"You do what M. Aymar says," she warned Josephine, "or you'll find yourself in worse trouble. Monsieur is doing his best to help Bertrand, and if you leave him alone, he'll get him to Paris for you."

The situation, of course, was beyond endurance. Vague rumors were beginning to circulate in the village, carried there by the Guillemins, that Bertrand had gone insane and had had to be locked in his room.

But Josephine, whenever she was in the village, did not flinch one bit. Her poor Bertrand was ill again. He had such delicate nerves. But he'd surely be better when the cooler weather came, and be in condition to go to Paris. If it hadn't been for the war, the Galliez situation would have been threshed out more thoroughly by the village gossips, but Bertrand was soon reported to have left for Paris, and other important and more startling matters came to the fore.

Chapter Nine

Bertrand, in his long enforced leisure, ruminated on his case, but could come to no conclusions. Sometimes it seemed to him that if only he were free to go out into the wide fields, he'd feel better. It was this being shut up in such confining quarters that made him so ill. He could hardly breathe. A fierce resentment arose in him. He would kill his uncle next time Aymar came in! But at other times, particularly in the morning, waking from a dream in which he had run madly for his life, pursued by a great white dog, or some similar nightmare, he would experience a sense of joy to find himself safely at home. His tensed body could relax, his panting chest come slowly back to normal breathing.

Urged by his uncle, who vaguely promised to take him to Paris, he opened his books and studied desultorily. There were many things he wanted to ask his uncle, when the latter brought him his meals, or came to take him out for a little walk. But Aymar always turned the conversation to other matters, discussed the war, or economics, state life-insurance and kindred subjects, or sometimes quizzed him in Latin and mathematics. Bertrand did not shine. His memory was bad at times. "The wolf has got the better of him again," Aymar concluded.

Most of his leisure, however, Bertrand consumed in day-dreaming. He liked to think of Thérèse and wondered if she would be willing to see him again. Often he would stand at his window and look down into the court. Françoise would frequently pass by but she would never look up. Then his mother, neat, trim, would walk past, look around quickly and seeing no one near, would throw him a kiss. That always touched him deeply. Or again it was Mme Guillemin bending over the well, her great round bottom bulging up beneath her red skirt which flamed in the sunlight. The sight of these women somehow always brought Thérèse to mind. He could not forget her standing before him in her shift and teasing him: "Take it off with your teeth." The mad delight of tearing off that last garment!

Occasionally his mother would stand outside his door and talk to him. "I'll get you out," she would promise. "You'll go to Paris. I have money for you." As a matter of fact she had lately drawn out all her savings.

One day, in the village, she learnt that Jacques had returned and was going to have a farewell dinner before he left on foot for Paris.

"No, I don't think we'll be able to come over," she excused herself to Mme Bramond. "Bertrand is leaving tonight to take the train from Arcy. No doubt he will see Jacques in Paris."

Josephine enjoyed her triumph. Poor Jacques was walking. But Bertrand was riding in the train. And Mme Bramond, feeling the sharp edge of Josephine's words, came back: "Jacques's name was ahead of Bertrand's on the list of those who passed the examination." She was hoping that that thrust would strike home, although it had been explained to her that the list was purely alphabetical and Bramond naturally came before Caillet. When her false arrow reached its destination and Josephine took leave, a bit discomfited, Mme Bramond had a further source of joy: that ignorant Josephine did not even know that the order of the names was not according to merit, but according to the A B C.

136

Josephine was determined now that Bertrand must leave that very night. She secretly fitted up a bag with clothes and food, placed money inside and waited impatiently for night to come. She knew that Aymar kept the key to Bertrand's room in the pocket of his waistcoat, and she proposed to steal it from there just as soon as he fell asleep. The affair was risky, but she meant to go through with it. She managed to whisper through to Bertrand: "Wait for me tonight. You're leaving for Paris."

"Paris," Bertrand thought. For the moment he was more anxious to go see Thérèse. But there would be women in Paris, too, he decided, and that provided him with an excellent topic for dreaming through the day, until the evening came.

Late at night, as he was lying asleep, he felt someone kiss him. He had been dreaming of Thérèse and for a moment did not fully understand that it was his mother, in her nightgown, who had opened his room and now was saying, between her kisses:

"My darling boy. Get up and leave quickly before your uncle discovers that I stole the key."

Sleepily he returned her kisses. "Wake up, child. I've got a bag packed with everything you need. Money, too. Quick! You must put a safe distance betweeen you and this prison. Oh, my darling baby. How long will it be before I see you again? I have a mind to go with you."

She had sat down on the bed beside him, had lifted him up and held him embraced against her bosom. And he, too, put his arms around her and hugged her tightly. He was trying desperately to fight off the fog of his dream. But it had his faculties enmeshed as if in a mist of spiderwebs. He was holding Thérèse and she was taunting him to take off her shift.

"Darling baby...Why, Bertrand! What are you doing?"

"Stop it, Bertrand!" she whispered as loud as she dared. "Bertrand, I tell you!" She struggled against his youthful muscular body, then she ceased and made no further resistance. A strange glow of satisfaction emanated from her sacrifice and caused her features to relax into an ecstatic smile. All the years of her life coalesced — Pitamont, Aymar, Bertrand. They were all one. They had melted into a single body, with many arms flailing about her, but with only one face.

When Bertrand awoke several hours later, he noted with dismay his mother lying naked beside him, her limbs flung apart in complete relaxation. Violently disturbed, he rose softly and dressed himself and opened the door. The hall was quiet and dark in contrast to his own room dimly lit by the night sky. He felt again that familiar sensation of wanting to run in the forest. He must get out. He could not quite recall what had happened, but he was filled with a sense of fear and shame from which he thought he could escape by leaving the house.

As he came out into the hall, the figure of his uncle, in a night-gown, suddenly rose before him and blocked his way.

"What are you doing out here? How did you get out? Get back to your room!"

Bertrand bared his teeth. "You can't hold me a prisoner forever!" he screamed. "I'm going to Paris! Let me go, I say! I want to get out! I'm dying!"

"Get back to your room. Get back—"

Bertrand lowered his head and dashed forward. He heard his uncle gasp as he bowled the man over, but he did not wait to learn what had happened. He ran downstairs. The front door was locked, but in the adjoining room, his uncle's study, the low balcony doors were flung wide open to the night winds. He ran through the room, leaped over the railing and six feet below fell lightly on his feet. Without knowing precisely what he was doing, he took the main road and followed it.

The noise of the commotion aroused Josephine. At once aware of what was happening, she rose to put herself within the safety of her room. She grabbed her torn nightgown, saw the bag Bertrand had forgotten and thought "He'll write and I'll send him money," and picking up the bag, she slipped into her room. The key which she had plucked out of the lock as she passed, she flung out of the window and into the bushes below.

Bertrand loped along at a fast trot, panting heavily. Finally he

138

flung himself down on the grassy bank bordering the road and lay there breathing in the dew and finding the coolness soothing. Some blades of grass were against his face. He opened his mouth and nibbled them off reflectively.

But in another moment he was all aquiver. His body tensed. Someone was coming along the road. He rose cautiously and retreated behind the hedge of a field. His uncle was after him! No. Through the darkness came an indistinct shape, a man with a knapsack on his back, treading with an even pace, and marking every second step with a tap of his cane on the ground.

A wild desire to lay his hands on that man coursed through Bertrand's body and set his brain aflame. His eyes were so hot that he could not blink without a stab of pain. Every part of his body was sore and so sensitive that every stitch of clothing on his back pressed on his skin like the point of a needle. He quickly disengaged himself therefrom, tearing the buttons off in his haste. As his clothes fell about him in a heap, he felt much better. But the sudden contact of his naked body with the cool wind called attention to a feeling of distention in his bladder. He relieved himself, making an are of his water away from his clothes.

Now he truly felt free and unencumbered, and with long, silent strides, raced after the man, who had disappeared into the night. In a few minutes he had caught up with the figure, indistinctly visible in the darkness. Instinctively his hands itched to be at that throat. With a cry, he bounded over the hedge and leaped at the man who turned, startled and defenseless, and crumpled up before the violence of the attack.

Though a moment before Bertrand's hands had itched to be at the man's throat, they made no move to seize and hold his prey. The tension was not in his limbs but in his face, in the masseter muscles of his jaws. His mouth had opened wide. His teeth had dug through cloth and flesh. His face was inundated with a warm fountain, which he licked at greedily.

He dragged his kill to the hedge bordering the road. It did not occur to him to use his hands for this task. He used his teeth and tugged. His arms and legs stemmed his body, pushed at the ground, and thus pulling backwards he reached the side of the road. There he began to devour bits of flesh torn from the throat. What he wanted was the flesh of the body, but the heavy cloth of the suit hampered him. As hard as he pulled he could not tear it off, and his teeth could not rip through the tough material. But already his appetite had been largely satisfied. What he craved now was sleep. His head dropped on the body of his kill. He dozed. How long he knew not.

But when he awoke, it was with a start. He was chilly and had had a bad dream, a tangled dream of blood and flesh, of fighting and of shouting and leaping. His hand reached forth to find the blanket which in his disturbed sleep he had evidently pushed off. But the blanket would not come. It must be stuck between the bed and the wall. He pulled. How heavy that blanket was. What was that white, heavy object, like a head of winter cabbage chewed by worms?

The ravaged face of his friend, Jacques Bramond, appeared plain before him. "Will these nightmares never stop?" he complained, and released his hold on the blanket. The head fell back. "Decidedly this is too real. Now how can I wake myself up? I know, I'll get out of bed."

But there was no stepping down to the floor from this bed. He was awake. This was reality. In the thinning darkness he saw the mutilated corpse. His own mouth was sticky with clotted blood.

"God, is it real?" he cried out. "Or will I yet wake up from this nightmare more horrible than any I have ever had?"

The sound of his voice was too clear to be denied.

He fell on the body and burst into violent tears: "Jacques! Jacques!" But Jacques could not answer.

"Oh! I knew it was real, I knew it was real! I knew I was kept locked up for a better reason than Uncle would tell me."

He wept. He gnashed his teeth. He tore out his hair. When his emotion had spent itself a little, his first desire was to run home to his mother. But a vague recollection of having done a horrible thing to his mother restrained him. "Was that reality, too? No, no! Never!—And yet…" No, he could not go home.

That might be as true as this. *This* caused him to burst out weeping again. What a monster he was! Truly fit only to be locked up forever. But with the light of day gradually sifting through the atmosphere, he began to think of caution. He must go somewhere. If he should be found here, by the villagers—by old Bramond himself! God forbid!

Filled now less with horror at himself than with fear for his own safety, he rose hastily and considered. A few hundred feet away was a forest. If he could drag the body there?

He was surprised at his own composure. He took the body by the shoulders and snaked it along through a break in the hedge, and across the field to the trees. "You were certainly a stocky fellow, Jacques," he found himself thinking. About a hundred yards into the woods he felt safe. With his hands he scraped away the soft leafy mold until he had made a shallow grave.

A new thought disturbed him. Perhaps he ought to remove Jacques's clothes. "I can't go back to the house for my own." Then he recalled, as if it were from a dream, that he had left his clothes in the meadow yonder, behind the hedge. "If all my dreams are true," he said to himself, "then I'll find my clothes there."

He left the body and ran back. There was no time to be lost. A distinct pearly haze of dawn pervaded the eastern sky. From the distance came the crowing of cocks. He almost wished that his clothes wouldn't be there. It would mean that at least some of his dreams weren't true. But his clothes, now damp with dew, were there where he had torn them from his feverish body. He dressed himself and ran back to finish his task.

At every moment the light increased and the business of burying his old playmate became more gruesome. The stiffened body was hard to manage. The knapsack was in the way. He removed it. "A good idea," he thought to himself. "There will be things in there that I'll need. He made a hasty examination of the contents. Food, linen, and, tucked away, a billfold with money in it.

He had a sudden notion to dump out the bread and wine and cold meat in the knapsack and pack in a limb or two of the dead body.

The idea so revolted him that he nearly retched. "Where do such ideas come to me from?" he exclaimed in horror.

He finished hastily with the grave, erased the signs of his activity as best he could by scattering leaves about. Then, shouldering the sack, he ran out to the road.

He walked all day, resting occasionally, heading, as far as he could judge, northeast, toward Paris. He avoided people and villages. Toward evening he found himself a good distance from his home and with a certain feeling of security.

At noon, that day, hunger had caused him to interrupt his flight for a moment. He had sought a cool, secluded spot, and had investigated more carefully the contents of the knapsack. There was a good quantity of various delicacies, cold chicken and hare. Old Bramond would have hare, Bertrand thought. There was a bottle of wine, several slices of bread, and a couple of early apples. And there was a small jar full of some paste, probably of liver and chopped greens. It made a delicious luncheon indeed. The wine was excellent and the cold meats most tasty. He ate with genuine appetite.

"I'll leave some for this evening," he thought. "There'll be plenty here for another meal." Satisfied, both with the present and with the prospects of the immediate future, he took a little nap and proceeded on his journey.

Evening discovered him hungry, true enough, but incapable of thinking of more chicken and hare for supper. He found himself turning over a strange thought in his mind': "Why didn't I take an arm from Jacques? Yes, he was my good friend Jacques, whom I've known all my life, but after all, he was dead, wasn't he? What good could my scruples do him, once he was done for?" Impassively, he ruminated on. "I'll know better next time."

The pangs of hunger began to be acute and he found himself skirting the villages closer, hoping for a stray child, and looking closely at the churches and their adjoining yards, scanning them for wreaths and ribbons and other signs of a recent burial. But night found him still wandering, unsatisfied, past dark farmhouses where the dogs barked strangely at his passing scent. He sought the

142

shelter of the woods. His body was racked with hunger. He yelped and whined at the moon that glittered coldly, cut by the silhouette of leaves and branches.

Only a few minutes after Bertrand had left the scene of that morning's crime, a young farmhand had come down the road. His shoe encountered a hard object that was flung ahead by the vigor of his stride. He picked up a handsome knotty cane. "Wonder who lost this?" he thought and walked on, making use of its swing and tap to grace and accentuate his walk.

Arrived at the scene of his work, he showed the cane to his fellow workers. "Look what I found. Nice, eh?" The workmen admired; but one man said: "Where'd you get that? Belongs to Old Bramond, the garde champêtre. Better return it."

"I'll have to, I guess," the young man said, a little sorrowfully, hating to part with the piece of polished wood to which his hand had already acquired a friendship.

"See that you do," said the older man. Intentionally, however, the young man allowed various matters to delay him a week before he brought the cane back to its owner.

"Where did you find this?" Bramond asked in surprise.

"Out on the road."

Bramond shook his head. "Hm." He showed the stick to his wife.

"What does it mean?" she asked wildly.

"Hm. Nothing, I guess. You remember he did not want it and stuck it through the straps of his knapsack? It must have fallen out without his noticing it."

"But we haven't heard from either him or Aunt Louise. Surely he's reached Paris already."

"Give him time, Mother. You know he hasn't a cent to spare. With the four others we've got, he'll have to go easy. He knows that too. And Aunt Louise is poorer than we are. Now, don't you worry."

"But I am worried. Oh, I wish we could have sent our boy to study in style. M Galliez told me Bertrand took the train at Arcy.

And M Galliez is going to follow just as soon as he can. Oh, I hope everything is all right with Jacques!"

Lovesick for his sweetheart at home, the young farmhand suddenly departed. He was even willing to lose a portion of his wages for not having worked out the week. This proved a strong argument against him, when, a week or so later, poor Jacques's body was discovered and this young farmhand was brought to trial. It was shown by clocking that on that morning he would have encountered Jacques at just about the point of the road which was nearest the grave in the forest.

If he was not convicted, it was only because, aside from the cane and the meeting on the road which would explain either the finding of the cane or the murder, the evidence was too scanty. And no motive could be established, though theft was brought up strongly by the prosecution.

Old Bramond was heard to mutter: "If he isn't convicted, I'll murder him myself!" But his wife could only think of the sadness of it: over and over, as she shook her head, she would repeat: "Just imagine, he didn't even get out of sight of the village. And we thought him in Paris, long ago."

Even the farmhand's girl back home had at least some suspicions and broke off with him, and the young man, though legally acquitted, found himself convicted by the community. Only Galliez had been decent to him, but when he knocked at the Galliez house he learnt that Monsieur was in Paris. He thought of emigrating, but he had no money, though the village credited him with having secreted Jacques's cash. He thought of joining the army, which was calling for men to join the colors to beat back the Prussians besieging Paris, but before he did so, he got himself drunk one night of desperation and hanged himself.

"Saved my gun the trouble," Bramond grumbled. "Well, that shows up his bad conscience."

He was told of a note that was left by the young man. It read:

I am innocent, but even my dearest Hélène thinks me guilty. How can I live?

"Hm," said Bramond in surprise. "The cheek of that kind to lie, even when they are about to appear before God's tribunal."

Only Aymar knew. That morning that Jacques was murdered was the morning Bertrand had run off. The manner of the killing, the tearing of the carotid artery, the mutilation, etc. There could be no doubt of it. And yet: What proof had he?

His first intention was to run off at once to Paris, where he suspected Bertrand must be, but he delayed several weeks. There was the trial of the poor farmhand. He must see that there be no miscarriage of justice there. He journeyed to Auxerre, where the trial was to be held, and having assured himself by a talk with the lawyers of the defense that the man could not possibly be convicted, he thought to have done his duty by slipping the poor fellow fifty francs and promising to do more if necessary.

Subsequently, in Paris, when several months later news began to come through again, he learnt of the truth and reproached himself bitterly. "If only I had set fire to the house that night," he thought. That phrase in the letter had been true: the Pitamonts leave a trail of misfortune that spreads out fanwise behind their poisonous course. If only he could have brought himself to make a complete confession to the police. But there was a strange shame here that he could not overcome. Oh, the terrible disgrace, the ignominy of it—possessing a mythical monster in one's own family, in this age of science and enlightenment!

Chapter Ten

Aymar slipped into Paris, September the third, a day before its investment by the Germans was complete. Long before he had reached Paris, he had come to understand that, with no clue to go by, it would be difficult to find Bertrand. "How, in fact, shall I discover him?" Then he thought, sadly but realistically: "He will leave a trail of crimes."

Aymar's first duty ought, then, to have been a visit to the police. But of this he naturally fought shy. What would he say to the police? For example: "I know something. There is a man who on certain nights craves blood so that he turns into a wolf and goes out to kill his prey." If they do not laugh me out of court, they will at any rate ask: "You have seen this with your eyes." And I shall say: "No, but I have proof of this fact from having lived with this man for nineteen years."—"What proof have you?" "There was a silver bullet, which was shot at a wolf, and was found in his leg."—"The mere sight of this bullet wouldn't convince us, but where is it?"—"I haven't got it, but he was born on Christmas eve and his eyebrows meet…"

No, this was mad. He would not even get that far, and if he did, what good would it do? In the end he could only be locked up for a fool, and "serve me right, for I'd be a fool to do it," Aymar concluded these thoughts.

The best thing would be to wait for circumstances to make the matter plain to a number of people. "Then I can appear with my further confirmation. And either there will be crimes such that the matter will come to light, or else there will be no crimes and I needn't worry."

Thus it was that several times a day Aymar looked through all the papers. Impatiently he turned away from the war news and sought the news of crime. But the war had crowded the latter out. Before the greater importance of thousands going to death, before a greater werewolf drinking the blood of regiments, of what importance was a little werewolf like Bertrand?

Nevertheless, one day there was a clue. A General Darimon had died. His death roused sympathy, for his end was tragic. On one day he had lost his only child. On the next he had suffered a most brutal attack, the criminal going so far as to desecrate the dead child, and on the following day he, himself, had expired. The criminal was being held at the Dépôt and would shortly be moved to the prison of La Grande Roquette to await trial.

The matter allows itself to be reconstructed from the data given by Aymar in his script, the newspapers of the time, the dossier of a certain Jean Robert, etc.

General Darimon had been a popular figure in Imperial Paris. After a life spent in seeking the satisfaction of his baser instincts, he had secured both a stable position and a new fortune by an excellent marriage to an heiress. Despite the gossips, he was genuinely in love and thoroughly willing to be completely domesticated, which is not surprising, seeing that he was near taking his retirement. His cup ran over when he was blessed with a daughter, who he could not doubt was to be the last fruit of his life.

In November 1870, when the girl was but five years old, she was carried off by so rapid an illness that there had been scarce time to call a physician, who, to be sure, could himself do no more than witness the last choked breaths of the hot, tortured body, whose fever cooled down rapidly to death's chill.

147

The church ceremony was impressive. The funeral cortége, for those days when horses were lacking, was nevertheless an endless file, so great was the company. Women and children wrapped in shawls against the cold streets, waiting in long queues to obtain their little rations of meat, watched the sad procession and found their lot a little easier to bear. Even shivering in the cold is a manifestation of life. It's when the cold no longer makes you shiver...

The little body was brought to rest at Pére-Lachaise. The workmen had removed the great slabs of stone from the vault and, on account of the lateness of the hour and the bitter cold, had gone home, expecting to close the vault on the morrow.

The stricken parent, with tears streaming over his cheeks, could not restrain himself from weeping out loud, and informing those around him that he had been a cruel father who once had even shouted angrily at his angelic daughter because she had scribbled over some important correspondence. For this he would never forgive himself. Why had he not saved those scribbled sheets and framed them? They would now have been the most cherished mementos of his life.

Among the mourners were many of the general's old colleagues who could not help recalling that this pitiful old man with his childish tale of woe had been for twenty years the most noted raconteur of risqué stories in France, with more than one such story of his own experience. The way that man could crack a chestnut in the company of young men and women so that the girls understood not a word while the men had to hold their sides! That had been, in fact, his favorite trick, his forte.

The hardest hearts melted at the sight of the father being torn away by force from the pit that had swallowed his child in its white coffin. The wife distraught, half unconscious, suffered herself to be led back to the long line of carriages with no resistance. But the general proved a problem for his friends.

Finally he stood at the door of the coach. Resolved, he suddenly went forward to the black-plumed horses and spoke to the coachman. "You will call for me at five o'clock tomorrow morning.

And every morning hereafter until I die. I shall see the sun rise here every day of my life." The startled coachman doffed his tall black hat and mumbled something incomprehensible.

Early in the morning the general was ready for the coachman who called promptly. Off they drove at a rapid pace through the dark, silent streets, where only a few trucks piled with cabbages and carrots were distributing the scanty rations of the siege-period. The drivers nodded on their seats, while the patient donkeys and horses trotted on philosophically. Behind, a woman or a boy snored, muffled in many shawls against the morning chill. It was a shrunken picture of a scene the general had often witnessed when coming home from some late festivity, but at the end of a night, never at the beginning of a day.

The general sat erect, dry-eyed. He was fulfilling a vow, the execution of which, by the demands it placed upon him, was already helping him bear his load of grief. As he drove on, it suddenly occurred to him that he was making a strange man a party to his vow. A man who would henceforth suffer the same punishment he had meted out to himself. This idea, which would never have occurred to him in his former days, was now so insistent that he was driven to act. He called out to the coachman to stop. Then he stepped out and hoisted himself upon the box.

"Drive on," he said.

The coachman, nonplussed, lifted the reins and let them slap down on the backs of his beasts. The night wind rushed past the two men. The general sat bolt upright. The coachman stiffened out of his natural droop.

"What is your name?" the general asked kindly.

"Jean Robert, at your service."

"Are you married?" the general pursued.

"Yes, your excellency."

"Any children?"

"Five, your excellency."

"Girls?"

"Two."

"Do you love them?"

"Ah, well, you see, monsieur, they're mine."

"Of course."

"And then they cost a pretty sum."

"They do that," the general confirmed and nodded his head.

"When they're tiny then of course they cost nothing for a while, but when you figure in the midwife…"

"To be sure."

"They've got little mouths but big bellies and they're always hungry."

"Strange, isn't it?" the general asked politely.

"Still, when they grow up and become men and women and marry, then you naturally expect them to take you in and take care of you in your old age."

"No good child forgets that duty," said the general sternly.

The coachman answered quickly: "I didn't forget my old folks, I can tell you that, but children nowadays are not what they used to be. No respect for their elders any more. And the newspapers full of crime stories."

"Yes, the good old days," said the general and sighed. "By the way," he said, as if the thought that had been occupying his mind all the while had only just occurred to him, "it's a shame that you should have to get up so early to drive me out to the cemetery. Hereafter I shall get up an hour earlier and walk."

The driver's face fell. His voice revealed his disappointment.

"Oh, not at all, your excellency. I am only too glad, too happy…"

"That's all right, my good man," said the general and patted the coachman on the thigh. "You've a kind heart. But I have no business depriving you of the company of your children in the morning, simply because I have lost mine. I shall walk." He sighed.

They jogged along through the darkness for a while in total silence.

"So it's over," said the coachman, and he too sighed.

"What do you mean?" the general asked.

"I mean it's finished."

"What's finished?"

"The good job, of which I had promised myself so much."

150

"I don't understand."

"We are paid very little, sir," the coachman explained. "And here I had a little extra work every day, at an hour when no one else would have required me. Moreover, I arranged all the necessary details and promised the caretaker some money for opening the gates at this early hour."

The general fell into a reverie.

As the carriage halted before the locked gate of the cemetery, the general, spurred by a sudden determination, handed the coachman his well-stuffed portefeuille.

"Here. In that you will find a good year's wages. Take it. It is yours. And I shall feel free to walk every morning and bear my grief alone."

The driver could not think of any other way to express his thanks than to get down on his knees and, with a choking voice cut by strangling sobs, mumble words that were incomprehensible.

"Come, my friend," said the general, to whom the scene was distasteful, "rise and let us be attending to business."

"Holà! Holà!" the coachman screamed.

"What's the matter?"

"I must wake up the attendant who sleeps in the lodge there. He promised to open the door for us."

"No, no. That won't do. Why should his sleep be disturbed? Besides, it is unseemly to shout in this place. Give me your hand and we shall soon be over the gate." To facilitate the climb, which was not inconsiderable, the coachman backed his vehicle against the gate.

The hour was now a little short of six. A morning mist, whitish-gray and luminescent, announced a chill dawn. The wet, leafless trees rained onto the cobblestoned walks. The two men had hardly dropped onto the other side when a dog rushed past them, took the high fence at one bound, resting for a second on the upper bars, and was gone.

"What was that?" the general asked, startled.

"The caretaker's dog, I think," said Jean Robert.

"My nerves are bad," said the general. They walked down the

151

path through the wall of fog, in which the white tombstones seemed to be only concreter portions of the general mist, roughly carved into the shape of figures hunched against the chill.

The feet of the walkers left the hard cobblestones and crunched along the pebbles of a narrower path—that crunch the only friendly sound in the dismal atmosphere. But even that friendly noise too often repeated grew ominous at last, took on an alarming note, seemed a threat. And from being the only sound in the cemetery, it came to be the only sound in the world. Crunch, *Crunch!* Crunch! The rhythms of the two walkers now agreed and reenforced each other, now broke and disagreed into a quarrel of crunches and then caught again, like dancers twirling in a complicated figure, like lovers kissing and bickering.

The general's ears were filled with the sound, his heart, his body, his mind were fastened on nothing but that crunching, crunching until his eyes caught sight of the grave of his child, a grave in strange disarray.

His eyes sought to penetrate the mist. His feet hastened on. O Lord! O God! Have pity on me! The white coffin lay on one side, the cover was wrenched off and broken. Of the body of his little girl there were left only horribly mangled remains, scattered over the ground. In the distance sounded the early cannonade of the besieging Prussian troops firing on the fort of Mont-Valérien.

Two hours later the caretaker discovered the terrible scene on his morning round. His dog, an old and silent beast that rarely barked, had run ahead and was excitedly growling and sniffing at the body of a man, General Darimon, and at the scattered remains of the body buried the previous day.

The police, notified, were at once busy on the case. Both the general's position in society and the gruesomeness of the crime demanded immediate attention. The general had been conveyed home where he lay in high fever unable to answer any questions, but the notorious cleverness of the Paris police rose to the occasion. In less than three hours, an officer and four men had set out, armed with a warrant, to a small street near the Porte Saint-Martin. They halted in front of a low two-story house of unappealing exterior. A central archway gave access to a dark staircase. Having posted his men, the officer, though timid by nature, felt compelled by his leadership to mount the steps, which he did, his pistol cocked. He took the further frequent precaution of stopping at almost every step and shouting out at the top of his voice: "In the name of the law!"

Finally he stood on a landing and knocked at the door that faced him. A slatternly woman with two small children clinging to her skirts and one held in the crook of her arm opened the door. With her free hand she brushed strands of black hair away from her dark, not unhandsome face. Then with a snarl of scorn on her mouth, she spoke:

"He's under the bed, the coward!"

The officer, his timidity turned to courage, even to actual bravado, before this display of greater timidity than his own, whistled to his men, who came bounding up at once.

"Drag him out!" and pointed to a large, unmade bed heaped high with feather mattresses and pillows.

What they dragged forth was obviously a man mad with terror. Clutched in his hand was a heavy billfold of red leather, bearing an elaborate coat of arms worked out in gold thread.

"Hm," said the officer and snatched the case.

Four thousand francs in bills on the Banque de France.

"Well, well," the officer laughed and said gaily, teasing the man who had now dropped on his knees.

"Yours, of course?"

"Mine!" cried the coachman wildly. "Mine, mine. Oh, don't take it away. We need it so badly. It's mine, I swear before all the saints of heaven. Don't you see how poor we are?"

"Of course it's yours, my friend. And did you think we'd be so cruel as to separate it from you? No, you must come, both together. Allons, mon cher croque-mort! En route!" The men prodded the coachman from his kneeling position.

Jean Robert threw a glance of despair at his wife: "And you, even you."

153

She turned her head away. "Take him away. The thief! The dirty dog! I slaved for him to the bone and bore him five children, because I loved him, because I thought he'd never steal again."

"Steal again," said the officer and whistled. "So that's it, eh? When?"

"He was in prison at Besançon for three years," she said. "Oh, how he swore by all the saints of heaven that he would never steal again if I but took him back! God, why was I fool enough to believe him? Now get out, all of you!"

After a visit to the Permanence, where his name and address, etc., were taken down, the coachman, Jean Robert, was led a short distance away, around great somber walls, wet with cold rain, to the Dépôt, where the prefecture of police was busy night and day. There Robert was left in a little cell to attempt to puzzle out the curious fate that had overtaken him. Rich suddenly and now poorer than ever. He had small success with his problem. But he did recall a thought given to him long ago by the priest who used to visit him in the prison at Besançon. There, when Robert would complain that he had played only a small share in the crime for which his associates had nevertheless received shorter sentences, this old healer of souls used to say: "My son, a guilty man must often bear the punishment that belongs to some other criminal. And so great is the sin of this world that sometimes even an innocent person must suffer; and so great is the virtue of this world that sometimes a sinful person will enjoy his life in peace. But these are exceptions. In general it is the great group of guilty people who suffer for the guilt of their kinds, while the great group of innocent are rewarded. The few exceptions must not blind us to the rule. And that rule is: if you transgress no moral law, you need never fear retribution."

So often had this kind and benevolent priest assured him of this fact that Robert had memorized the words if not the import. Now, however, he saw their meaning: If you violate no law, if you commit not the slightest infraction of rules, you are absolutely safe. It is the borderline people, those who have been neither great criminals nor

154

great saints, who have reason to complain of the severity of justice, for it often strikes them harder than they deserve. "My son," the priest used to warn Robert, "avoid even the appearance of sin."

Robert was forcibly reminded of this caution when an officer came to lead him before the juge d'instruction, in a small chamber nearby. A few benches, a special chair for himself, a greffier busy writing: "Par devant nous, Gustave Le Verrier, juge d'instruction, sont comparus: Jean Robert, cocher attaché aux services des pompes funèbres," etc., although Gustave Le Verrier, the examining judge, was as yet nowhere to be seen.

When he came, however, there was no escaping seeing him. He was immense. He was mountainous. His ample robes swayed about his body with the grand freedom and magnificent folds of stage curtains. His enormous roseate face, with its light beard through which the pink of his flesh shone, was wreathed in smiles. He looked upon the prisoner with such benevolence that the sun of hope rose in his dark interior.

"Quel temps, quel temps affreux," he muttered, but in a booming voice, and sought the prisoner's eyes for confirmation.

And when Robert did not know what to do or say, the judge leaned forward, his gigantic face came nearer to Robert, its cavernous mouth, lined with lustrous teeth and rosy gums on which the saliva sparkled, seemed to exhale an immense: "W E L L? And you have nothing to say?" until Robert gasped:

"Oui, monsieur le juge…rotten weather, rotten weather, indeed!"

Then the great body withdrew, the wreath of smiles came forth again and the fat lips trumpeted, while the little glittering eyes buried in fat held the prisoner: "But we're due for a change," with a deprecating gesture of his white, sausage-like fingers. A pronouncement which Robert enthusiastically seconded.

After some preliminary formalities and some questions addressed to the commissionaire and to an austere gentleman who was the conservateur of the cemetery (Robert knew him from a distance), the judge demanded of the culprit:

"Do you not know Article Thirty-seven of Heading Seven?"

"No, monsieur." Robert trembled.

"What! You are a coachman in the funeral service and do not know that private hiring of coachmen is forbidden?"

"Yes, monsieur, I know that."

The judge glared at this man who knew and didn't know at the same time. "And Article Thirty-eight? Do you know that one?"

"No, monsieur."

"That entrance into a cemetery at night is forbidden?"

"Yes, monsieur, I know that, but..."

Positively this was too much for the judge. "Do you know or don't you?" he bellowed.

"I know, I know," Robert repeated weakly.

"Then tell me what are Articles Forty-eight and Forty-nine under Heading Ten?"

Unable to express himself quickly, Robert faltered: "I don't know."

With that the judge gave it up. He sank back, shrugged his shoulders, and said in tones of plain disgust: "Forty-eight forbids dogs; Forty-nine forbids the walls to be climbed. And seeing that you know nothing of the very rules that apply to your own occupation, and which are posted everywhere so that you may familiarize yourself with them, I doubt if you would know Article Three-sixty of the *Code d'Instruction Criminelle.*"

As Robert made no answer, the judge's voice rose: "Speak up!"

Robert hastily confessed his ignorance.

"*Sera puni d'un emprisonnement et cætera,*" the judge intoned. "Whoever shall have rendered himself guilty of violation of tombs or sepultures shall be punished with imprisonment from three months to one year and with a fine of from sixteen to two hundred francs. This is not to limit the punishments accorded for any other crimes or infractions which may be associated thereto.—This last sentence applies to the theft of the pocketbook," he generously added in explanation.

"And let me read you the decision of the *Cour de Cassation* of June twenty-third, eighteen-sixty-six: 'For violation of sepulture to be a crime the culpable intention of the violator must be shown.

156

But mere violation of sepulture necessarily implies the intention of insulting the dead.'

"The law has furnished us with delicate pincers, there," the judge admired. "The crime of violating a tomb must rest upon the intentions of the culprit. To be sure. But these intentions are plainly culpable if the tomb has been violated." He smiled with satisfaction. He appreciated the subtlety of the law. His face again oozing friendship, beaming with love, he addressed the prisoner:

"You see how our beneficent laws extend their protection even over the dead. No corpse has anything to fear in France."

Meekly Robert hastened to confirm that.

Next the question of the theft of the pocketbook was taken up, and when the law had been expounded on this matter too, Robert was asked to make a statement. The greffier took down Robert's tale of how he had indeed been guilty of wishing to earn some additional money and had planned to share this money with a certain few employees whose aid in the matter was indispensable. Aside from that, however, he had done nothing. The general had given him the money. The grave had been discovered already violated. The general had fainted and he had fled in terror.

With this the examination was completed. The judge had now no further duty but to decide whether there was need for holding the prisoner for a trial or not.

This decision was not far to seek. Honesty and innocence never involved contradiction. Only crime involves men in such a tangle of knowing and not knowing. The man was plainly guilty and must stand trial. Meanwhile he was ordered transferred to the Grande Roquette prison: "... within a stone's throw of the scene of the crime at Père-Lachaise," so the judge phrased it, and there Robert was to await the recovery of the general who was to testify against him.

Robert clasped his hands in prayer. "But the general knows I am innocent!"

To which the judge allotted one of his kindest smiles. His huge face fairly burst with kind joviality. "Then, of course, he will say so at the trial."

"But my work—my family?"

"This is a court, my friend, not heaven. The law punishes crime, it does not reward innocence."

As Jean Robert was being led out, the judge observed: "Why is ignorance of the law so universal?" He shrugged his shoulders. It was as if an earthquake had lifted mountains. The great folds of his robe flowed like the tide. And the majesty of the law arose to retire for a moment in the recently installed lavatories flushed by water, even as in the best English manner.

Unfortunately, at this inopportune moment the general chose to breathe his last. The newspapers naturally recalled the harsh fate that had struck him in these last few days and so the matter came to Aymar's notice. "Bertrand did that once," he observed to himself, thinking of Vaubois. The more he thought it over, the more convinced he was. He hastened to the prison to see Judge Le Verrier.

Introduced, he began at once: "I think I know the criminal of Père-Lachaise. I mean I think I know who is responsible for the mutilation of the child's body."

"Really?" the judge smiled broadly, but without that warmth that could light up his face like the door to a furnace.

"A young man with whom I lived for many years and who has shown that propensity on previous occasions.

"What is his name?"

"Bertrand Caillet."

"Of Paris?"

"I think he is living in Paris now. He ran away from home."

"So?—But you know that we have apprehended the criminal already?"

"I know, but the man you have may not be guilty of that act."

"That will be a matter for the jury and the judges to decide," the juge d'instruction observed coldly.

"But perhaps the man you are holding may know something of the real culprit. I mean of Bertrand Caillet. *There* is a man who should be behind bars. Once he begins to commit crimes, you will not hear the end of him; there will be a whole series."

158

The judge bent forward until the chin of his great head rested on the top of his desk. And now he spoke, while his head bobbed up and down as his chin moved in the formation of his words.

"And if I held *you*, would there be any further crimes?"

"Me? Why, what have I to do with the matter?"

The judge pulled his head back. Decidedly the world of men, untrained in law, was full of contradictoriness. First they knew, then they didn't know; first one thing, then its opposite.

"I thought you had something to do with this case! But if you have nothing to do with the matter, then what are you putting your nose in here for?" His voice rose to the volume of thunder.

Aymar shrank back, muttered some excuses and hobbled out as fast as he could.

But he continued to watch the papers, and he was rewarded on the following day with another violation of a fresh grave at Père-Lachaise. Then there followed spoliations at the Montmartre cemetery and more again at Lachaise. Despite his unkind reception by the juge d'instruction (he shuddered to think what might have happened had he explained the real nature of the case to that man), Aymar determined to see the conservateur at the cemetery of Montmartre. The latter was a kind old man, and when his clerk brought him the purpose of Aymar's visit, he admitted him at once and introduced him to the conservateur of Père-Lachaise who happened to be present.

"We'll be interested in hearing what you have to say, for we've just come to an astounding conclusion."

"What is that?" Aymar asked, unwilling hastily to presume that they had discovered the werewolf.

"Tell us first what you have to say."

"There is a young man, a distant relative, who back in our province showed a similar penchant."

"Hm."

"He has lately come to Paris, and I am looking for him, since I know, somewhat, how to restrain him."

"Hm."

"Well, and I imagine that this would be his work."

"I'm afraid your case has little to do with ours."

"Why?"

"A very careful examination of footprints around the desecrated graves shows that both here and at Lachaise the matter involves, not a young man, but—"

"But a wolf," Aymar interjected, "—or a dog," he added quickly.

"How did you know? We hadn't thought of a wolf. What makes you say that?"

"Well, you see, he, ah, well, he has a trained dog (part wolf, you understand), and that dog helps him."

"I see," said one of the two gentlemen. He asked Aymar for various information, names, details, etc., to which the latter answered the best he could, while the conservateur took notes.

"Well, we expect to see the end of this soon," he confided to Aymar. "We are placing, every night, heavy spring traps near every newly dug grave, and the marauder, man or dog or wolf or all three, will soon find himself within a pair of uncomfortably powerful nippers."

"The only trouble," said the other, "is that the war will soon move into our cemeteries. Both here and at Lachaise cannon are to be mounted, so that Paris will be in a position to resist if the outer fortifications should fall, which God forbid!"

"You would think," said the first of the two gentlemen, "that people are in great haste to die, the way there's one war after another in this world. Do they imagine that if they don't kill each other they are likely never to die? I assure you they are under a mistaken notion if they do. Since I can remember, I've never seen a day without a funeral."

The lugubrious and reminiscent turn in the conversation allowed Aymar to conceal his fright: poor Bertrand, mangled in a powerful steel trap. Well, why not? One way or the other, it had to end.

He went home and waited. But nothing happened. Apparently the violations had ceased. Five days passed and inquiry at the cemetery revealed no further attempt to disturb any graves.

160

The conservateur said: "Either we are mistaken about the theory of a dog, or else he can smell our traps. More than likely, you are right, M Galliez, and it's a man. Perhaps one of our own personnel or at any rate in communication with our staff. How else account for the fact that these nearly daily spoliations suddenly ceased on the placing of the traps and in the last five days there has not been a single repetition?"

Chapter Eleven

The issue of the seventeenth of November of *Galignani's Messager* contained among the faits divers an inconspicuous item that by chance came to the attention of Aymar, as he was perusing this sheet, and naturally struck him at once.

"Tales of wolves depredating Paris are always afloat in times of war. Here is a legend that will not die. The severity of the coming winter, heralded by the recent cold, and the famine that now reigns in our poor city, have again conspired to revive this imperishable legend. In the outlying quarters there is talk of a wolf, some even say droves of wolves (!), and one informer would have us believe that a specimen wolf was actually secured and taken to the Jardin d'Acclimatation for identification. What happened there is left vague. It is never wise to submit a legend to a scientist like our esteemed A. Geoffroy Saint-Hilaire."

The article provoked a sudden spasm in Aymar. He was at once certain that the story did have a foundation of truth and that that foundation was nothing less than Bertrand. Remote connection indeed. But in the frame of mind he was in, weeks in Paris, with no clue to Bertrand except a series of horrible crimes which no one but himself ascribed to a wolf-man monster, he was capable

162

of seizing upon the slightest clue and finding everything in it, as a microscopist discovers whole populations in a drop of foul water.

"How should a wolf come into Paris?" he asked himself. Through the German lines? Ridiculous! Ergo that wolf was our Bertrand. He formed in Paris! A far jump, but no farther than Newton made from the falling apple to the eternally falling moon. Yes, here was a spoor. Definite and direct. Moreover, the slightest chance was worth investigation. He made up his mind.

The famine in Paris, of which the newspaper article spoke, had at this period reached considerable proportions, if we may be allowed to speak of nothingness reaching magnitude. Although the question of feeding Paris had come up at once upon the opening of hostilities, Paris being almost a frontier city and exposed to the advance of the enemy across a short distance of French territory, nothing much had been done until the night of August 4–5, when the danger became acute. The government had just received a telegram announcing the defeat at Wissembourg.

M. Henri Chevreau, who had lately replaced the famous and infamous Haussmann, beautifier of Paris, as Prefect of the Seine, gathered together a committee of municipal counselors and functionaries and moved to gather into the city a sufficient supply of foodstuffs, meats, hay and grain for horses, salt, wine, etc. Although the legislative body was repeatedly assured that everything had been done to safeguard Paris from famine during a long siege, and although over six weeks elapsed before the city was completely invested, nevertheless a shortage of food and consequent rise in prices declared itself almost at once. Government rationing could not help. The poor took the matter philosophically and intelligently as they always do. They noticed that every time after an announcement of peace negotiations, false though the announcement might be, food at once reappeared in quantities on the stalls and prices sank. Everyone who was in a position to do so was hoarding food, hoping for greater profits, but partly scared into releasing their hoards upon the prospect of the siege ending suddenly. There were indeed great quantities of food in Paris, but private profit was manipulating the market.

The name of Geoffroy Saint-Hilaire also caught Aymar's attention. "Saint-Hilaire?" he said to himself. "Especially that combi-
nation: Geoffroy Saint-Hilaire. I wonder now. Could that be the
same fellow I used to know?" If so, his task was easier. Geoffroy
Saint-Hilaire could not have forgotten him and would extend him
every courtesy. It must be the same. The Geoffroy Saint-Hilaires
were always connected with zoölogy.

That very afternoon Aymar betook himself to the office of the
director of the Jardin d'Acelimatation.

The director was too busy, it seemed.

"Tell him," said Aymar, "that I used to know him when he was
never too busy."

The clerk returned to the director's office. A moment later,
Geoffroy Saint-Hilaire—grandson of the famous Geoffroy Saint-
Hilaire, the news of whose discoveries had seemed to Goethe more
important than the fate of kingdoms—appeared and said hurriedly:
"Monsieur..." as though he wished to expedite matters and return
to his work as quickly as possible. Then he hesitated: "Tiens, c'est
toi, Aymar!"

They embraced.

"*Et alors?*"

After a few phrases concerning their respective fates, Aymar
wished to come to his point:

"I hear from the newspapers," he said, "that a wolf was brought
here."

The director laughed nervously. "A wolf? Oh, yes. Ha, ha! The
newspapers, of course." Then he became quite serious: "Are you
interested in that wolf?"

"Yes, deeply," Aymar exclaimed. Then struck at his own
emotion, he sought to explain: "That's precisely why I came. You
see, I'll explain."

"No need," said the *directeur* quietly and seriously, "my friend,
I'm afraid I see all too well." He hesitated, while Aymar shivered.
"Let me see now," he continued. "Hm, I'm very busy now, but your
visit is most opportune. I'm invited to dinner along with Maubert.
Did you know him? Maubert, the big Maubert? No? Well, anyway,

164

he can't come, so you must go with me. Meet me here in two hours. We'll be going to dinner together. Yes, you must meet me here," he concluded hastily. A bit nervously, Aymar thought.

"But the wolf?"

"Yes, precisely. The wolf," he said mysteriously, and slipped back into his office.

Aymar, amazed, thrilled, vainly turning over a hundred speculations in his mind, returned home to dress and then back to meet his old friend, sharp two hours later. "He knows all," was his thought, but when the directeur appeared he certainly gave no sign of it.

Geoffroy Saint-Hilaire took Aymar amicably under the arm and led him to the gate where a coach was waiting. They drove off at a good clip.

"Where to?" Aymar asked.

"To Dr Anatole de Grandmont."

"The wolf?" Aymar asked.

"Sh!" his friend replied.

The trajectory was short. In a few moments they had alighted and entered a fine old house. The dining-room, visible beyond the drawing-room, was splendidly illuminated, the table set for ten sparkled with fine china and glassware, with silver and gold-plate, all set on a snowy cloth.

Aymar was introduced. "Poor Maubert couldn't come. I've taken the liberty to bring an old friend, M Aymar Galliez, an old Republican. M le docteur Anatole de Grandmont, our host, M de Quatrefages, and M Richard du Cantal, vice-presidents of our society.' M Demarets, the famous—"

"We know each other," said Aymar. They shook hands.

"M Decroix, our celebrated propagandist for the use of horse-meat."

"Richer, stronger and better for the health," said M Decroix severely.

"M Graux, whose father made sheep grow silk."

"M Degient."

---

* The Société impériale zoölogique d'acelimatation.

"M Giraudeau." *

It struck Aymar that there was something about this gathering. It was natural, of course, that they should all be interested in animal husbandry, but there was something else. A constant whispering and chuckling and in general an import to this meeting which he could not fathom. Once he heard: "You'll go through with it, of course."—"I'm afraid I'm weakening rapidly," replied the person thus addressed.

Finding himself near his friend, Geoffroy Saint-Hilaire, and therefore safe, Aymar spoke up:

"About that wolf."

"You'll learn in time," the directeur cut him short hastily.

Could it be, Aymar wondered, that the whole mystery had been uncovered and that it was this that elicited this buzzing of suppressed excitement?

At this moment the host called the company to order.

"Gentlemen! Your attention please! I see that the purpose of our dinner this evening has not remained as secret as we wished it to be. It little matters. You all know that this is a moment of great danger to our beloved patrie and to our dear city of Paris, the jewel of Europe. Here we are, near two million of us, and of food there is a sad lack. Our enemies know it and are depending on this factor to cause our undoing. But God willing, we shall manage to hold out until the provinces gather their forces and come racing to our rescue, under the leadership of our staunch Gambetta.

"We too have our little work to do. We too can help. We too gentlemen, have a little plan. It is not an invention that shall blow up armies, it is not a scheme for a sortie en masse, it is none of the plans of our dear Trochu or any other of our brave generals. It is, my dear friends, a contribution of zoölogical science to mankind. Not only to our stricken city, no. To all the world, at present limited in its choice of foods to a very small number of animals.

---

* It was this M Giraudeau who achieved a species of notoriety during the famine, when cheese was absolutely unprocurable for love or money, by mounting a small slice of fromage de Brie on a gold scarfpin.

166

"This is an historic occasion. We shall all have reason to remember it. The world will honor us for this brave step. This bursting of bonds that only silly prejudice has forged and tradition tempered.

"Gentlemen, let this be a merry occasion. We, Columbuses all, about to explore a new world, discover a new taste in dishes and a new nourishment in foods. Let this, as I say, be a merry occasion. Have you heard the joke that is taking Paris by storm? It heralds a new era. Let us fling away our old hide-bound notions and plunge in with a smile.

"The joke? Yes, here it is: Our good bourgeois of Paris, hard pressed for a bite to put between his teeth, has sacrificed his dog on the altar of the great god appetite. He and his wife sit in silence and consume their beloved fox terrier. The wife looks up after a while and notices her husband carefully placing the bones beside his dish, even as he had always done.

"'Why, what are you doing?'

"'Ah,' he catches himself up, and sighs. 'Too bad,' he says, shaking his head. 'Fido certainly would have enjoyed these bones.'"

Though the joke was not new for some of the guests, there was a complimentary burst of laughter and the company filed into the neighboring dining-room and took seats. Aymar was beginning to understand. Only beginning.

The soup was excellent. The guests kept saying as much again and again, especially M Decroix, the advocate of horse-meat for human food. And the reason was at once plain. No sooner was the course cleared than the host announced that the soup was:

"*Consommé of horse, with millet.*"

In came the relevés (the appetizers). More exclamations of delight. The cook was called in to receive congratulations. Aymar, a little muddled, tasted the dishes, found them pleasant and wondered. After some lively discussion between the guests, the host, reading from a slip of paper, announced:

"We have had: *Skewer roast of dog's liver, à la maître d'hôtel*; and *Minced back of cat, with mayonnaise sauce.*"

Aymar controlled his stomach. But of course it was only a joke.

He turned to his friend for assistance, but Geoffroy Saint-Hilaire was busy making notes on the back of a letter. Came the entrées. Which, subsequently, were revealed as:

Braised shoulder and undercut of dog with tomato sauce;
Jugged cat with mushrooms;
Dog cutlet with green peas;
Venison ragout of rats, sauce Robert.

The roast followed, borne in great platters, while Aymar was ready to sink under the table. If his scientific companions had not been so objective in their demeanor, tasting, criticizing, discussing, comparing, he would have given way long ago and collapsed. The roast was:

Leg of dog and raccoon, pepper sauce;
Salad: Begonias with dressing and cold boiled mice;
Side-dish: Plum-pudding with rum and horse-marrow.

And still they came, dish after dish.

Finally the repast was over. The wise ones had only tasted each food, lest they be gorged. When the company sat back, with sated appetites, Geoffroy Saint-Hilaire was invited to read his report:

"The soup was excellent. Some found the millet a little hard, but none had anything but praise for the savor;

"Our repugnance for dog's liver, roasted on skewers, was quickly forgotten when we had tasted this truly delicious preparation. Lamb kidney was held to be its nearest equivalent, but below dog's liver in tenderness;

"Second helpings were frequent for the minced back of cat. This is white meat, vaguely recalling cold veal, but more pleasant. Recommended for invalids;

"Braised shoulder and undercut of dog were highly appreciated and judged to be not unlike the flesh of chamois;

"The jugged cat, though a little tough, was so flavorsome that had not the number of dishes been so large, many would have gladly called for more;

"Too much vinegar (I believe the other guests will bear me out in this) was used on the dog cutlets. This meat is rather stringy, but not bad;

"Not a single one of us had a word other than praise for the exquisite ragout of rats. It is only to be compared to the flesh of swallows;

"The leg of dog is extremely edible, though a bit coarse in texture. The best parts were those least well done, left bloody; few cared for the raccoon, which was without flavor;

"The begonia salad was reminiscent of sorrel. I believe we have here an excellent corrective for a too exclusive salted meat diet. This should be investigated; cold mice are deceptively like prawn-meat; some accused the cook of practicing a trick on us;

"The great success of the evening remains the ragout of rats. I cannot understand how the world has so long refused this delicious food. I, for one, am converted. Hereafter, famine or no famine, my menu shall be frequently adorned with rat-meat, and my guests will learn to love it as I. Yes, I foresee a great new industry, for once the savage rats are exterminated by our epicures, rats will have to be bred in farms and breeding will improve them, if indeed one can think of any improvement.

"From this room let the word go forth to the public. *The rat is good food!* Do not imagine that one must have many rats to make a meal. A rat, skinned and boned, leaves nearly eight ounces of meat, of which one ounce is liver, very fat and succulent. Two rats will take care of a modest family. And one trial will convince and convert.

"A single criticism and a single warning before I conclude:

"The criticism: Our cook did bravely, but he erred in his attempt to conceal a different flavor of meat with heavy sauces. These meats will soon become appreciated for their own peculiar flavor.

"The warning, which I shall have posted on the walls in our city: 'Rat-meat must be boiled before preparation to prevent trichinosis, which has occasionally been observed.'"*

---

* Here as everywhere one must note the trail of business. As the Société of the Jardin d'Acclimatation found it more and more difficult to secure food for the beasts in its care, they were sold to enterprising butchers and fine restaurants who could, as a result, offer, though of course at enormous prices, such rare meats and fowl as cassowary, ostrich, dingo, tapir, kangaroo, etc. Of interest is the sale of the two elephants, Castor and Pollux, who went to the wealthy butcher Deboos for 27,000

The dinner had consumed such a length of time that the guests soon separated. Aymar steeled himself, managed to express effusive thanks for a delightful meal and a rare experience.

Geoffroy Sainte-Hilaire sat down amidst a salvo of handclapping. Porto was served now, in the English style, and Aymar seized his glass and drank eagerly to quiet his rebelling stomach.

"Of course," said Geoffroy as soon as they were outside, "this is only a beginning. We have not touched the insect world." He expanded his chest with pride and satisfaction. "Come, let us walk a bit. The night air is refreshing." Aymar found it so too.

"Yes, insects. Have you ever tasted a bedbug? Sweet, you know! Bad odor, though. But locusts! Like nothing you ever tried. We'll need new terms when we come to that. Yes, man is omnivorous. Zoölogists have always classed him and the bear together in this respect. Why, then, has he been hitherto so timid when he has but to reach forth his hand? Columbuses! Old Grandmont struck the right note there."

Aymar hesitated to interrupt this almost elegiac flow from the scientist who for the moment seemed to be speaking with the gift of prophecy. Shyly, he ventured: "And the wolf…"

Then Geoffroy Saint-Hilaire did a curious thing. He turned toward his companion, and, grasping his hand, declared with emotion: "I know, my friend, I understand. Let us say no more."

What did he understand? Aymar wondered. Really, did he truly understand? Since the supper, Aymar had come to doubt it. "They

---

francs. These ponderous beasts, for twenty-five years adored by the children of Paris who had ridden on their backs at 50 centimes a ride, went to grace the platters of the Jockey Club and other eating places for the rich. The two elephants, facing their doom, were nonplussed. Having been subjected to nothing but kindness all their lives, they could not suspect anything but kindness in the motives and actions of those who now led them into the slaughterhouse. There was some discussion as to how the killing could best be done. Finally, a powerful fellow swung an enormous mallet with all the might of his bulky muscles. The heavy wood crashed into the forehead of one of the elephants. The beast swayed, while blood spurted from a great dent in his brow. He looked puzzled for a moment, but only for a moment, and then he regained his lifelong assurance that only caresses and food emanated from the two-legged animal. Eventually a sharpshooter was employed to kill the brutes with well-placed bullets. The meat sold for upwards of 142 francs a pound.

have all become wolves," he thought. "Bertrand has infected them, but of my wolf they know nothing. Still when a man says he 'understands,' you bow your head in gratitude." Aymar bowed his head. They walked along in silence.

"If I had known, my dear Galliez, you can believe me... Do you think it was cruel of me? But, ah, ah, come to think of it: it was just like the joke Grandmont told us."

"What was?"

"The joke about the dog."

"The joke about the dog?"

"You see, I knew at once, when you came about the wolf, that you knew it was no wolf. And when you said how deeply you were interested in the matter, I realized at once."

"You realized what?" Aymar asked, still not following.

"That he was your dog. Of course, anybody could see it was no wolf except that newspaper man. He wanted a story. And we wanted a dog for our cook. And then I thought: If I say nothing, wouldn't that be cruel? And the happy thought struck me: I might take you along, and at least you would be in on his funeral. Better than nothing, wasn't it? Too bad, of course, but—"

The "happy thought" pierced Aymar like a blade of cold steel. The wolf or dog had been served at that infernal supper! Bertrand! They had eaten Bertrand! His flesh was *delicate in savor, although a trifle stringy!* God Almighty!

Horror tingling in every nerve of his body, he ran off without a word.

"But, Galliez...forgive me!" he heard the directeur's voice shouting after him. But Aymar fled as if a pack of wolves were snapping at his heels, his stomach revolting. In a dark recess he stopped and retched till he was weak and clean.

But it was only when the morning papers came out with another horrible and gory crime that Aymar felt better. They hadn't killed Bertrand. Bertrand was still alive. Witness this:

"In the rue de Budapest, lived La Belle Normande, so-called, or rather so self-dubbed, in order to attract customers from that province, an honest prostitute, highly respected in her own quarter, if nowhere else. Last night a young man of prepossessing exterior, in the uniform of the Garde Nationale, so the concierge states, came home with La Belle Normande. The two retired and were not heard of again until his handiwork came to light. This morning La Belle Normande requires a successor to the affection of her numerous countrymen in Paris. She, herself, is dead. Slashed by a rough, coarse instrument. Literally ripped apart. So she was found, lying in a pool of blood, on the floor of her room. Nothing seems to have been stolen. Has the London Jack the Ripper crossed the Channel? The police are combing the battalions of the Garde."

The nature of the deed betrayed the real culprit. So Bertrand was in the National Guard. Why, of course. Every young man was there.

Chapter Twelve

Aymar had deduced correctly. Bertrand was in the National Guard. Where else should a young man be, who was in Paris during the siege, but in the National Guard, where he was sure of his daily solde? The workshops were empty, there was not a job to be had, but no man need worry with the National Guard ready to take on anybody who was willing to sign his name. As to actual service, that was another matter. When it was decreed that the soldiers were to elect their own officers, discipline was done for, since the officers were for a large part more interested in pleasing their men and in conserving their offices than in planning an effective resistance against the Prussians.

Bertrand, having soon exhausted his money in a round of debauches in search of a repetition of the pleasure he had had with Thérèse, was easily persuaded by a chance acquaintance to join the National Guard, which he did under a very slightly altered name, which explains why Aymar could not find him on the registers.

In the turmoil of that period there was not much time for clerks to make investigations. Many men enrolled in several battalions under different names, and collected so much more pay. Only a stupid few neglected to have wives and children and thus lost the increases which went with a family to support. The elected officers, too, were willing to plug their lists, and receive pay for a thousand men when they could muster only eight hundred, pocketing the difference as well-merited earnings for their astuteness.

But it is not right to demand virtues from the poor who must starve to practice them. It would be better to ask what the rich of Paris were doing. No doubt about it, they were doing their share of patriotic work and being well rewarded for it as the rich generally are.

Bertrand, in these days, was hard pressed to satisfy that hidden appetite which he had only recently come to understand clearly. But now fully aware of the reverse side of his nature, he regulated his life so as to satisfy this need without endangering his safety. He rented a cheap basement room, far in the rear of a house. A window, which he could leave open, allowed him to escape and return unnoticed at night. During the day he locked the window carefully, going to the trouble of purchasing and affixing a new lock. He did the same for his door and thus guarded himself from any possible intrusion by the concierge, a busybody who wanted to mother him, look after his room and mend his clothing.

He knew when an attack was coming on. During the day he would have no appetite. It was particularly the thought of bread and butter that nauseated him. In the evening he would feel tense and both tired and sleepless. Then he would arrange his window and lock his door, and having taken his precautions, he would lie down. Frequently he would wake in the morning, in bed, with no recollection of what had happened at night. Only a wretched stiffness in his neck, a lassitude in his limbs that could come from nothing but miles of running, scratches on his hands and feet, and an acrid taste in his mouth argued that he had spent the night elsewhere. On one such occasion, however, full conviction awaited him when he rose. Under his bed he caught a flash of white. It was a human forearm! A man's. The fingers were clutched tightly into a fist. Hair, as if torn from a fur coat, protruded from the interstices between the fingers.

174

He racked his brain. Where? Whom? Evidently a man with a fur coat. Vague pictures of himself leaping gleefully through snow and slush, with a wind laden with icy crystals sweeping through the deserted streets of night, moaning among the chimney tops, and catching the breath from one's lungs at turnings, came back to him. But a man with a fur coat? He couldn't remember any man with a fur coat.

He did, however, recall that as a concession to his nature he had followed a late funeral to the Cimetière Montparnasse. It was a dreary cold day, heavily clouded, with the feel of snow in the air. The shivering mourners trudged behind and Bertrand marched with them. The relatives and friends did not bother about the young man in the uniform of the National Guard, who seemed to be mourning in his own quiet way. At such moments one respects the grief of others and is satisfied with any mental excuse: a café friend, one to whom the deceased did a kind turn once upon a time, and so forth. It even added a glamor to Bertrand. A glamor which was heightened by his shyness, by his rapid withdrawal when the ceremony was over.

Only one old man had spoken to Bertrand. He did not interrogate Bertrand much. He seemed more anxious to do the talking himself.

"Are you a friend of Madame or of Blaise?" was his only question, but this was but a precaution, for when Bertrand answered by chance, "Of Blaise," the man continued at once:

"A scholar, if ever there was one. The kindest man you ever met. God only knows whatever led him to marry such a young girl, when he was nearly fifty! And I warned him too: Blaise, I said, again and again, you're an old fool. A young and lively girl like that will kill an old fellow like you. She'll suck the life-blood out of you. You won't be able to stand the pace. But he was bent on it. She had him bewitched.—Still, I never thought that the end was to come so soon. Barely three months of married life.

"And you know," the old man continued, sinking his voice to a confidential tone, "there is something about this that I don't like. Two days ago, he was in excellent health. I saw him myself, and

175

spoke to him, too. The next day dead and the next buried. Why this unseemly haste? And as for the widow, she seems more concerned about striking an elegant pose of grief than genuinely indulging in her sorrow. Ah, well. Blaise, my old friend, it will be a long time before I forget you."

When Bertrand had recalled this conversation, all the other details of the night came back to him. The open pit, which because of the late burial had been left unfilled, the coffin, which now was covered with a thin layer of earth and snow. And then the horrible fight with a corpse recovering from a heavy drug!

And then he understood something else. Not fur from a coat, but *his own* fur! Those grayish and brownish hairs were his own! Then it was not just an illusion that he changed; it was not a mere alteration of the desires of his muscles, but a real transformation!

Could one believe that? How, with paws, could he have pried off a heavy coffin lid?

This was a point on which he would have liked to assure himself, but a decision to take note of the matter on the next occasion was of little avail. Even when he awoke outside, and found himself lying beside a new grave or beside someone whom he had evidently attacked in the street, he could not recall whether he had been a beast or only a man acting like a beast. Apparently, on these excursions, he was incapable of rational, human thoughts, but not for all that devoid of the cunning necessary to the accomplishment of his purposes.

When he had first come to Paris and still had remnants of the money taken from Jacques, he had frequented the maisons tolérées. But he soon had to abandon this form of amusement, for the girls of Paris were experienced in their line and, like barbers, charged exorbitantly for every deviation from the normal, for every added attraction.

On the slender pay of a soldier, Bertrand could not afford expensive amusements. He sought in the streets for cheaper material. Occasionally he was successful, more often not. Then bursting with a sullen rage he would deceive a woman of the streets with grand promises. These amorous exploits frequently ended in murder. This was especially the case when it became impossible to find fresh graves to despoil.

Of his life as a soldier there is little to be said. The military annals of the National Guard are an empty book. Bertrand saw little fighting. He paraded frequently, he saw festivities, he listened to much talk on this and that plan to save Paris.

He made few friends of his comrades. In the late afternoon when his duties were finished, he generally went to a canteen, sipped a glass of wine and ruminated morosely about his disease.

One canteen to which he was accustomed to go was especially favored by the soldiers, not so much for its wines as for a young girl who donated several hours of service to it, almost every afternoon. She was of more than human beauty. She was slight of stature and could not have been over seventeen; within these limits, her physique was of that perfect variety which transcends clothes, and would have looked as graceful and strong draped in the blanket of a savage as she did in her expensive clothes.

Her dusky face was a perpetual delight, for a permanent smile transfigured it and revealed teeth whose whiteness was flawless. Her quick black eyes wandered from man to man and she had a pleasant word and laugh for all. She was Mlle Sophie de Blumen-berg, daughter of the famous banker.

Many of the men, particularly the officers, of course, made attempts to draw her into something more than mere banter, but she would not allow herself to be led astray. When her coach drove up and the footman descended to open the door, she slipped out of her apron, took off her military cap, wrapped herself in her furs, waved her muff in a gesture of good-bye and was off.

Frequently an officer, recognizable by his gaudy uniform as a military person of importance, and by some actually known to be Captain Barral de Montfort, appeared to escort Mlle Sophie. They were a distinguished pair. He, perfect in his smart, military bearing, she, in her exotic type of beauty.

One envies such people, but in the same breath one wishes

heaped upon their heads all the joys that life can offer and yet so insistently refuses to most of us. For such people seem as if selected by nature to be showered with the best gifts.

She, herself, wanted of life an endless succession of new wonders, new pleasures and surprises. And indeed, all her life had been such a succession for her. And she had that infinite capacity to enjoy, without which a princess must remain unhappy even in the finest palace of the world.

During their drives together, she took pleasure in teasing Barral. She told him of how all the men adored her. She described some of them. Insisted upon their handsome physique. Declared they would outshine Barral, if they were permitted to wear his bright blue uniform with its gold braid adornments.

Seeing that she was pleased if he appeared annoyed and jealous, he did his best to frown and find angry words to say to her. Mme Hertzog, Sophie's Aunt Louise, who tried to be present as often as she could in order to chaperon, remained frozen and indignant during these playful quarrels, which she found in very poor taste indeed. She found, in fact, the whole canteen business highly disgraceful for a daughter of the aristocracy, and could not approve of a patriotism carried to such excess. Such patriotism, she correctly divined, was a mere excuse for looseness of conduct.

But Baron de Blumenberg was incapable of refusing anything to his daughter, his only child. Furthermore, a display of patriotism was always a good business policy. He had been patriotic under the Empire, and was patriotic again under the government of September Fourth. He would even make a gesture of patriotism to the Commune. Good business demanded as much.

He had contributed a large sum of money to the maintenance of the canteens, but the personal appearance of his daughter was an even more effective gesture. Besides, the daughters and wives of the best families of Paris were engaged either in canteen work or in nursing.

At dinner, Aunt Louise never failed to bring up the question of Sophie, her neglected education, her work at the canteen, her freedom, "one might almost say promiscuity."

178

And later, in the evening, when she prepared to return to her apartment, there was more quarreling because the family allowed Sophie to stay up so late. Barral de Montfort took his leave and accompanied Mme Hertzog. In the carriage she confided to him:

"You're too good for that crowd, even if you are Christian."

He did not know whether to feel flattered or insulted.

"Ever since those artists have made bad morals fashionable, the world is fast degenerating. This war is only another proof of it."

He murmured a polite agreement with her thesis.

"I recall," she said, drawing in her chin with indignation, "when that fellow Courbet put his picture of a naked woman in the Salon. I was there when the Empress turned her back on it in horror. Of course all Paris was congregated in front of that picture. Since then there's been no stopping the dégringolade. Bad pictures, bad books, and the most shameless goings-on."

He said, "Terrible," with the proper inflection.

She looked at him severely. "I had good fun in my youth, without being improper."

It was on the tip of his tongue to ask her how.

"I suppose your generation would find me very prim."

He would have liked to say: "Sophie is perhaps more prim than you, if you only knew her."

When he had returned to his own apartment and removed his cape and sword, he sat down and thought of Sophie. Sophie's dress of tightly laced white velvet faintly tinted with lemon, her trailing skirt of white satin and frills, as if she had stepped out of the surf and a wave had dashed after her with a foaming white crest. And out of this calyx of whiteness, her beautifully curving shoulders and bosom as if of polished bronze, her bare brown arms, her dark laughing face, her hair in ebony ringlets.

It was his duty as well as his pleasure and privilege to write to her every night, and think of new ways to describe her waxy black eyebrows rising in decisive curvatures from her perfectly modeled brow. It was his duty to find new comparisons for her teeth, white like gardenia petals, or better still, like forest roots broken fresh and glistening from the ground. It was his nightly duty to write down all these things, interspersed with his professions of love, and mail the letter to her so that she would have it to read in the morning.

When the few dinner guests had departed and the baron had retired to his bureau where he generally slept, the baroness to her boudoir, then Sophie itched to do something. But what was there to do? If she went to Papa he would welcome her with a smile, caress her, talk inanities of the days when she was a little baby. If she went to Mamma she would be received with inquiries about her health, talk of clothes, and most certainly with a round scolding interjected at some point in the conversation.

The great apartment was quiet. The massive furniture gleamed, the brass fittings of scrolls and sphinxes glittered under the gas-light. Somewhere behind a door, she knew, a sleepy servant was yawning and waiting for her to depart so that he could extinguish the lights.

She picked up a few magazines from the drawing-room table, a few books from the library, and went off to her own room. She read until her eyes ached, and yet there was nothing to interest her. She undressed and read in bed, and put off until the last possible moment the turning off of the gas-light on the wall, the blowing out of the candle on her night-table.

At last she took her courage in both hands, reached out and turned off the jet. The continuous hissing noise of the escaping gas, a noise of which she had not been conscious until then, stopped. The great porcelain soot-catcher dropped its bursting whiteness and shrank into gray. The whole room was as if suddenly yanked out of the beautiful present and pulled back into the Dark Ages. The single candle cast yawning shadows. The corners of the room, swathed in darkness, retreated into a distant mysterious gloom. A little life still remained, huddled about the candle.

She blew that out. Darkness engulfed her. Even the Middle Ages vanished. She had retreated to the pitch-black of prehistoric times. She cast herself back among her pillows and prayed that sleep would come soon. But her nerves were too taut. She had to listen to a dozen incomprehensible noises and trace each one to its source. She had to dissect a score of vague shadows, hulking threatening shapes, and determine the reality of each. She suspected each new shadow that her peering eyes carved out of the general blackness and was not content with the reassurance that she had been wrong a hundred times before. She looked and looked until all the darkness of the room was alive with swirling shadowy figures, products of visual fatigue. And she told herself as much, but each new shape looked more real than the last. They were but waiting for her to close her eyes, to come plunging down on her. No, she would remain awake all night. She did not dare close her eyes in sleep.

In the same manner in which darkness concluded the day, death concluded life. She exhausted herself in sterile attempts to pierce the mystery of the tomb. What was it like to be dead? It was like this: Darkness. Intense darkness. And shadows among shadows. And a vast fear. No. It wasn't like that at all. It was like complete nothingness. Absolute blankness. But within this nothingness a something more horrible than the mind can imagine.

That was death. Lying underground in a coffin. Her imagination had already put her there a thousand times. In Père-Lachaise, in the Jewish portion of the cemetery, not far from the entrance, next to the mournful monument of Rachel, the tragédienne. There were the plots belonging to the Blumenbergs and the Hertzogs. She recalled the day Uncle Moïse, the husband of Aunt Louise Hertzog, had died. The cortége had gone through the rue du Repos. The street of rest. Strange name, fascinating and revolting at the same time.

She would lie there. Mother and Father would lie there. Perhaps she would lie there first. She could hear, in her ears, her father and mother crying. She could hear her mother saying: "So young! And just married!" And her husband Barral was there. She could hear him swearing vengeance.

When she had reached that thought, she decided that all her imaginings were really silly. Why should he be swearing vengeance, and against whom? But her heart still bled from her gruesome thoughts. Of course it was all too silly. How could she be married to Barral and be buried in the old family plot? She would be buried with him, of course. Wives did.

Somehow that was reassuring. To be buried with Barral. Besides, it showed that there was no truth in her imagination. No prophetic power. That picture of Barral swearing vengeance in the Cimetière Israélite of Père-Lachaise couldn't ever be true.

Then she thought: But Barral's parents, who lived in the country and were known to be but slightly pleased at their son's affair, might not let her, a Jewess, be buried in a Christian cemetery? And the whole story took on once again its threatening aspect and descended on her chest like a heavy stone.

In the morning there was not a shred left of her dreams. Daylight filtered in through the draperies of the window. She was lying in her lovely bed with its gilt cupids. Above her head was her familiar azure ciel-de-lit, spangled with gold stars and illuminated by a white moon stitched with silk.

Gone were the crazy dreams of cemeteries, of Barral swearing vengeance, all the stupid cobwebs with which darkness litters the brain. If she rose early, before her mother, she might have her mother's maid to help her dress and arrange her hair. And soon the mailman would come and bring her Barral's description of her loveliness on the previous evening and his assurance of eternal love. Such were the dreams of the day.

The nights might become even more horrible. The Germans might move their gun-emplacements to within a few miles of the ring of forts and drop their bombs into the very city. Then one had to go to bed without any light at all, or only the slightest illumination, and sleep was often impossible. The winter nights were cold and long. It required effort not to scream out in anguish. But then the day was all the more to be enjoyed. Every second must offer her a laugh, otherwise life would bring no compensation for the inevitable night.

Thus her days were full of laughter and her nights full of anguish. But, so she used to think, "I, at least, have the compensation of wealth. What do the poor do?" She had Barral. What did those poor girls do, who had no letters from Barral?

182

During her hours at the canteen, she thought of Barral. He would come and fetch her. She would see him from a distance. Either on foot or on horse, but always in a bright blue uniform with golden aiguillettes.

The men, too, saw him coming. They nudged each other and smiled. But there was one young man, neither very handsome nor ugly, with only great brown eyes to recommend him. Every day, Sophie noticed, while the others smiled, he remained sullen.

Once, when she bent to rinse a glass, she looked full into those sad eyes. There was something strangely moving in them. Something that brought her night-thoughts to mind. She looked away because she feared he might have seen into her eyes and that he might have read there the thoughts he had called up, her thoughts of terror and of death.

But again and again, at the canteen, when she thought he wasn't looking, she would glance at those eyes, wide open, under heavy brows. Almost always his glance shifted quickly toward hers and he caught her eye. Then she would look away. But a moment later she would look again. There was something compelling in his eyes. Something of that strange compulsion of an abyss. That invitation of the void, of great heights: Come, cast yourself down. Just let yourself go. How do you know it isn't sweeter than anything you have ever imagined or experienced in life? Why do you fear? Why do you fear what you do not know as yet? Come! Come!

Oh! The opium-sweet attraction of death!

She knew that attraction. How many times had she not revolved such thoughts in her mind, at night, when she had extinguished the gas and blown out the candle. During the day, when away from the canteen, she rarely thought of those eyes, but at night they haunted her. They were there before her in the darkness, and had that strange phosphorescent glow that the eyes of some animals have. Those eyes mingled with her night-thoughts. They were her companions during the long ugly night. They were with her in the Jewish cemetery at Père-Lachaise. She was not alone at night any longer. Those eyes had rescued her from her lonely nightmares.

She asked those eyes: What of the grave? What of the moldering bodies in the grave? And the eyes had an answer. The eyes said: Wherever you are, I will be with you. Night and day. Life and death.

In the morning these thoughts were gone. She had Barral's letter, and as she planned what visits, what shopping she might do during the day, her light laughter resounded again and again. Even in his bureau, her father could hear her. He smiled and shook his head. "Gay little chick. How can one be so perpetually light-hearted? Especially our Sophie, who was, so to speak, born out of the grave. God bless her."

But in the afternoon, when she entered the canteen, her eyes began to seek for him at once. If he was not there she was almost glad, but not quite. She found herself looking around expectantly, hoping to see him come in. Hoping with that tremor of mingled fear and desire. And while she smiled at the men as if she had not another thought in the world but pleasure, gaiety, amusement, she looked around.

He came. He always came. He sat alone and brooded. Brooded on the crazy fate that had made him half a man and half a beast. Sometimes he thought he would consult a doctor. It might be that there existed a cure for such cases as his. But no. His case was unique.

Besides, it was silly to think of such things. He could not go to a doctor. He did not dare. The number of his crimes barred that way forever. Perhaps if he were wounded, taken to a hospital, there might be a possibility of interrogating a physician.

He used to pause at the bookstalls and examine medical texts, but what he discovered was of little value. He learnt that his disease was known, that is to say, it had a name, but observers classed it either as a fraud or as a delusion, and as far as curing it goes, no one had any suggestions to offer except that the medieval method of burning was an unmerited cruelty.

He began to think that this rejection of the cure by fire was as superficial a decision as that which rejected his disease, and that there was, on the contrary, much to recommend the stake. He contemplated seriously the necessity of taking his life.

These thoughts had grown more frequent when he stepped by

chance into the canteen where Sophie worked. He saw her and was at once in love with her. Thereafter he came every day. She represented to him all that he was not. All that he could never be. She was the epitome of that which he had lost and could never recover: the joie de vivre.

Then he began to notice that she was observing him. And one day when their eyes met he had the feeling that there was a bond between her and him. He shuddered to think of the filth from which he dared look up to her purity, and he vowed seriously that he would reform himself. He decided that hereafter he would gorge himself with human food during the day, so that his ghastly appetite of the night would diminish. But that first night, despite the gorging, he woke up from his sleep, his body tense, robbed of all desire for further rest, his skin aching to feel the freedom of the night air, his limbs yearning to touch the ground, his jaws to bite and rend. For a while he fought with himself to keep her image uppermost in his mind.

He panted through his opened mouth. And he felt his tongue, his tongue, the short and bulky tongue of man, begin to flatten and lengthen. "God help me!" he cried. But now that tongue was curling out of his mouth, was hanging over his teeth. Unable to resist any more, he sprang from his bed. He went to a corner of his room, muzzled under a piece of cloth, and dragged forth an arm, a human arm. The last of the two arms he had taken from La Belle Normande.

He sank his teeth into it. His eyes glared around suspiciously. Low growls came from his throat. For a while there was silence, then there were more noises, the slap of the hard, dead hand as it hit the floor, the crunching of a bone, and occasionally a sharp tick as a ring on one finger struck wood.

At last his hunger was appeased, but he had no recollection of it. Morning found him in bed, his head heavy, his neck aching, his tongue furred. It was difficult to get up, but having succeeded at last, he began the disgusting task of cleaning up the remains on the floor. He dressed himself and went out to join his regiment.

As he traversed the courtyard, the fat concierge came dashing out: "Monsieur, monsieur. Leave me your key, finally. I would like to clean your room."

"Here it is," he said darkly, "but in that case, I'm moving."

"Ah monsieur…" she said.

"How many times have I told you that I don't want my room cleaned? What do you think I had my own lock put on for? So you could come in and disturb me whenever you pleased?"

"Ah, mais–"

"Well, do you want the key or not?"

"Ah, mais, voyons…"

"Merde alors!" he exclaimed and walked off.

"Peuh!" she breathed. "Quelle bête féroce! You'd think I wanted to spy on him. Well, I bet he has something to conceal, if he keeps his door locked that way." Self-righteous, her lips compressed, she returned to her interrupted scrubbing.

When his duties were over, Bertrand went to the canteen and sat sullen, filled with horror at himself. "You've besmirched yourself foully. How dare you even come into the same room with that pure being?"

He wished with all his strength that he might turn into some loathsome insect, a spider, for example, and that he could run beneath her foot and die crushed under her sole. "No," he thought, "she would not even step on me. Even a poisonous bug she would let live. She's too good."

But though he tried to restrain himself, he did at last look up. Her eyes were upon him, but she shifted her glance quickly. Her gaze wandered back, however. As if magnetized, her eyes looked into his, and his looked into hers. It lasted but a fraction of a second, but it might have been years.

That evening he made a deep vow, and when he reached his room he wrapped all the flesh and bones he had and, adding a stone for weight, made a tight package which he contrived unnoticed to sink into the Seine.

"No more of that," he said. "No more. Never. I swear it by your eyes."

He was in love. He was in love. As he wandered home a woman

186

accosted him, but he shook his head violently. "Ugly creature," he said to himself. He was through with that sort. He had suddenly become very prim. He went home and slept soundly. In the morning he woke up from a dreamless sleep.

"I'm cured!" he wanted to shout to the sunlight that in the early morning found its way into his room. "I'm cured! She has cured me. With her help, it needed only a good effort."

In the afternoon at the canteen he was moved to rush up and thank her, but he did not dare. However, he found a piece of paper and wrote: "You have rescued me from my nightmares. You are an angel." But for two days he carried the scrap of paper around and did not dare give it to her.

Finally, one afternoon, when he saw her coach driving up and the possibility about to be lost for another day, he walked rapidly past the counter and pushed the paper across to her. She snatched it and hid it away in her sleeve as if she had been expecting a message from him, as if she had been secreting billets-doux from him all her life.

Before she rode off with Barral she had a chance to glance at the note: "You have rescued me from my nightmares." The effect on her was electrical. How did he know? How did he know about her dreams?

She was not in the mood for Barral's gaiety. But she dissembled. It had come to be natural for her to be perpetually smiling and laughing. She could do it despite her trembling heart.

"Sophie," said Aunt Louise shaking her head, "will you never be serious?"

Sophie stopped laughing. She was struck by the similarity of their thoughts. She, like Aunt Louise, had been thinking: "Is that all you have, Barral, jokes and smart replies and pretty nonsense? What do you think of at night?"

She could formulate the answer he would give to such a question. "I think of you all night long, and if God is good I dream of you too in my sleep." A pretty conceit and nothing more. A good fellow, this Barral, but shallow and silly. And she held that reply against him without ever giving him the opportunity to make it.

For several weeks Sophie and Bertrand confined themselves to an exchange of notes. But these protestations of mutual dreams and love soon ceased to satisfy. She craved more intimacy.

In the evenings at home, with Barral, and generally under the watchful eye of Aunt Louise, Sophie nearly yawned. "If Barral would only leave," she thought, "then I could go to bed and be with my Bertrand's eyes." She was no longer so afraid of the dark, no longer so afraid of death, since she knew her fate shared.

Once Aunt Louise left them alone for a minute. And Sophie, unaware of what she was doing, ceased her light chatter. She was thinking: "Poor Barral, I'll be leaving you soon." And under a sudden impulse of pity, she laid her hand in his. Frightened by this open declaration of affection, a token greater than any she had ever shown him, he clasped his fingers round hers and was so weak with love that he could not say anything. With astonishment and a joy so deep that it was painful, he saw her eyes fill with tears, he heard her say: "Poor Barral."

Aunt Louise entered and suggested that it was late. He took her home, feeling all the while as if he were floating on clouds, and when he had reached his apartment, he forgot to take off his cape in his haste to sit down and write to Sophie. He filled more pages than ever. He described his emotions a dozen times, swore his love in every paragraph, and when he went out to post his letter, it was three o'clock, but he was in no mood for sleep that night.

In the morning Sophie took his letter to her room and sat down, intending to read it. But her thoughts carried her off to Bertrand. She wondered how best to arrange a meeting with him. It grew late, and time to hasten off to a silly appointment which she regretted ever having made, except insofar as such appointments kept people from discovering her secret.

But before she left home she must write a note for Bertrand. Why not say that she would come to his house? Yes, she must do that. Soon, almost any day now, the siege might be over and with that the canteens and a large measure of her freedom. She wrote the note and was about to hurry off. Then she remembered Barral's letter which she had not yet read. "Bah," she said, "some other time," and threw it unopened into a drawer of her secretaire.

188

That evening Bertrand could scarcely control himself from shouting with joy. She was coming to his house. *She,* yes, she. She was actually coming into his room. She could only spare a half-hour, but she would come sharp at the dot and they would be together and alone.

The night no longer had any terrors for him. He knew he would sleep through, and if he dreamt at all, it would be of her. In the morning as he was leaving, he bethought himself:

"Mme Labouvaye!" he shouted into a dark hole.

"Oui, monsieur! Oui, monsieur!" the concierge shouted back and came running out, her ample bosom dancing with the motion imparted by her strides.

"Voilà la clef," he said. "Please clean up thoroughly."

She was too astonished to speak.

In spite of himself, he smiled. He could smile now that he belonged to the human race again. "Someone is coming to see me."

She understood and laughed with him. "Ah, monsieur," she said, drawing out her words. Then she chuckled: "I'll clean it. I'll scrub your room so clean you will be able to eat off the floor."

He shuddered, controlled himself, and smiling a goodbye, walked off. She remained looking after him, standing out in the chilly winter air. "Hmm. And so that's all he wanted to make him act more human? Those young fellows take that sort of thing too seriously. But after all, what else is there to life?"

Sophie came on time. He met her at the corner of the street and showed her through the maze of courts and dark corridors to his room.

"I'll remember, next time," she said and smiled up at him.

Within, she noted the ugliness of his chamber. The window that did not look out upon the sky, but upon walls. The chairs that were hard and uncomfortable.

They sat together on the bed and held each other's hands. And they were silent, filled with rapid thoughts and emotions, but embarrassed. What should they do now that they were together? They did nothing, just sat and looked at each other.

At last, in a voice that was hoarse from its weight of love, he excused the meanness of his quarters. And she, in a voice warm and throbbing, expressed some equally trite remark.

They may have been sitting thus for some twenty minutes or more and exchanging remarks that were far from inspired, when a strange thought obtruded itself into her mind. What was she doing here in this room? Who was this young man whose hand she was holding in her own, clasping it with force as if she would have sooner parted with her life? Why...?

A strange terror took hold of her, the kind of a terror one has when, just before waking from a bad dream, one's whole being shrieks: This can't be true! and yet fears that it may.

Abruptly she dropped his hand and rose.

"You're not going yet?" he exclaimed.

"I must," she said.

"Don't," he pleaded.

Her eyes were darting around the room as if she imagined she were trapped in a cage. And indeed she did feel trapped. She must get out! She had put herself into a living nightmare. She had entombed herself alive! She made a move toward the door, but he caught hold of her hand again and held her.

"Let me go," she cried in a whisper.

He wanted to let her go, but his fingers wouldn't loosen. He drew her slowly back toward himself. She held her hand before her face as if she would ward him off. Her eyes were wide open in terror.

"Don't hurt me!" she begged. "Oh, please don't hurt me!"

Thereupon he suddenly released her. "I wasn't going to hurt you," he said in a pained voice. He looked away and said: "You may go if you like. Shall I show you the way to the street?"

Her momentary terror vanished. What had she been afraid of? She was filled with contrition instead. Impulsively she put her arms around him.

His own arms remained at his side. It was now his turn to be frightened. He realized that for a moment at least he had lost control of himself. He did not dare clasp her in his arms. It would be better if he never saw her again. Better still if he killed himself quickly.

190

"Bertrand," she said softly, entreatingly.

He did not answer.

"Bertrand," she cried out in despair, "don't you love me?"

He sighed out: "I love you so madly it were better I—"

"Then quick, put your arms around me," she interrupted.

He obeyed.

"You must hold me tighter," she said.

Again he obeyed.

"Tighter still," she whispered. Such a bliss flowed through her from the feel of his arms about her, from his body pressed close to hers, that her head grew dizzy, her breath came and went. Her body tensed and then seemed about to dissolve in liquid. About to dissolve, but not quite. If only he would press harder. If only he would crush her. Tear her! Mutilate her!

"Hold me, hold me tighter still," she panted. And still she was on that point of dissolving and could not dissolve. In desperation she cried out: "Hurt me! Bertrand, hurt me!"

Then she felt his arms closing around her like a vise. And within this circle of pain she experienced a strange exultation, as if a bird within her had been released and was filling her ears with a wild singing. And it was as if all her body dissolved away. She breathed heavily.

They were still standing near the bed.

"You're hurting me," she said at last. At once his arms loosened. She looked up at him. Looked first into one of his eyes and then into the other. She was searching there for an explanation of the joy she had just lived through. There was nothing, only strange, big, brown eyes under heavy brows that were out of place on so boyish a face.

She was grateful to him. She wanted to give him some sign of her gratitude. What could she say? What could she do? They were sitting on the bed again and holding hands.

"What large nails you have," she exclaimed.

"Don't look at them," he said, "they are ugly."

"You mustn't say that. They are not ugly. They are very beautiful and so shiny. But why are they so big?"

"Because..." he said and halted. "Because it's—it's a disease."

"A disease?"

"Yes."

"What kind of a disease?"

He was on the verge of casting himself at her feet and telling her all. But he restrained himself and sought for a way to turn the conversation. "It's called onichogryphosis," he said.

"Onicho...what?" she asked.

"Onichogryphosis," he repeated.

Her laughter tinkled through the room. "You must write it down for me."

"Let us look at *your* nails instead," he suggested. "Like polished jewels." He put them to his mouth and kissed them. He felt tempted to nip her fingertips with his teeth, and he did so, but ever so gently.

And yet he had hurt her. She had wanted to exclaim and draw her fingers away, but she didn't. Was not this the way she could show her gratitude? She insisted: "Bite them, if you want to." And as he hesitated, she asked: "Do you want to?"

He felt as he had once when as a little boy he had confessed to his mother of a pain in his groin and she had wanted to see.

He conquered his shame and answered. "Yes, I do." But with that his desire had expired. "Some other time," he said.

"Next time," she corrected. "Tomorrow."

She rose. "Oh, how late! I shan't be able to go to the canteen."

The short winter afternoon had faded into a gray cold twilight. They hurried out into the street to find a cab for her.

Barral was waiting at her home. Aunt Louise was there too and maintained the silence of intense indignation. Her mother began to scold at once. Barral, however, was so relieved from his worry that he could only say: "Thank God, you're safe. Thank God."

"Where were you?" her mother asked. "You have made everyone miserable; the whole house is upset on account of you."

"Just strolling around," she said carelessly, and went off to her room.

After dinner she sat alone with Barral.

"I was so worried," he confessed. "I thought a German bomb had

192

hit you and I determined to wreak a bloody vengeance on those Huns."

She smiled. "Good Barral." And for the second time in their long courtship, she laid her hand on his. Deeply moved, he clasped it and spoke in a trembling, earnest voice:

"Darling, what did you think of my letter? Did you think I was bold?"

"Why, no," she said hesitatingly. He mistook the meaning of her embarrassment. "Why should I?"

"Then dare I? Dare I?" he cried.

"Why, Barral!" she exclaimed.

"Will you please...I mean, may I...kiss you?"

She smiled again. She felt so immensely superior to him. "Of course you may," she said gently.

He took her head between his hands and looked her in the face. "My dearest Sophie," he said in a choking voice. She was interested to know what could happen. He laid the mildest kiss ever on those sweet lips whose virginal purity he feared to soil. Nothing had happened. No bird sang a deafening song in her ears. Her body did not grow tense nor threaten to dissolve. Nothing. His kiss was reminiscent of the milk diluted with sweet warm water which her nurse used to give her to drink at night.

He went home and wrote her the most impassioned letter he had ever penned. He poured out his whole heart into it. He asked her pardon a thousand times, confessed to a dozen schoolboy peccadilloes which made his lips unfit to touch her pure mouth. Would she, could she ever forgive him for having concealed his miserable past from her? He swore, by high heaven, that ever since he had laid eyes on her two years ago, he had been clean as a new-born baby and would ever remain so.

She threw his letter unopened in her bureau drawer.

As her joy in her new love grew, and each time she went to Bertrand's room her body experienced some new exultation, she ceased to care whether anyone knew. More than that, she wanted to flaunt her love before other people. "Look!" she wanted to cry. "Look what happens to me when my lover holds me in his arms!"

She felt at times as if she would like nothing better than to invite everybody into Bertrand's chamber, undress before them and ask: "Do you find me pretty? Look then, for all this beauty I give to him. See how he holds, kisses me, caresses every part of my body? Is there anyone else in the world who has such a lover?"

The men at the canteen were not long in discovering her secret. They said to each other: "She was ready to be made. I don't understand why we left it to that young snot, Bertrand. Any one of us could have ousted that sky-blue popinjay, de Montfort."

They grew bolder and cracked remarks which were far from innuendoes. She laughed and that heartened them. She was a good girl, that Sophie de Blumenberg, even if her father was a millionaire. "She's of our kind," they concluded and smiled at each other. Goodwill and jollity reigned in the canteen when she was there.

Barral, however, was long in understanding what he certainly did not want to understand. He had, of course, noticed how of late Sophie's eyes sparkled and then veiled as if in a fever. He had noticed that never before had she been so bewitchingly beautiful. He had noticed that she had grown chubbier, had filled out. But he set this down to the natural attainment of maturity. And when he understood, it was too late to do anything. The siege was over, armistice was declared, France must cede Alsace and Lorraine and pay billions of indemnity. And then came the revolution and the declaration of the Paris Commune, and Barral had undertaken a delicate task, that of spying, which prevented him from any violent action in his personal affairs.

Chapter Thirteen

Writing as he did, when the cataclysms through which Paris was passing were at their height and fresh in everybody's mind, Galliez makes little attempt to fill in the historical events of the moment. I have been at some pains to remedy this omission, for our day has forgotten these matters. Moreover, it seems to me that the temper of the period has a great importance in this tale. Galliez, too, now and then lets fall a hint that the atmosphere of the times played a not inconsiderable share in these strange events. Though sometimes he inclines to the very opposite, that is, he intimates that the times were an infection spread abroad by Bertrand, and by others like him.

He says: "I now recognized a meaning in my aunt's, Mme Didier's, wish, expressed in her will, that I study for the priesthood. Was it the germ of religious belief thus sowed in me that protected me from Bertrand? I do not know. But this much I have observed. Few people have come in contact with him without suffering.

"I have often wondered if several such monsters might not, by geometrical progression, infect whole nations in a few days. Like that walking, stalking image of cholera in Eugène Sue's romance. Yes, this would explain so much that is inexplicable in history."

So it would, and certainly Paris seemed to be infected, though the cause is more easily traced to the horrors of war than to werewolves. The bitter winter, with multitudes starving, with babies dying like flies, with shells bursting in all directions, was an experience likely to weaken many characters. The city was full of hate and suspicion. A man of a too Germanic name or of a too Germanic cast of countenance was likely to suffer for what was scarcely his fault. Every strange house was peopled with spies. Poor people who took to sewers for warmth and refuge from a wintry night might wake rudely to find themselves vehemently suspected of planting bombs to blow up the city.

An old woman, about to commit an indiscretion ordinarily beyond her years, hung her torn skirt before her window to dim the light of her candle and guard herself against betrayal. But the strange configuration of light, as seen from the outside, collected a crowd on the street, who saw in this mixture of dots and dashes where the light came through the torn garment a secret code, a signal to admit the Prussians to Paris. Instead of keeping her shame a secret, the poor woman found her room invaded and her sin the latest joke of the street.

One dark night during the bombing a distant light in the east, evidently a signal lamp hung on some tall structure, caused a mob to chase clear across Paris. In vain an amateur astronomer attempted to convince them that they were chasing a planet of the solar system, only distantly interested in mundane matters through the bond of gravity.

Once, upon the report of a patriotic amateur spy, a squad proceeded to the apartment house at No. 3 Place du Théâtre Français, armed with warrants of search and arrest. This was a serious business. It was said that at certain times a black and white flag was to be seen hanging from the fourth floor. The squad returned rather shamefaced. The black and white flag was really blue and white and hung from the window of the Consulate of Honduras.

But if sometimes these suspicions ended in laughter, more often they terminated in corpses.

Still, all things must have an end. Louis Adolphe Thiers became chief executive, the armistice was signed, the peace treaty was ratified and the Germans made their brief triumphal march through Paris. The long siege was at last over. The heart of Paris bounded. Profiteers who had too long held on to their stocks of food were caught now by the raising of the siege, and hastily threw their produce on the market, flooding the stalls. Prices tumbled. There was a hint of spring in the air. Life was a delight.

But the pall of hate and suspicion would not lift. Mobs smashed the shops and cafés that had remained open to trade with the Germans. There was talk that the government had betrayed the city. The National Guardsmen, nearly four hundred thousand strong, complained that treachery had prevented them from being properly employed. And they did not want to be demobilized. Demobilization meant starvation.

But the new government evinced itself as stupidly reactionary. The moratorium on debts which had saved the poor during the war was to be lifted. For now that the national enemy no longer threatened, it was time to put the poor back in the harness, and the momentary spell of making them think that French economic slavery was to be preferred to German economic slavery was no longer to be continued.

However, the popular notion that the Thiers politicians had betrayed their country to Prussia was erroneous. It was decidedly not true. A real politician, and these were real politicians, never betrays his country to an outsider. He betrays it to himself. He is the enemy within.

Bismarck had proposed to disarm the National Guard by offering a loaf of bread for every rifle. His offer was refused by Favre, who later regretted it. For the National Guard refused to disband, refused to begin again the weary business of looking for work at reduced pay, long hours and no future. They demonstrated before the Hôtel de Ville. They threw up barricades. They shot a couple of generals. The Thiers government fled to Versailles, gathered its forces and returned to give the city its second siege. Paris had the Commune. It wasn't what the people were after. But the people are always like that. Like a righteous man raising his axe to scotch a snake and gashing his shin instead. That is a picture to be found on almost every page of history.

The Russians have made a national holiday of March 18th, when the Commune was formed. But they are worshiping a legend, though it is true that the Commune was a mistake from which a new generation of revolutionaries was to learn a lot. The Commune was a proletarian government, yes, but so is a hobo camp. The Commune was never anything but the gnashing of teeth of men annoyed at their impotence and failure. Among these men were many lovers of mankind, many old workers in the field, men who had spent much of their lives in prison for their political opinions, men who went here to their martyrdom, but there were also many incompetents, opportunists, personally ambitious, and more traitors than most governments have had to wrestle with.

Aymar, like most old Republicans, particularly those who had taken part in the revolution of 1848, was offered a post in the Commune government. He declined several and finally accepted a minor post involving few duties and no pay, under Courbet, the painter, who had been appointed Director of Fine Arts by the Republic, and continued as such under the Commune. Aymar was glad to renew an acquaintance which went back to the days of Balzac in the brasserie of the rue Hautefeuille.

A fissure, however, had split him apart from most of his old associates. He did not see eye to eye with them on the question of religion, as formerly. He was as anxious as ever to divorce the priesthood from politics, education and industry, but he could no longer find in the phrase: Religion is just a superstition, the forceful argument he had once thought it. But on this matter he kept his mouth shut. It was not a safe thing to speak, as Aymar had more than one opportunity to discover. For example, during the Piepus affair.

Aymar accompanied Courbet one day shortly after the insurrection to the magnificent hôtel which the Baron de Blumenberg inhabited at the Place Saint-Georges. They found the palace almost emptied of its famous collection of objets d'art. Courbet's fame rather than his frankly boorish demeanor entitled him to be received by the baron himself, who apologized for the appearance of the house. They were leaving for a summer vacation in the country, he said. The stocky, jovial genius took his pipe from his mouth and guffawed. A lot of people were finding it convenient to take their summer vacations early, he remarked. As yet the way out of Paris was free and many, aware of what was coming, were taking refuge before the storm burst.

Courbet's visit was one connected with his position as President of the Society of Artists, and as Director of Arts. He was concerned with the safety, from the fury of the mob, of the art work in the house of Adolph Thiers nearby, and that in the houses of other famous collectors. In the back of his mind was the thought that all collections of art should pass into the safekeeping of the State. In particular he wished to enrich the collection in the Louvre.

It was upon this occasion that Aymar Galliez was introduced to and first saw a certain Mlle Sophie de Blumenberg, a ravishing beauty of about seventeen.

In his script, Aymar Galliez recalls this visit only briefly in connection with its subsequent importance. It would, therefore, be well for the reader to linger here a moment in the company of the author and take a closer look at the Blumenberg ménage.

The Baron de Blumenberg was one of the most prominent citizens of Paris. His patronage of art, his charity, his lavish hospitality concealed with a pretty varnish the nefarious manner by which he had accumulated his millions. His generous right hand was extended in such a friendly gesture to the people of Paris, rich and poor alike, that the actions of his left hand went unnoticed.

True, the pamphleteers had found him out. He was the target for their naïve but biting wit. They exaggerated his paunch, which infuriated him. It is said that Courbet allowed himself to be bribed to treat that paunch leniently in a portrait he was commissioned to make.*

The baron was greatly pleased to see high-priced artists depict him more as he wished he looked. He was that childish in his emotions. But in concocting a wily business scheme, in putting through a contract in which one harmless-looking clause, buried deep in the writ, meant a million to his privy purse, for that there was no better brain in Paris.

The September revolution and the fall of the Empire had not disturbed his position. With a graceful flourish he turned Republican. A matter of no greater difficulty than stepping from one cow pasture into another. He was still Baron de Blumenberg. He still had his money and his power.

Even the Commune did not disturb him seriously. Knowing the bad finances of the revolutionary party, he, like Baron Rothschild, quickly donated a million in cash, and in exchange did much as he pleased. The Commune rarely had the courage of its opinion. In fact the opinions of the Commune were still in dispute the day it perished.

On the day of Courbet's visit, the baron was putting himself into safety. There was great commotion in the house. A hundred bronzes were being packed into boxes, a hundred rugs and tapestries rolled up, a thousand pieces of linen and lace folded into trunks. An endless stream of muffled vases, paintings, chairs, etc., issued from the portals below and found a place in huge vans. The driver's whip cracked and the objets d'art rushed off for their vacation.

Mme de Blumenberg raced from room to room, gathered up her precious bibelots, superintended the shipping of her furs, her fans, her ostrich plumes. She carried under her arm a precious handbag bulging with jewels. She was a tiny, birdlike woman, trim and quick, with brilliant birdlike eyes, and sudden birdlike motions. She skipped around, hopped upstairs and down, and from garret

---

* Several such stories are told of Courbet's willingness to prostitute his famous Realism for money. For example: that a famous Mussulman employed him to do a woman realistically depicted in the act of love. In this painting, said to be still extant, all unimportant details such as head, limbs, hips, breasts, etc., were omitted as having no bearing on the central theme.

200

to cellar there was not a crumb that escaped her. No servant in her employ had ever managed to subtract so much as a minute's worth of time or a centime's worth of property. She often used to say that if she were ruler of France the government would have been run on half its budget. There can be little doubt of that. Only it did not occur to her that as head of French finances her policy of strict economy would have reduced her husband to beggary.

"I hate to leave this behind," he was saying later in the day, when Courbet and his assistant had gone off with certain valuable gifts to the Louvre and the house was almost emptied of its contents, "but I guess we can't take everything." He contemplated sadly the enormous Érard piano of rosewood and ivory inlay.

"Edmond, mon cher," his wife exclaimed in tones of exasperation, "can't you find something more useful to do? Of course we can't take that. No one else can either, though.—Here, you two," she turned to a couple of aproned men, "this goes and that. Quick now! We haven't all day."

"Remember when I gave you this?" The baron sighed. He lifted the lid, the inner surface of which showed a ship foundering in a violent storm, done in ivory and various natural woods, and surrounded by a scroll of leaves in which amorous mermaids were disporting. He sighed and tapped a key. In the empty room it emitted a plaintive note that hung trembling in the air.

"Edmond!" she admonished. He caught her arm and pulled her over to the piano.

"Remember?" he asked.

"Of course, of course," she said, irritated.

"That marvelous, terrible shipwreck." He sighed again.

"How romantic you are," she sneered and attempted to free her arm.

"Don't," he pleaded. "Don't go.—After all, it was the only time in my life that you gave yourself to me." His voice broke a little with emotion.

"You'll remind me of it some other time." But he had passed his arm around her waist and restrained her.

"I'll always remember it."

"How can you, among all the others?" she teased.

"You know they mean nothing to me. Just the distraction of a busy man. You have been my only love. I have often wondered what it might have been like, if you could have returned all my affection."

"Haven't I managed your house? And as for women to sleep with, you can have all you want for a couple of francs. Experienced girls, too—in their line."

"The only time," he mused, half to himself, and passed his free hand over the scene of the shipwreck. "We all thought we were doomed. That awful storm, the rigging swept away, the hulk leaking in every joint, the captain and the crew in despair. And we two, certain that we were to die on that trip which was to have been our honeymoon. During the first days of the trip, I had thought it was only maidenly modesty that had made you refuse to receive me; I was to learn better later.—But with death in sight, you were kind enough to give yourself to me, because it was my last wish. Ah! All these years of your coldness will not erase that one embrace."

"As for me," she said, drily, "I regret it to this day.—Come, are you through reminiscing?"

"How can you regret it," he asked, "seeing that Sophie came of it? I shall never cease to wonder that life, and such joy in life as Sophie shows, could have come out of the embrace of two who thought they were about to die."

"All you think of is Sophie," she said. "And of how much you hurt me, that you conveniently forget. And all those dreadful months of seeing one's body bloated and knowing that the day is coming nearer and nearer when one must split oneself open. *That* is what *you* should have had as your share, for yours was all the pleasure. All I had was the pain."

"To think," the baron continued, "that from such a terrible experience, snatched from the very grave as it were, should have sprung our light-hearted Sophie, gay and insouciante as a linnet, with never a dark moment, never a thought of death."

202

"While we're on the subject of Sophie," the baroness said, "you might go have a talk with her."

"What's the trouble now?" he complained, and regretfully turned down the lid and the scene of the sinking ship, which commemorated the most poignant moment of his life, when death had turned itself miraculously into life.

"Another one of her follies. She wants to stay in Paris!"

"Wants to stay in Paris? How ridiculous! Where would she stay?"

"With Aunt Louise."

"What nonsense!"

"Well, see what you can do with her. I've exhausted my art."

The baron traversed the great empty halls to his daughter's room. She was sitting on a bare bench at the window. When she heard her father enter, she looked up with a smile.

Radiant, warm creature, he said to himself. Lucky the man who will have her for his wife. How she will love him! Lucky Barral. The baron was moved by a strange emotion that was not jealousy, for it was not painful, but it was related to jealousy.

"You have been having another quarrel with your mother," he said.

"Why, no. What about?"

"She just told me that you refused to come along with us. Well, I'm glad that's settled." He was indeed glad. He was so genuinely fond of his wife and daughter that the slightest misunderstanding between them was enough to spoil the day for him.

"Of course it's settled," she said carelessly. "I'm not going. I'm staying with Aunt Louise."

"But, child," he expostulated, "why didn't you say so before? We would all have stayed together. Why, we've moved every stick of furniture. Besides, I'll never be able to persuade your mother to change her plans. You know your mother. Now, why can't you two ever agree?"

"But, papa darling, you needn't change your plans. I'll be well taken care of at Aunt Louise's."

203

"Ah, I see," he smiled suddenly. "Of course, why didn't I think of that. He's staying too. Isn't he?"

She blushed and bit her lower lip. "Yes," she answered. "He's staying too."

Lucky Barral, the baron had to think again. Yes, stay, he blessed them mentally. Stay and a benediction on both of you. Give yourself, give your whole self to the man of your choice and make him happy, as I was happy only once in my life. The train of thought nearly brought tears to his eyes, and he felt impelled to sit down beside his daughter and put his arms around her. "You don't remember when I used to take you from your nurse's arms and carry you around the room. Ah, you were the sweetest baby in the world. You wouldn't go to bed, you wouldn't eat, and ah! you wouldn't do your little business, unless I first gave you a ride around the nursery.—Ach! how I wish I could do it now."

She hid her annoyance and suffered his caresses for a moment.

"Then you will take care of Mamma, and make it good with her?" she said, and took the occasion to free herself from his arms.

He rose with a sigh. "I'll see what I can do." The unpleasant prospect caused him to mop his brow.

She jumped up and gave him a hug and a kiss. "My good papa!" she exclaimed. He left the room treading on a cloud.

Just outside he met Barral and impulsively wrung his hand.

"There's a surprise for you," he said. "A big surprise! Go, Sophie is waiting to tell you."

Barral, who had seemed worried, looked up with relief. "What kind of a surprise, sir?"

"Sophie will tell you," the baron insisted. It would not do, he thought, to deprive her of the joy of telling Barral herself, that she was going to stay in the city.

Though Barral had come to say good-bye, that had not been the chief cause of his worry. On the contrary, within the last two days he had come to feel rather pleased that Sophie was leaving, for in the face of the growing conviction that there was some truth (not much truth, of course), to what all the men were repeating about Sophie, he could have imagined no better solution than her

204

departure from Paris. That would put a stop to her friendship with this young guardsman.

What might the surprise be? Barral wondered. "Perhaps she has decided to accept me when I ask her." The thought was almost too much for him. With his heart beating audibly, he knocked at her door.

"Sophie," he breathed as he entered, and could not say any more.

They conversed in staccato sentences. Neither was at ease. Barral was debating, should he drop to his knee? Should he speak out boldly? At last he determined to speak: "Now that you are about to leave Paris, my dear Sophie, and I shall be remaining here, away from you, and occupied in dangerous work—there is something I should like to ask you."

"But I shan't be going, Barral," she objected.

His stream of language which had been flowing so limpidly ceased at once. Thrown over the tracks thus, suddenly, he was for a moment completely at a loss.

"You don't seem pleased," she commented.

He turned his head away and muttered: "If I could be sure it was for me that you were staying…" She had not heard him.

"What did you say, Barral?"

"I said—I said," he summoned his courage: "The men around the canteen are saying such ugly things about you."

"Really?" she answered. "What, for example?"

His courage petered out: "Just…well just ugly things," he concluded lamely. "Of course," he added in great haste, "I don't believe a word of it."

"But what?"

"But I thought I'd tell you."

"I see," she said.

There was a moment of silence. He squirmed, unsatisfied.

"Of course it's just gossip," he said, and awaited her confirmation.

"What's just gossip?"

"What they say."

"But you haven't told me what they say," was her calm and altogether too sensible riposte.

Nervously he pleaded: "Tell me only that it isn't true!" But she insisted relentlessly: "That what isn't true?" Spurred on by some malicious spirit, she wanted him to bring the words to his lips. She craved the strange joy of hearing her love for Bertrand issue from his mouth. She would have that pleasure, at least, granting the impossibility of flaunting more intimate proof of her love before him. She had experienced a great many new sensations in these last weeks and still she wanted more. Now that she had broken into a new world she was insatiable for ever new joys.

A great wave of pain passed through him. "So it's true," he murmured. "But how can it be true?" He was a man who has run to the harbor and found the ship he was to take already far out to sea, and who now stands on the shore saying over and over again, as if a lie well rubbed in could act as a balm to the hurt of truth: "It can't be true. No, it can't possibly be true."

And then anger rose in him. "I know what I'll do,'" he declared. "I'll kill him. I'll find out where he lives and kill him."

Inspired by her cruelty, she encouraged. "Find us some time when we're both together and you can pierce us both with one thrust."

"Not you!" he stuttered, all undone. "But I'll kill him."

"That comes to the same thing," she said. "For we two are only one and if he dies, so do I."

"Very well," he said. "Then you can die too, for I'll get him."

"So that's how much you love me?" she sneered. "That's how much your letters were worth? After all the times you swore undying love for me. And to think that I was taken in by those cheap promises." She turned her head away as if in disgust.

He was thunderstruck. The boldness of her argument quite took his breath away. Her defection was pushed into the background. The question now was: Had he lied in his letters, or had he told the truth? Which?

Thoroughly whipped, he whined: "Then what am I to do?"

206

"If your love was ever real, you will continue to love me," she answered. "My love for him will never waver, I can tell you that."

This was even more crazy than her first argument. But he accepted it. "I'll always love you," he declared in a low voice.

"You are good, Barral," she praised. "And I shall continue to give you what I have always given you: my companionship. I never gave you more, never promised you more. And for my sake and the sake of your love, you will be kind to Bertrand and never say anything of this to Father or Mother, or Aunt Louise, or anybody."

He gulped and promised.

In a daze he found his way home. When he had taken off his uniform, he threw himself on his bed. But he felt very uncomfortable. And he did not want to sleep. What was it he wanted? Something was missing in the room. He looked around, his thoughts in strange confusion.

Then he knew. His letter. He must write Sophie a letter. And he sat down and wrote. Wrote of his love and her beauty, and his pain and anguish, and his eternal fidelity. And early in the morning when he had posted his letter, he felt more his usual self.

Captain Barral de Montfort, disappointed in love, heartbroken, launched himself into his work with viciousness. The task of spying for the Versailles government was a delicate one. He found in its intricacies the necessary antidote to his misery.

Moreover, if he could not, true to his promise, take direct vengeance on Bertrand or on those other gossiping guardsmen of the 204th battalion, he could attack them from another side. And he was after their blood. The thought that they would suffer from his work spurred him on. These were the people whom his activity was going to destroy.

But though he went at his task with great energy, he did not fail to protect himself from suspicion. For example, though as a member of the staff he could have secured valuable information at the staff meetings, he deliberately avoided being present and secured his knowledge elsewhere. In that way no one could think he was snooping.

Cluseret, chief of staff,* noticing de Montfort's absence from the meetings, accused him of negligence and threatened to have him dismissed. He was generally taken to be merely a light-hearted officer, interested more in his uniform and in making an effective appearance on horseback than in war.

---

* Cluseret, famous soldier of fortune, fought under Garibaldi and later in the American Civil War on the side of the North. Lincoln promoted him to a generalship. He took part in the Franco-Prussian war and Commune, and being subsequently sentenced to death, he fled to Mexico, where he remained until the amnesty. He returned, entered politics and for some time served in the French legislature. He had talent as a painter.

Chapter Fourteen

I have referred already to the Piepus affair. Although of itself unimportant except as background, it is so illustrative of the temper of the period that it may be of value to dwell on the matter for a while. Aymar Galliez, in his script, makes several references to the Piepus mysteries. And these having become famous in history, there is no difficulty in filling out his remarks and giving them the breath of life. And still another reason for going into the Piepus affair with some detail:

Aymar had been in Paris now a good eight months and still he had not once seen Bertrand. Moreover, for the last three months there had not been a single crime that he could confidently ascribe to Bertrand. Frequently he said to himself: "Bertrand is dead. Yes, he must be dead." And how easy to be dead in such a period! The Germans had bombed Paris for a good long month. Hundreds had been killed. And in the relatively few battles in which the National Guard had played a part, military inefficiency had sacrificed thousands. "Bertrand is among those poor devils," Aymar thought and was moved. He recalled the little baby of whom his aunt had been so fond. He recalled the boy. His soft hairy palms. His large brown eyes, liquid and appealing like those of a dog.

And then, suddenly, he came face to face with Bertrand. Aymar had pursued so many clues that he had come at last to consider himself a permanent spectator at all scenes of crime. His friendship with so many revolutionaries, serving in important offices, guaranteed him a degree of immunity in these nervous days, though occasionally he was taken for a spy and once came near being put in jail.

On the second of April, the short-lived government of the Hôtel de Ville (the Commune) decreed the nationalization of all property held by "dead hand" (that is to say, the lands and buildings of religious institutions which are passed on by mortmain – and the police were ordered to search and list all such property and all organizations hitherto in possession thereof.

It is claimed that the prefect of police, Rigault,* was only anxious to secure important clerics as hostages, to exchange for Blanqui held by the Versailles government, but ostensibly the accusation was that such societies as the Jesuits, etc., had secreted large stores of guns and ammunitions, a political canard still effective today.

The notion that there must be something mysterious within the gray stone walls of a convent or monastery; some secret victim immured, praying to hard-hearted, hymn-chanting monks for liberty and finding only sneers beneath the brown cowls; or some delicate maiden hidden away where the walls will absorb her laments, a maiden forced to give in to the brutal lust of celibates who must outwardly conform to impossible vows; or else a treasure, or ghosts, or inexplicable apparitions accompanied by mysterious sounds—I say, such notions are centuries old and will not die.

The newspapers of the day, apparently having nothing better to do, revived these old tales. "The delegate to the ex-prefecture

---

* I should say rather the delegate to the ex-Prefecture of Police, since the odious prefecture of police of Imperial days had been abolished. The ex-prefecture continued, however, to function under its new name, with Raoul Rigault delegated to take charge.

of police," we are told by one sheet, "has evidence that the high clergy of Paris has betrayed France to Rome, that during the siege the clergy acted as spies for Germany."

Among the churches searched for caches of guns and bullets was that of the Fathers and Sisters of the Sacred Heart of Piepus, two societies which owned adjoining buildings in the rue de Piepus. The story ran that eighteen hundred chassepots (a newly introduced rifle), were hidden there, along with the great "treasure of the Fathers." On the seventh of April, the place was searched. Nothing was found. Nevertheless, one newspaper announced the discovery of "arms, munitions and a workshop for the manufacture of bombs, with some bombs in construction."

The public clamored for more news. On April 12th, a second search was made. But the mysterious underground chamber could not be found, though trenches were dug everywhere and the walls pierced in dozens of places.

At this juncture, with the legend about to perish, a fortunate stroke of a workman's pick uncovered human bones in the garden of the convent. Bombs and chassepots were forgotten before this more horrible discovery.

In line with this gruesome find, directly implicating the convent not only of violation of the law against burial outside of official cemeteries, but also of the suspicion, which grew stronger every moment, of wholesale murder, was another strange discovery. Up in the attic were three small rooms, clean, but iron-barred, and in each of these rooms a gray-haired woman, unable to speak intelligently, or muttering gibberish and voicing threats and loud shrieks. In short, three insane women. What were they doing there? How had they gotten there? There could be no doubt upon the matter. These poor women had formerly been beautiful girls, pensioners, no doubt, in the convent, and for expressing some opinion of their own or for refusing to obey some cruel order they had been shut up here so long that they had lost their reason.

Worse than this was to come. It was to be shown that there existed secret relations of a most sordid, but readily comprehensible

211

nature, between the monks and the nuns. What this commerce was is easily guessed.

Among the possessions of the nuns was found a crib! Yes, a small baby crib! Worse still, in the cell allocated to Rev. Father Bousquet, superior-general of the brothers, who was, for the moment, absent from Paris, was found a treatise: a manual of *practical obstetrics!* Of all things. In addition, a chest of human bones! And upstairs in a kind of garret, iron instruments of strange and frightening shapes, and peculiar beds with ratchets and winches. And still a further discovery: in the crypt of the nun's chapel were found eighteen coffined cadavers in all states of decay.

The case was complete. The newspapers presented it with all the lugubrious details painted in vivid colors: "Why was poor Sister Bernadine shut up in a kind of cage, so small that if she dropped her needle she could not stoop to pick it up? What is the meaning and purpose of this iron crown, this racking bed, this corset of steel? These are parts of the arsenal of torture, necessary adjuncts to a branch house of the medieval Inquisition, flourishing in Paris of the nineteenth century."

One paper recalled that ten years before a man had fallen asleep in the Piepus church, and remaining unnoticed, had been locked up for the night. Hours later, he was aroused in the dark by an indescribable moaning.

An observant reporter noticed that all the eighteen bodies were of women and that their bodies seemed disarranged in their coffins. The corpses were evidently recent. The abundant ash-blond hair of one woman was particularly striking. It was said that a wine dealer of the neighborhood recognized her as his daughter who had disappeared some years ago. "The gaping jaws of these human remains," wrote the reporter, "when brought up to the light of day, take on surprisingly fantastic appearances. It seems as if these fleshless bones craved to speak, as if they yearned to recount the tragedies that had terminated their lives." And filled with inspiration, the reporter himself wrote what these bodies could not utter: "See," they (the cadavers) said, "see our poor heads, all bent either to the right or to the left. Is that not proof that we were buried before our bodies had stiffened in death?" He went on to describe ghastly midnight orgies held by the monks in the crypts, under the vacillating flare of torches. It was a tale of girls lured by promises of special religious festivals, the attendance of which brought safe-conduct to heaven.

However desirable this promissory note to future bliss might be, there was not one girl who wanted to call for payment, for many years to come. But the wine had been heavily drugged. The sacred wafer had been formed of flour mixed with the dust of dried soporific herbs. And the priests wreaked their horrible, perverted lust on the maidens who, dulled by the drugs, resisted only weakly, until the curtain of complete loss of consciousness descended upon them.

When the effect of the narcotic had dissipated, the feeling of life returned and the girls woke to find themselves in a dark, confined space of which the horrible nature gradually dawned on them, only to extinguish in the final blotting out of death. And there, in their premature graves, their bodies remained, along with the evidence of their final struggle: bodies contorted, jaws distended, fingers crooked, signs of their agony, their chests gulping for air, their hands seeking for freedom.

"But justice," says our writer, "advances inexorably, majestically! However deeply hidden crime may be, it must some day come to light. Advance! All you good and kind-hearted citizens of Paris and gaze on these black deeds of the infamous clergy. Gaze! And either lie down in your coffins alive like Charles V, or rise up like Lazarus from your long sleep of laissez-faire. Here, before this charnel house, mount guard! And let this be your luminous pharos to guide mankind to the sublime association of harmonious," etc., etc., etc.*

Another journal grew expansive and rhetorical on the crib in the convent. What poor babies, products of the union of monk and nun, had here been lulled to sleep, separated by only a few feet, a few walls, from the altar of the Virgin? What became of

* *Journal Officiel,* May 21, 1871.

these children? The aim of the monks was surely not to keep them alive, as living evidence of a disgraceful breach of holy vows. No, their intentions were only too plain. Alas! When the mothers, nuns cruelly deprived by a stupid religion of their right to parenthood, had grown fond of their offspring, and could look at the image of Mary and the infant Jesus, and understand something they never had known before: the tug of a baby's mouth at the nipple of the breast, a tug which reaches to the heart, then the monks tore the baby from the mother's bosom, slew it or cast it into some ditch. And if poor Sister Bernadine, or Celestine, went mad with grief, they locked her up in a cage in the garret, where her crazy lullabies, intermingled with frantic shrieks for her baby, died among the rafters of the roof.

Later the monks bethought themselves of a better system. They would study obstetrics and learn the art of aborting, and thus safeguard themselves against babies. The empty crib was put away. It was no longer necessary. Nuns and monks now could conceal their misdeeds behind permanent angelic smiles.

Decidedly a breath of folly was sweeping through Paris. The public flocked to rue de Piepus. Aymar among others. Etienne Carjat, "employing the miraculous aid of electric light," photographed the skeletons in the crypt. In shops a drawing of the secret funeral was exhibited for sale. Other convents were ransacked, other monasteries. More horrible discoveries! Chains fastened to walls, handcuffs, straitjackets, etc., all evidently destined for the adoration of recalcitrant Venuses.

Of course, all Paris was not so stupid, but the unthinking mass, accustomed to playing the sounding board to the tune of the journalists, responding first to one sentiment and then to its opposite, was stirred profoundly by these romantic tales of horror.* At the Paris Medical School, many students must have known that a Bousquet, nephew of the superior-general of the Piepus

---

* One of the three crazy women was brought to the barracks at Reuilly. The woman at the canteen charged a ten-centime admission. If the Commune thought to improve her lot...

214

brothers, had recently submitted his thesis on obstetrics in partial fulfillment of the requirements for a degree, and he must have told his friends about the matter. But they chose to keep quiet. He, too, said nothing. It had become dangerous to speak out of turn. Dr Paillet, physician to the Sisters, had been arrested as "an accomplice in the crimes of Piepus."

In the neighborhood there must have been many who recalled the annual theatrical representation given by the nuns of the birth of Christ and the visit of the Magi. And it could not have been difficult for them to realize that the crib was a part of the permanent stage properties. But they kept quiet. And they were justified. On the tenth of May a young lady who dared emit some skeptical reflections anent the origins of the skeletons in the crypt was arrested and locked up.

What ignorance was abroad that a coffer of bones was not recognized as a reliquary with the remains of a saint in it? One man, bolder than the rest, sent the police a marked copy of Dulaure's *History of Paris*. The buildings on rue de Piepus were constructed over a former cemetery part of this cemetery was still in use,* the rest was built on or converted into garden space. The Reign of Terror of 1793 had buried here 1,306 guillotined aristocrats in a big ditch. Perhaps the police couldn't read.

Ancient pupils of the convent did indeed appear to declare that the instruments of torture, the beds of Procrustes for racking victims at the "branch house of the Inquisition," were only orthopedic devices, employed in the treatment of crippled children who were taken care of by the nuns. The three crazy women, it was shown, were old sisters who had lost their reason and were most kindly treated by the convent. But this evidence was not spread abroad in the papers.

Dr Piorry, professor at the Academy of Medicine, was commissioned by the Commune to draw up a medico-legal report. He delayed sending in the results of his observations until the Commune was a matter of the past, and a free opinion was

---

* The Piepus cemetery is still open to visitors to Paris and is worthy of a trip.

safe. Then he published his paper. The eighteen corpses were all of old women, not of young girls. They had been buried long ago. How long, the doctor could not say, but certainly a great number of years. There was no evidence of any recent crime.

But when this article appeared, the comedy of Piepus had long reached its seemingly predestined tragic finale. Raoul Rigault, chesty little fellow, strutting in his bright uniform, always ready to offer his snuff to his friends, appeared on the scene one day and ordered wholesale arrests. Rigault was a genius, a born detective, who from his earliest days had determined some time in his life to be chief of police. He had achieved this, but his insatiable ambition and his evil disposition were also his ruin.

Rigault wanted important churchmen as hostages, for the Versailles government was holding the aged revolutionary, Blanqui, and the chief of police thought it might be possible to effect an exchange of prisoners.

A long line of monks and nuns were led off to the ex-prefecture. Here, too, a number of other clerics had been brought, in particular Monseigneur Darboy, Archbishop of Paris, Lagarde, his grand vicar, and a host of lesser priests.

Rigault examined them personally.

"What is your profession?" he asked a Jesuit.

"Servant of God."

"God? What is your master's address?"

"He is everywhere."

"Write," said Rigault to one of his secretaries. "So-and-so, styling himself servant of God. Citizen God, a vagabond without fixed address." He caressed his luxurious growth of beard and mustache.

The archbishop sought to make an appeal. "My children—" he began, spreading his arms.

Rigault interrupted him: "There are no children here. Only citizens."

The archbishop halted and then wished to pursue.

Again Rigault interrupted him. The police had enough information, he said, to show that the priests were plotting with the government of Versailles, that the priests were responsible for recent skirmishes in which the National Guard had been worsted by the Versailles troops. There were traitors, that was certain. Information was leaking out. At last they had the guilty ones and meant to hold them.

And as the prelate wished to reply: "Enough," said Rigault dryly. "You fellows have been getting away with it for eighteen centuries. Since you refuse to confess your conspiracy, the matter will be investigated. In the meanwhile, I shall hold you."

He picked up a sheet of paper and wrote: "The director of the Dépôt will hold incommunicado the two calling themselves Darboy and Lagarde." On the walls of the vacant churches, signs were placed: "Stable for rent."* The religious houses were turned over as meeting places for the political clubs.

The police were right in one respect: there was treachery, there was conspiracy. No government was ever more conspired against, no government ever so riddled with treachery, as the Commune, but in looking for the infection in the priesthood and in religious organizations, the police missed the real nest of vipers, the Café de Suède, from which the net spread out over the whole Commune.

Paris was full of men to whom the revolt was purely an opportunity for speculation. The Thiers government at Versailles knew the prices to be paid and was ready with its money. Men occupying high posts in the Commune came to the Café de Suède and received the gold. Captain Barral de Montfort, on the staff of the 7th legion, an honored officer of the Commune's military forces, sat there at his little table and conversed casually under a heavy cloud of cigar smoke. To all appearances it was only apéritif time, and a moment for sprightly repartee.

But from all over agents came to see him there. He received them as friends, talked of indifferent matters, slipped them a few bills on the Banque de France. The price was agreed on: For opening a gate, five thousand francs, to be debited to the prefect of police at

---

* "Since Jesus Christ was born in a stable," wrote Rochefort, the witty journalist, "it can be no offense to the most religious-minded to see their churches turned into stables."

217

Versailles; ten thousand francs for a battalion, to be charged to the Ministry of War; three thousand francs for a man—the Home Office paid for that. This was the activity that went on while the police exhausted themselves hunting for an underground communication with Versailles, dozens of possible tunnels being suspected, but none found. This was the activity that went on while the police pursued nonexistent murderers of cadavers dead a hundred years.

When the business meeting at the Café de Suède was over, the glasses empty, the trays full of silvery cigar ashes, then Captain Barral de Montfort arose and, before returning to his military duties, took a cab or else walked to the canteen where the 204th battalion congregated.

An astonishing dark-haired beauty looked up at his entry.

"Well, what is new today, Sophie?" he said casually.

She looked around to make sure that she was not observed and then whispered:

"I hear that troops are being taken away from the redoubt at Hautes Bruyères and the advance post of Cachan."

"Hm! That's a stupid move."

"Any good to you?"

"Might be. If they're weak there, then that's the place for us to attack."

She smiled slightly: "Let me know how it turns out. And if I've done my work well, if I've paid, you do your share."

"You can rely on me," he declared solemnly. Then they spoke of indifferent matters. She took off the apron that protected her fine dress and they went strolling out hand in hand.

"You still love him?" he questioned. There was a bitter expression around his mouth.

"Why, of course," she said carelessly.

"You're a liar, he replied. He stopped at a lonely corner and took hold of her shoulders. "Why do you lie!" He shook her and raised his voice: "Tell me why you lie?" He would have screamed if he had dared.

"Don't be a fool," she said, annoyed.

"Huh! Do you think I haven't any eyes to see? Your face is getting paler every day. More and more like a lacquered mask."

"Why must you always be annoying?"

His face distorted as if he were going to cry. "You don't know that I love you?" he asked sadly, quietly.

"You're a good boy, Barral. I wish I loved you too. But it's too late, now."

"Don't say that," he exclaimed. "Why is it too late? Come, we'll leave this terrible city. I can get out any time I want to." And as she made no answer but only looked away into the distance as if she yearned for something beyond the possibility of reach, he continued hastily, "Come, we'll go together to the country, to my little place at Vallauris."

She cut him short. "Let's take a cab. I must hurry; he'll be waiting for me. He's doing guard duty at the Piepus and he will be relieved about this time."

He muttered something under his breath. She did not catch his words, but she gathered their import. "Don't you dare touch a hair on his head! Mind you, if anything should happen to him, I'll kill you, whether you did it or not."

"I promised I would do nothing to him," he said, "and I'll keep my promise.—Look, will you give me your address?"

"What for?" she asked suspiciously.

He wouldn't answer for a moment. But later, seated in the cab, he repeated his request.

"I don't see what you can be wanting my address for. I suppose you want to tell Aunt Louise where I've run off to."

"No," he said soberly. "It's something else. I want to write to you. You know how long I've been in the habit of writing to you every night. Well, I can't stop. And as for handing you my letters personally, that's not the same thing. There was so much pleasure attached to that act, of going out late at night to post a letter to you."

"That's sweet of you, Barral. You are always very sweet."

A lump rose in his throat. He pursued his advantage. "And of course, once you left Mme Hertzog's, it wouldn't do to send the letters there, because I know you'd want her to think that we were together."

"You're really very sweet, Barral," she repeated, deeply touched. And she put her hand on his. "You're far too good for me. Oh, you haven't any conception of how rotten I am. Of the terrible things I do. Oh, Barral, you should be thankful that I'm going out of your life." As she said this, she was conscious of something more than sympathy for Barral. She was conscious of a touch of pride. She felt superior to the "sweet" Barral. She was so very, very bad.

Chapter Fifteen

The writer apologizes for the confusion of the last chapters. His excuses are that the chronology in the script is none too clear, and further that the elucidation of the events in the story was none too easy.

Aymar, so we have said, first came face to face with Bertrand during the Piepus affair, and though in our elaboration of the Galliez script we went off the track in the last chapter, we intend to come back to our duty in this one.

Aymar was vaguely acquainted with Commissaire de Police Clavier, who was in charge at Piepus, and one day stood for a moment talking to him outside the buildings which were being investigated, when a soldier came running up to inform the commissaire of the discovery of cadavers in the crypt. Clavier hastened inside and Aymar followed. Some workmen, aided by soldiers of the National Guard, were bringing the coffins up to the light as fast as they could be dug out of the ground of the crypt below.

At the sight of one of the soldiers a cold shiver ran down Aymar's back. It was not only the recognition of Bertrand, his face red and perspired, laboring under the heavy load of a coffin that made Aymar shudder. It was something else.

A few months ago he had been walking along a street of the Bastille section, and as it happened was thinking of Bertrand, which was only natural, and was wondering if he were not completely mistaken and Bertrand was not in Paris at all, never had been perhaps, and it was so thinking that Aymar suddenly noticed a large red sign over a shop. White letters proclaimed: "Guerre à outrance!" ("War to the bitter end!") It was a cat, dog and rat butcher shop, a chain of which existed in the city.

As he passed the door, he peered in. A group of housewives wrapped in shawls were waiting to make their purchases. The butcher's wife was wrapping the meat in old paper. The butcher was swinging the heavy cleaver which was rouged with blood. His great jowly face was tensed and red, in sympathy with the effort of his swinging arm.

Aymar walked on, but the vision of that face remained with him, lying like a picture on transparent paper over the tenor of his thoughts. Three blocks later he exclaimed, "Why, that was Father Pitamont!" He hastened back to assure himself, but when he looked in again, the butcher did indeed look like Father Pitamont, but Aymar was no longer so certain it was he. After all, it was many years now since he had seen the priest. Alternately, as he looked, Aymar felt certain and uncertain. It might be Father Pitamont, and then again...Disconcerted, he walked off.

And now as he looked at Bertrand straining under the weight of a heavy coffin, he had that same strange alternating sensation: It might be Father Pitamont, and then again...,But it was only Bertrand grown a little older and heavier. Aymar's blood was pounding. Here was the moment he had been waiting for. What should he do? Yell? Leap on Bertrand? Rouse the vaulted chapel with curses hurled at the monster? Instead of anathemas, only ironic words came to his mind.

He stood in the crowd about the cofim, while the lid was being pried off. Bertrand was directly in front of him. He touched the

222

young soldier on the arm, and when Bertrand turned around, Aymar said quietly: "Appropriate work."

Bertrand, startled, breathed, "Uncle..."

"This is your peculiar talent, eh?"

"Uncle..."

"I say, your specialty, isn't it?"

Bertrand pushed himself out of the crowd, which was glad to flow into the space he left. He went over to a bench and Aymar followed.

"I knew I'd find you here," Aymar pursued.

Bertrand looked up with an innocent expression in his brown eyes. His clean-shaven face, seen from close, was still youthful, attractive, so Aymar thought. But when Bertrand opened his mouth to ask, "How did you know that?" then the sight of his white teeth, with the large interlocking canines, made Aymar conscious of what lurked below the handsome exterior.

"Are you asking how I knew I'd find you here? And do you think that I have forgotten you and your tastes?"

"You are cruel."

Aymar laughed in staccato. "You are evidently nothing but kind-hearted."

"I have suffered," Bertrand returned.

"And those whom you slew? They did not suffer, I suppose. Do you think I have not watched you, even if from afar? There was, let me see: Jacques, first of all. What? Have you forgotten him? Well, I suppose when you have so much to recall, when one is so terribly busy..."

"Uncle," Bertrand pleaded, his head lowered.

"And here's one you can add to your list," Aymar said, suddenly recalling. "When mail came through again after the armistice, I received a letter from Françoise. By the way, it never occurred to you to write, did it? Seventeen years of good care and food, and then off one goes."

"You were holding me a prisoner," Bertrand defended himself meekly, his head still bowed.

"And I did wrong, I suppose?"

"No," the soldier breathed.

"Hm. Well, I'm glad to hear you admit as much. That helps. Ah, yes. As I was saying, Françoise wrote to tell me that the farmhand who was accused of murdering Jacques was acquitted. But the whole district was united in thinking him guilty. Life was made unbearable for him. He hanged himself."

Bertrand sighed.

"In the matter of digging up the miser, Vaubois, it never occurred to you that the shepherd, Crotez, would be accused of the job. Or in the matter of General Darimon's daughter, that a poor *croque-mort,* the coachman, Jean Robert, would go to jail for it, and his family become destitute? How many others have suffered through you, I cannot say. I blame myself for keeping quiet in these matters. I should have shouted your guilt from the housetops. But I was ashamed. Yes, ashamed. Like a man who is afraid of being surprised in a privy. That's it. I did not want people to know that I was even remotely connected with such a monster as you."

"Uncle," Bertrand pleaded.

"Yes, monster," Aymar continued, working himself into anger, his voice rising now to a hoarse whisper. "Yes, a monster, the man who could murder prostitutes like La Belle Normande. For that was you, too, wasn't it? Confess! All those murders were yours!"

Bertrand bowed his head. His whole body began to tremble.

"You beast!" Aymar cried in a subdued voice. "You—you loup-garou!"

At this Bertrand pushed his knuckles between his teeth to strangle a wild desire to shriek, a shriek which came forth only as a whine. The public, clamoring around the newly discovered crimes of the monks, the eighteen coffins of young girls, paid no attention to the two who sat apart. Nor did the officers, quite accustomed to the lax discipline of the National Guard, concern themselves with Bertrand.

The young man's body was shaken with violent tremors. "Not that!" he sobbed. "Oh, isn't it bad enough to know oneself a werewolf, without having it thrown at one as a reproach?"

224

Aymar was moved. He had been cruel. It was the boy's misfortune, not his sin. "I'm sorry, Bertrand. For years I tried to spare you from knowing. I tried to help you. I would not even tell your mother what was wrong. It was a hard task at times."

"Mother never knew?"

"I don't think so."

"How is she?"

"Well, I guess she's all right," Aymar said lamely.

"What do you mean?" Bertrand asked, his suspicions aroused.

"Nothing. You know, one doesn't get much mail these days."

"Tell me," Bertrand insisted, "I want to know."

And Aymar thought: "Why should I try to conceal his mother's shame from him? It's such a small matter compared to the others." – "Your mother," he said, taking a long breath, "was seen to be pregnant and it made much scandal in the village, and Jacques' mother especially talked a lot and accused me of sinful relations with your mother, which, of course, wasn't true, I mean it wasn't so-" He stopped, filled with memories.

"Go on."

"Well, Françoise wouldn't stand for that, and she had seen young Guillemin sneaking around the house, so she took a long chance and accused him. Your mother confessed it was so, but Guillemin denied it at first. But it evidently was true, for one day they ran off together."

"Where to?"

"No one knows." Aymar shook his head and sighed.

Bertrand also shook his head. "That too," he said slowly.

Another shame for the lad to bear, Aymar thought, and nodded sadly. Then, in a flash, he understood: "What? That too?–Bon Dieu!"

"Yes," said Bertrand, looking up and straight at his uncle. "That too. But it is all past. All over now. Thank God for that."

"What do you mean, all past?"

"It's over. I'm cured," he answered simply.

Was he trying to escape, Aymar wondered? Or really, was he cured? "How?" he asked.

"I don't know. Yes, I do. A girl. I'm in love. She cured me. She keeps me from—" He didn't finish.

Could this be true? No, impossible. And yet, Aymar argued, the crimes had dropped suddenly. Was this then the explanation? Love? The miracle of Love? The love for a good woman?

"Who is she?"

"Her name is—Well, I would rather not say. But you will see her, for she will come to meet me here. I'm off duty at five. I shan't introduce you. But you will be able to look at her from a distance. She is rich, and very beautiful and so good. Ah, you cannot have any conception of how good she is. No, you cannot have any conception."

"Hm," said Aymar and smiled. Cured by a love affair. And just like Bertrand to turn into a loving swain. For such is the irony of life. Aymar had no doubt that this affair was pure and sickly sweet with sentiment.

A number of old fairy-tales, connected by Grimm* to werewolf-ism and for that reason brought to Aymar's attention during his study of the subject, leaped to his mind. It was a story of endless variations: the prince turned into an ugly lizard or a frog, or some other loathsome or dangerous beast, requires the love of a pure virgin to turn him back to human shape. Of course, no one will consent to marry a frog. But at last one pure and innocent girl, filled with pity, consents to a wedding and takes the frog to bed—the frog who thereupon ceases to be a frog and becomes a prince. And the two, of course, live happy ever after.

And was this nightmare, too, to end with a dawn all of rose and pearl and perfume? And was Bertrand to live happy ever after? What truth was there in the old stories?

Was that the way to cure them?

Beauty and the beast. Yes. There was deep wisdom in those old tales.

"I see her there, outside now," Bertrand declared in an excited whisper. "Come and look at her, uncle, from a distance. She is the most beautiful thing you ever saw."

* *Deutsche Mythologie.* Göttingen, 1835.

226

Bertrand ran out and greeted Sophie with a kiss. They clung to each other as if they had been apart a year.

Aymar watched from the portal of the church. He saw a young officer pay the coachman and move away, his head bowed, as if he had nothing to do with this scene but take care of that one detail. Evidently her brother. Truly she was a beautiful thing. Hadn't he seen her somewhere before? But where?

And Aymar watched Bertrand and his love go off hand in hand. "And the sheep shall lie down with the wolf," he quoted, "and they shall beat their swords into plowshares." A real calf-love, he mused. And then said to himself, cynically: "I wonder…"

It occurred to him: "Suppose I talk with that young officer. Perhaps I shall discover if I did right to let him go, after having hunted for him so long."

He approached the officer, who was standing on the sidewalk as if he were waiting for another cab to come along so that he could pay another coachman.

"Pardon me," said Aymar. "Would you mind if I asked you a question?"

Captain Barral de Montfort ceased at that moment to be an unfortunate lover and became a spy. "Not at all," he answered. "But whether you'll get a reply is another matter."

"Entendu," said Aymar. "Do you know that young lady?"

"Perhaps."

"Do you know the young man?"

"No."

"Well, many thanks for your courtesy," said Aymar. "I hope I didn't trouble you too much."

"Pas de quoi," said Montfort. But as Aymar turned to leave, the captain bethought himself: "À mon tour maintenant: Do you know the young lady?"

"No."

"Do you know the young man?"

"Perhaps."

Aymar smiled and the captain smiled.

"I think," said Aymar, "that if we put our fragments of knowledge together, something might come of it. Come, let us sit down somewhere."

They found a café nearby, took seats and ordered drinks. But the conversation did not want to go forward, the reason being that each wished to receive more than he gave. Barral was not anxious to reveal the woeful tale of his love nor, was Aymar ready to divulge the truth about Bertrand. He spoke vaguely of a mysterious and obnoxious nature, but said nothing of crimes.

"I see," Barral said at one point, "that you have none too high an opinion of your nephew. That coincides completely with my own. Let me tell you something that I have observed," he continued. "When first she went with this fellow, she began to show an unusual flush on her cheeks. I was struck by it, for it increased her beauty, but I was also frightened. To those hectic spots was added a queer, hard brightness in her eyes. I thought at first these might be symptoms of the onset of disease. But no, she was, as ever, in perfect health. Later I came to understand. She was bewitched. How else explain that a beautiful girl, the gayest, happiest creature you ever saw, pampered all her life, brought up in a luxury *inouï,* should take to such a sullen, poverty-stricken boy?"

For some obscure reason this annoyed Aymar. He now took up Bertrand's defense, not vigorously, but to a certain extent.

As if to excuse himself, he said, "Why haven't you communicated with her parents?"

"Well, you see," said Barral, obviously embarrassed, "she made me promise not to tell."

In love with her himself, Aymar decided. Poor fellow. And worse fool, I, to let Bertrand go on unhindered.

After an hour of this sort of desultory conversation, they rose, neither quite satisfied with the results of the conversation, and both imbued with a sense of fatality. Barral, who had begun the conversation with much hope, seeing the end approaching, could not restrain himself from crying out: "But, monsieur, isn't there something you could say to your nephew? Isn't there something you could do?"

Aymar patted him on the shoulder. "My friend, that's your

228

job. But let me warn you. Do something! And do it quick." And with that he hobbled off, feeling content that, on the one hand, if Bertrand was still a criminal, then by this last warning he had done his duty in that the young captain would be urged to some really desperate move and thus solve the whole problem; and that, on the other hand, if Bertrand was now reformed, then he had done right again by not forcing matters. But in the long run, he feared, such straddling was not likely to prove the best course. Years of shilly-shallying, however, had made straddling on the question of Bertrand a permanent habit.

Barral, watching Aymar go off, wanted to run after him and cry out: "Why do you say that? Why have you only hinted at terrible things? Come, you must help me. We must work together!"

Instead he went home and began his usual evening letter to Sophie. This was the only restful and beautiful moment of the day. Then the duplicity of his secret service was over, Bertrand faded from his mind, he concentrated on recalling exactly how Sophie had looked on such and such a day, it might be two years ago. He wanted to recall the exact dress, the color of the taffeta, the nature of the design on the ribbons that hung in garlands, from bow to bow, around the voluminous skirt. He wanted to recall the precise words of their conversation that evening, and puzzled his mind to find quotations from his letter of that night.

All that was back in the past and impossible to lay one's hands on, but it was surprising how suddenly things would leap out of the dark and stand before one's eyes as if they had happened only yesterday.

Reliving the past, thus, he had all the pleasure of wooing Sophie again and of thinking his love returned. His memory was naturally good. He did almost all his spy work by word of mouth and memory, and thus avoided keeping papers that might furnish incriminating evidence.

Late at night when he had finished his missive, he went out and posted it. Then it occurred to him: Was there really such an address? And did she live there? If there was actually such a number on the street, then the likelihood was that she had told the truth.

He went tramping through endless silent and chilly streets to the indicated address. The distance was considerable, but he did not mind. At last he found the place. The number was correct. Which was their apartment? he wondered. He crossed the street and looked up. All the windows were dull black squares, dark against the stone work. To the side there was a narrow passageway. Perhaps their window fronted in that direction? No. Everything was dark. They were probably asleep. Asleep. In one bed. Side by side. Or not asleep—lying awake in the dark—

He almost groaned aloud with pain. At that moment a faint glow came from the base of the building. Behind that half-subterranean window someone had lit a candle. He had been heard and people were going to open the window and examine. He was about to flee. But no. The window remained closed, and still aglow from the candlelight that filtered through a dense white curtain, probably a piece of sheeting.

Supposing that was their room? He bent down and peered. One could see through into an interior, but so faintly that nothing was recognizable. There were voices. They came through a slit made for ventilation. Male and female, it seemed. But they spoke in such whispers that it was hopeless to determine whose voices they were or what they were saying.

Emotionally exhausted, Barral left at last. The candle still burned. "Bah!" said Barral, "probably a mother and her sick child." But he didn't believe it. He felt certain, on the contrary, that that was their window. He reeled through the streets like a drunkard. His mind was in a turmoil. "I mustn't ever do this again," he said to himself, "if I were seen, it would be up with me. And after all the precautions I've taken not to be suspected as a spy!"

Yes, behind that curtained soupirail, they lay. The evening's embraces had tired them. They slept.

Suddenly Bertrand awoke. He was frequently a light sleeper. The slightest noise outside would rouse him. He lay, wide awake, hoping for sleep to take him back again.

The room was dark and cool but he could not find any sleep in himself. He tossed about, annoyed. His body was on fire.

230

She heard him and turned around. "Can't you keep quiet?" she said impatiently. Every cell of her body ached for slumber.

He sighed.

Thereupon her pity was aroused. "You poor child," she said compassionately, and put her arms around him. They kissed. He nipped her ear playfully. They held each other tightly embraced. "Please…" he murmured, and was annoyed at himself for asking. Why had he done that?

"If you must," she said, resigned. "It's on the table."

Angered at himself, and at her for acquiescing, but incapable at this point of restraining himself, he rose and lit a candle. The sharp blade of the knife flashed orange.

He uncovered her. There was scarcely a portion of her body that had not one or more cuts on it. The older ones had healed to scars that traversed her dark skin with lines that were visibly lighter than the surrounding area. The newer ones were angry welts of red, or hard ridges of scab. In the candlelight the latter were like old jewelry or polished tortoiseshell.

Suppressing a moment's hesitation, he bent over her body…The blood welled up, ruby-red. He put his mouth to it at once and drank greedily. His lips made ugly sucking noises, as he strove to extract all the blood he could.

Her fingers played with his hair, meanwhile. "Poor little baby," she murmured. Her mind reeled, filled with unsubstantial pictures, with broken threads of unconnected thoughts.

Now they were locked in each other's arms again.

Sleep separated them at last. They lay exhausted, their limbs still entangled, the sweat of their embraces drying in the night breeze. The candle burned unheeded, until the flame expired in a mass of molten wax.

In the morning, when daylight woke them up, he was a different person. He looked with horror upon his deeds. With his fingertips he touched her wounds and wept.

"I'm killing you," he moaned. "What a fate!" He slapped his brow with the palm of his hand, that hairy palm.

She laughed through her own tears. "Don't be foolish, Bertrand. Besides, I'd gladly die for you." An inexplicable stab of pleasure accompanied the thought of death.

He would not be consoled. "If I had any humanity, I'd kill myself, before I'd as much as scratch you."

"Don't, Bertrand! Don't! What would I do if you left me?"

His fingers sought for the latest wound he had made. When he had found it, he shut his eyes lest he be tempted to look at it. "I did that?" he murmured. "I did that. How could you let me? Why did you not kill me at once?"

"Don't be foolish, Bertrand," she repeated, and erased his dark thoughts with kisses.

The sun was out and it was time for pleasant thoughts. The night was over and the crazy thoughts of the hours of darkness must return to the graves which exude them.

The concierge came running out to them as they were crossing the cobbled courtyard.

"Madame," she cried, "a letter for you."

"A letter?" Bertrand wondered.

"Yes, a letter," said the concierge, and smiled at them.

Sophie recognized the hand at once. It was only Barral's daily letter.

"It's nothing," she answered the suspicion on his face. "You may read it, or better still, throw it away."

"Shall I?" he asked, his hands about to tear the letter in half.

"If you don't, I shall, so that's settled.—Now let's have breakfast. I'm famished." The sound of the paper tearing was pleasant to their ears.

They were both in high spirits at breakfast. He talked of what he would do when the war was over. He would return to the study of medicine. "Uncle has plenty of money," he said.

"And me. Haven't I any money?" she returned. "Father will give me millions, if I just say so. Besides, it will all be mine some day anyhow. We'll go and live in my room at home." She thought of her pretty bed, with the azure canopy. There were times when she missed the polished luxury of her former surroundings, the paintings, the rugs, the colorful marbles, the bronze and gold and grained woods smoothed to the luster of a mirror.

"Perhaps," he thought aloud, "I could learn to control myself, or find someone else for my bad moments, and keep my love pure for you."

That hurt her. Hurt her down deep in her intestines. She realized at once, as if she had experienced such a sensation before, that she was jealous of this "someone else" who was to give Bertrand a part of herself.

"Don't say that. Never say that," she said softly. "You are all mine."

"But—" he began.

"Hush," she cautioned. She brushed the picture of another girl and Bertrand from her mind and returned to her former thought: That then was jealousy, terrible pain that made all food suddenly distasteful. And she thought of Barral. "Poor soul," she said. "Is that what he suffers?" At that moment she would have been capable of giving herself to him, of giving herself to everyone who might have needed her. To the whole battalion that looked at her with lusting, hungry eyes. All those bearded and unshaven faces that wanted the smoothness of her cheeks. All those hard arms that craved to crush her soft body. All those calloused, dirty hands that wanted to touch her with intimate caresses.

And all that love for the whole male world that welled up in her rose and bunched itself into her lips. And she leaned across the little table and planted it full on Bertrand's mouth. He sensed the gift. He sensed that her love, which she might have given to anyone, to everyone, that greater love she had chosen to bestow upon him and upon him alone. He was deeply stirred and left speechless amid the maelstrom of his emotions.

"Never, never speak of another to come between us, Bertrand," she said. "You do not know how that hurts."

"I know," he replied, "only—"

"Hush. Was it not I who first offered myself to you? Was it not I, again, who bought the knife, because you were afraid your teeth were too painful? There is nothing I would not do for you."

In the silence that followed, she thought suddenly of her father and mother. Had they loved each other that way? Had her mother ever offered up her body to her father in this manner? The thought had poignancy to it. Somehow she could not reconcile the picture her mind called up. She could not believe that her father and mother had ever shared a bed. And yet they must have, at least once. But it could not have been such a bed as she and Bertrand shared, down in a cellar, a miserable couch so narrow that their bodies must be intimate all night. Did her father and mother ever wake up to find the candle burned down to the neck of the wine bottle in which it was stuck?

Chapter Sixteen

They had clasped each other as two children will in the dark when they are oppressed by the fate which they sense must overtake them some day or other. And they continued to cling to each other with all the despair of drowning people. They felt themselves being sucked under, into that eternal night of nothingness which follows the brief day of life. Their souls were too weak to have a tight grasp on their bodies, and it was as if, knowing how soon death was to rob them of this delightful housing of flesh which protected the weak flame of their spirit, it was as if knowing that this life must be brief, no matter how long it lasts, for anything which must come to an end is brief, that they laced their arms about each other and would not let go, that they put their lips together and feared to sunder them lest something slip between, that they desired nothing, night and day, but he to inflict pain and she to feel her body bruised and cut, so as to realize keenly at every moment that they were truly alive, alive at least in this little moment of now, no matter how dead or deprived of humanity they must be in all the future moments to come.

A night of love, a day of companionship, did not satisfy them.

Their thoughts played on with each other during their moments of rest. He grew insatiable. Her body was a fountain of blood to him. And it was as if her body responded to his needs. She grew heavy, sultry with blood, like a nursing mother with milk.

When she walked her body swayed. She could not control the movement of her hips. It was as if she still had him in her arms, and indeed in the bruises on her body she still carried the feel of him. And that is why, when she was alone, he being on duty where she could not follow, which was rare for they clung together even at the ramparts, she would bring her arm to her mouth and kiss some place he had hurt.

Curiously, but comprehensively, this perpetual intimacy allowed them to face the prospect of death with courage. She frequently begged him, now that the Versailles troops were surrounding the city and waging vicious warfare against the Communards, not to expose himself to danger.

But when he asked her, "What will you do if I am shot?" she answered, "Shoot myself, too." And neither of them quailed. They could die together. Whatever there was beyond the grave, even if it was nothingness, would at least be shared. The thought of outliving or being outlived would have been intolerable.

Such was their mood that they often spoke of committing suicide by jumping off a roof while holding each other in their arms. Such a death would not really have been death, it would only have been a wilder form of caress than any they had hitherto practiced.

She had permanently affiliated herself with the 204th battalion as assistant cantinière, in which function the men were more than ever fond of her. She fitted in well in her new position. She had grown, to a certain measure, coarse. Her lips were heavier and curved in a loose pout as if about to expel a curse. Her abundant hair, on which she had formerly lavished much attention, she now gathered together into a hasty knot. Her complexion was no longer so much tan as swarthy. But these changes had not diminished her beauty, they had only altered it.

There was a kind of desperation in the air. One could sense the approach of the end. At this point many of the Commune began to lose their heads. Courbet had the great bronze Vendôme Column, glorifying Napoleon's victories, torn down. A great munition factory was blown up by a traitor. Many lives were lost. In this atmosphere of violence it is not strange to note that a scientific delegation was appointed whose chief task appears to have been the collection of inflammable materials, petroleum, sulphur, dynamite, resin, along with quantities of rapid fuses, all of which were to serve to burn Paris to the ground in case it was about to be taken.

And worse still. Gas bombs, designed to asphyxiate, or others made to spatter acid, were manufactured, though with little success. Rings, each with a small rubber sac of poison and a tiny hollow needle, were designed to be used by prisoners against their captors, a little scratch being sufficient to slay. Few of these were actually made and none appears to have been used, but if little came of these devices, they remain impressive signs of the desperate condition of the Communards.

And the two in their little basement room could feel the strain more than others. Bertrand especially. The scent of death all about made him want to howl. He would find his throat forming itself to let out a wild cry, but he would catch himself in time. His mind kept repeating, "I'm cured. I'm cured," but he knew that he wasn't and he knew that it was only at the expense of Sophie that he kept the beast within him at bay.

He would wake up at night and say to himself: "Don't let me weaken! God! Don't let me weaken!" He repeated all the snatches of prayers he knew, and called upon all the saints. At last, despairing, he would seize the knife. Sophie slept on. Of late she did not always wake up when he made demands upon her. In her sleep her body gently pressed itself against his. She moved sluggishly, her muscles relaxed, as if actuated by a dream.

He would find himself dissatisfied almost at once. Then a mad longing would course through him to have done with these little sips and proceed to the central fountain, there in the soft part of the neck, and feel again that sensation of being inundated with a warm flood as the blood comes spurting from the carotid artery.

Then he would shake his head madly. "No, no!" he would cry behind his clenched teeth. "O God! keep me from that!" And all night would be a long struggle to crush a desire that rose again and again, stronger after each fall. Again and again he would attempt to slake his mad thirst, but the amount he could secure was insufficient. "I'm killing her slowly anyhow," he raged, "why not have done with it!"

Once, indeed, so overpowering was the desire of his teeth to get at that throat that he leaped out of bed, hastily donned his clothing and ran out. "If I must," he thought, "at least let it be someone else than she."

Within a few blocks he ran into a man. He found his hands and feet leaving the ground, propelling his body through the air. He found his teeth seeking for a throat. The man fought with a sudden strength summoned up by terror. Guttural cries, choked snarls escaped from Bertrand. His clothes hampered him. He knew he had done wrong to put them on. He found himself floundering on slippery cobblestones, a heavy knee pressed into his stomach, and a fist crashing through the defense of his arms and beating against his head.

When Sophie woke up, late, she thought at first that Bertrand had only hurried out to buy something for breakfast. But when a considerable time had passed she began to feel troubled. Had he gone out to join his battalion at the fight now raging near the Porte Saint-Cloud? Mme Labouvaye, the concierge, had not seen Monsieur. Sophie ran to the headquarters of the battalion. The shop that had served as such was closed. No one could give her any information. She dashed here and there, looked into every canteen, interrogated every official-looking person. Pursued a dozen misdirections.

Evening found her exhausted mentally and physically. Her hopes aroused a hundred times only to be destroyed as often. At last, footsore and hungry, but careless of her comfort, she returned to their room. As she crossed the court, she was certain that he would be there, waiting for her. But the room was dark and empty, and the disorder was precisely the same she had left.

238

She promised herself better success in the morning and lay down to find rest. But sleep would not come to her. She missed the body beside her. She missed the reassurance of Bertrand's presence. She found herself doing what she had not done for several months: carving the darkness into terrifying shapes, peopling the shadows with crouching figures about to leap upon her. She could see them moving into positions of advantage, waiting for an opportune moment to leap at her throat and kill her. Why was not Bertrand here to guard her? "Bertrand, Bertrand!" she moaned.

Would she never see him again? Was this the end? Were they to go to separate graves? Would she then truly lie in the Cimetière Israélite? And would the picture she had so often dreamt come true? Her parents weeping beside her coffin. Barral swearing vengeance. She could actually hear the weeping. Yes, she could almost hear Barral's words. And now they had lowered her into the ground. She could hear, yes, now she could hear, could hear distinctly the earth thrown spadeful after spadeful on the lid which covered her.

She rose in horror. Sweat covered her body. She gasped for breath.

How stupid of her! It was only someone walking about in the room overhead. Some laborer in heavy, hobnailed boots.

She heard another sound. This, at last, was Bertrand coming home. Finally! Thank God! The footsteps grew louder. She was about to cry out, "Bertrand!" Then they turned off, diminished down a long neighboring corridor. Extinguished.

The swarming darkness closed in on her again. She rose and lit the candle. There was only a little stub left and it soon burned out. The petroleum lamp had a wick that wouldn't turn up. Besides, the supply of oil in the base was down to a smear.

The candle flickered its last. Sophie had nothing left but a few matches and these she husbanded, lighting them at long intervals. Inevitably they must be used up. But somehow she fell asleep. In her moist, warm hand the sulphur heads of the matches softened and coalesced. She woke up in the morning with a mass of evil-smelling chemicals adhering to her palm. There was no sign of Bertrand.

239

He had, as a matter of fact, been put under arrest. Since he was a soldier and his captor a soldier, his case was left for the court-martial.

That morning as Aymar was walking he met Colonel Gois. Aymar congratulated him. "I saw, a few days ago, that you were nominated president of the new courtmartial."

"As it happens," Gois replied, "we are having our first session. There are some interesting cases to be tried. Several traitors, a madman who tried to bite a comrade—"

At this Aymar interrupted: "A madman who tried to bite a comrade?"

"I know nothing about it," said Gois, "but if the case interests you, come along."

On the way he revealed his intentions to Aymar: to reestablish the severity of the revolutionary tribunal. "What is the sense of a court-martial, if it is to be a mere board of pardon?" he complained. "The court-martial is losing its revolutionary character of rapidity and severity, and the fault is in the public that comes to the session. We should function behind closed doors and kill five innocents before allowing one traitor to escape. I guarantee you our military reverses would cease at once.

"Yes," he continued, "the mistake we made was to abolish the guillotine. We threw away there the most valuable tool revolutionaries have ever had at their disposal."

He was not particularly concerned about Aymar's interest in the madman who was to be tried that afternoon. Perhaps his mind was full of other matters. The hundreds of confiscated sheets, pillow cases, etc., all of the finest linen damask, and the fine furniture, etc., which he had had transported to London, to be there a kind of nest egg in case the Commune should fail. Or else he was wondering about his speculation in garlic, of which there was serious shortage. Or are these tales mere anti-Communard inventions? Who can say? Certain it is that his closest friends had little respect for anything pertaining to him except his throat, which was capable of accepting without a murmur as much live brandy as he cared to throw down it, and that was by no means little.

240

Absent-mindedly he fussed about his papers and finally furnished Aymar with a pass to see the madman. "*Il est permis au citoyen Galliez de communiquer avec le Bertrand Chaillet détenu pour la cour martiale à la prison du Cherche-Midi,*" signed it and passed it over to Aymar who, seeing the name, was now certain of the matter.

"Just the addition of an *h* after the *c* was enough to hide him from me," he thought. Aloud he said: "There's a good deal I can tell you about this man. I should like to write out a little report for you."

"It will be welcome," said Gois. "But I'm not sure that there will be time to go into the matter very deeply. In cases of that kind I like to show clemency to balance my severity in more important matters."

Aymar hurried off to see Bertrand. A National Guardsman brought him to a small room, not originally intended for a cell. Inside, seated on a cot, was Bertrand, his features almost unrecognizable behind purple blotches. A strait-jacket immobilized his arms. He did not raise his head from its sunken position.

"Bertrand," said Aymar softly.

"You, uncle?" Bertrand asked without moving.

"Bertrand," Aymar repeated with compassion. "You, here? What has happened?"

"Nothing. Leave me here. I want to die."

"Where is Mlle de Blumenberg?"

"I don't know. I don't want to know. I must never see her again. I have done enough harm in my life."

"Is she safe?"

"I hope so. But I know that I ruined her life. Do you recall when you used to give me raw bloody meat and said it was for my anemia? Well, I know now that it was just a ruse. But it didn't work."

"What are you implying?" Aymar urged. Under his interrogation, Bertrand rapidly explained Sophie's sacrifice for him. He concluded:

"Don't try to save me any more and don't let Sophie know I'm here, for I cannot trust myself. It is best that I die."

"I have long had no intention of saving you. Bien au contraire. If you had not assured me, at Piepus that time, that you were cured,

I can tell you I would have had you then where you now are. And I shall do my best to see that you do not escape this time. Good-bye, Bertrand."

"Good-bye, uncle," the boy

Aymar's heart was wrung. Could he really leave the lad thus? He was not only sacrificing Bertrand, but all those hours of instruction, all those long years of training. Could one forget such things utterly, and separate thus with so few words?

"Isn't there something I can do for you?"

No answer.

"Take a message to Sophie?"

Bertrand shook his head vigorously. Then he said: "Say good-bye to Françoise, she was always good to me, and to my mother, if you ever see her."

Aymar, his eyes misted with tears, limped out and took a cab home. "Yes, let this be the end of it," he thought, and set to work at once to prepare a damnatory report.

He had purposed, at first, to confine himself to a rapid sketch of the implicating crimes. He had intended no more than an outline. But he was carried aw subject and allowed his personal feelings a sha brief. It was a ridiculous thing to do and he was ashamed of it. But these matters had fermented in him too long. They burst through the cold phrases in which would have liked to set down the plain narrative of a criminal career. Willy-nilly, he was swept away by a flood of emotion that translated itself into a heated harangue, full of misplaced rhetoric, but a natural rhetoric nevertheless, for it flowed from his pen-point as if it were born there and not in his brain.

And as he went on he warmed to his subject. He permitted himself remarks that were blasphemous to the minds of the Commune, he developed arguments that at this point in history were plain heresy. Then he cast aside all fear and launched himself into his subject with all the fire and vigor he could command.

After all, there was a point to be gained. Colonel Gois had said: "In cases of that kind I like to show clemency to balance my severity in more important matters." This must on no account

242

be permitted. Bertrand must be sentenced to death. To this end Aymar made a display of all his research, attempted to show that the punishment of burning at the stake which the Church had meted out was not to be rejected as mere medieval cruelty, but to be examined on its own merits.

"The vast strides of our generation in the conquest of the material world must not mislead us into thinking that when we have plumbed the physical world to its depths we shall thereby have explained all there is to explain. The scientists of a former day strove mightily to fathom the depth of the spiritual world and their successes and conquests are all but forgotten.

"Who can estimate what thanks we owe to those courageous priests of old who went into the forbidding Druidic forests and with bell and book and swinging censer, exorcised the sylvan spirits, banished the familiars, expelled the elementals, cast out the monsters and the devils of old Gaul? Who can estimate the debt we owe to them for helping to slay all the strange and unnatural beasts that formerly cowered in every dark cranny and recess, under ferns and moss-covered rocks, waiting to leap out at the unwary passer-by who did not cross himself in time? Not all of these monsters were equally evil, but all constituted unwelcome interferences in the destiny of man.

"If today the lonely traveler can walk fearlessly through the midnight shadows of the silent forests of France, is it because of the vigilance of our police? Is it because science has taught us to be unbelievers in ghosts and monsters? Or is not some thanks due the Church, which after a millennium of warfare succeeded at long last in clearing the atmosphere of its charge of hidden terror and thus allowed for the completer unfolding of the human ego? We who have profited thereby should not allow pride to blind us to our debt. Future clearer thinkers will support my contention.

"Yes, if today we feel safe from the diabolic terrors that afflicted the benighted folk of former days, let us not take pride as if we had merely outgrown a childish fear. Let us examine the matter without bias.

"Evil exists. And evil breeds evil. The horrors and cruelties of history link hands down the ages. One deed engenders another, nay, multiplies itself. One perpetrator of crime infects another. Their kind increases like flies. If nothing resists this plague, it will terminate with the world a seething mass of corruption.

"Let us beware of judging hastily. The Catholic Church is said to have burnt 300,000 witches, until the world exclaimed in horror: 'What gross superstition! There are no witches.' And truly there were none. At any rate there were no more.

"But now the bars have been let down, the doors are opening wide and monsters of old, in new disguises, will soon throng the world. The new terror will not lurk in the forest but go abroad in the marketplace; it will not attack lonely wayfarers but will seize the throat of nations. There will be wars such as the world has never seen, and inhumanities such as no one has dreamt of. And the dark blood of life will flow in cataracts, and the cries of those 300,000 witches will be only as the twitter of birds to the massed groans of dying mankind."

Flushed with labor, for he had written in great hurry in order to finish before the trial, and flushed too with the embarrassment that comes of having uncovered secret places in his heart, he ran off to the building set aside for the councils of war, at the corner of the rue du Cherche-Midi and the rue du Regard.

Colonel Gois was visible, but busy. It was past seven o'clock and the session of the court-martial was to begin at nine in the evening. Colonel Gois took Aymar's brief, asked a few questions which Aymar parried as best he could, saying, "You'll find everything in there," and having received the colonel's assurance that the document would be read, he left.

Well, that was over and done with. If it was a mistake, it was now irreparable. And in that fact there was more consolation than in debating whether to do or no. Relieved, Aymar took a seat in the large uninteresting hall in which the trials would soon take place. For the moment the room was empty. A few lamps suspended from the ceiling attacked the gloom. The shadows retreated slightly and massed themselves in the corners as if to gather their strength and return a swarm of bats, to strangle the feeble lights.

244

A few National Guardsmen, bayonets fixed, saw to the orderly seating of the public which began to fill the benches. Ladies, expensively gowned, took the first row.

Finally Gois entered and immediately the cases were brought up. Minor matters: theft, lack of respect, brawls. Then came the meat of the evening. Jean-Nicolas Girot, Captain of the 74th, accused of insubordination by the chef d'escadron, Gandin. The lawyers argued. Then Girot spoke.

He admitted the facts. His company had been on duty at the Porte Maillot under fire from the enemy for three days. It had been promised them that they were to be relieved. The men were weak from constant exertion and from lack of food. But no sooner had they been relieved and marched off than they were ordered back. "In my conscience," Girot concluded his defense, "I found the right to disobey. As chief of my company, I arrogate all responsibility."

President Gois suspended the audience for a moment and deliberated with his associate judges. They soon produced a verdict which Gois read aloud. It was a succession of Attendu que... attendu que, that is to say "inasmuch as the accused admits the charge; inasmuch as the Porte Maillot is where the enemy is now concentrated; inasmuch as the political past of the accused, no matter how glorious (Girot was an old Republican), cannot excuse him from fulfilling the military duties he has accepted to perform, etc., etc. We declare the accused guilty of having refused to march against the armed rebels of Versailles.

"Wherefore the court, after due deliberation, condemns Citizen Girot, Jean-Nicolas, to the punishment of death, which shall take place—"

In a loud voice the condemned man cut across Gois' readings with a sharp, impertinent, "Thank you, gentlemen."

Another case was rapidly called up lest the public demonstrate. And a public once invited to demonstrate takes to that weapon all too readily.

It was past midnight before Bertrand was brought up. The room by that time had become infernally hot. The lamps smoked. The air was stifling. The spectators squirmed a little impatiently. The sight

245

of Bertrand did not move them. There was nothing unusual about him, neither his hangdog expression nor his hands tied behind his back, the strait-jacket having been reinoved.

The case was rapidly reviewed. The single witness, his arms in bandages, his face badly slashed by tooth and nail, was invited to recount his story. Then Bertrand was asked for a statement, but refused to make any. By agreement both sides had dispensed with lawyers, so that matter was soon concluded.

After a moment's deliberation, President Gois rose to speak. Aymar's heart began to pound for the president was holding up Aymar's script as if he were about to read from it, and indeed he did read from it, but in a way that altered Aymar's intention at every point.

"Here," he concluded after a rapid and attenuated summary of the facts given by Aymar, "is a case that would have been led to the stake in former days. The Catholic Church, ladies and gentlemen, burnt three hundred thousand of these. Think of it! Three hundred thousand people whose only crime was that they were afflicted with a disease, people, therefore, who should have been handed over to competent doctors, not to the executioner. The Commune, enlightened and guided by science, does not propose to confuse physical or mental illness with deliberate violation of social laws. Indeed, it is the aim of the Commune eventually to treat all criminals as if they were sick people and cure them by the application of medicine and hygiene. And that fortunate day will come, once the rebels of Versailles and their allies, the priests and monks, have been exterminated.

"It is that brood that for centuries has fostered the belief that only their crosses and prayers, their torture chambers and their flaming fagots and stake, could hold the devil in check. And this young man, deluded by I know not what disease into thinking himself a mad dog, would have been an example for them to exhibit as proof of the existence of the devil and of the need of priest and aristocrat to hold the Evil One in cheek.

"We deal differently. Here is no self-interest seeking to oppress a people and hold it in subjection by means of enforced and cunningly

246

inculcated ignorance and superstition. Here is progress, freedom and intelligence. This court therefore agrees that inasmuch as the accused is suffering from an illness which leads him to go mad at times; that inasmuch as he shows by his present demeanor that his violence is only temporary; that inasmuch as this court tries only crimes and does not propose to cure disease by jail or execution, that this court therefore decrees that the accused be turned over to the infirmary at the prison of La Santé for treatment, and there be guarded until cured.

"Read in public audience of the court-martial…" etc.

"Talk! Talk! Talk!" Aymar muttered in disgust at seeing his own words quoted against him. "Talk one way and talk another. All words, words, fighting words, and none of us knowing anything."

There was in truth a great deal of talking that day. That same evening in the Hôtel de Ville the "American" Cluseret, formerly head of military affairs, was being tried for high treason. The trial seemed never to want to come to the point. The committee, formed for the purpose of judging this professional revolutionist who had brought his sword to the support of a dozen wars in as many countries of the old and new world, was in the majority for freeing the general, but even more anxious to employ this occasion to attack the minority that had framed the charge against him.

There were endless speakers, there was endless bickering. Every detail of the events of the last few weeks had to be gone over and gone over again.

It was late at night. Vermorel was speaking. The inquest, he declared, had shown the falseness of the charge against Cluseret, but "the ease with which we can arrest a military chief when he seems to be doing our cause harm, that is the important point of this trial. That, it seems to me, is one of the best symptoms of the soundness of the Commune, the best proof of its strength!"

A pale, agitated man had come into the hall. He held a telegram in his hand and waited impatiently for Vermorel to cease, but as the latter showed every sign of launching out into a long address, he cried out, annoyed:

"Make it quick!"

247

Everyone turned to look at the rude interrupter. It was Billioray, member of the Central Committee. In the silence that followed he ordered all unimportant officers out and all doors closed. Then he read the telegram. It was from General Dombrowski and announced that the Versailles troops had forced an entrance into the city and were pouring in.

The trial was resumed, but the speakers had their minds elsewhere. No more flowing orations. In short phrases the matter was concluded and brought to a vote. Twenty-eight to seven voted for immediate release. Cluseret was now admitted to hear the decision.

He thought it incumbent to say a few words, but no one listened. The hall emptied itself. The days of talk, talk, talk were over.

The members of the Central Committee departed into the night. Some were thinking of their families or of themselves, and these hastened to find safer quarters. But others, heroic to the end, went to superintend the throwing up of barricades, and sought in a last desperate resistance to die for their cause.

Chapter Seventeen

At a later period Aymar added several postscripts to his defense of Bertrand Caillet, known as Bertrand Chaillet of the 204th battalion of the National Guard. We have quoted elsewhere part of one to the effect that the uprising of the Commune was due to a kind of infectious disease. The following paragraphs, too, are of interest:

"After the trial and conviction of Bertrand, Colonel Gois returned my manuscript.

"'Mon cher M Galliez,' he said, 'there are ideas in this thesis of yours which you would have done better not to express, and that is why I am returning this to you. Destroy it. Such things are dangerous.'

"I replied stiffly, for his plagiarism of my work had annoyed me not a little and his present schoolmasterish reprimand struck me in a sensitive spot: 'They seem to have been good enough for you to have used,' I said; 'but you are right. I have noticed myself that the Commune is afraid of ideas. However, I have never allowed timidity to restrain me from exercising that freedom of thought and expression which an earlier, and more successful, Commune once procured for us.'

"To my surprise, for I knew his intransigence, he smiled and put his arm around me. 'Come, Aymar, you really don't seriously believe all the things you wrote there, do you?,

"As a matter of fact, I didn't and yet I did, so I answered evasively: 'And what if I do?'

"'Hm,' he said. 'And are you going to be a priest?'

"'Perhaps,' I answered.

"'You? Aymar Galliez? You in a soutane with a cross hanging over your belly? No, I can't believe it!' He laughed.

"We had a few words of rather friendly discussion. Knowing me of the party, he was unwilling to be too severe but he warned me to be careful of speaking out of turn. Indeed, he, himself, was a dangerous man, and he is one of those whom I have set down as infected by Bertrand, and he was to prove it shortly.

"I did not think then that I was to see *him* under a soutane, and with a cross hanging over his belly, sooner than I was to find myself in such attire."

This rather curt conclusion to the fate of Gois in Aymar Galliez' script is readily expanded, for the history of the last few days of the Commune has been meticulously compiled.

The reader will recall that the delegate to the ex-Prefecture of Police had arrested many people, especially of the clergy, to keep as hostages. The avowed and widely published threat was that the Commune of Paris would kill two hostages for every one of their party shot by the government of Versaillles.

The chief purpose of the Commune, however, seems to have been to intimidate Adolphe Thiers to return Blanqui, who was being held a prisoner by the Versaillists. The captive Archbishop of Paris, threatened with death unless Blanqui was returned, himself wrote a letter to Thiers, in which he pleaded that Blanqui be exchanged for himself. Among other things he said that Blanqui, the Communist, was of no value to the Commune and not to be feared, for the Commune followed none of his ideas. "If he were associated with the Commune, far from being a help, he would only be a new element of discord in the party."

But Thiers refused. The efforts of the American Ambassador failed, as did the efforts of many others. Some Communards claimed that Thiers wanted the archbishop killed so as to rouse the populace against the Commune. This seems really far-fetched, and if the Commune suspected as much, nothing was easier than not to slay the archbishop. But perhaps it was too late to exercise clemency. The Versailles army was marching on Paris. A gate was taken, the army poured in, barricades were thrown up. Terrific street-fighting ensued. Every window might conceal a Communist with a gun, fighting like a cornered rat. This last week was one of no mercy.

There is such a thing as a drunkenness that comes from a surfeit of bloodshed. The mob of Paris, outraged by endless murders, howled, but only for more blood, like a man drunk with liquor who, while lying wretched and puking under the table, still craves another drink and yet another.

On the 24th of May, on the third day of street-fighting, a firing squad had come to the prison of La Grande Roquette and demanded six hostages, among them the archbishop, to be executed immediately. For what? It was too late now for a dramatic warning to Versailles to release Blanqui. This was the end. The army of Versailles, circling like a python, was slowly crushing the Commune to death. The ribs of the city were cracking. The air was full of flying death. "While we are still in possession of the archbishop, let us execute him. Tomorrow may be too late." So the Communards thought.

On the 25th, Clavier, the commissaire who had been in charge of the Piepus affair, came to take the banker, Jecker, out of his cell. The director of the prison wished to see an order before he would consent to release Jecker. Clavier had none, but being of a compliant nature, he wrote one out in the spot and signed it, too. The director accepted the paper at the point of a pistol and found the combined argument exceedingly valid. The banker, who was suspected of having made and concealed millions, had actually

251

been ruined in his Mexican speculation by his fellow bankers, for there is no more loyalty of caste among capitalists than in any stratum of society, although more power for ill and good.

Clavier marched out with his prisoner, and after a fairly long walk, found a quiet and convenient spot, placed his captive against a wall, and while the latter pleaded softly, "Don't make me suffer," the order was given to fire. Some gamins of the neighborhood amused themselves by kicking the dead body.

Curiously, the firing was heard by Colonel Gois, who happened to be passing along an adjoining street. He felt this to be a kind of poaching on his special province, he being the head of the court-martial. The two thereupon agreed to join forces.

Clavier and he first had lunch, then they met by appointment and proceeded once more to the Roquette prison. Revolvers were loosened in the holsters and a list of prisoners demanded. The director had learnt his business by this time and complied at once.

Gois read out the names and marked down fifty, ten being clericals (four of them monks arrested at the Piepus comedy), forty being guards and agents of Imperial days. Fifty. That was all he wanted. He did not have men enough to handle more.

In the prison there was much commotion. The inmates had seen seven go to their death and were frightened. To reassure them and obviate resistance, the guards repeated that this was to be a mere change of prison. Many believed. "We are going to take you to the mairie of Belleville, because they have no more bread here for so many prisoners." Moreover, the number of names called out was in itself reassuring. One, even six, might be placed before a firing squad, but fifty!

The jailers, passing down the line, unlocked many cells from which no inmates were called out. This was done because several of the older jailers had run away and the men left did not know the prison. Thus was opened the cell in which Jean Robert was locked. His term had long expired but still he was in jail. So that though his name was not called, he thought it an excellent idea to step out as if he heard himself called. There might be a possibility of escape. For months now, he had had no news of his family. He saw men

252

hastily making bundles of their effects. He quickly snatched his own overcoat, his only possession, and ran out.

No effort was made to control the prisoners. The men were simply hustled into a line and marched off to the sound of fife and drum. Some of them were bareheaded. But most had had time to dress and to tie up a few things in a kerchief. The captive guards of Paris of Imperial days took pride in marching smartly. The priests, hindered by their soutanes, dragged behind. All around were the Fédérés, the men of the National Guard, adhering to the Commune, guns held in readiness.–Jean Robert, his limbs stiff from years of sitting on the box and months in prison, walked among the clerics.

Robert's first surprise was to note the crowds on each side of the street. The shouts of anger, the vegetables that came flying, along with kicks and fisticuffs. What was it all about? Why were they shouting: "Death to the hostages!"

"Where are we going?" he asked the monk walking beside him.

"To Golgotha," the latter answered curtly and resumed his muttered prayers. The coachman, though he had worked for years in Paris, could not recall any place with that name. He wanted more information but was a little shy of interrupting the prayers of the monk a second time.

The guards, fearing that the mob would snatch the prisoners to a sooner death, secured reinforcements from a barricade manned by the 74th battalion. From then on the way was quieter. The column moved up the rue de Paris and turned into the rue Haxo, escorted by an enormous and constantly growing mob.

"No escape for me. Well, another prison, then," Jean Robert said to himself, and resigned himself with a sigh. Indeed the number of men with guns, the number of escorting boys who had joined with the march, grew every minute. A hundred pairs of eyes were constantly fixed on every prisoner. Jean Robert shrank a little within himself. What if it were to be discovered that he was not supposed to be with this group and he were excluded? Even a change of prison was a novelty to be enjoyed.

At this moment the whole column marched through a long and

broad archway into a courtyard and past several small houses, issuing from thence onto what was half an ornamented garden, half a vegetable patch. The prisoners were bunched up against a wall at the higher end. The mob that had poured in continued to howl for the death of the hostages.

Jean Robert's slow mind began to understand. The escort of the National Guard had protected them from the brutal mob only to bring them here to die in more military style. Surprised, he shouted out, "But they are going to shoot us!" A great fear clamped itself around his heart with claws of steel. He made a move to run forward.

A guard with a far-off, dreamy expression on his face pushed Robert back roughly to the wall and held him there with the stock of his gun, while he continued to think of something else.

"But I'm not guilty! I'm —" Robert cried,

"None of us are guilty," said the young monk quietly, and sought to lay a consoling hand on him.

"But —" Robert shouted, and angrily shook off that kind hand that wished to force him gently into death. His eyes were popping out of his head. There was a lump in his throat so big that he couldn't talk without great pain. The saliva drooled from his mouth. "I don't want to die!" he exploded violently.

"Hush," said the monk. "We must all learn to die."

"But I don't want to die!" Robert cried again. Sweat was beading his brow from the terrible strain of uttering words.

Below in the garden, the soldiers were disputing about the firing. Some members of the Commune made a vain last effort to stop the crime, but it had gone too far. The public so long urged on by their leaders to shout for blood had become infected with the lust for murder. "Let's get out of here," the members of the Central Committee whispered to each other. A moment later, when the shooting began, there was not an important official in sight.

The guards left the prisoners to join the firing squad.

"Here!" Robert shouted, and was about to run after his guard who was moving away. "I'm not one of —"

He got no further. The guard, now distinctly annoyed, forced

254

him back with a vicious blow in the pit of the stomach. Robert clasped his hands over his belly, his mouth yawned for a breath which his paralyzed muscles refused to give him. In an agony of pain, he dropped to one knee.

And the guard moved off and out of range.

The monk, seeing Robert kneeling beside him, turned quietly with his fingers raised: "Ego te absolvo ab onmibus..." The formula for conditional absolution.

Robert was still struggling for air when the firing began. Some fruit trees, still half in blossom, were in the way. Soon their pretty spring foliage was torn to shreds, their branches hung broken, their bark scored and burnt. In lulls while the men reloaded, the wind brought snatches of a waltz from a nearby encampment of German occupation soldiers, who were amusing themselves out of doors in the pleasant weather.

When the victims lay in heaps, revolvers were drawn and endless coups de grâce administered. Bayonets were brought into play. Later, autopsies were to reveal bodies with sixty, seventy bullets in them and as many bayonet wounds.* Many of the firing party, too, bore wounds, inflicted by their own careless comrades.

When the execution was considered complete, Colonel Gois and Clavier investigated. They had lined up fifty men, but they counted fifty-one bodies.

Gois shrugged his shoulders: "Decidedly there's one too many."†

They did not wait to examine into the matter more carefully. There was need for hurry. Step by step, barricade after barricade, the Versailles troops were wresting the city from the Communards.

---

* These enormous figures are thus fairly credibly explained: The moaning of the great heap of dying and dead hostages would not cease. And it was impossible to tell where the sounds were coming from, so that there was nothing to do but keep on firing and stabbing until there was complete silence.

† See Laronze, *Histoire de la Commune*, p. 625, and Vuillaume, *Mes cahiers rouges au temps de la Commune*, p. 116 *et seq.*

There were still 315 hostages left at La Grande Roquette prison. On the following day a man named Ferré tried to secure them either for a firing squad or as volunteers for fighting on the barricades. But the fighting in neighboring streets was coming so close that he gave up in the midst of things and left the prison with almost every cell door open. The majority of the inmates thought themselves likely to be safer in jail than outside and for greater security proceeded to barricade themselves within their prison. Some tried to escape, and these bold ones fell into the hands of Communards who executed them at once. The next morning the marines had captured the district and the hostages were liberated.

Then began those terrible moments which were so like cataclysms of nature, like earthquakes and avalanches, that words seem incapable of describing them. The retreating Communards had set fire to various public buildings. Groups of men and some of women went about destroying the best structures in the quarters that had to be evacuated. Among these mad women who were setting fire to the best that Paris contained was Sophie de Blumenberg.

On this, the last day before the end, Sophie had not left the 204th battalion. She had taken a pair of boots from a dead boy. They fitted her small feet. Somewhere, too, she had picked up the overcoat of a Zouave uniform.

Several days before, the 204th had been called to protect the barricades of the 9th ward. The battalion was almost wiped out there, for the Versailles forces seized a barricade in the rear, rue Caumartin, and poured a deadly fire into their unprotected backs. Sixteen of the company, taken prisoners, were executed at once and within sight of the remaining few who had been able to retreat to another barricade.

The few survivors of the 204th were now standing about the mairie on the Place Voltaire, and talking about the event, as they had been ever since it had taken place. Sophie, unashamed of her love, continued to make open inquiries. Now, though no one could remember having seen Bertrand on that morning, they nevertheless added his name to the list of dead. It made the disaster the more impressive and formidable. "Dead along with the others," they commented briefly and shook their heads. They made no attempt to twit her. Their present great desire was to discover how such a calamity could have overtaken them. It seemed to them impossible that their defeat was a natural result of the chances of war. They suspected treason. And this suspicion, after lighting on any number of people, fell at last on Captain de Montfort, who had ordered them to that position, who had specified the placing of the barricades and who had left the one in the rear insufficiently manned, evidently on purpose.

As soon as the men began to build upon this supposition, they found more and more valid reasons. Three were outstanding. First, Montfort's aristocratic ancestry and demeanor, his love of cantering around on his horse in his blue and gold uniform and shouting down his orders from above, all convincing evidence of relations with Versailles. Second, his natural jealousy of Bertrand, which would be likely to lead him to treachery in an effort to erase his rival. Third, his insistence on that day, during a little altercation among the officers, that the barricades should be here and there and manned thus. Usually he had taken little part in discussions of military strategy.

To this was added a story which was true, and which someone now thought of for the first time. A few days before, Captain de Montfort had come up to the Ministry in the rue Saint-Dominique. He was slightly drunk and in an ugly mood. His wild gestures caused the guard to raise his bayonet and prevent the captain's entry. Montfort was beside himself with fury. He called down curses on the whole guard. And noticing that they were from the 204th battalion, which he knew was Bertrand's, he sneered: "The two-hundred-fourth, huh? You fellows seem to be a rare pack of scoundrels. That's a battalion that needs a good purging."

Sophie cared little about the decimation of the 204th at the Madeleine, but the fact that Barral had gotten rid of Bertrand in this fashion made her sick with grief. A grief which rapidly boiled over into a wild desire for vengeance.

It was Captain Barral de Montfort's misfortune just then to

come riding along on horseback in the direction of the barricade on Boulevard Voltaire. And Sophie, seeing him first, pointed him out with her finger, yelling: "There's the dirty traitor!" He heard her voice and reined in his prancing steed.

With cries of: "Kill him! Kill the traitor!" a dozen soldiers raced up to him, a score of arms seized him and yanked him from his saddle. He was tossed, thrown about, dragged toward the mairie, until his beautiful uniform was a mass of rags, his features lost amid bruised and swollen flesh. Sophie, catching a glimpse of him through the mob that surrounded him, opened her mouth in horror. She wanted to run away but restrained herself: "Serves him right, the traitor!" She had completely forgotten that for several months now she, herself, had been aiding Barral in precisely this sort of treachery.

The mairie was crowded with women sewing sacks to hold earth for the barricades. Ferré and Genton, two officers there, decided that a trial must be held. "It must be regular, men," they shouted over the tumult. The captain was taken out on the square, which was massed with soldiers and curious spectators. Many did not know what was happening. But they heard the cry of traitor and took it up.

It was slow business plowing through the mob with a prisoner whom everyone wished to injure. Progress was further impeded by a long line of hearses, draped in red flags, which were climbing up the hill to Père-Lachaise. "His turn now!" someone cried. And the impatient mob repeated the phrase in a hundred variations.

Genton and Ferré kept repeating to the men who barred the advance: "It's got to be regular. We must be just. The Commune has decided to bring him up before the court-martial." This assurance, and the commanding position that Genton seemed to occupy with his scarlet sash about his waist, allowed the escort and their prisoner to finally cross the square and reach the rue Sedaine.

A shop on this street had become the new headquarters of several battalions. A revolutionary tribunal was improvised on a moment's notice. Colonel Gois took charge. Genton and Ferré assumed the rôle of assessors. It was a mere parody of justice.

There was not an iota of evidence to implicate Barral de Montfort. He had been vain, yes; imperious, yes; and negligent, perhaps; but of communications with Versailles, of treachery of any kind, nothing.

The judges wished to save Montfort, whom they knew well and whose cousin Edouard Moreau was a member of the Central Committee and one of the big men of the Commune. But in the face of the mob, they did not dare proclaim him innocent. The prisoner himself would not speak, could not perhaps speak. His eyes were closed by puffy bruises; blood ran from the corner of his tightly shut mouth. He sat in impassive silence. Only once he murmured, but so low that his voice scarcely carried to the judges: "I'm innocent. Who dares call me a traitor?"

None of the judges could believe him guilty. They were, in fact, certain of his innocence, and that being the case they ought not only to have said as much, but they ought also to have extended protection to him. They did neither. True, they found him guilty only of negligence, and ordered him merely degraded from his captaincy, but they specified that he should be sent to the nearest barricade and take his share of the fighting. One of the assessors added, as a sop to the mob: "If he shows signs of cowardice, bash in his head." The hint was sufficient. And the mob saw to it that it was carried out. He was left lying for dead, in a ditch, covered with the mud and phlegm that was thrown and spat on him by the crowd. The crowd. The same crowd that barely eight weeks before had made a bonfire of the guillotine, on this same Place Voltaire, and had welcomed with wild acclamations of joy the news that the legislators of the Commune had abolished capital punishment.

But the odor of blood was in the air. The feel of approaching death roused the worst that hides in man. The Versailles troops had taken the whole left bank. They were beginning to encircle the remainder of the city still in the bands of the Commune, and wherever their assaults carried a barricade, they set up at once their temporary booths of methodic, pitiless, thorough repression: court-martial, summary execution. And their revenge was as 50 to 1.

At this crisis of the expiring Commune, it was natural that the most violent members should seize the reins of action, for at such moments the milder men think of retreat or else grow desperate along with the others. The blame for the firing of Paris will never be fixed on any one man, but it can be blamed on the Commune as a whole, and excused, if such actions demand excuse, by the strain of the moment. It was wrong to burn the treasures of Paris, valuable libraries, irreplaceable archives. It was wrong, not because these things have half the value that is placed on them, but because the burning was the mere gesture of a beaten man taking a spiteful blow at his opponent's children. Yes, if the burning of libraries, museums, archives, would abolish poverty, I'd call the exchange cheap. But this had no symbolic meaning, nor any real value.

Nevertheless, the burning was carried out with a certain amount of planning. Since the men were needed at the barricades, women were enlisted for the job. They were provided with petroleum and with torches that were formerly part of the equipment of the policemen. The job was a dangerous one, but many volunteered for it, some attracted by the ten francs a day which was the pay allotted. Of such was Épouse Jean Robert, wife of the coachman Jean Robert, who worked in the company of her two little children (two left of five), whom she could not well leave behind. Now that she was earning money, her children each held a fat cut of cervelat and nibbled on it. They had starved for months and now for once they were no longer hungry. And though their bellies rebelled against more food, they couldn't keep their teeth from wanting the feel of food again and again, as if to reassure themselves that this was true.

Others joined because they were enraged at Versailles. Their husbands had been killed, or some other great loss had struck them, and they were anxious now to deal a blow no matter how or where, but preferably against the rich, their permanent oppressors. "These things we can never have, these great mansions, these halls of fine furniture," they said, "let us burn them! They shan't have them either!"

And Sophie? She joined because she wanted to die. She joined because she itched to go mad. She joined because those of Versailles, whom she had so often aided by her information, had betrayed her Bertrand and killed him on the barricades; yes, and if only she could have been fully certain that he was dead, if she could have seen his body, she would have killed herself at once, too.

Aymar, during these terrible days, kept as much to his rooms as possible. Still he could not restrain himself at times from going out to have a look at things. He used to go up the Boulevard des Batignolles to a place where one could get a good look at Paris. A number of people used to meet there. They would watch the great fires which in the twilight changed from black and white photographs to colored lithographs. The dun smoke first took on red and orange glows and then, when night was complete, disappeared completely and one saw only flames and sparks.

The people would guess what was burning. From the distance it was hard to say. The Tuileries, the Louvre, the Palace of Justice, the Hall of Accounts, the palace of the Legion of Honor, the Palais-Royal, etc., etc. The heat of the conflagration was such that it reached out to quarters that were still being defended. There was fire at the Chateau d'Eau, fire at the Boulevard Voltaire, fire at the Grenier d'Abondance. The Seine, already red with blood, rolled through Paris like a dragon with fiery reflecting scales. Straws from the granary, papers from the records, flew burning through the air.

As the soldiers of Versailles took new positions, they organized fire squads and were assisted by the fire department which the Communards had prevented from functioning as long as they remained in charge of these districts.

While the great bulk of the city was soon in the hands of the Versaillists, the Communards still held on to a number of positions, the town hall of the 11th ward, Belleville, the Buttes Chaumont, etc.

During the night of May 27-28, the last fierce fighting took place. A terrible guerrilla retreat of the Fédérés, from tombstone to tombstone in Pére-Lachaise. Finally, a last remnant of 128 of the Communards were forced against a wall and shot. When the sun rose on the 28th, Pentecostal Sunday, the civil war was over, except for a house here and there from which still came stray shots fired haphazardly, and except for a single barricade on rue Romponneau where a lone Communard planted a red flag, and defended his position for a short time. He fled; the red flag was torn down and the tricolor hoisted.

On the other side, the side of the Versaillists who by their victory became the legitimists, the cruelty had not been any less; on the contrary, though lightly passed over by historians, their deeds were vastly more impressive.

Why drag eighty wounded men out of their beds in the hospital improvised at Saint-Sulpice and shoot them to a death which many were headed for anyhow? Why shoot the attendant doctor, Faneau, along with them, his only guilt the crime of staying to care for them?

Line them up and shoot them! At the market of Place Maubert, in the courtyard of Cluny at rue Charonne, at rue Brézin. The corpses thrown into ditches, not in small numbers, at the most fifty, as the Communards had done. That was picayune. No, in hundreds.

Then order was introduced. The rule went out: no more killings. Prisoners must be court-martialed. And they were court-martialed. The speed of killing was slightly reduced. For the courts at least took the formality of marking down names. But few escaped. For the interrogatory was brisk. No witnesses, no defense. A couple of questions and off went another group of wretches to a convenient wall.

Mistakes? Well, of course, considering the haste. Vuillaume was shot by two different squads; actually he escaped to write his famous books. Who were the two shot in his stead? – Délion wrote: "I saw him perish. His demeanor was most cowardly. He could scarcely talk for rage." How well one can understand that cowardice and that rage. Courbet, one reads elsewhere, was shot after identification. Who was that? And what was the nature of the identification?

The paper *Gaulois* came out with the story. "They arrested Billioray at Grenelle. He defended himself, writhed on the ground, begged for mercy. He was done to death where he lay." In another district, someone cried: "There goes Billioray." At once the man in question was arrested. He denied his identity vigorously. Brought before Captain Garcin, he still persisted in his denial, but a dozen witnesses were ready to swear to it. Captain Garcin asked: "Do you still deny—"

"Yes, yes!" the man screamed wildly. The whole matter was done so quickly that only a few seconds passed before the fellow was lying mortally wounded in a pool of blood. It was then, albeit a little late, that someone searched his pockets. Letters showed that he was a draper's assistant named Constant, who had had nothing to do with the Commune. But he was so badly wounded then that it was deemed advisable to finish him off.

Who was the man at Point-du-Jour who was also executed as Billioray? The real Billioray was arrested a week later and subsequently condemned to prison for life.

A Dutch traveler, unable to express himself well in French, was brought before the court-martial established at Le Châtelet. The large sums of money on his person were considered proof that he was an important Communard about to escape beyond the frontier. He was executed at the caserne of Lobau.

Varlin was executed on that Pentecostal Sunday. Arrested and tried and shot in as many minutes. So great was the crowd that the firing squad was unable to handle their rifles properly. The man remained standing. A second volley. He fell. And the crowd clapped their hands.

Aymar made no effort to escape. He walked about and saw and felt a strange exultation. "Burn!" he cried within himself at the fiery flames that leaped to the sky. "Kill!" he shouted to himself when the men lined up in front of a wall dropped to the rattle of musketry.

"I was not so wrong," he thought, and derived a curious joy from the violence raging about him. He wanted it worse. He wanted the whole world to go up in flames and blood. It wasn't worthy of being anyhow. "Rise up! Danton! Marat! Robespierre! Why aren't you here to see that the job is done right?"

Aymar soon discovered that he was talking nonsense. The

Commune shot fifty-seven from the prison of La Roquette. Versailles retaliated with nineteen hundred. To that comparison add this one. The whole famons Reign of Terror in fifteen months guillotined 2,596 aristos. The Versaillists executed 20,000 before their firing squads in one week. Do these figures represent the comparative efficiency of guillotine and modern rifle, or the comparative cruelty of upper and lower class mobs?

Bertrand, it now seemed to Aymar, was but a mild case. What was a werewolf who had killed a couple of prostitutes, who had dug up a few corpses, compared with these bands of tigers slashing at each other with daily increasing ferocity! "And there'll be worse," he said, and again he had that marvelous rising of the heart. Instead of thousands, future ages will kill millions. It will go on, the figures will rise and the process will accelerate! Hurrah for the race of werewolves!

He was thinking such things and exulting one day as he walked through the streets of the city. The executions were now over. Only arrests were being made. Bands of soldiers and police were systematically ransacking every home. Every suspect was arrested at once. The least suspicion was enough. A mailman denounced a family because it received more than its usual mail. The grocer denounced another because it bought an extra sausage. So-and-so was taken in because he didn't answer quickly enough. Another because he walked too fast, or else too slow. No reason was too insane to provoke an arrest. No excuse too slight for suspicion. In three weeks the police received 379,523 anonymous letters of denunciation.

Such events, such sights and thoughts, raised not only pity in Aymar's heart, but also a wild sense of satisfaction. The grand and delightful balm of "I told you so." This was, after all, the proof of the pudding. See those soldiers busy clearing the streets of cadavers? See those corpses being tossed into a foundation that had been prepared for the erection of a school? Or perhaps for a church, or for the building of a house in which more families of werewolves were to breed?

The police service was still unorganized, but squads of soldiers

264

saw that bodies were placed discreetly out of sight, that is to say, they were laid side by side, off the main thoroughfares, and some spades of earth thrown over them in order to conceal blood-stiffened clothes. A little earth and a little time was enough. And the race of werewolves would forget.

Homo economicus rose up amid the smoldering ruins and began to flourish again. One man went up and down street after street with a handcart. At the sight of a body, he would stop, uncover himself piously and mutter a brief prayer. Then he would wave his hat before he put it on again in order to chase away the flies, and with a rapid and practiced hand, he would strip the corpse of its footgear and throw boots or shoes into his cart. The harvest was plentiful.

Some suspicious people stopped him, questioned him. He replied politely, "For official identification," and went about his business. Aymar, seeing him, said briefly: "Eighteens, eh?" and enjoyed the startled expression on the man's face.* "A minor werewolf," he thought, and laughed to himself.

Altogether these were enjoyable days for Aymar. He saw a priest going down one street and whistled. Under the soutane and the cross, Aymar had recognized Colonel Gois, the terrible slayer of the hostages, for whom everybody was on the lookout. "I'll give him a scare, the wolf in sheep's clothing," Aymar thought, and approached him with a Latin phrase:

"Pax vobiscum! If it isn't our old pastor fidus Gois."

Gois shivered: "For God's sake, Galliez!" he pleaded in a trembling voice.

But Aymar couldn't control at least one joke: "You'd have shot yourself on sight in the old days! Well—"

Yes, these were enjoyable days for Aymar, enjoyable until he was arrested. And even to that there was some enjoyment. In groups of a hundred fifty to two hundred, tied hand to hand or elbow to elbow in rows of four, the prisoners were marched out of the cellars of the

---

* A pun in French. Resoled shoes are twice new, that is to say, "deux fois neufs," which is also two times nine or eighteen.

265

Luxembourg to the ramparts, and from there down the long road to Versailles. Day after day, until some 40,000 had made the journey.

Side by side marched old fighters, some in uniform, others in sketchy workman's costumes, hastily donned. Their faces were lined and feverish, and they all looked like drunkards, as men always do when they are unshaven. Old men stumbled along, linked to weeping children, or to girls in fantastic uniforms, who had snatched up a rifle to defend the barricades, or to gray-haired matrons, preserving their dignity with difficulty as they walked beside servants in calico and aprons, all somehow caught up in the rebellion, or by mistake numbered among the prisoners. And here and there a figure in redingote, erect, sober, a man with the face of a scholar or an artist, who had added his beautiful dreams of Utopia to the sad fiasco of the Commune.

This column of rags and remnants moved slowly along the dusty roads, beneath the fierce heat of the June sun. The guards rode on horseback, loaded guns across their knees, like gauchos conducting cattle to the slaughterhouse. Short halts were made at Sèvres and again at Viroflay. And then the troops entered Versailles through the gate of Paris.

Now came the most terrible part of the journey. The march through the regal city of Versailles, between lanes of closely packed people, a fanatic multitude, void of all sense of balance, void of pity and of intelligence. The city of the rich here demonstrated that it, too, could form mobs as mad as those of the poorest quarters of Paris. Not bare, dirty or calloused fists were shaken at the cohort, but neatly gloved hands, hands of demi-mondaines in lace gauntlets, and hands of bankers in yellow kidskin. And voices that spoke correct French howled: "No prisoners! Death, to the bandits!" and the fine-clothes rushed the line, broke through the protecting file of horsemen. And the snobs and the elegant ladies, seizing the opportunity to strike a blow without fear of retaliation, lashed out. The men prodded with their canes and the women swung their pretty parasols, or removed one glove to let their sharp nails leave furrows across the face of a young girl. "Pétrolouse!" they shouted. For though only a handful of women had actually done incendiary

266

work, all the thousand and more women arrested were suspected of having burnt a palace or two. Even the six hundred fifty children seemed demons.

And Aymar chuckled. "Moro werewolves!" he exulted, oblivious to the blows that rained upon him. "The world is full of them. How is it that I once thought they were rare? I was once one myself—and didn't know it."

Versailles couldn't accommodate all these prisoners. They were guarded in great courts, halls, cellars, under the months of cannons, while Thiers vainly thumbed his history books to find a solution to the problem of taking care of this mass. Great batches, transported in long cattle trains, were sent to fortresses on the coast and summoned separately to their trials. Scores were to be condemned to death, hundreds were to be sentenced to imprisonment for life, thousands were to be deported to tropical islands.

Chapter Eighteen

Where shall I end my tale?

This has neither beginning nor end, but only a perpetual unfolding. A multi-petaled blossom of strange botany.

Why should I not end here? Why should you want to know of the death of this werewolf rather than another? Consult your mortuary registers. Were these men and women? Or were they only disguises, disguises that concealed nameless monsters, warm incubators of infamies which would congeal your blood if brought out from their bowels into the light of day for you to see? The earth does not swallow the dead, but only their corpses which were the envelopes of their hates and crimes. These are never buried, but live on imperishable to write more gruesome records every generation.

What is it you would know? Sophie? The records of the Ministry of War, the *Gazette des Tribunaux,* inform us that she was condemned to be deported as implicated in the case of Barral de Montfort. He, himself, came to the trial, limping and his right arm

268

withered by a shot through the nerve. He wept out of one eye. The other was dry and closed. It had been eaten by flies as he lay for dead in the ditch beside the barricades of Place Voltaire.

The transport *Danaë* sailed on its interminable journey to New Caledonia, a journey lasting five months, without Sophie. Her father had brought his wealth into play and saved her from the penal colony.

His surprise had been great when he returned to Paris and learned of what had happened. Only one letter had come through to him. It was from Aunt Louise Hertzog and it told of the disappearance of Sophie. "And Barral de Montfort," Aunt Louise wrote, won't tell me where Sophie is, but obviously he must know."

The baron had read the letter with mixed feelings. But after he had considered for a while, he had decided: "Let fire burn." And thinking of his wife and of Louise Hertzog, he had added: "And let ice follow the rules of ice, if it so desires." And then he had chuckled: "Lucky Barral. If only I were in his shoes.—Ah, well, life goes on. A few years more, or maybe only a few weeks, and where will we be? Let her have her fling." He had looked across his desk to a mirror hanging on the wall and he had noted the growing whiteness of his remaining sparse hairs.—And as for Sophie, she had had her fling.

She did not know whether Bertrand was dead or alive. She did not care. She wanted to kill herself but could not summon the courage to meet death. The horror of the night was so strong in her that she took care not to go to bed too sober. Nor alone, if she could manage it.

Barral's heart was numb with pain at the sight of her conduct. He spoke to her in gentle reproach one day, when they were alone.

"Those men—" he stuttered, "those—how can you?"

"Why, you too, you poor fool!" she said gaily, and dragged him down to her on a couch.

He went home bewildered, entranced, all his old love reawakened and doubled. He forgave her everything. And next day begged her to marry him.

"What?" she asked, astounded. Then she wept. "Faithful, loyal Barral," she said. "After all I've done to you."

They set the date of the marriage for the morrow, and that gave her the necessary impetus to kill herself with gas that night.

Instead of accompanying her to the mairie for a civil wedding, he followed her body to the Cimetière Israélite at Père-Lachaise. Her father wept silently, her mother noisily. As the earth was spaded over her, Barral could not restrain his anger. He pointed his good arm to heaven and swore that he would have his revenge.

Aymar was released shortly by virtue of a non-lieu, but was summoned again at once to testify in the trial of the painter, Courbet. This bluff genius had been responsible, during the Commune, for the tearing down of the Vendôme Column, that huge bronze column surmounted by a figure of Napoleon. While the column was being pulled down to the applause of the populace, Courbet was heard to say: "That column is mad at me. I'll bet it's going to fall on me and crush me." It did not fall on him, it fell precisely on the bed which engineers had built to catch it, but it did crush him.

Before the tribunal Courbet maintained that he had acted out of no hatred for the Little Corporal, but purely out of artistic motives. "That bad imitation of Trajan's Column annoyed me. I was ashamed to think that visitors should look upon that as one of the glories of French art. And then no consideration for perspective—and that statue of Napoleon done seven and a half heads tall, just because the rules say so, whatever the actual proportions of the little fellow were."

The president said: "You were moved then purely by artistic zeal?"

And Courbet answered: "Simply that."

He was condemned to six months in jail. And the cost of reconstruction, which came to over 350,000 francs, was charged against him. He had not that much money, so his paintings were seized and sold at auction. Today they would fetch enormous sums, and even in his own better days, but for the moment his fame was in eclipse. Even with his furniture thrown in, only 12,000

270

francs were realized. And the Salon refused to exhibit him any more, holding him morally unworthy. He ran away to Switzerland, but France continued to pursue and dun him. He died at last of a broken heart. And his death was passed over without a word. Courbetism and realism were for the moment out of style. The Impressionists were in.

As soon as Aymar was free he visited Bertrand at La Santé. The head physician was dubious about the possibility of release for the prisoner.

"He is in good health, but he has moments of rage. Then he smashes the furniture or attacks the guards." The physicians saw nothing mysterious in Bertrand. He was just another case.

"Moments of rage?" said Bertrand bitterly to Aymar. "Why not? Who wouldn't in this awful hole?"

"You don't seem so anxious to die any more, do you?" Aymar asked.

Bertrand hung his head, as if an unwillingness to die were a shame. Imprisonment had made him keen for liberty and life. "Please, uncle," he begged, "get me out of here. They treat me so miserably."

Aymar smiled: "Get you out? How can I? And do you think you ought to be out? Wolves belong in a cage in the zoölogical garden."

But then he thought: "Why should this one wolf be shut up for an individual crime, when mass crimes go unpunished? When all society can turn into a wolf and be celebrated with fife and drum and with flags curling in the wind? Why then shouldn't this dog have his day too?"

"Do you ever think of Sophie?" Aymar asked.

Bertrand closed his eyes as if in deep pain. But after a second he shrugged his shoulder. "Sophie. Yes, Sophie. Or any woman, for that matter," he concluded fiercely.

"They don't provide women for the prisoners, eh?" Aymar asked.

Bertrand breathed heavily.

"Well," said Aymar, "I shall see what can be done, but first tell me.

271

Do you ever...well...change?"

Bertrand hung his head again.

"Indelicate question, eh? Like asking a girl if she—Yes, I quite understand."

Though outwardly bitter, Aymar was sorry for Bertrand. The prison of La Santé was considered a model one, being only recently constructed, but metal and stone make at best a chilly abode. The director, with whom Aymar consulted, suggested that if Aymar wished to remove his nephew to one of the pay asylums licensed by the State, the permission could probably be secured.

It was thus that Bertrand found himself transported to Dr Dumas' sanatorium at Saint-Nazaire. Aymar, himself, had gone to inspect various places and had picked out this quiet retreat. Here, if anywhere, Bertrand would be comfortable and well taken care of.

The first aspect of the place was inviting. There was a large garden with old, spreading trees shading soft lawns. An old brick wall overgrown with ivy surrounded the estate with a sufficient but gentle barrier. Within the enclosed area were a main building of handsome exterior and several smaller structures. Inside were pleasant large rooms with windows looking out onto the park.

The patients were mild creatures. They had, perhaps, a tendency to think one thought over and over again like a wheel turning idly after the belt has slipped off. Or their minds followed some strange personal logic, their thoughts were off in a world of illusion, shut up in a private universe, or sunk into a permanent stupor.

Some sat in comfortable chairs on the terrace. Others strolled on the lawn, strutted about impersonating Shakespeare or Alexander, or else chased imaginary butterflies.—When visitors came to inspect Dr Dumas' establishment, these were the patients they saw. And the sight was almost pretty: children playing in a garden.

These were the show patients. It was intended that visitors should picture their dear ones in this scene. Yes, here would be an excellent spot for Mother who has lost the ability to direct her muscles, who can no longer control her bladder or her bowels, or lift her cup to her mouth.

272

"And can you cure them?" Dr Dumas is asked.

He is a handsome fellow. Well-built, serene, with the bearded face of a distinguished scholar. He replies evasively, but majestically.

"That depends on the individual case. We can *cure* some. We can *improve all.*" He points out some of the patients sitting in the shade of the great chestnut trees and gives their case histories. It is enough to convince his visitors. And so poor Mother's last dwelling place is fixed upon. She will be better off here than at home, the sons and daughters assure themselves. "And we can see her every second Saturday afternoon and any other time upon written notice. Of course, the price is steep, but Mother is worthy of the best. Good old Mother. Some day she will be cured and we'll come and take her home again."

But there is more to this hospital than the park and these droll troubadours who are exhibited to visitors. On the top floor, for example, there are certain rooms which are never shown to visitors, and which on visiting days are locked and barred, with the windows tightly shut. If the relatives of a patient in these rooms come to visit, the afflicted one is hastily washed up and made presentable, the violent ones are drugged if necessary, and brought into a special visiting room below.

"Yes," says the doctor. "I can note improvements. Of course, to the medically untrained—" And when the relatives are leaving: "Now not too frequent visits, please. It upsets them too much emotionally. For best results our carefully worked out routine must not be broken."

In these upstairs rooms are the patients with disgusting, beastly habits. Those who pollute themselves, who make constant obscene motions, those who argue and fight acrimoniously with an imaginary foe. Those who must be prevented from killing themselves and thus robbing the doctor of his fee.

In one room you may see a poor wretch who grovels on the floor, clinging with his nails to the flooring in mortal dread lest he drop to the ceiling. He has lost all sense of direction due to a disease of the inner ear and knows not up from down nor left from right. He cannot walk, he cannot lie. There is no longer any balance in him. But Dr Dumas has succeeded in keeping this man alive for three years.

In another room is a patient who must be fed, who must have her every want attended to. She is the daughter of a nobleman. She looks like a dwarf Chinese woman. She is over forty years old and has been in various asylums all her life. She is harmless, but disgusting, and there is no sense in attempting to tend to her every want. Once in a great while, when her white-haired father drives up in his fine barouche, an orderly throws the little runt into a tub of water, she is divested of her smelly clothes, scrubbed clean and brought down to the visiting room. Her father contents himself with a perfunctory look, hands over a check and leaves. He has heard of people paying through years for the care of a patient who has long departed to a better world and he is determined not to be taken in.

Elsewhere in these garret abodes are epileptics given to violence and horrible shrieks, sufferers of syringomyelia, whose limbs decay and drop off painlessly, melancholic individuals who must be chained in order to prevent suicide, and more horrible types without labels who are simply beasts unfortunately born from a human womb and therefore credited with a soul, and these are merely kept in a cage, for their locked rooms into which food is thrown are nothing else than that.

To Bertrand, intelligent, mild-looking young man that he was, Dr Dumas first assigned a nice room on the second floor. Bertrand was immensely pleased. And that very first night he made an attempt to escape. But Dr Dumas was no fool. He gave all his patients this very opportunity only to see how they reacted. The orderly, Paul, a brawny fellow who had gotten his muscles in a blacksmith's shop, was on guard. At midnight he saw Bertrand leap from the low balcony and go racing through the bushes. Paul ran to head him off, tackled him and thought to pin him to the ground with ease. But Bertrand had a vigor beyond his appearance and an unaccountable strength in his soft muscles. Moreover, he brought

274

his teeth into play and his fangs ripped through the cloth of Paul's uniform and tore the flesh to ribbons. Paul howled with pain but held on. The two other orderlies came racing to the rescue and Bertrand was finally subdued.

"So that's the kind you are," said Dr Dumas. "I thought as much. Well, we'll teach you. Take him up to the top floor. Give him the corner room. If you can learn to behave, you'll come down again."

It did not take Bertrand long to realize that he had exchanged his nice cell at the hospital-prison of La Santé for a genuine hell-hole. His new room contained only the minimum of furniture; a narrow cot, a chair and a small table. By standing on the table one could barely reach the sill of the only window, an oval, barred œi'l-de-bœuf.

He kept his rage under control for a while. He promised himself that he would get that fellow Paul yet. And if he ever had his hands on Paul again that would be the end. He licked his teeth at the thought. And of course he'd tell Aymar all about it when Aymar came, and Uncle would see to it that he got a better room.

In fact, there was no sense in waiting two weeks for Uncle's visit. He could write to him at once. There was no pen and paper. Bertrand called out for an orderly. There was no answer. He banged on the door. But sounds didn't travel far in this solidly built house. Moreover, the third floor was completely isolated by doors at the top and bottom of the staircase. And as for noise, as for shrieks and banging and all manner of sounds, these were far too common to disturb the orderlies even if they should chance to be on the upper floor.

Maddened by the unsuccess of his efforts, Bertrand lashed out in fury. He threw the chair against the door, until that flimsy piece of furniture was in pieces. He ripped the cover of his bed to pieces. Then he subsided in tears. He promised himself to be wiser in the future. To control himself and play the mild-mannered youth, which, he had learned at La Santé, achieved the best results.

A round, barrel-like fixture on the door clicked. On a little shelf was his food. No orderly came into his room. Perhaps an orderly would never come into his room. They would leave him here forever and tell his uncle he had died. Yes, now he regretted the nice cell he had had at home. What good had it done him to run away? He had only succeeded in getting into La Santé. And from La Santé he had come to this. From bad to worse.

But the second Saturday came around and with it the prospect of being able to unload his misery to his uncle. He had counted without his hosts.

In the evening he found himself lying on his bed. His room had been cleaned. There was fresh linen on the bed. His mind groped through the clearing mists of a drug and remembered as if in a dream his uncle's visit. He recalled being led downstairs by Paul. Yes, by Paul! He recalled the visiting room, his uncle seated opposite and questioning him, and himself sitting there stolidly and unable to do more than smile.

This time he lost his head completely. He smashed, he tore, he howled, until he fell exhausted on the floor and slept. When he woke up, feverish, tense, he groaned to know himself alone and unable to find release.

He listened: There was a noise in the adjoining chamber. It could be faintly heard. It was the little mongoloid cooing to herself. Bertrand did not know what the origin of the sound was, but the soft feminine voice enchanted him, drew him with the power of a siren. He threw himself against the wall. "A woman!" he screamed. He kicked and scratched. Impossible. The wall was not a simple partition but one of the retaining walls of the house, of solid brick and heavy plaster surface.

The noise he had made had evidently frightened the owner of the voice. Bertrand fell to his knees. "Please, sing some more! Please... please...I'll be quiet." But the owner of the voice remained silent.

So great was his necessity for hearing that voice, sole link with the feminine world, that he learned to control himself, especially in the evening, when it generally sang its flat, gentle, monotonous tones. Its timbre was surely only vaguely like Sophie's rich and resonant voice, but Bertrand came to think of it and speak of it as Sophie.

"Sing to me, Sophie," he would say. "Sing to me. Do you recall

276

how we used to go walking in the evening, hand in hand? Do you remember...?" And the mongoloid crooned soft accompaniment to his reminiscences.

The prospect of seeing his uncle was another hope that aided him in keeping himself in check. He had puzzled out the mystery of the drug. Of course they administered it to him in his food. It was only necessary to keep good track of the days as they passed, and avoid eating on Saturday.

His trick worked. On Saturday he did not touch his food, hungry as he was. Instead he waited quietly for the afternoon visiting hours. At last he heard footsteps outside. The key squeaked in the lock and the door swung open.

It was Paul, the enormous lumbering orderly who, a month ago, had defeated Bertrand's attempt to escape. And now Bertrand made a terrible mistake. Evidently he should have gone meekly with Paul, as if truly drugged, and then revealed his grievances to Aymar. Instead, blinded by his desire for revenge, he leaped on the surprised orderly and would surely have killed him if his screams had not attracted another orderly who ran to his comrade's assistance. Between the two, Bertrand was subdued and tied up.

Then Dr Dumas was summoned. It was a simple question of the injection of a drug by means of a hypodermic needle, and a meek, mild and stupidly smiling Bertrand, neatly attired, was led downstairs.

When the drug wore off, Bertrand knew that he had missed his second opportunity and that another would be hard to find. Mad with disappointment he sank his teeth into a leg of his table, and splintered the wood. When he had made a heap of ruins out of that, he attacked the sheets and blankets of his bed. He took off his shoes and chewed up the leather, cracked the buttons on his clothes. He twisted his spoon, the only implement that was served with his food, into knots, and crushed his tin plate.

And the following fortnight found him drugged by an easy trick. For the two previous days he was starved. He howled with hunger. His empty belly growled. He fell into light dozes from which he woke with vivid dreams of food. And then, there in the revolving tray was a plentiful, appetizing meal. He knew, yes, he knew that it was visiting day and that he should not touch a bite of it, but he couldn't resist. He gulped down every morsel. As through a dark glass, he saw Paul enter and grin at him.

Dr Dumas was incensed at all this breakage. "No more linen or blankets for him. Take off his clothes after visiting hours. Let him go naked. And as for his food, throw it on the floor. No more dishes!"

You can't very well throw soup on the floor. But you can throw a piece of meat. And the orderlies had discovered Bertrand's love for meat. It got to be quite good sport to starve him for a day, then open his door suddenly and fling in a bone covered with shreds of flesh.

The orderlies, armed with whips or clubs, would stand in the opening and watch Bertrand pounce upon his food and crouch on the floor to gnaw off and bolt the meat in chunks, and then to crack the bone for the marrow fat. For greater amusement the orderlies liked to offer Bertrand some especially hard bone, the heavy thigh bone of the horse, for example. The sound of enamel grinding against bone filled the room with a sinister crackling. The orderlies trembled and retreated as far as they could. And they held the handle of the door, ready to slam it shut at the least sign of danger.

In this they were well advised, for on several occasions Bertrand, irritated by their laughter or excited by their applause, suddenly leaped at them. Once he was rewarded by having his face caught between the door and the jamb, so that his cheek bones were nearly crushed in. But on another occasion his teeth managed to reach the leg of Paul, and slashed through the cloth, but without catching the flesh.

Paul had had enough. He had long thirsted for vengeance, anyhow. One day, knowing the doctor absent, he procured a heavy whip from the stable. Bertrand was drugged and chloroformed and tied to the bedpost, where he slumped over the ropes that sustained him, for he was completely unconscious. They took turns beating him, now lashing him with the fine thong, now clubbing him with the butt. Bertrand groaned softly. But he did not wake, though

278

blood spurted from his bruised and shredded back. For weeks after, though, his days and nights were one long torture.

Of all the patients, the men took a peculiar delight in annoying Bertrand. On the days when he was starved, preparatory to being drugged, they used to stand outside his door and listen to his mad bellowing. That amused them. And then when he had been drugged, they found some strange pleasure in manhandling him. He was docile as a sick child. The orderlies scrubbed him, put soap in his eyes or tweaked his nose. He responded with a silly grin. Once an orderly thought of a clever trick. He put sharp tacks through the soles of Bertrand's shoes so that points projected through. And thus Bertrand, oblivious of pain, was walked along the hall and down the flights of stairs to the reception room where his uncle awaited him.

To his uncle's greeting he gave no answer. Stood by glumly until Aymar forced him into a seat. Aymar tried to question him. Bertrand continued to glare angrily. Or if his face broke into a silly smile, the effect on Aymar was only the worse.

He tried kindness. "Answer me. Answer me. Please, Bertrand, answer me. Bertrand, look at me. Are you angry at me? Did I not always do my best for you? No father could have struggled harder. And what, after all, did I have to do with you? Neither your mother nor father was any relative of mine. But you came to belong to me, and I came to love you and feel responsibility for you. You were mine, but only as a stray dog sometimes attaches himself to a passerby and will not be shaken off."

Bertrand grinned.

"Well for you to smile," Aymar continued. "It was I who had all the pain and disappointment. It is I who now bear all the affront of your ingratitude."

Bertrand's smile faded. His face darkened into a scowl.

"Yes, scowl if you like. But you will be sorry. For I shall not see you much longer. I have received papal dispensation and will soon take holy orders. Then I may be sent far away. To China, to South America. And you will be left here. Will you write to me at least? Probably not. You have answered none of my letters so far. Your brutish nature has swallowed all the learning I gave you. Do you recall how I taught you your letters, cutting the alphabet out of various colored papers, and how you first thought that every letter from red paper was A, because A had been cut from red paper?

"So you will not forgive me for having brought you here, where you are surely better off than in that prison asylum? Here it is expensive and beautiful and you have the freedom of that great garden, and the care of a famous doctor who means to help you, if he can, which I doubt, but at any rate.

"Well, speak, finally! Answer me! Or are you dumb?" Aymar rose and yelled into that stolid scowl. He postured, gestured, pleaded.

Then he mopped his brow. "I am going crazy myself," he thought. "It is plain that the poor boy is totally off."

He went into the corridor and called an attendant. "Good-bye, Bertrand. Who knows if I shall ever see you again." Bertrand meekly followed the orderly without so much as another glance at his uncle.

Aymar knocked at the doctor's office. Dr Dumas greeted him with a smile.

"Come in, M Galliez. Come in. Have a glass of porto with me."

Aymar was only too happy to sit down and talk to a human being for a change. Dr Dumas was indeed a kind and intelligent man, one with whom one felt at once at home.

"And how did you find your nephew, M Galliez?"

Aymar sipped his porto and answered sadly: "I'm afraid he's not doing very well." He shook his head and sighed.

"Well, well," said the doctor, "such cases, you know, are devilish hard to treat. You must repress their beastly side and that robs them of their joy in life. They grow angry at the whole world and sulk or else mock you in secret.—Here, let me fill your glass."

After a few glasses of porto, Aymar was feeling more mellow. "What disturbs me, what, in fact, wounds me deeply, is that he will not even talk to me. And why does he never answer my letters?"

"Ah, well, M Galliez, one must put up with such things. Gratitude is rare enough among the sane. For myself, I cannot approach him without raising a scowl on his face. And yet, you know yourself

280

how much care and attention we give to our patients here. What kind of a life is this, after all, to devote oneself, sacrifice everything, in order to relieve the suffering…"

"You should feel ennobled by that, my dear doctor. To attempt to relieve the world's ills, from whatever side. Oh, by the way, you know, I intend soon to take holy orders."

"Really?" the doctor was shocked, but recovered quickly. "Then allow me to congratulate you. May I drink to your future? There is nothing finer than the career of priesthood. I am not one of those blatant medicos who are so vociferous in their denunciations of the Church. As a man of science I must be unbiased, as a student of the soul, I know that religion is a potent force."

Aymar was pleased. There was something he had had on his heart for a long time. Could he entrust it to Dr Dumas?

"I've wondered. I know, of course, that your patients may have mass said to them, if they so desire, but do you, ah, systematically attempt to open their hearts to religion? Do you, for example, try to teach them to pray?"

"You have hit there on one of my pet theories, monsieur. I am gradually working toward that."

"I neglected that myself, in former years," said Aymar, "but since the terrors of the last year I have become deeply convinced that man must return to the simple faith of his ancestors, back to what we in our modern sophistication and pride term vulgar superstition."

Dr Dumas nodded his head in agreement, and filled the glasses.

"There is something," said Aymar, "that I have been wanting to ask you."

"Certainly."

"Yon have watched my nephew carefully?"

"Why, monsieur!"

"I am implying no criticism," Aymar declared quickly, "but you know, of course, that I have had my nephew in my care for many years?"

"Yes."

"Well, have you ever observed him change?"

"Change? What do you mean?"

"I mean into a wolf."

"Into a wolf?"

"Why, yes. You know, of course, that he is afflicted with lycanthropy?"

"To be sure, but that is a mere name."

"I beg your pardon, it is the truth."

"Ah, come, M Galliez. You would not have me believe that your nephew does more than delude himself? You know, his disease is quite common. I have in fact made a study of it. And given considerable attention to the huge mass of testimony in the medieval werewolf trials. There is, in all this testimony, full proof that no one ever saw a werewolf, and the patients themselves confess that they only felt like wolves."

"Whatever may have been the case," Aymar returned, "–and I am not prepared to agree with you, for I have studied the matter myself–I am certain that my nephew has been a wolf, and does change into a wolf."

"And you have seen him do it?" the doctor smiled.

"No. But I am convinced he does."

"Have you seen the wolf?" Dr Dumas insisted.

"No, but–"

"You seem easily convinced then."

The two men, a little flushed from the wine, slowly raised their voices. The doctor could no longer pretend to be a friend of religion. He began to berate the Catholic Church for having burned the werewolves. Aymar defended the Church, claiming that the burning was a kind of sanitary device to stop the infection. Somehow D.D. Home* came into the discussion. They went astray here for a moment, while the doctor recalled how Home used to give séances before Impératrice Eugénie. He used to cause

---

*Famous American spiritualist and physical medium (1833–1886). He was examined by Lord Crookes, the celebrated physicist who was convinced of Home's power to levitate himself, etc.

harmonicas to float in the air and play tunes by themselves. "Do you believe that?" the doctor asked.

"The Church says that this is the work of the devil, though similar phenomena occur in the lives of the saints. In any case, I should want to see it with my own eyes."

"Well, of course," Dr Dumas agreed. "Precisely. But here we have a case which you confess no one has ever seen. Not you, yourself!"

"I have never seen the wolf, true enough," Aymar came back. "But I have as many good proofs as I want. I have, or rather I once had, a silver bullet which was shot into a wolf by the garde champêtre of our district, and that silver bullet I extracted from the leg of my nephew. I saw his deeds. I heard of his dreams. I have seen, many people have seen, his footprints. I have heard his breath and his snort. There are stranger things. Shall I mention one of many? After he removes his clothes, when the change is about to overcome him, he finds it imperatively necessary to urinate. He has told me of that. Now I ask you, has my victim of lycanthropy read Petronius and other more obscure sources, to know that this is a universal trait of werewolves before the metamorphosis, and why should he want to follow their hints as to the manner of the ceremony? Nonsense."

"I can't quite see the point you wish to make, monsieur. I do not deny that the symptoms of the delusion are alike in all its victims. On the contrary, the symptoms would be alike. And if urinating is one of them, why, then of course it belongs there, like a fever in diphtheria. Moreover, the act of urinating can be explained more simply by the cold air striking the skin of the body. A lowering of temperature invariably brings on the desire to rid the body of the larger amount of moisture required in a warmer atmosphere. It is akin to a sudden condensation and precipitation."

"Why not to the sudden necessity of getting rid of an excess of moisture because a wolf naturally carries less? Good Lord, doctor, do you think I lived twenty years with this thing without debating with myself every single minute point? Ten years would not suffice here to recapitulate the entire story of the origin and mystery of this creature. I was as unwilling as you to accept the facts. I am not by nature gullible."

"I take for granted your original incredulity. I ask myself only how you ever changed. How could you ever come to believe that he was metamorphosed into a wolf? That is per se preposterous!"

"Certain things. Many things, some small in themselves, but all of them together presenting an invincible argument made me change my mind. His birth on Christmas Eve, for example."

"Statistics will show, I am sure, said Dumas eagerly, "that thousands born on that day have had lives no different from the rest of us. Are you going to bring up astrology?"

"Not at this moment," said Aymar, "but science has still not explained many phenomena of human character and emotion."

"Would you set limits to science?" Dumas raised his voice. "Man is a compound of chemicals and some day we shall write the chemical reaction of love!"

"Tommyrot!" Galliez retorted. "Man is a union of spirit and matter. In the instant between life and death, for example, what leaves the body: a chemical?"

"No, but the chemical order or aggregation is altered there."

"Ha, ha! So we do have a remarkable change of form, here."

"What do you mean?"

"Simply that the alteration from man to wolf is no greater than from life to death."

"Rhetoric, monsieur!"

"That's no answer. Are you at loss for a scientific argument?"

"But, man!" Dumas bellowed. "Consider what you are saying: that a man can turn into a wolf. A wolf, remark you, that has no sweat glands, whose bones and teeth, hard bodies, mind you, are all differently shaped, whose every cell and every hair and nerve—"

"And why not?" said Galliez, flourishing his wine glass. "Do not such changes take place in nature? Have you never seen water change to ice?"

"Oh, come."

"Have you never seen two gases unite suddenly into a snowy powder?"

284

"Yes, but—"

"And a worm change into a showy butterfly?"

"Yes, but in a whole month of time."

"What difference does time make? Is not time infinitely divisible? If a wheel can turn once a year can it not also turn a million times a second? The life of some animals is the twinkling of an eye, while of others it is a century."

"I concede you that," said Dumas slowly, "but you have mentioned the butterfly. Have you ever seen it turn back into a worm?"

"No, but if, as you said, life is a chemical reaction, is there any reason why it should not be reversible?"

"No," the doctor said slowly, for he was beginning to recall his professional discretion. He'd better not argue himself out of a patient here. He swung slowly around until he was agreeing with Aymar.

"And those eyebrows that meet," Aymar pursued.

"Yes, I've noticed that, but I took that for a sign of hereditary syphilis."

"Not at all," said Aymar. "And those nails."

"A common enough sign."

"Interlocking teeth set with little spaces between."

"Of course, there are wide variations in the dentition of man."

"And those hairy palms."

"Very strange, that, isn't it?"

"Not so much any one of these signs, but all together. It is as if the beast in him peeped forth here and there.—And then, of course, his actions, more than anything else."

"Hm," said the doctor. "You know, M Galliez, that what you say there interests me immensely. It unfolds a remarkable new theory for all the inexplicable manifestations of morbid and abnormal psychology. The intrusion, even in partial degrees, of lower forms of life into the human form. Of course, attractive though the idea is, I cannot accept your conclusions fully. But I intend to study the matter."

From this point the discussion grew more and more one-sided

and even more flattering to Aymar. When he arose to go, it was with renewed and increased faith that in Dr Dumas' sanatorium he had found the ideal spot for Bertrand. In fact he felt a little concerned for the doctor. "I hope you can do him some good, Dr Dumas, but let me give you a little friendly warning. Be careful. He's a dangerous criminal. Watch out for him. And if you must approach him, remember to cross yourself."

"Thank you for your advice," the doctor replied. "I shall avail myself of it. And may I communicate to you the results of my observations?"

He stood at the door and as he watched Aymar go off with a more unsteady limp than usual, he snorted quietly: "I may have two patients yet, out of that family."

Bertrand, when not in a rage and not drugged, had now no pleasures in life but these two: the singing of Sophie, and the hope of revenge on Paul. As for communication with his uncle, that had best be given up, even as a dream. For it was plain that they would never let Aymar up here, and equally plain that they would never let him down unless he was drugged. If not by food, then by an injection. And as for writing, there was no possibility of that; not only was material lacking, but how to post a letter, even should one succeed in writing it?

Often, when ruminating thus over his miserable fate Bertrand was overcome with sadness, it might happen that the faint singing of Sophie would sound through the wall. The bitterness would vanish from his grief. Tears would come to his eyes. "Sophie," he would say to himself, "Sophie." And he would lie down on his mattress, which was on the floor and constituted his entire bed, in fact his entire furniture, and imagine she was in his arms. Her black curls were in his face, her soft, moist lips against his, and her slender arms about his body. And the dream would last until the singing ceased. Then he would beg: "Sing again, Sophie. Sing another song." And if, as sometimes happened, the flat, drawn-out notes rose again, then he was almost certain that she knew he was here, in the room next door, and that she knew he wanted to hear her sing.

After a while the singing alone was not enough. The mere dream of Sophie no longer held. He must get into the next room. But how? He formulated a hundred bold plans and rejected all. He discovered, however, that he could manage to leap up to the oval window, catch on to the sill, and by digging his toes into the wall, almost hitch himself up to a seating position. If only his toes could secure a better hold on the wall. With his fingernails, with a splinter of bone, he remedied that. Two little niches now served to give him a good purchase on the wall and actually to seat himself on the sill.

Chance favored him there. The entire framework of the oval window, bars and all, was loose in its setting of stone. Evidently the workman who had made a permanent opening above the glass, for ventilation, had loosened the frame from the plaster and not bothered to repair his damage. Or else time had shrunk the wood to its present size. In any case, one could take hold of the bars and pull out the whole window as if it were a stopper. Having made sure of this, Bertrand waited feverishly until late at night to explore further.

Just outside the oval window, to the right, was a steep roof, and from this projected a dormer window. That led, evidently, to Sophie's room. On the other side was a blank wall, so that escape on that side was impossible. But the dormer window might be reached. The steep roof was dangerous, but accessible. Trembling with excitement, Bertrand made his preparations. He rolled up his mattress lengthwise, into a cylinder, and pushed it through the opening until it dropped to the ground below. "We'll jump on that," he determined. "We'll either hit it and run off together, or miss it and die together in suicide, as we so often planned."

It happened on this night that Paul was in a mood to be with a woman, and this was unfortunate, for the patient who had been accustomed to receive him for several years now had just been removed by her relatives. The only other possibilities were two female patients, who were, so to speak, the property of the other two orderlies. Paul debated whether to affront the jealousy and anger of one of his comrades or attempt to sneak out of the asylum and get to the village. Then the little mongoloid occurred to him.

287

That'll be fun, he promised himself. He knew she was fond of candy, so he took some up with him and expected no difficulty — nor did he encounter any.

His pleasure, however, was short-lived. He heard a noise at the window, looked up and had no time to escape a dark form that hurled itself at him. In a second the combat was over. The blood spurted from his torn artery in a high wide arc and splashed onto the floor. The arc diminished, sank back to its origin, where now the blood only welled up in ever slower pulsations.

Bertrand lay there in a kind of stupor, from a surfeit of ecstasy. At last he roused himself, struggled against the sluggishness of his mind and looked about in the dark room. In this chamber, lit only by the moonlight from outside, he saw a strange, dwarfish woman with a heavy brown face and stringy gray hair. She was seated on the bed, naked, and sucking at a stick of barley sugar, and because it was good, she began to coo to herself.

His mind was incapable of accepting this. "Sophie!" he said, bewildered. "What have they done to you?"

There was a noise outside in the hall. Without puzzling out the matter, he picked her up and cried, "Come, Sophie, let us die together." And holding her clasped tightly in his arms, he stepped upon the sill and leaped for the mattress lying on the lawn below.

"My most profitable patient, too," Dr Dumas said, and sighed.

Investigations being annoying things at best, the doctor suppressed the triple death as much as he could, filled out appropriate death certificates, dated them differently and held the funerals at a week's interval. There were only two funerals. Dr Dumas had long been anxious to dissect the mongoloid and wrote for permission to the marquis, saying that he would pay the usual price. "The old skinflint will be glad to earn a couple of francs."

But the old skinflint was not. "The remains of Mme la Marquise de la Roche Ferrant must rest in the family vault," he declared proudly and sternly. And when one comes to think it over, why not? Alive and in the family castle, she might have been a source of annoyance. But whom could she disturb or embarrass in the family tomb?

Barral de Montfort came just a week too late to the asylum, in search of Bertrand. He had been delayed by trouble with his eye. When he heard that Bertrand had just died, he cursed his fate. He had promised himself so much from his revenge. "Death," he exclaimed bitterly, "robs me of both my love and my hate."

He wanted to see the grave. For a tip, an orderly took him over to the cemetery and pointed out the mound. Barral bent down over the fresh sod and, rendered furious by this climax of frustration, muttered viciously: "I'd like to dig you up, you dog, and spit in your face."

This completes the elucidation of the Galliez script.

Appendix

About this period, that is to say, 1875–1880, the question of municipal hygiene was much to the fore. The great researches in microbiology, in the causes of disease, in sanitary engineering demanded that municipalities take an active hand in improving the hygienic conditions of populous centers.

Among other matters the disposal of the dead elicited much argument. The practice of burial was attacked as unhygienic, and proponents of cremation demanded state action making incineration of corpses not merely lawful but required. The practice long followed, and still followed, of burying stillbirths and embryos in privies or otherwise privately disposing of them, was forbidden by law in numerous places.

The history of municipal government shows that little attention was paid to such matters until the nineteenth century. Apparently one of the first attempts to show the insalubrity of intramuros burials in great cities was that of Drs Fernel and Houllier of Paris who in 1554 expressed fears concerning the Cemetery of the Innocents, a great charnel field which in 1186 had been allotted for the burial of the deceased of Paris. Here great pits were dug and the coffins placed solidly side by side and one upon the other until some two thousand were buried, or rather exposed, for only with the placing of the last coffin was the pit covered with soil.

During its existence this cemetery, swollen by the addition of two million bodies, rose ten feet above the level the surrounding territory and at places overflowed the walls. Old pits were frequently opened and the bones thrown into great heaps. Subsequently some of this vast mass of human relics was put in the Paris catacombs, which were really former quarries whence fine stone was extracted.

To make matters worse, this great Cemetery of the Innocents was surrounded by a vast gutter into which the surrounding quarters of the city were accustomed to cast the ordure of the houses. In those days latrines were generally on the top floors only, and when these were cleaned the matter was thrown into the moat about the cemetery, from whence it was upon occasion removed.

Such was the mephitic nature of the ground and air in this region that citizens complained they could not keep birds in cages, the poor beasts dying promptly within a week of being brought into the houses of the neighborhood. Moreover, it was impossible to go down into the cellars with a candle or lamp: any flame was at once extinguished in this noxious underground breath. Barrel-makers and other workers having to labor in cellars were frequently seized with such spells that they came near dying, and gradually these regions were abandoned, especially when it was found that the sweat of the walls was positively poisonous and would raise ill-smelling suppurating boils if it came into contact with the bare skin.

Despite this, the city had become crowded with poor people who could find no other shelter than this horrible cemetery. Many dug themselves subsoil grottoes in which they practically lived, with what effect on their general viability one may well imagine.

Perhaps worse than this was the habit of burying people in churches. The limited space and the desire for financial gain among the clergy caused the bodies to be withdrawn as soon as possible, even before complete decomposition, and stored elsewhere in the church, in the garret, etc.

In 1870 the work of De Freycinet on municipal sanitation, together with the necessity of providing for more cemetery space in Paris, caused considerable discussion on the matter of hygienic burial grounds. The recent Franco-Prussian War, too, had precipitated the question of the disposal of great numbers of dead in a sanitary fashion.

Among others, M. Coupry *fils,* an architect of Nantes, patented a hygienic cemetery construction, the "*système Coupry*" which he proposed to install in his Cimetière de l'Avenir.* A test of Coupry's method was carried out in a portion of the Saint-Nazaire cemetery. Here a number of bodies were buried above the device which facilitated the circulation of air beneath the coffins and drained the soil of waters, and an equal number of corpses were buried as near to the test portion as possible and allowed to remain for varying years in the soil. In this system the deleterious gases which collect in the underground pipes are brought to an oven and there burnt. For its best operation the Coupry system demands burial in simple wooden coffins without the use of antiseptic substances, embalming, impregnated sawdust or charcoal, since the purpose of the system is the rapid disintegration of the body to a skeleton, with the complete disappearance of all the corruptible fleshy parts.

It is, of course, well known that the French Revolution began the practice of forbidding church burial by state legislation of the 23rd of the month Prairial of the year XII, and limited the creation of new cemeteries to beyond the city walls. It forbade the burying of one coffin upon another and limited the burial to five years, except for those who wished to pay exorbitant sums for perpetual burial plots. Further, the depth of burial was stipulated so that noxious gases would not reach and contaminate the outside air.

Since then France, particularly the Prefecture of the Seine, has interested itself constantly in the betterment of burial grounds, and it early appointed a commission to investigate the Coupry

---

* Cemetery of the Future.

system. The report published by Dr P. Brouardel and O. du Mesnil contains a complete study* of this system.

For the purpose of their report, the above-mentioned members of the committee appointed by the Prefecture of the Seine, Commission d'Assainissement (Board of Health), exhumed ten bodies, five Coupry, five plain, which they subjected to a complete examination.

Thus:

Sieur G...(Baptiste), 53 years of age.
Died March 20, 1876. — Buried March 21, 1876. — Exhumed, May 25, 1881. — Again exhumed June 9, 1881. Length of inhumation: 5 years. In untreated portion of the cemetery.
This cadaver (see accompanying photograph)† is absolutely intact. It has been transformed into corpse-fat. Bad odor.
Autopsy was performed by Professor Brouardel.
All the viscera have grown thinner, and are flattened out against the walls of the thorax and abdomen.
Only the heart is still voluminous and perfectly recognizable.
All process of decomposition seems to have been halted. Apparently the body will remain in this state indefinitely.
A single insect of the Staphilinides family: a Philonthus ebeninus *is found in the coffin.*

Contrast this with a body disinterred from a treated section, where it had remained but a year:

Sieur B...66 years of age (see photograph).‡
Died May 21, 1880. — Interred May 22, 1880. Cerebral congestion. — Length of inhumation: 1 year and 18 days.
Body was not shrouded.
No odor spread by body.

---

* See copy in the Forty-second Street library, New York.

† Not reproduced here. The reader may consult the original.

‡ See preceding footnote.

Skeleton is almost completely relieved of all soft parts.
Head is separated from body.
The destruction of the fleshy and soft parts is complete.
Numerous insects are found in the coffin. Anthomysides, Ophria
cadaverina *and* lemostoma. *One fly, quite alive, had just come forth
from the numerous nympheas of the* Ophia.

However, the reader of this book can hardly be interested in the
above details.* The author's reason for introducing this report is
to quote a small portion of it which seems to have some relation to
our story.

Among the bodies exhumed was one:

Sieur C...(Bertrand) Cerebral hemorrhage (not illustrated).
*Died Aug. 9, 1873.—Buried Aug. 10, 1873.—Exhumed June 10,
1881.—Length of inhumation: 8 years, 2 months.*
*The following case was reported to the conservateur of the
cemetery and by him forwarded to the department of criminal justice.
Evidently a case of grave robbery, or a grim prank of the fossayeurs
(gravediggers).*
*The body of Sieur C...was not found in the coffin, instead, that
of a dog, which despite 8 years in the ground was still incompletely
destroyed.*
*The fleshy parts and the furry hide are found mingled in a fatty
mass of indistinguishable composition (adipocere). A nauseous odor
spreads from the body.*
No insects.

---

* The economic motive here is not to be concealed, and intrudes upon the hygienic.
If bodies will, by the "*système Coupry,*" form skeletons in one year, the five-year
burial period may be reduced to one year with a consequent greater turnover in the
cemeteries and an increased income to the State.

294